NO MERCY

Kathryn Johnson

Affairs of State: Book #3

No Mercy

This novel is dedicated to women of the sciences...whose intelligence, ingenuity, and dedication make this world a better place.

Also by Kathryn Johnson:

Mercy Killing
Hot Mercy
The Gentleman Poet: A Novel of Shakespeare's "The Tempest"

Writing as Mary Hart Perry:

The Wild Princess
Seducing the Princess
The Shadow Princess

Cover art by Earthly Charms

ISBN-13: 978-0692492772
ISBN-10: 0692492771

Kathryn Johnson

Everything that night was going perfectly, until the door that was supposed to be locked crashed open and the man with a gun stepped through.

Dr. Kate Foster turned in her seat at the computer terminal and stared at the intruder, her mind still caught up in the data from the satellite, circling high in the sky above Earth.

Normally, thirty or more scientists and techs caromed off of each other, jockeying for a screen, barking into headsets when anything critical happened. But it was three in the morning, most of the team at home in bed. Tonight it was her and a core staff, seven of them in the NASA Command Center, leaving most of the cubicles unoccupied. No one had expected anything more exciting than a routine telemetry adjustment.

No one had foreseen a man in a black jumpsuit with a gun.

Or the two armed figures in camouflage who followed him into the room.

Vernon poked his shiny bald head up from his cubicle at the far end of the room. "Sorry, sir, authorized personnel only in this area." Which sounded absurd. More like a teacher warning students not to run in the corridors.

Belatedly, she realized the partition around Vernon's desk must have blocked his view of the short-muzzled automatic weapons held hip level by the intruders.

Then everything happened at once.

Cambridge screamed.

Tommy stood up beside Kate and whispered, "Oh, shit."

And Kate's dawdling brain snapped into gear.

She slipped one hand beneath the terminal's desktop. Found the smooth plastic panic button. Fingertips of her other hand hit three keys in succession on the board in front of her. The central monitor flashed once. Then every screen in the lab went black.

No Mercy

Her heart hammering in her chest, Kate stood up and turned to face the intruders, who still hadn't said a thing. Maybe they thought their weapons made their presence a clear enough threat? She had seen guns like this before, but only in movies or on TV. Uzis? Ugly, black things with wooden stocks. Far more terrifying in real life.

"What do you want?" she asked, struggling to come up with an explanation for how an armed trio had invaded a guarded compound and made their way into a supposedly secure laboratory. *Maybe this is a drill of some sort?* Practice for a real emergency. A Special-ops team brought in by NASA to support the compound's usual security detail.

Please, God, let it be.

"Which one of you is Dr. Foster?" the man in the lead growled in an indefinable accent. His features and coloring could have been either Middle Eastern or South American. Dark eyes slid around the room to members of her team, fixing momentarily on each shocked face.

No, she thought, *not a drill*. The backs of her legs prickled with the urge to run. But these strangers, these incredibly dangerous-looking people were between her and the door. She sucked in a shallow breath, consciously willed her hands to stop trembling.

"I'm Kate Foster." Somehow she kept her voice from cracking. "Listen, there's absolutely nothing here of value to you. No money. No drugs. If it's weapons you're after, we have access to nothing like that. This is a telemetry research laboratory." *I bet you don't even know what that means!* In all fairness, 99 percent of the world wouldn't.

"Shut up." The man in black waved the muzzle of his gun menacingly. "Go!" he barked over his shoulder at one of the figures who'd followed him into the room. A woman, Kate noted.

She stepped around behind Kate and started hitting keys on the keyboard. "Nothing. God damn it, Zed, the bitch locked it down!"

"We're just running tests on a satellite," Kate tried to explain.

"It's a peacetime scientific experiment involving microwave energy," Frank Hess added helpfully, moving up to flank Kate from the opposite side as their baby-faced intern, Tommy. As though the two of them could protect her by their mere proximity. "No onboard arms of any kind."

Hess, her senior scientist on Project Heat Wave, had worked with her on other NASA operations. A brilliant man but he had a temper. When annoyed, he sometimes acted irrationally. She glanced sideways at him. His face was flushed, as if he considered the intrusion a personal affront.

Not now, Frank, she prayed silently. *Keep your cool for once.*

The one called Zed ignored the middle-aged physicist. "Sit down, Dr. Foster," he said. "Turn your computer back on."

Her mind whirled, trying to make connections, to understand what had brought him here.

Zed. Was that a nickname? Or a code? It was what Brits called the letter Z. Maybe he was from England, although his accent didn't sound right. Her penchant for trivia dredged up stupid little facts. Zed came from the Latin word zeta. It literally meant "weapon." *What mother would call her son that?* So he'd picked a macho name for himself.

"Sit!" the man commanded.

Kate snapped out of her trance. Before she could move, Hess stepped between her and the gun pointed at her. "Leave her alone, you bastard!"

"Frank." But Kate's warning came too late.

The man in black swung his free arm. Kate swallowed a scream. Frank ducked but the vicious blow struck the side of his face. Its impact knocked the physicist off his feet with as little effort as if he'd been a gnat. He crashed into the side of a metal desk, then fell to the floor.

No one else in the room made a sound. No one moved.

For the first time, it struck Kate that it was possible none of them would leave this room alive. *Oh, God!*

Frank gave a low moan from the floor, one hand pressed to his inflamed cheekbone. He looked up at Kate through bleary eyes, and she thought she read an apology there. For not being able to do the manly thing and be a hero? Or maybe it was a plea: *Do something!* As if she could make these people, this nightmare, go away.

No Mercy

"Dr. Foster, if you will." Zed motioned toward her chair, his mock politeness an absurd contrast to the violence of his attack seconds earlier. He aimed a crooked smile at her. She caught a glimpse of obscenely white, perfectly straight teeth. *A terrorist with good dental hygiene?*

Why was she even thinking such things? Her stomach clenched, then heaved. She swallowed back a mouthful of bile. Where had these people come from? What the hell was going on?

"Let us now talk to your satellite." Zed pointed at her monitor.

"I. But I—"

She glanced with concern at Frank, who had managed to pull himself back up onto his feet. He wobbled once, then leaned against one of the terminals, a stunned, unfocused look in his eyes. A trickle of blood dripped from one corner of his mouth. *She* was the senior project manager. It was her responsibility to make sure he was all right. That none of the others would be harmed.

"Let my people leave," Kate blurted out.

"No one is leaving this room until I say so," Zed snarled.

Her mind raced, still reaching for possible reasons a bunch of crazies would target her project. This made no sense whatsoever. Unless... "If all you want to do is destroy a satellite to make some kind of political statement—"

"Sit!" Zed leveled the muzzle of his gun at her heart.

She sat.

Tommy Leonhardt, jaw set, eyes narrowed, stood alongside her chair. As if, he'd decided that he now had to do the job of two males, with Frank Hess eliminated as her protector and no one else stepping up. She gave him a look and subtle shake of her head. *Don't. Do. Anything.*

There had been the obligatory classes on what NASA called Catastrophe Management. How to evacuate buildings safely in case of a fire, earthquake, flood, whatever. How to lock down their rooms and barricade themselves inside until help arrived, should terrorists somehow infiltrate the guarded compound. But there hadn't been time for any of that. It had happened too fast.

Kathryn Johnson

Were these, in fact, terrorists? A homegrown ISIS faction? As a scientist, she needed an explanation. Data. Proven facts. *Maybe not terrorism at all. Industrial espionage?*

She knew that ASEC, Alternate Sources Energy Corporation, the company providing most of the funding for HW-1, faced tough competition from other groups hoping to expand into the field of renewable energy resources. And that's what HW-1 was all about—harvesting energy from the sun, and then amplifying it and sending it to gathering stations on Earth. Fortunes could be made from the kind of technology her research team had been involved in for the past five years.

But an assault team and automatic weapons? That seemed a bit rash for the world of corporate crime. *And where the hell is Security?* They must have received her alarm signal. Were they even now on their way here? Kate's heart gave a little flutter of hope at the thought. Maybe all she had to do was stall for just another minute or two, and then they'd be rescued.

When she didn't move, Zed slowly swung the muzzle of his Uzi to the left, within inches of the Georgetown University crest on Tommy's gray sweatshirt. Night shifts, they dressed casual. She sensed the boy's lanky body stiffen.

Kate spun around in her chair and clicked on her computer's power. She entered her password. Without it, no one could access the satellite's onboard computer. The booting-up process started. Desperate, she tried to think of more ways to stall for time. Without seeming to stall for time. It would take only another minute or so before the satellite's memory and control systems came online.

How long had it been since she'd pushed the damn silent alarm? How many more minutes before Security came to their rescue? And when they suddenly appeared, what then? A hostage situation?

She felt sick to her stomach. Her palms itched, hot and damp with sweat. A wave of nausea flowed over her, like oil slicking in an iridescent sheen over water, blurring her thoughts. She was going to throw up all over the keyboard.

No, can't do that. If she went to pieces, it would only make matters worse.

No Mercy

The initiation screen came up—a sky-blue background with the familiar NASA logo. Kate hesitated, her fingertips hovering over the keys.

"Go on, do it." Zed's voice was a low vulpine growl. He leaned over her, spoke into her ear. "Now, madam! Contact your satellite. Last warning."

Kate shot a quick look around the room at her team.

Cambridge Mackenzie stood, still as a doe caught in headlights, between two cubicles. Her brown eyes enormous, her dark skin glowing with visible perspiration. Their eyes met for an instant. Cam blinked then shook her head: *I don't know what to do, either.*

Kate didn't have to look at Tommy, not even an arm's length away, to know he was scared, but also hyped. She could feel his energy pulsing through the air between them. Only twenty-three, fresh out of college, he was the one she most feared doing something crazy now that Frank had been cowed. Would he try to snatch a weapon away from one of the intruders? Attempt to wrestle one of them to the floor? She touched his arm lightly, letting him know he must hold back.

And the others? How to get through to them that they must do nothing, absolutely nothing, to antagonize these armed people, whoever they were? She considered the volatility of each member of her team.

Frank, second in command of the project, might explode again, despite Zed's warning blow. She could imagine him cursing these people, ordering them out of the lab. This was turf. He'd defend it. But he wasn't a stupid man. She didn't think he'd take on an Uzi. *No, probably not.*

David Proctor? He stood quietly, taking in the scene. She didn't expect any interference from him. He was a thirty-six-year-old workaholic with a wife and two kids. Put him on task and he'd run forever, the Energizer bunny. But he wasn't one to think outside of the box or to take chances. He'd play it safe.

Vernon Hernandez? She didn't know him well enough to say what he might be thinking at this moment. He'd transferred from the Applied Physics Lab in California only a month ago. He was farthest away from the guns, and looked almost happy to have a couple rows of cubicles between them and him. But if the trio opened fire, spraying the room with bullets, the flimsy aluminum-and-burlap partitions would be no protection.

Last of all came Amanda Becker, their Earth mother. Fond of tie-dyed anything, a little on the plump side, with four grown kids and one grandchild. One of her boys was a Catholic priest. As the team's support tech she made sure they were on schedule, reserved their time on the antenna, and kept the project log. She looked ghostly white now. Her lips quivered and moved as though she were whispering her rosary.

Pray for us all, Amanda.

Kate's own family flashed into her mind. Christmas in Chicago with her parents, brothers and sisters and their kids. All of the cousins would be there, too, including her favorite—Mercy O'Brien.

They'd grown up together, she and Mercy—closer than most sisters. It had been months since they'd last seen each other. Her parents had passed along news that wasn't entirely clear to Kate. At the time, Mercy had been involved somehow with the FBI, or was it the CIA? Something to do with busting a human trafficking ring. And then her cuz had rushed off to Ukraine. She still hadn't learned the details about what had gone on there. She understood it had something to do with Mercy's mother, Aunt Talia, but everything had sounded very hush-hush.

She wished she had her cousin's quick, practical mind. Mercy would have known what to do in a situation like this. All of the science in the world couldn't help her now.

Her computer gave a little hiccup, as if the remind her: *I'm ready!*

"I need to know what you intend to do to this satellite before I bring it online," Kate said. Destroy it; she supposed that was their intent. She pressed her palms over her stomach, to comfort and calm it with their warmth, to hold the nausea at bay.

The woman in camos stepped forward. She swung her arm up, the butt of her weapon rising over Kate's head. "Do as you're told or—"

"No!" Zed roared. "She's too important." He turned back to Kate. "I do not have time to play games, Doctor. No questions. Do as I say or, I promise you, there will be consequences."

No Mercy

Kate closed her eyes for a fraction of a second. *Consequences.* Slowly, she began entering her codes.

The third intruder had stood silently beside Zed since they'd entered the room. Now he looked at his watch. "Two minutes gone."

She glanced over her shoulder at his face. If they came out of this alive, she'd need to be able to describe the three. A long, jagged scar ran from the outer corner of the man's left eye, and across his cheek to his chin. He wore a wool skullcap. She couldn't tell the color of his hair or, indeed, if he had any. She kept her fingers moving on the keyboard: Click, click, click. Slow, slow, slow.

"She's stalling." The woman slapped the side of her weapon with her palm, her impatience palpable. "Five minutes max, remember. We gotta *move*."

So, Kate thought, they're racing Security's response. They know about the alarm.

But what the hell did they want with her satellite? It still made no sense, taking such an awful risk. And for what?

She looked around once more to see the frightened eyes of her team, searching for guidance. From her. She had none. If she stonewalled any longer, one of these creeps might start shooting her people. Zed appeared fully capable of doing just that. So did Miss Uzi. But if she cooperated—then what?

"We're in," Kate said and pushed back from her console, feeling utterly, stupidly helpless.

Zed took a piece of ordinary-looking paper from his shirt pocket and held it out to her. "Here are your instructions."

She unfolded the sheet and scanned the sophisticated lines of script—the language programmers used to talk to their computers. It didn't matter whether that computer was set up in the next room, launched in a satellite to circle Earth, or built into a space probe and shot off to the edge of the universe.

Tommy shifted closer to read over her shoulder. "Oh crap! They're changing the FARM?"

The Frame Acceptance Reporting Mechanism enabled scientists on the ground to communicate with and command the satellite. They weren't out to destroy the HW-1 after all.

Kathryn Johnson

She turned around to face Zed. "You're *hijacking* my satellite?"

Zed didn't respond.

"One minute left," the man with the scar announced in a monotone.

"Do it!" the woman screamed. "Type, bitch!"

When Kate didn't move, Zed lowered the muzzle of his Uzi to her chest. The steel circle poked the valley between her breasts. The sensation of cold metal came through the thin fabric of her blouse. She shuddered. Never had she felt this close to death. And yet she couldn't ignore one thing: *Others—maybe many others—will suffer, if I give in now.*

"*Now*, Doctor," Zed said.

Kate drew a shaky breath and shook her head. "No. I won't do this. Please, if you leave now you may still have time to get away before—"

"Do it or I will kill you!" Zed's dark eyes flared with rage.

Somehow she had to make him understand how useless this plan of his was. "I have no idea what you intend to do with my satellite. But I have a feeling it won't be used for a humanitarian cause. I won't help you do anything to hurt people."

"You don't value your own life?" he sneered. "What about the lives of your friends here?"

Her entire body throbbed with apprehension. *No. No. No!*

"If you kill us all," Cam shrieked, "there will be no one to carry out your demands. You *need* us, you bloody idiot."

Zed seemed unperturbed by her outburst. "Ah, but perhaps by the time a few of you have been sacrificed, those remaining will have a change of heart?" He angled his body toward Frank but kept the gun's muzzle pressed into Kate's breastbone. "Or maybe someone else will be more reasonable without needing to see bloodshed. What about you, sir?"

Frank dropped his hand away from his swollen jaw and narrowed his eyes at the man. "I wouldn't help you even if I could, you clown."

"You might." The muscles of Zed's gun hand and wrist tightened. "If I put a bullet through your boss."

Hess flashed the man a wry smile. "If you kill her, you'll never get in. She's the only one with the fail-safe code." Such

No Mercy

information was closely guarded. But Kate realized he just might have saved her life.

Zed didn't miss a beat. His long arm reached out. He seized the physicist by the front of his shirt. "Is that right, Mr. Smart Man? Then maybe she needs a demonstration of the seriousness of the situation."

Before Kate could react, Zed shoved Frank back against the nearest cubicle partition and swung his weapon toward him. A look of horror flashed across Frank's face. "Oh, God, please no!"

Zed fired a single round at the scientist. A bloom of red seeped through the right shoulder of his shirt. Frank clapped a hand over the wound and collapsed on the floor, sobbing.

Before Kate could do or say anything at all, David Proctor lurched forward. Camouflage Woman fired a burst into his back. The deafening chatter of the gun cut off cries of protest from Kate and her team. Blood sprayed everywhere. David slammed down, face first, on the floor.

Later, in thinking back on that night, Kate was never sure whether the young father had been trying to make it out the door, rushing to help Frank, or desperately attempting to wrestle away Zed's gun.

For a stunned moment, there was only silence. Kate stared in horror at the two injured men. Victims of her delaying tactics? Frank had assumed a fetal curl on the floor, gripping his bleeding shoulder, moaning in agony. David, she suspected, was already, perhaps mercifully, dead.

"Now, Doctor," Zed said, in an eerily calm voice, then shifted his gaze back to Frank Hess. "Do I finish off this little worm, too? Or maybe choose another of your friends to further prove the seriousness of my intentions?"

Monster! Kate stared at the man. Then shook her head. Her throat felt as if she'd swallowed razorblades. Could she even speak? "That won't be necessary," she croaked.

Kathryn Johnson

Chapter 2

Daniel Rooker pulled his black Ford F-150 into a parking space outside of the guardhouse. Security at NASA-Weston's research facility had become a pain in the ass for outside contractors like him. He supposed it was unavoidable; 9/11 had changed the world. Every government and defense industry installation had been locked up tight as a clam that sees the soup pot coming. Even a civilian terrorist consultant with top-secret clearance had to identify himself to gain access.

Tonight it looked as though he wouldn't have to wait long for his dated clip-on pass. Only a few cars in the lot, no line snaking out through the guardhouse door.

Inside the glass-walled office he could see two guards behind the desk. Another pair manned the nearby gate shack, waiting behind bulletproof glass to screen personnel driving or walking into the facility. In the wee hours of the morning, no one was coming or going. It was, he imagined, yawn duty.

Rooker walked into the office. Ed Green gave him a grin and mock salute. "Evening, Colonel."

"It's just Rooker these days." Not that Green needed to be reminded they were both civilians these days. They'd known each other since Marine Corps days, another lifetime.

That was way back before Rooker started freelancing and then started his own business: Worldwide Security Services— WSS. Back before Rooker started slipping in and out of Afghanistan, gathering intel for the CIA. But when you were in the security business, rank was remembered and moved along through life with you.

"I hear you guys have a ticket for me."

"Don't know why they keep making up new badges for you." Green lifted a cardboard box from beneath the chest-high laminate countertop. He started flipping through plastic holders. "Must cost 'em a fortune."

No Mercy

"Only if they're stupid enough to buy them for a hundred bucks a piece."

The second guard chuckled. "Like the ten thousand-dollar file cabinet?" That snafu had been all over the news a week ago. Now there were more rumors of fraud involving government purchases. The GSA was investigating. The *Washington Post* hinted at a separate Senate investigation."

"Hey, why you here in the middle of the night, buddy?" Green said. "Couldn't wait to pick it up in the morning?"

Rooker shrugged. "I was in the neighborhood."

The Cove, his regular hangout, was just down the road. Live music and energetic women on weekends. Weeknights, the bar was pretty well dead. Fine with him. When he wasn't actually working he preferred his own company. He'd lost the last two guys he could call real friends—one to an IED on a mountain road, the other to marriage. (An old joke he no longer thought very funny.) He'd grown up in a string of foster homes. Still had no family. Rooker supposed it was better that way, given his line of work. No one to worry about him.

"This place is a zoo mornings, everyone checking in. I have a nine o'clock with Davis Jessup."

Ed pursed his fleshy lips, eyes widening. "Chief of Operations, pretty impressive."

Rooker looked across the counter to the second guard. He was repeatedly smacking the heel of one hand against a buzzing control panel. "What's the problem?"

"This crappy alarm system is going nuts again."

"It's not supposed to sound off like that?"

Ed shook his head with a look of disgust.

"Not for no reason, it isn't," the other guard complained. "Been doing this off and on for a week now. Even the electricians can't figure out why it's misfiring."

Rooker frowned. "Shouldn't someone check out the location?"

"You mean drive clear over to building twenty-two again?" Ed said. "Waste of time."

"If anything was wrong over there," the other man added, "the cameras would've picked it up. Our guys on monitor duty would be raising hell. We're covered."

Kathryn Johnson

Rooker let this settle in his mind for a moment. They were probably right. Nothing more than a false alarm, something mechanical going haywire. "Where are your monitors?" He wasn't as familiar with the layout at Weston as he was with the region's military installations and federal offices in downtown DC.

Green shrugged and shoved the badge box beneath the counter. "Backside of the building. Be my guest. Take the shortcut down the hall." He triggered the lock on the door marked Personnel Only.

Rooker could still hear the wonky alarm going off, even after the heavy metal door clacked shut behind him. The pale lime walls of the hallway stretched out ahead of him—doors opened into a break room, a janitorial closet...toilet. He couldn't help thinking: *Someone wants an alarm ignored, best give the thing plenty of obnoxious play time before the critical moment.*

Like the kid crying wolf. After a while, no one pays any attention.

He passed the break room, stinking of stale coffee and microwave pizza. Passed the lavatory. Farther down, a door was marked: No Admittance/Security Only. He tried the knob, even though it was fitted with a key-card system. Locked.

"Rooker, WSS," he called out, knocking. "Everything kosher in there?"

"Hey, Rook!" a voice he recognized said from behind the door. Pete Genovese opened it for him. "Haven't seen you in like, forever."

"Not since Kandahar," Rooker said. They exchanged solemn looks.

Those were bad times. Worse for a young Daniel Rooker than his lonely childhood. Worse than his troubled teen years or the grueling training at Parris Island. Those years in the desert hill country were what had set his course for the rest of his life.

He buddy-punched the Italian, two heads shorter than him, and grinned. "Got yourself a cushy civie gig, I see."

"Yeah." Genovese laughed. "Never thought I'd see the day anyone would pay me to watch the tube. Man, nothin' ever happens here. All I can do tonight to stay awake. Want coffee?"

No Mercy

Rooker shook his head. "Just thought I'd check and see if anything looked funny in Building two-two. Their panic alarm keeps going off."

"Yeah. Was doin' that last night. Day before, too."

The second man in the room, seated in front of a wall of monitors, said, "You'd think in a place like this, crawling with scientists and computer geeks, someone could rig an electrical connection without shorting it out."

Rooker laughed, because it was the thing to do, not because he was about to take a wonky alarm lightly. He already had a bad feeling. He eyed the closed-circuit TV screens. They spanned the width of the room, from desk level to ceiling, each numbered according to buildings on the NASA campus, he assumed. He found the one he was looking for, watched as the cameras cycled through interior and exterior views.

A shot of the main entrance, an empty hallway outside elevator doors, an unoccupied computer lab, an auditorium, another lab, a couple of offices with immense file cabinets, a library of sorts (also unpopulated), the power plant with AC units and emergency generator. Nine views total, before they repeated. Nothing unusual. No people visible. In fact, the building appeared to be completely unoccupied.

"Hold on a minute," Rooker said. He jogged back down the hallway to Ed Green in the main office, his head buzzing in harmony with the rogue alarm. "Do you have a log showing who is actually in the compound now and where they're supposed to be working?"

"The gate does."

"Ask them if anyone has signed in tonight for building twenty-two." Rooker's pulse doubled, making him feel he should be running, without knowing where to or why. *Trouble,* he thought. *Maybe big trouble*.

Green sighed. "Man, you're like my old bulldog Jo-Jo. Get hold of a shoe, and you just won't let go."

Rooker waited while Green made the call. He could see the two men in the guard shack checking a digital tablet, one with the phone wedged between his shoulder and ear, his lips moving.

Ed said into the phone, "Thanks. No, just checking." He hung up. "Only Dr. Foster and her crew. Seven total. She told me they'd reserved antenna time for tonight—had to book time when it was available."

Rooker swore.

Both men stared at him. "What?" Green said.

"Come back here with me."

Seconds later, Rooker was staring at screens again, Green and Genovese flanking him. Images cycled smoothly from camera to camera to camera.

"I still don't see anything," Genovese said. "Everything looks normal."

Rooker nodded. "How many cameras are in twenty-two?"

The two monitor-men looked at each other. "I think it's ten...yeah, ten," Genovese said.

"Only nine are showing images." Rooker squinted at the screen. There it was again—the blip. A brief, nearly imperceptible dead space between views, as if something had been there but no longer was. "One camera's been cut out of the cycle," he said. "Someone's tampered with the system."

"Aw hell," Green muttered and rushed out of the room.

Within minutes, Rooker knew that the entire base would be on alert and locked down—no one in, no one out. Every guard on duty scrambling.

Blood pounded in his head. *Go-go-go!* his body urged. But he needed one more piece of information.

"Do you have a camera in Dr. Foster's laboratory?" he asked.

"Yes, sir." Genovese, all business now, looked confused. Then his eyes widened. "Crap! That's the missing one."

"That's where it's happening." *Whatever it is.* Rooker bolted out of the room.

Out in the parking lot he climbed into his truck. Green and two other guards slammed into an SUV. "No sirens!" Rooker shouted out his window. "We go in silent."

No Mercy

Kate's hands were shaking so hard she kept hitting the wrong keys. Painstakingly, she entered the scripts indicated on the intruders' note. *Terrorists,* she mentally corrected herself. Because that's what they had to be, right?

Homegrown or imported? Aligned with ISIS, al Quaeda, or some local sleeper cell acting on their own? Whoever they were, they seemed to know a hell of a lot about her satellite and sophisticated coding. The strings of data they'd given her would communicate through an antenna on the ground to the satellite overhead. With every keystroke she was beginning to understand more about what these people intended to do with her satellite. The possibilities were chilling.

Camo Woman stood over Kate, watching every flick of her fingertips. "Don't even think about changing anything," she warned. "I'll know if you do."

Would she? Or was that a ruse to force her to cooperate? Kate glanced up quickly, really looking at the woman for the first time.

The sleeves of her camouflage shirt had been torn off to reveal muscular arms that looked capable of lifting a small car. She was Caucasian, but maybe with some Asian mixed in. Her white-blond hair was spiked. Black eyeliner thickly circled pale lavender eyes. She looked like a throwback to an '80's rocker. Benatar on steroids.

"You think I'd chance your gunning down another of my people?" Kate couldn't keep the revulsion out of her tone.

Hess moaned. Out of the corner of her eye, she could see him struggling to move into a sitting position, his back supported by the blood-spattered partition. If he didn't receive medical attention soon, there was every possibility he'd bleed out. She dropped her hands from the keyboard and started up out of her seat.

"Sit!" the woman commanded.

"He's hurt! For God's sake, let me or one of my team help him." She tried not to look at or think about David. *Be practical. He's past help. Save the others.*

"No!" Zed barked. "Everyone will stay away from him. If you did as I asked, we wouldn't have had to shoot either of them."

"You bastard!" Cam sobbed. "How can you let the man suffer like this?"

"He won't suffer for long." The woman gave Cam a smug smile.

What does that mean? Did the trio intend to murder all of them before leaving the building?

The woman glowered down at Kate. "Keep working, bitch."

Kate risked another quick peek to check on the rest of her team. Zed's timekeeper was herding them to the far end of the room. They sat down beyond the last row of cubicles. At his order they turned to face the wall. Would any of them survive this night?

Where the hell is Security!

"Six minutes gone," their timekeeper announced. He gazed with a bored expression around the lab, apparently no longer all that concerned about the timed goal they'd set for themselves. Maybe he was on drugs or something. The scar on his cheek glowed an electric blue in the fluorescent light. She would remember that detail, for all the good it might do.

"Hurry up, Doctor!" Zed roared.

"At least let me cover Dr. Hess with something," Amanda called from the back of the room, her voice surprisingly strong. "He's bleeding and must be in shock. Show a little kindness. You're getting what you want."

"I'll be all right." Hess ground out the words between clenched teeth. "For God sakes, don't give them an excuse to start shooting again."

The woman standing over Kate adjusted her stance. Kate glanced up cautiously. Her guard's attention had shifted to Zed, who was striding down the room toward Amanda and his other prisoners.

Kate's fingers flew, taking advantage of two precious seconds of distraction. She prayed she remembered the encryption codes correctly. Within seconds she had scrolled down the screen and was back to inputting the last bit of information from the page Zed had given her.

"Finished," she said, lifting her hands from the keyboard with a flourish that would have done a concert pianist proud.

"Move." The woman pushed Kate out of the chair, took her place, and scanned the screen. "She's done it. We're gold!"

Zed turned back around, grinning. "Let's go."

Kate could only stand by and watch as Camo Woman slipped a USB flashdrive into the computer. She hit a few keys, copied data onto it, then slipped the little silver stick into her pocket.

"Come on," Zed snapped.

The woman turned toward Kate with a malicious gleam in her eyes and lifted her gun. "First, we finish the job."

Kate planted her feet and faced her assailant. She wasn't feeling brave. But she was, after all, a scientist. And scientists deal with fact, not emotion. Fact #1: There was nowhere for Kate to hide. Fact #2: She had no weapon and no combat skills. Fact #3: She wasn't even sure that she deserved to live if the decisions she'd made had cost one or, possibly, two men their lives. She didn't even want to think about the even worse scenario.

Kate watched the rock-gangsta-terrorist woman's finger curl around the gun's trigger. Her heart tripped then felt as if it had stopped beating entirely. Swallowing, Kate said a silent goodbye to her parents, her sister and little nieces, cousin Mercy...the world.

The gun's muzzle jerked to the right by inches, then fired a deafening clatter of rounds. Kate's computer exploded in a mass of sparks and metal shards.

Kate was still shaking when the woman stepped back, grinning as if pleased to have terrified her. "Insurance," she said.

"Seven minutes," the robo-stopwatch announced, even as Kate was still absorbing the miracle that she was still alive, still trying to catch her breath. He turned to Zed. "We take him, right?"

"That's the plan—one hostage. Might as well be Mr. Big Mouth."

Kathryn Johnson

Kate's eyes flew wide as the two minions moved toward Frank Hess. "No, wait!" she screamed. "What are you doing? You have what you came for."

"Stand back!" Zed warned. "He's coming with us."

Kate's knees liquified. Her heart raced. The pair hoisted the wounded man to his feet. Frank Hess's tear-streaked face contorted with pain. He shot Kate a terrified look as the three intruders shoved him, staggering, ahead of them and out of the room.

The door slammed shut behind them.

For what seemed an eternity, no one in the room moved. Or breathed.

Then Tommy leaped up from where he sat on the floor and charged the length of the room at Kate. "Why'd you let them take him? Jesus, he's dead meat now!"

Cam sprang to her feet and quickly caught up with him. She grabbed his arm and pulled him to a stop. "Quit that! How do you think she was going to stop them? Cross that maniac one more time and they might have killed us all."

"But Frank," Amanda whispered. She stayed seated but turned to lean her back against the far wall. "Poor, poor soul."

Yes, Kate thought, *poor Frank.* What did they intend to do with him? Use him as a human shield if they have trouble getting past the guards? Her terror morphed almost instantly into fury.

"Where the hell is Security?" She dove for the door.

"Wait!" Vernon shouted. He moved toward her at a determined pace, his eyes wide with fear, arm outstretched as though to grab hold of her from twenty feet away and yank her back from the door. "Don't go out there, Kate. What if they're still in the hall? What if they get cornered by the guards and have to double back? Better to barricade ourselves in here and wait for help."

Kate hesitated. He was right. She couldn't help Frank or recover the USB with the satellite's control data without help. The best she could do for now was to protect her team. *What's left of my team.* The words rang hollow and accusing in her mind. Never in her life had she felt so heartsick, angry, and powerless.

Vernon and Cam started shoving furniture in front of the door. Amanda ran to David, settling her plump body down on her

No Mercy

knees, like a partridge on its nest. She held her fingertips to his throat, as if she still wasn't convinced he was dead. After a moment, she closed her eyes, bowed her head, and whispered, "Dear God."

Kate picked up the phone and punched in Security's extension.   "I don't believe it."

"What?" Tommy said.

"The line's *busy!*"

Kathryn Johnson

It seemed forever and a day, but when Kate checked her watch, only two minutes had passed. Just a hundred-twenty seconds from the moment three killers left the HW-1 Command Center to when stealthy running steps approached the barricaded door. The knob jiggled. Someone shoved hard from the outside. The door didn't give.

"They've come for us," Amanda breathed. "Praise the Lord!" She started to weep, and Kate knew she was thinking of her children.

"Don't open the door yet," Tommy warned. His freckles stood out against the pallor of his skin, making him look even younger. "We don't *know* it's Security."

"Dr. Foster?" a man called from beyond the pile of furniture. "Are you all right?"

The voice didn't belong to any of the intruders, she felt sure. Neither did it sound familiar.

"Who are you?" Kate said.

"Daniel Rooker, Worldwide Security Service. I'm accompanied by NASA guards. If you're able, open the door." Relief filled her chest, tightened her raw throat, burned behind her eyelids. *No, no tears yet*. Not even tears of relief. There was still hope the guards might stop the three intruders before they left the grounds of the installation with the stolen data. Besides, there was Frank to think about.

"Move everything out of the way!" she shouted.

They'd only cleared away half of the small mountain of desks and file cabinets before two men on the outside slammed the door open the rest of the way, forcing open a passage.

A dark-haired man in jeans and T-shirt climbed over the mess and into the room, his eyes darting left, then right, then ahead. He wasn't exceptionally tall but seemed, to Kate, to fill the room with his presence. He held a gray metal pistol. Kate thought she'd be happy to never again see another gun.

No Mercy

"They've gone," she gasped. "You have to find them. They took valuable—"

"Into the hallway," he ordered, as if he hadn't heard her. "All of you. Now!"

She stared at him. "I said, they're gone."

"Right. Out of here, lady."

A half-dozen security guards rushed in. Kate and her team were pushed unceremoniously out of the lab, into the corridor, where another asked each of them their name and checked their photo badges.

Kate leaned against the beige wall and closed her eyes, exhausted beyond words, her head pounding, only vaguely aware of the sounds of the men knocking around inside cubicles, roughly shoving aside anything in their way. Checking, she supposed, to make sure the terrorists had indeed left.

Someone inside the room said, "Called for an ambulance. Won't do him any good."

David, she thought, tears blurring her vision. She forced them back. *No time for mourning now.*

When Rooker reappeared, he was talking into his cell phone. He kept repeating the same word in response to whatever was being said to him. "Right. Right. Right."

"Has Security caught them?" she asked when he flipped the phone closed.

He shook his head. "If we'd had more warning—"

"More warning?" She choked on the words. "Your warning system is worthless! I triggered the silent alarm the moment they broke into my lab. A good fifteen minutes passed before you showed up. What the hell were you all doing—taking a freaking coffee break?"

He drew a slow breath and observed her with irritating calm and a steady blue-eyed gaze. "This isn't helping, Dr. Foster."

"I demand to know why no one responded to my alarm. Do you people always move like mimes on holiday?" She didn't care whether or not she was being fair, or professional, or even logical. Not with one man dead and the life of another, *plus her life's work*, at stake.

Rooker seemed unfazed by her accusations. "As it was explained to me, the alarm has been acting up all week. The men on duty assumed it was another false signal."

"The cameras!" she shouted. The calmer he acted, the angrier she got. "What about them?"

"Someone sabotaged the one in your lab." He started to turn away as if to follow the other guards, most of whom now were rushing down the hallway. At the last moment, he swung back to face her. "We've sealed off the compound. No one's getting out." His eyes slid sideways to the door behind her. "Who was injured in there, besides the man we found dead? I saw a lot of blood across the room from him."

Kate drew a breath, counted to ten, and then filled him in on the scenario that had ended with the intruders escaping with the USB...and the only copy of the data that enabled a conversation with her satellite. Her throat felt raw, shredded. She couldn't stop her voice from shaking. She feared a flood of tears was a blink away. "They shot Frank Hess, my lead physicist, then took him hostage. What will they do to h—" But she really didn't want to think about *that*.

Rooker looked away from her. "We'll find them. But if by some chance they've gotten away, I'll need to know why this USB stick they took is so important." She opened her mouth to speak but he plunged on. "I also need to know any details you can recall about the intruders' physical appearance or behavior, anything that might help us identify them. Write down everything you can think of. Have each of your people do the same. Your Security office will have forms to fill out, too."

She stared at the man. How cold and totally devoid of compassion he sounded. He might be on the white-hat team, but the least he could do was offer her some kind of reassurance.

"You want us each to file an incident report tonight?"

"Yes."

Kate sighed. "I don't think you quite grasp what my team and I went through tonight. We were *held at gunpoint*." She gave each word the weight it deserved. "We were threatened with the loss of our lives. We watched while two men—colleagues and friends—were ruthlessly gunned down.*"

No Mercy

"Right. And you'll get your people to hand in their reports immediately, or Security will hold you on-base until it's done." His tone was scalpel-sharp, not a sliver of sympathy.

Kate drew a steadying breath. "Fine. I'll make sure every member of my team hands in a report. Furthermore, I'll instruct them to do it in simple English, no long words, so that even *you* can understand."

A muscle twitched in the man's jaw. Another sign of his irritation with her? She didn't care. Anyway, he was being a jerk. He deserved to be brought down a peg...or three.

Kathryn Johnson

By the time Kate was allowed to send her people home it was nearly four o'clock that morning. They'd each given statements to the chief of security. An FBI forensic team arrived from DC and closed off the entire Greenfield, Maryland compound. She waited breathlessly for word of the intruders' capture, along with the missing USB stick and their hostage. But although the entire base had been searched, no sign of them turned up. They seemed to have disappeared without a trace.

Standing next to her car in the parking lot in those quiet, pre-dawn hours that always seemed to her so very peaceful, Kate felt utterly exhausted. She could barely summon up the strength to press the key fob and unlatch her car door. It was as she reached for the door handle that she glimpsed a figure moving soundlessly along the perimeter of the dark, tree-lined pavement. She froze, held her breath.

Get into the car! she told herself. But she couldn't make herself move.

Whoever it was, he—she was sure it was a man, given the broad shoulders and height—didn't walk as much as shift from one position to the next. He seemed little more than a shadow, glimpsed between tree trunks and moonbeams. Then out of the gloom and into a pool of yellow halogen, cast by the lamps surrounding the parking lot, stepped the annoying Daniel Rooker.

She breathed again. "Have they found anything?"

He came toward her without speaking. She examined his face, wanting to see good news there. He didn't look particularly tired or worried, even under the stress of a failed search. But his expression was virtually unreadable. If anything he appeared so completely focused on something other than her that it took him a moment to register who she was.

"We've located how they got out, and probably in," he said. "The perimeter fence behind a storage trailer at the north end of the property has been cut."

27

No Mercy

She knew the place he was talking about. "But that's clear on the other side of the compound from my lab. How did they get way over there without being spotted by the guards?"

"Tunnels."

"Tunnels?" She pressed fingertips to her throbbing temples, feeling as if there wasn't enough sleep or aspirin in the world to release the pressure. "Those abandoned underground passages from Cold War days?" Back in the nineteen-fifties people believed that bomb shelters dug a few feet below ground level really could protect them from the holocaust.

He nodded. "They link a half dozen of the older buildings and lead to subterranean shelters. One tunnel ends at a recently unsealed hatch within feet of the fence." He looked away for a moment. "Who knew about them, doctor?"

"Lots of people, I suppose. They aren't used anymore, of course." Kate frowned. "How can you be sure that's the way they escaped?"

Rooker turned back to face her, his gaze still scrubbed clean of emotion. "Blood. Fresh."

She shut her eyes and shivered. Frank's, of course. And that's when she decided she couldn't take one more second of this. "I'm going home now. Goodnight."

She desperately needed to shut herself away in the comfortable cocoon of her little condo. There was nothing more she could do here. She'd wait at home for word of Frank Hess's fate, praying he'd be rescued. And she'd hope to God that whoever was sent in search of the trio that stole her satellite would find them.

And if they failed on both counts? *No, no, no! Stop thinking like that!*

She swung open the car door and dropped wearily into the driver's seat.

Rooker stepped up behind her, preventing her from closing the door. "If you'd held out for a few minutes longer—"

"Don't even go there, Mr. Rooker." She stuck the key into the ignition and turned it. The engine gave a familiar, strangely soothing rumble.

"I'll damn well go where I want. It seems to me you could have done more to—"

Anger and resentment swept away her fatigue. "If you feel compelled to blame someone other than those three crazies who broke into my lab," she said, "try pointing your finger at NASA Security. No one told me the alarm system was malfunctioning. I pushed their damn panic button, followed protocol. After that, all I cared about was trying to keep my people alive."

He opened his mouth as if to object, but she rushed on.

"As important as HW-1 is to me, my team—those six human beings—mean a hell of a lot more to me. And that's what I'll tell our Chief of Operations at the briefing that will no doubt happen tomorrow." *Today*, she corrected herself, because she could already see wispy pink-purple trails of dawn in the eastern sky.

Kate grabbed the car's inside door handle and yanked hard, hoping she'd crush the man. Unfortunately he stepped to one side just ahead of the heavy door. She slammed it hard, hit the lock button.

"Neanderthal," she muttered under her breath, hit the gas and sped away, ignoring the 25-mph speed limit.

The traffic report blared from the radio-alarm clock. WTOP's announcer reported the usual rush-hour mayhem on the DC beltway, with accidents on I-270 and massive commuter delays along I-95N, coming in from Virginia. It was 7:15 a.m. and she'd had barely three hours of sleep.

Kate tossed back the bed clothes. The message light on her landline phone was blinking; she recognized the number. The CoO's office had called a half hour earlier. She'd slept right through five normally irritatingly loud rings before voice mail silenced them. She couldn't recall that ever happening before, light sleeper that she was.

Kate retrieved the voice mail and was rewarded with a sinking feeling in her stomach. As she'd expected, the Chief wanted her in his office ASAP. But, according to his assistant's message, she was also scheduled for a formal briefing at NASA-Weston at 11:00 a.m. with Homeland Security. It would be an agonizing day crammed with explanations and, no doubt, accusations and buck-passing, as a result of the security breach.

No Mercy

There would be a formal press conference, the media hyping things up even more. She might even lose her job over this mess.

One thing she was sure of. The government and NASA would want to limit information released to the public. They'd probably try to make the break-in and assault on her team the story. Maybe even admit that the control system of a satellite had been tempered with. But nothing would be said to the press about possible dangers to the public.

Fine. Let them spin the story their way. But if anyone pointed the finger of blame at her and her staff, she'd defend them with her last breath. She and her team had done the best they could with an impossible situation. Losing Dave Proctor and—she had to be honest with herself in the light of a new day—probably Frank Hess, weighed heavily on her. But she'd try to focus on the lives she'd saved last night, and on the one step she'd been able to take to protect the integrity of the HW-1 project. The step that no one other than her knew about, so far.

By 8:00 a.m. Kate had showered, pinned her still-damp blond hair into a dignified twist at the nape of her neck, dug her best navy-blue pant suit out of the back of the closet, and dressed. The nausea of the night before had left a burning sensation at the back of her throat. Her head pounded with a relentless jackhammer rhythm. The only thing that gave her strength to face the day was the thought that Frank, if he was still alive, would be having a far worse day.

She left the coziness of her Delft blue-and-white bedroom—bed piled high with white eyelet pillows and cozy down-filled comforter, with delicate watercolor prints on the wall—that had soothed the traumas of many a difficult day. In her tiny kitchen she made herself a soft-boiled egg and ate a single slice of dry toast with it, hoping the light meal would stay down. Amanda had once teased her, saying the Space Shuttle had a larger kitchen than Kate's. But she spent so little time at home, and besides, she was the only diner she cooked for.

As Kate ate she stared at the bulletin board beside her fridge. Tacked to it were five colorful mission patches—reminders of her earlier projects with NASA. Beloved, exciting missions that had taught her so much. It struck Kate again, the possibility that her career might be over. She'd surrendered control of a valuable asset—a multi-million-dollar satellite. Colleagues had died and been brutalized. She'd let NASA down.

People were fired for far less.

Before leaving home she tried to call Dave Proctor's wife. A message in her voice mail had informed her that the Chief had contacted the family's minister, and the two of them already had broken the news to Gloria Proctor. This morning when Kate called, a neighbor answered the family's phone.

"She's not able to talk to you now," the woman said, her voice tight with grief. Kate asked that the woman pass along her condolences. She promised to call back later to see how Gloria was doing and answer any questions she might have.

Frank Hess was unmarried, and no one knew of close relations. There was nothing she could do but hold out hope that he'd survive the ordeal and be freed.

She then called each of the team members who'd been with her in the lab last night. She saved Cambridge Mackenzie for last. She repeated a version of her previous conversations: "Don't even think about coming in today. The CSI investigators won't let us into the lab until they're finished there. Stay home and rest with your daughter. Try not to think about last night."

"How are the others doing?" Cam's voice sounded distant, as if reaching out to her through a Chesapeake Bay fog. Kate had never known her to be anything but strong and sure of herself. Being confronted by one's mortality could change a person.

"Vernon was sleeping. His wife answered. She said he was as upset as she's ever seen him. Tommy and Amanda are, I guess, managing as well as can be expected. Tommy's dad was with him. Amanda has her entire tribe around her."

"Good. So, what are you doing today?" Cam asked.

"I meet with Jessup in his office at nine to prepare for a briefing of the top dogs."

"He won't be alone," Cam said, "probably have attorneys and who knows what else with him. You want me to come with you this morning?"

"No. You stay with your little girl. You need each other now. Give her lots of hugs for me."

"Uh-huh." Cam drew an audible breath, as if she was considering saying something more. Whatever it was, she apparently decided against it. "You take care of yourself, hear? Don't let those macho types dump this on you."

"One already tried." She pictured Rooker's arrogant expression, heard in her mind his accusatory tone. *The nerve of the man!* "I'll give it my best. Wish me luck."

"A truckload."

Kate's hand hovered over the receiver one last time after she'd hung up from speaking with Cam. She ached to talk with her father. Mom would react emotionally to the incident, no doubt thinking how close her daughter had come to death. Her father was her rock. Just hearing his voice would clear her head. But she couldn't discuss classified information with him or anyone else. She decided against calling them just yet.

Twenty minutes later, as Kate parked her little red VW Golf outside Building Five at NASA-Westin, she considered the uselessness of her advice to the team. Tell someone *not* to think about purple cats and they immediately picture purple cats. The brain works in perverse ways. Her own advice had been less than successful even for her. The horror of the previous night stalked her like a wild animal, gnawing at her subconscious, interfering with her ability to focus on the critical tasks of the day.

Regardless of the motive behind the hijacking of HW-1, it was up to her to arrive at possible strategies for reclaiming the satellite. At least until they took her job away from her. But until she was given access to her lab there was little she could do. She didn't even know what options remained for contacting the sat. Had her last-ditch effort, while the intruders' attention had been diverted, even worked?

Walking from the parking lot toward Headquarters, Kate again tried to concentrate on rational solutions. But the terrifying sequences of the night kept playing over and over in her mind, a nightmarish instant replay that always ended the same way:

Zed casually turning his weapon on Frank Hess as he pleaded for his life.

A hail of bullets peppering Dave Proctor's body as Kate stood helplessly by.

The ear-splitting cackle of their weapons.

Blood. So much blood.

Kathryn Johnson

Her stomach knotted and cramped, worse than the night before. Kate pressed a fist to her abdomen as she shoved her key card into the building's lock pad. She rushed through the sun-streaked marble lobby of HQ, eyes straight ahead, focusing on nothing.

Then *it* was there. Her nemesis. Out of the deepest recesses of her memory rose an image of another gun. The one that had changed her young life.

She forced herself to keep on walking, moving blindly through the crowded lobby toward the elevators as she fought off the past. But that was impossible. One didn't just walk away from tragedy. The damage a bullet was capable of doing to human flesh was obscene. It stuck in the memory. Forever.

Suddenly, it wasn't just a memory of the weapon that she saw. She was back in that other time, recalling every ghastly detail she'd struggled all of her adult life to suppress.

That afternoon, she had heard the shot nearly at the same moment as Meghan's scream. At first she'd thought it was part of the children's game. Kate had actually been laughing when she ran up the stairs and into Meghan's bedroom, and saw the little girl lying in a widening crimson pool.

They'd said it was her fault. Kate's fault for not watching the two younger children she'd been babysitting carefully enough. Even those who tried to be kind to Kate had whispered similar words when they thought she couldn't hear them. She'd believed them. *My fault...my fault.*

Kate blinked away tears as she stepped onto the elevator. Thankfully, no one else joined her for the ride up. This isn't the time for guilt, she told herself. Remorse for the past would have to wait its turn. She had enough to deal with now.

The satellite—HW-1. Why did Zed's gang want it? That was the question that haunted her. What did they think they were going to do with it? She had several ideas, all of them horrible.

The corridor outside of the chief of operations' office on the third floor was deserted. No one stood chatting outside of the break room or swapped gossip around the water cooler. People were staying out of sight, in their offices. As in a classic Western film, Main Street had cleared before the big gunfight.

No Mercy

Kate took a deep breath for courage before letting herself into Jessup's outer office. His administrative assistant didn't look up from the file drawer pulled out in front of her. Kate's lips automatically twitched up at the corners in greeting, but Sara Brown in her conservative pinstripe suit wasn't smiling today.

"Go on in, Katie. They're waiting."

Kate swallowed. "Who's with him, Sara?"

"Max Archer." Still no eye contact. A bad sign.

"I don't recognize the name. Who is he?"

"Homeland Security. He replaced Evermont last week."

"Oh, right." Her throat felt so raw she could hardly get the words out.

"And some kind of special investigator. The FBI, I think, though I'm not sure." Sara finally moved her attention from the files to glance uneasily at Kate. "Someone said she was with a terrorist task force."

Kate nodded. The situation had certainly gone high-profile fast.

"I heard about Drs. Hess and Proctor. I'm so very sorry."

"Thank you, Sara," Kate murmured. "I guess that means you haven't heard any good news. They haven't found Dr. Hess yet?"

Sara shook her head, blinked, and looked away.

Kate knocked on the chief's door then let herself in. The conversation in the room stopped. Kate kept her head down and moved toward the only empty chair.

"Dr. Foster." The CoO's voice was cool but polite. "We're glad you're here, and that you weren't harmed last night."

Jessup was, she'd often thought, a man who would disappear if he stood against a beige wall—sandy-colored hair combed back from a colorless moon face, a tan suit and shirt with matching tie that lay over a concave chest and round paunch. Short and otherwise physically unimpressive, he surrounded himself with proof of his own importance. Diplomas, honorary degrees, and awards papered the entire wall behind his desk. Another wall displayed photographs of himself with various political, sports, and entertainment celebrities.

Kate was more interested in the other real people in the room. Max Archer's face was unfamiliar to her, but had a lot more character than Jessup's. Heavy eyebrows, a prominent nose, eyes that pierced her. He was tall, slender, and looked like a man who worked out religiously, although his steel-gray hair revealed his age to be at least sixty.

The final member of the group Kate recognized immediately. Mercy O'Brien. Her very own cousin. Kate hid her shock but couldn't help smiling. She restrained herself from rushing up to Mercy and hugging her while spilling out everything about last night.

She doubted it was luck that landed the cousins in the same room. Mercy must be here for a reason. Terrorist task force? Was that what Mercy was involved in these days? Or was the FBI, or whoever Mercy represented, now invested in the management of Earth-orbiting satellites and the possible risks to national security from sats that were armed, regardless of who owned them?

But now wasn't the time to ask such questions. She told herself she must be patient.

Introductions were made. Kate tried to look each person in the eye as she greeted them, but found it hard to do, even with Mercy. How could they not blame her for what had happened, for the men who had died, when she in all honesty blamed herself?

"Dr. Foster. Kate," Mercy said.

Kate looked up at her and gave her another weak smile.

Mercy observed her with what appeared to be genuine sympathy. "We're grateful you were able to come in and help us get a full picture of what occurred in your laboratory last night. And, by the way, the gentlemen in this room know that we're related." She smiled and Kate felt the lump in her throat swell with gratitude. "I'm here partly for that reason, to put you at ease, but also because the Department of Defense has asked my employer, Red Sands Consulting, to coordinate communications between government entities ."

"I see," Kate said stiffly.

"I'm sure you'd rather spend the day at home. It must have been terribly traumatic to everyone last night."

Kate nodded her head. She still couldn't trust herself not to tear up at the memory. "I'm sure we'd all rather be elsewhere." She set her briefcase on the floor beside the empty chair, obviously intended for her use. Her hand shook as she released

No Mercy

the briefcase's strap. She steadied herself by gripping the polished wood of the chair arm, and sat down.

Jessup flattened his palms across printed pages on his desktop and cleared his throat. "We've all read your report, Dr. Foster. It must have been a terrifying experience."

"It was—" she swallowed once, then again, holding herself together "—as Mercy has said, for all of us."

"Yes, well..." Jessup murmured, then glanced at Archer.

The Homeland Security man turned to face her, as if reacting to a cue from Jessup. His bullish face remained free of emotion. His eyebrows looked so oppressively weighty Kate doubted any incident, no matter how horrendous, could lift them in shock.

Archer said, "The President has been informed of the incident. He is, of course, most concerned."

Kate cleared her throat. "He should be." All eyes were on her now. And there were important points she had to make before they booted her out the door. "To date, over eight hundred satellites orbit the Earth. Any one of them, in the wrong hands, could be potentially dangerous." But very few of the "wrong hands" in the world, including groups like ISIS and al Quaeda, had the knowledge to be able to manipulate such sophisticated projects to their use. That ability was limited to an elite few of the highly trained scientists in the world.

Kate spent the next few minutes briefing Archer, Mercy, and her boss, who was relatively new to the Heat Wave project. "The HW-1, initially launched three years ago, was a prototype designed to test the use of microwave energy as a reliable alternate energy source. If successful, our work will enable the launch of a fleet of fifty or sixty similar satellites—massive structures assembled in space over a period of years, each with an array of solar panels and parabolic mirrors."

"A *renewable* alternate energy source," Archer added.

Kate nodded. "Yes. Positioned around the Earth, these satellites could collect solar energy, convert it to microwave energy, and beam it to ground stations. The conversion to electricity could provide power to light cities, run transportation systems and industries. Free energy to replace fossil fuels—oil and gas—as they dry up or become too expensive." No longer would America and Europe be dependent upon oil from other countries. *If* the theories of scientists such as Kate proved workable.

Archer folded his hands in his lap. "What I don't understand, and the President is having trouble grasping, is why such a dangerous mission was being pursued without proper safeguards, and without informing the White House in advance."

Kate's mouth dropped open. For a moment, she couldn't form a response. He'd taken her by surprise. She had known that someone, or some group, would be singled out as a scapegoat. Was the government going to blame NASA, giving yet another reason for cutting funding for space out of the budget? Then she thought about all she and her team had been through the previous night. This interview—or *lynching*—was, by comparison, a piece of cake.

Kate said, "No one involved in Heat Wave has ever doubted the safety of the mission. HW-1 is merely a prototype, designed to emit a safe level of microwave energy. In fact, to redirect or bump up the level of energy would be extremely difficult. Heat Wave is designed to be used solely for controlled experiments in energy disbursement. The satellite was never intended to be used as a weapon or at a level of output that would be harmful in any way."

Jessup nodded his head in solemn agreement. "Security was more than adequate for civilian-funded experiments of this kind."

Archer frowned down at his hands, then shot an accusing gaze at Jessup. "What once was adequate is no longer enough, sir. The President's advisors believe we now have a loose cannon poised above Earth. The military has experimented with many forms of energy. Human beings exposed to ultrahigh levels of microwave emissions suffer illness, severe burns, and even death." His face reddened and voice rose until he was nearly shouting. One fist came up, as though he was tempted to pound his fist on the desk for emphasis, but he held himself back. "Germ warfare without the germs, that's what this could come to. Invisible. Odorless! Used as a weapon, microwaves would be undetectable until it was too late!"

"Now wait—" Kate interrupted Archer's tirade. "I think we're getting ahead of ourselves. First, whoever has control of

No Mercy

the HW-1 needs access to highly technical knowledge in order to increase the level of emissions and concentrate them to a lethal dose. They'd also need a means of pointing the energy at their intended target." She was thinking the onboard lasers would do the trick, but decided this probably wasn't the time to mention that.

"But—" Archer tried to interrupt.

Kate cut him off. "This isn't like a video game or *Star Wars* where you just aim and fire death rays. Even if the people who took HW-1were capable of manipulating the satellite to their use—a destructive use—it would take time for the effects to be felt in the targeted area. We'd have a little warning. Theoretically, people could be evacuated."

Archer was shaking his head. "Unacceptable. You're assuming whoever ends up in control of the satellite *doesn't* have the technical know-how to use it as a weapon? We can't take that risk."

Jessup nodded his head solemnly, taking Archer's lead. "That's true, we must assume the worst case scenario. Why snatch it if they don't know what to do with it?"

"Fear," she said. "Isn't that the weapon all terrorists count on? Create mayhem. Terror. Disrupt society and make governments vulnerable."

"You're saying—" Jessup again "—just the threat alone would be enough for them? They don't have to actually do anything other than claim they'll use it?"

"It's possible," she said.

"But what if they *do* modify the satellite, actually turn it into a weapon?" Archer glared contemptuously at her. "The technical knowledge and strategies of ISIS, and other large terrorist cells, have improved exponentially in just the past year. Say, they threaten to strike downtown Boston. So we—what? Evacuate the entire city? Another day they threaten to strike the White House, or Congress. Do we move everyone out of Washington, D.C., and into West Virginia? Or do you recommend we simply call their bluff and wait to see if they'll actually kill thousands of people with a rogue satellite? You can't suggest this as a solution, doctor!"

Kate swallowed, her heart tripping over beats. She looked toward Jessup for support. He avoided her gaze and said nothing. The man was an administrator, not a scientist. It was cover-my-ass time.

Mercy had been silent throughout the emotional exchange. Now she said in a quietly reasonable voice, "All of your fears, gentlemen, are based on the premise that this Zed is actually able to access the HW-1's guidance system. Dr. Foster has said that she doubts they have the wherewithal to do that."

Archer looked from her to Kate. "I thought your report stated that they've stolen the encryption codes and blocked us out."

"They have. We are shut out, at least temporarily. But so are they."

The two men stared at her as if she were a talking wedge of cheese.

Mercy's lips twitched as if she was controlling her urge to smile. Kate could almost hear her working out a tactful way of educating the two men. "Perhaps," her cousin suggested, "portions of Dr. Foster's report were somewhat technically worded for the lay person. I believe she mentioned a minor program adjustment she made while the intruders were too occupied to notice."

Kate began to breathe a little easier. She had an ally. *Bless you, cuz.*

"I embedded an extra code to buy us time. It may give us a chance to reclaim HW-1 before they can bring it online."

Jessup sat up straighter in his chair, shot Archer a beige smile, then turned to Kate. "You jammed their program?"

"Yes, sir."

Smiles all around.

"Then we're sitting pretty." The angry flush across Archer's face faded. "Why didn't you say so in the first place? They can't get in without knowing your code. Is anyone on your team aware of it? Is there anyone else you've told it to?"

"No, sir."

"Wonderful. All we have to do is make sure they don't get to *you*, doctor." He chuckled, enjoying his own humor. "Perhaps the FBI will assign you a bodyguard."

No Mercy

Mercy was shaking her head even before Kate could object to the plan. "I don't think that's quite what Dr. Foster means when she says we've bought time. I've had experience with cases involving cyber crime. Hackers, no matter whether they're college kids pulling pranks or foreign governments intent on shutting down an enemy's banking system, often are incredibly inventive and elusive; some we've been tracking for years and still haven't nailed. A good hacker can break down almost any code, given enough time."

Archer looked far less pleased now.

Kate said, "I had literally seconds, no time for anything fancy. I did what I could."

No more smiles.

"How long do you believe we have?" Archer asked glumly.

Kate's gaze tracked across the room to the vertical lines of sunlight cutting between slats of the window blinds. Light was power, and any power could be used for good, or for evil. The problem was—doing harm was almost always easier.

"With luck, we might have a week to locate the stolen memory stick. Without it, only a few days."

"At least we know who has it." Archer stabbed a finger toward the papers on Jessup's desk. "The description of the intruders is in your team's report, along with the leader's name, Zed. All we have to do is track the fuckers down."

Mercy made an impatient sound. "Those descriptions of the three intruders may mean nothing. My people at Red Sands think they might have been disguised. They weren't wearing masks to hide their identity. According to Kate's team, at least one of them was rather outlandishly attired. The men might have been subtler, wearing a false beard or makeup."

Kate smiled. She hadn't thought of that. But now it seemed likely that Mercy was right.

"Or," Mercy continued, "they might merely be mercenaries, not terrorists at all, hired by another party. Freelancers. Their plan being to sell the stick to the highest bidder as quickly as possible. We just don't know yet who we're dealing with— militant extremists, a hostile country, religious fanatics?" She shrugged. "So far, no one is claiming responsibility. And no demands have been made."

"What about my associate, Dr. Hess?" Kate asked, worried that no one had given her an update on his situation. "Mr. Rooker, the security expert who arrived with our *tardy* guards—" she couldn't help getting in a small dig "—said he thought they'd ditch Frank after they'd gotten safely out of the compound."

Mercy shook her head. "State and local police are searching and questioning anyone who might have been in the area last night. The Bureau has also assigned agents as support. Nothing so far. I'm sorry." She hesitated. "How serious was his wound?"

"I'm not a medical expert," Kate said. "He lost a lot of blood, but he was hit in the fleshy part of his right shoulder. So maybe the wound wasn't life threatening." A futile wish on her part?

"The CSI crew went over your lab, top to bottom. They didn't find the bullet, so it didn't pass straight through him. He'd be in better shape if it had. If he receives medical attention soon, he might make it."

Might. Or he could bleed to death in whatever ditch Zed threw him. Her heart ached at the grim possibilities.

Then it came to her—a thin thread of hope.

"There is a reason, other than insurance, for keeping Frank Hess alive." All eyes were on her again. "I assume they have their own computer experts. Someone who knew what they were doing wrote those scripts they forced me to enter. The first step was to clear the PSCIF, Power System Command Inhibit Flags. That cut us out of the loop immediately. HW-1 would then be vulnerable to commands from any source, if properly entered. The next encrypted commands would capture the command database. But to reprogram the satellite's computer would require a scientist with specific knowledge of Heat Wave's systems."

Mercy nodded her understanding. "It makes sense, then, that they'd grab one of the senior scientists on the project."

"And now that I've interfered with their immediate access to the system," Kate added, "they may decide to keep Dr. Hess alive long enough to help them break the code and reprogram."

Mercy gave her a reassuring smile. "That's good news then. Buys us time. Buys him time." But her expression almost immediately darkened. "Just keep in mind that traveling with a wounded man won't be easy. They'll have trouble hiding

No Mercy

someone hurt that badly. He'll attract attention, and they can't afford that."

Kate felt heartsick. *Be honest,* she told herself. *There's no guarantee they haven't already killed Frank.* They might not even realize they need him.

Kathryn Johnson

It was to the credit of her cousin that Kate was able to pull herself together over lunch and arrive halfway sane at the briefing that afternoon. After Mercy had informed Archer that she'd personally report any breakthroughs in the case to him, she whisked Kate off to the cafeteria for hot tea and a sandwich.

"I don't think they realize the gift you've given them," Mercy said after they were seated at a corner table, away from most of the other diners. "Not many people would have had the presence of mind to disable the program, given the pressure you were under." She studied Kate's face. "And you're sure they didn't notice?"

"If they had, would they have left when they did?"

Mercy shrugged. *Who knew the minds of people bent on violence?*

"No, I'm pretty sure they didn't have a clue," Kate said. "I imagine they'll be pissed when they discover they can't do whatever it is they intend to do with the satellite." She sipped from the heavy white diner-style mug of steaming Earl Grey, her favorite in times of stress.

For lunch she'd grabbed a tuna-salad sandwich on wheat bread, comfort food from her childhood. The chocolate layer cake had looked tempting and ended up on her tray, but she doubted she'd be able to eat it. Sweets felt like an undeserved reward.

"I'm glad you were there this morning," Kate murmured. "It really helped. The briefing this afternoon will be bad. Do you think you could—"

"I have to leave, sorry."

Kate winced as if she'd been jabbed with the fork on her tray. "Oh."

"You'll do fine. Just don't hold back. Let them know how bad it really was. They can't blame you. If anything, it was a failure of security. It happens. Heck, the Secret Service has let intruders get past them and into the White House!"

"Right." Kate sighed. Everything she'd ever worked for was on the line. She didn't think she could feel any worse. "I guess I was just hoping you'd be there, you know—for moral support. I can plot a satellite's launch trajectory, alter an orbit, chat with a computer on a space probe halfway to Jupiter, all while making peace between squabbling physicists." She let out a wry laugh. She wasn't bragging. These were tasks that had become as natural to her as making a peanut-butter sandwich. "But *this...this* brutal violence..." She shook her head.

"Dealing with psychos isn't your job." Mercy laid a hand over hers, a brief reassuring touch. "Listen, you'll probably never again have to face a situation like this."

"I know that. But—" Kate observed her cousin over the rim of her cup "—in a way, it's *your* job, isn't it? How do you do it? How do you survive dealing with inhumanity and bloodshed every single day? It must not only be an emotional drain. You're risking your life."

Mercy studied her roast beef sandwich and let out a soft laugh. "Most days the worst injury I'm likely to suffer is a paper cut. I'm knee deep in paperwork. Or I'm closeted with other agents who work for Red Sands Consulting—all of them adrenaline junkies like me. We're all dying to get out into the field. But when you *do* get thrown into the really ugly stuff— well, sometimes you just wish you were teaching kindergarteners."

"You carry a gun." Kate glanced at the gap beneath Mercy's jacket that revealed a shoulder holster, and gave an involuntary shudder.

"Yes."

"I couldn't."

"You could and would, if you had to."

"I—" Kate hesitated. Never, not once in her life, had she talked to anyone about *this*. Her nightmare. A nightmare come true. Had her aunt, Mercy's mother, been given the details of the terrible accident? "Maybe Aunt Talia never told you about this, about what happened a long time ago when we were kids."

Mercy tilted her head and observed her. "I remember hearing something about an accident. A child in your neighborhood being hospitalized. But we were out of the country at the time. Mom was on a photo assignment in France and took me with her. Go on."

"It had to do with a gun. I don't think I'll ever forget it." Kate's fingers curled tighter around her cup. She hurt. God, how she hurt at the memory. She had meant to tell the rest of the story, the whole thing. But she couldn't. Not now. Not yet. Never? She waved her hand in front of her face. "Anyway...after that, I swore I'd never touch a weapon of any kind."

"But you do," Mercy insisted. "Every day."

Kate stared at her, uncomprehending.

"You work with sophisticated equipment launched into space. Tons of that stuff circles over our heads every day."

"Sure, but—"

" From the little I've heard about that satellite of yours, and others too, I'd guess many have the potential for causing unimaginable damage here on Earth."

"If misused, yes. But we take precautions." Kate shook her head. "A satellite is nothing like a gun."

Mercy huffed. "There's absolutely no difference. It's just that your weapons aren't strapped under your jacket, they're in the sky."

"No!" Kate shifted in her seat, uncomfortable that her voice had sounded so loud. But no one else was seated near enough to hear them. She put down her cup, afraid of dropping it. Her hands had begun trembling uncontrollably, like last night. "The HW-1 was designed for peaceful purposes; to help, not to hurt people. If I'd ever thought it might be turned against human beings—" Her throat closed up with emotion. She couldn't speak. Her eyes burned but she held back threatening tears.

Mercy reached across the table and squeezed her arm. "My only point is that we live in a violent world. We can't foresee every new threat before it appears. You were amazing in that lab last night, looking out for your people and doing your sleight of hand trick with the computer. And, just now, with Jessup and Archer, you held your own and—" She hesitated, her eyes skittering away across the room.

No Mercy

"What?" Kate asked, turning to see what had caught her attention. Nothing, it seemed. Just a half-dozen NASA employees moving down the food line. Her cousin had changed from the carefree little artist she'd known when they were school girls. These days, she seemed always on the alert.

"I'm going to give you a tip, Katie. But you must promise to forget you heard it from me."

Kate frowned. "That sounds rather espionage-y."

"It's what I do." Mercy grinned, a little wickedly. "Two things you should watch out for—The Press and General Albert Kinsey."

"Because...?"

"Remember, *not from me*." Mercy drew a breath and lowered her voice as two scientists Kate recognized from a neighboring lab passed by. "Someone leaked word of the break-in to the *Washington Post*. Two of their most aggressive investigative reporters have already started nosing around and found someone who's talking to them. So the word is out that a NASA satellite is no longer under NASA control."

Kate was horrified. "Don't reporters realize that they'll create panic if they release that to the public?"

"Eventually, it will, if they find out what we already know and announce it to the world. But, so far, no one in the media has gotten hold of enough details. It's all very vague and technical to them, like the Hubble Telescope snafu."

Kate winced. She'd played a very minor role on Hubble's later years; some of her colleagues had been more intimately involved in that highly publicized project. "That was a huge embarrassment for NASA," she admitted. One member of the scientific team had confused centimeters with inches in a key calculation. (Thank God it wasn't her!) No one caught the mistake until after the telescope had been launched, and then it was too late. The entire multi-billion-dollar project had been jeopardized.

"Luckily," Mercy said, "the explanations in the media were so technical, the public soon lost interest in the story." And eventually, Hubble had been rescued. Was still sending home valuable data. "With any luck, that's what will happen after this incident. If whoever has possession of the codes on that memory stick is unable to use them, everyone will just forget about it."

Kate finished her sandwich and brushed crumbs from her fingers. "Right. Well, math and physics admittedly aren't very sexy. At least not for the general public." She eyed the cake, but her stomach warned, *Don't even think about it*.

"Exactly. And our dear government's higher-ups have already made it clear to your CoO that absolutely no information about the HW-1 should be released without vetting it through the Bureau and Homeland Security." Mercy locked eyes with her. "The longer we keep this as quiet as possible, the better. With any luck, we can round up your intruders before they do anything rash."

She knew Mercy was trying to make her feel better about the situation, but it wasn't helping much. "And General Kinsey. Why is he a problem?"

Mercy leaned in closer and lowered her voice another notch. "Kinsey will sit in on the briefing this afternoon. He's pushing for an alternative to recovering control over the satellite."

Kate stared at her. Was she really saying what it sounded like? Her mouth went desert-dry. "He wants to destroy Heat Wave?"

Mercy finished her tea and glanced casually at her watch as if she hadn't heard Kate. "I have to go, and you're due for that briefing. Keep your cool, you'll be fine."

But, Kate thought, would her satellite be fine? Would all of her hard work, five years out of her career and her life, be for nothing? If destroying the satellite was the only means of keeping people safe, she'd have to accept the sacrifice. Of course, she would. At least one of her team had already given his life. But...

Far more was at stake than a science experiment. Demolishing a satellite while still in its orbit entailed astronomical risks. *Bad pun,* she thought belatedly. She'd have to make sure that everyone involved, including the military brass, understood what those risks were.

If they didn't get it, she'd have a fight on her hands. One she couldn't afford to lose.

No Mercy

The second meeting of the day promised to be far less genteel than the first. Kate walked into the room to see a dozen people already seated at a long mahogany table in the austere, white-walled conference room. She was willing to bet that every person present would be looking out for their own special interests, determined to give no ground.

A recipe for disaster. Decisions as to the fate of Heat Wave had to be made swiftly. That would mean compromise. If they failed to take action... She just didn't want to think about the consequences.

She took in faces, quickly attached names to them when she could. Davis Jessup, her boss—of course he'd be here. Homeland Security Director Max Archer. General Albert Kinsey (in dress uniform, bedecked with a striking collection of medals). ASEC rep Jerry Reingold, whose company funded the HW-1 project. And two men she assumed were the computer geeks sent over from the FBI, whom Mercy had mentioned at the end of their lunch. There were also three other individuals she didn't recognize—and one she, regrettably, did know.

Daniel Rooker.

She sat down, set her attaché case on the table in front of her, and snapped it open. Everyone was looking at her as if she had dropped the ball in the last inning of a tied Orioles game and the other team had scored. The general and Rooker were outright scowling. Apparently she was to be the scapegoat *du jour*.

So you want to play rough, she thought, taking out her notes. *Fine.* As terrified as she'd been earlier in the day, now she was at least ready for them. If they fired her for last night, or for what she was about to tell them, so be it.

Kate read her prepared statement aloud, describing in detail the incident in her lab. She added as much as she knew about the current status of the HW-1, no longer controlled by NASA but not yet under the direction of its captors. While her lab was still closed down by the investigation, some of the FBI's computer fraud squad had taken over the task of scanning radio chatter in a range used to contact the satellite. If they picked up a signal they might be able to trace it to Zed.

As Mercy had predicted, General Kinsey was quick to speak up as soon as she finished her statement. "The Pentagon appreciates your cooperation, doctor. But we propose to make short work of this problem. Even as we speak, our people are determining which of our long-range missiles is capable of taking out this rogue satellite—"

"Now wait a minute, sir!" Jerry Reingold exploded from his chair, his narrow face livid with rage. "ASEC doesn't want to endanger innocent lives, but that satellite is worth five-billion dollars and represents technical advances that could someday save this country from being without vital energy."

"I'm afraid more is at stake than the satellite itself," Kate interrupted, her voice a good deal calmer than that of either man. "Even if our military possesses a fire-ready missile capable of reaching HW-1's orbit, you'll risk untold lives if you try to shoot it down."

Kinsey scowled at her. "Isn't such an assumption beyond your expertise, doctor?"

The room went as silent as a tomb. But at least she had their attention.

Kate said, "To plot a trajectory for the missile and accurately intercept Heat Wave would take time and planning. Days, maybe weeks. And we don't have the luxury of time." She spoke slowly, choosing her words carefully. "This is a huge high-orbital sat bulked up with lots of equipment—solar panels, huge parabolic mirrors. It's not a little communications job perched just outside of the Earth's atmosphere. The specifications are in my report." Even Kinsey was being a good boy now, listening to her. "Then there's the wreckage to consider."

Jessup nodded, evidently seeing where she was headed. "Some of the debris knocked back into the atmosphere won't burn up on its way down to Earth. Chunks of metal may scatter across populated areas."

Kate nodded her head. At least for the moment she had her boss's support. "It would be like playing Russian roulette with rubble, raining house-size shrapnel down on random targets." Kate made eye contact with each person around the table, one by one. "Some of it might land in the ocean—that's the best we could hope for—or it might end up crashing down in the middle of a densely populated city, a school, church...there's no telling where it might end up."

The general turned to a man seated directly behind him. His aide, she assumed. They whispered to each other then Kinsey faced the table again, his expression stormy. "Clearly that's not desirable. However, if we have no alternative but to—"

"When I accessed the HW-1 last night during the invasion," she interrupted, "I was able to put the sat in what's called a Safe-Hold status. This is only temporary, until Zed's people hack through the code-block I attached to the program last night." She was trying to keep her explanations simple enough for all in the room to understand. "If I'm allowed back in my lab, my team and I will scan for ultra-high-frequency signals attempting to communicate with the HW-1. If we find any, we'll attempt to track the signals to their source. That's where Zed, or whoever has taken possession of the USB date, will be. As far as I know, the FBI has already started working on tracking them. But we're the ones who know the satellite."

Rooker spoke up for the first time. "If Dr. Foster gives us the coordinates, I can mount a team to make the physical apprehension."

Good, two allies.

"ASEC would certainly support that strategy," Reingold added quickly. *Three!*

"You'll need military backup," the general stated firmly, protecting his turf.

Rooker gave the general a steely look of his own in return. *One dog facing down another.* "I believe that's the Department of Homeland Security's call, sir. We coordinate through civilian law enforcement. Right, Mr. Archer? DHS has the authority to either call for or deny military response."

The Homeland Security Director gave a stiff nod.

If this hadn't been a life-or-death situation, Kate would have been amused by the testosterone battle being waged. But the important thing was—decisions were being made. She could see a plan of attack evolving.

She sat back in her chair, able to breathe again, relief flooding through her. *Thank God.* She had been able to reason with these people. Now she'd let others at the table hammer out details of a cooperative effort. She could return to familiar tasks, to her science, *her* turf—which was a comfort. The laws of nature and the universe: in today's brutal world, they were all that made sense to her.

An hour later, Kate walked out of the conference room, intending to briefly return home before going to her lab. Hopefully, by the time she got back to the compound, the forensic team would have finished their work and given her permission to enter her lab. Jessup had told her that he thought they were almost done.

She was crossing the parking lot when she saw Jerry Reingold coming toward her. He flicked the flame of a lighter toward the end of his cigarette, his red hair like a beacon in the sunlight. "You know what they'll do when it comes down to it?" He blew a puff of smoke into the air; it drifted toward her.

She stepped out of the noxious cloud. "No, Jerry, what will they do?"

"They'll go through the motions of trying to find our sat-jackers, but in the end Kinsey will get his way. Those military types can't conceive of a solution that doesn't include firepower."

Kate winced. Was he right? But it didn't help to assume the worst. Or to give up the hunt.

"Well, at least we've bought some time," she said.

Kate studied the and felt not unsympathetic. His eyes were red-rimmed, complexion sallow. He'd probably been awakened in the middle of the night with the news that his company's baby had been stolen. When disaster struck, heads often rolled. There was a good chance he'd lose his job over this fiasco. ASEC and NASA would gang up on him if it meant appeasing federal investigators. Jerry was at the bottom of the food chain. And she wasn't much further up.

No Mercy

"Do you know anything about this so-called security expert—Daniel Rooker?" she asked. "The one who seems to have been given the job of tracking down Zed."

"Tough looking character isn't he?" Jerry knocked ash onto the pavement and watched the breeze blow it away. "Heard his name around. He's a free agent, terrorist consultant. One of our competitors hired him for a high-risk overseas security job. Don't know the details. I've also heard he specializes in finding people who don't want to be found." He drew deeply on his cigarette. "Word is, he's good but doesn't always bother bringing in the missing once he's found them. Not alive anyway."

She widened her eyes at him. "Really? You don't mean he—"

"If it's a question of the government wanting someone badly enough, for a crime of some sort, yes he probably gets to choose how the hunt ends." He looked away. "Gives me the willies, he does."

"Then maybe he's the right man for this job," she said. She still didn't like Rooker's attitude. *But when you're dealing with monsters, maybe you have to become a little bit of a monster yourself.*

"I don't know. Seems to me, it'd be a mistake to send out commando types like Rooker on a job like this."

"Why?" She dug her car keys out of her purse.

"All muscle, no brain. What if they find this Zed, or whoever now has your USB? What if these terrorists have twenty or thirty memory sticks in their pockets, or they've already downloaded the data onto a computer? You think Rooker will even know what he's looking for or how to retrieve it?" He dropped the cigarette butt on the pavement and crushed it under his foot. "You ask me, it's pretty hopeless."

Kate frowned. This possibility had occurred to her. But she hadn't wanted to think about it until the immediate danger of a missile being sent to destroy HW-1 had been shelved.

"Or," Jerry continued, " say that by the time Rooker tracks down his quarry, the HW-1 has already been deployed. You think Rambo types like him are going to know what to do to stop it?"

Now she felt truly sick to her stomach. "You mean, one of my scientists needs to accompany them?" Just the thought of

Kathryn Johnson

involving her own people with Rooker and his mercenaries, to face untold danger, made her head throb again.

"Not just *any* scientist." Reingold gave her a look.

And now Kate realized where he'd been going with all of these worrisome speculations. "Me? No thank you."

He held up a finger as if emphasize his words. "If the same thoughts occur to NASA and Homeland Security, you may have no choice, my dear."

No Mercy

Chapter 8

The day seemed never to end.

Kate had driven home in the late afternoon to change into work clothes and make herself a sandwich to take with her for supper in the lab. She was exhausted, her head pounding, neck and shoulders aching, but told herself she'd feel better once she was back at work, doing something useful.

She was almost out the door when her cell phone rang. It was NASA-Weston's public relations officer.

"So far we've been contacted by the *Washington Post* and CNN," Mitchell Pasturnak said, his tone clipped with urgency. "I've been fending them off for hours, Dr. Foster. They want a statement." He was accustomed to announcing shuttle launches, the discoveries of new galaxies and black holes, footage of the Mars landers. Exciting stuff the public loved. No one in PR wanted to deliver bad news. "If we don't give them something, they'll think there's a cover-up."

Kate had hoped Mercy was wrong about the leak. Guess not.

"I'd like to take the heat off of you, Mitch," she said. "But you have to put them off a little longer. It's 'no comment' for now. Anything I say has to be cleared through Homeland Security. They haven't yet decided how much to tell the public."

"That's what I thought." Pasturnak sighed loudly into the phone. "My people will keep the wolves at bay as long as possible. But once word gets out to the world we're cooked. Just think what the network news people could do to us!"

"I know. I'm hoping we'll retrieve Heat Wave before then. Just do the best you can."

"Right. One more thing."

"What?" *Breathe,* she told herself.

"Security tells me a media van and a second vehicle are parked just outside of the main gate. The guards wouldn't allow them inside when they flashed press cards. A reporter claimed he had an appointment with you."

54

Kathryn Johnson

She sucked in a breath, appalled by their audacity. "That's a lie."

"I thought so. But it's a pretty good bet they've staked out each of the facility's gates and, once they know what you and your car look like, you'll be treated to company on your next drive home."

With a sinking heart, she thanked him and rang off.

So, maybe I just won't come home tonight. She'd take extra meals with her, stash them in the lab's break-room fridge. The small couch in her office across the hall would suffice for a bed until this nightmare was over.

She rushed around the house, gathering up toiletries, two changes of clothing, anything she could think of she might need. Taking one last look around at her cozy condo, she longed to stay and barricade herself in here, where she felt safe, surrounded by the things she loved. Not holed up in the place that reminded her of violence and death.

Twenty minutes later, Kate could see from the end of the corridor that the crime-scene tapes across the doors to her lab were gone. She unlocked the door and let herself in.

It seemed eerie, seeing the place entirely empty. Heat Wave's command center was always manned 24 hours-a-day. She surveyed the familiar banks of electronic equipment, ranks of overhead monitors, unoccupied cubicles. Usually people moved with purpose from station to station. Screens flashed black-and-white data or colorful images. The click of keyboards, whir of hardware, and hum of conversations filled the long room.

Today, the place was utterly silent. A space-age ghost town.

Thankfully, someone had cleaned the blood-spattered floor and removed the panel Frank Hess had fallen against, smearing more blood over it. The remnants of her destroyed computer were also gone. But she couldn't forget the horror of witnessing the unprovoked shooting of two men she'd worked closely with, day after day. Dave had only recently joined the project, but Frank Hess had been a familiar face around NASA-Weston for many years.

She tried, without much success, to push aside grim thoughts.

No Mercy

Oh, Dave...Frank, I'm so very sorry. Was there something she could have done differently? Words she might have said to prevent bloodshed?

Kate collapsed into the nearest chair, at Cam's console. She dropped her head into her hands and, finally, let the tears fall. Until this moment she'd been able to hold herself together by a thin thread. Now she allowed herself cleansing sobs as the madness of it all struck her full force. The worst part was how utterly helpless she'd felt that night against the intruders' brutality.

All of her life, her ability to create order out of the complexities of a modern world had given her satisfaction, made her feel safe. Science gave her power. The universe and everything in it operated according to a strict set of rules. By studying these natural laws, she could make sense of her life. She felt in control. Logic ruled.

But when something like this happened...

Guns. Violence. Guilt...always the guilt. The other time had been many years ago. And now there was this.

At last, she dried her tears and found the strength to stand up and walk around the lab, booting up computers until the room glowed amber and green as monitors came alive. Each station interfaced with various functions within the HW-1 satellite, orbiting 36,000 kilometers above Earth. In similar control rooms, monitors linked with immense telescopes watched the skies millions of miles away. Still other NASA computers gathered data from probes on their way to Jupiter, circling the sun, or retrieving data from deep space light years away.

This was her world. An exciting and beautiful place full of galaxies, stars, nebulas and seductively mysterious black holes. This was where she'd always felt protected by her science.

She tried not to think about Dave and Frank. Tried to find comfort in hope.

In her heart she desperately wanted to hold on to hope that Frank, at least, had survived. That he would be found.

At one time they had started to date. Nothing serious, just friends who worked together, going out for a drink or a quick meal at the end of the day. She had wondered if more would come of their relationship.

Kathryn Johnson

But, then, their chief project engineer had announced he was retiring, leaving the position open. She and Frank competed with others for the same job. He had more years with NASA, but she had pursued the job aggressively. In the end, the powers that be had chosen Kate for her more-recent degree in aerospace engineering from Purdue. After that, Frank seemed to lose any interest in a social relationship with her.

Now she had to face the very real possibility that the physicist was already dead. Rooker was right, she reluctantly acknowledged. Frank was human baggage that Zed and his gang couldn't afford to keep for long, regardless of his possible usefulness.

A hard rap on the door behind Kate snapped her out of dark thoughts. "Yes?" She'd automatically locked the door—standard protocol.

"Open up, Doc, or I'll huff and I'll puff, and I'll blow—"

"You have a sick sense of humor, Rooker." Kate's suddenly galloping heart took a while to slow down after recognizing the raspy baritone. She wondered if he smoked, or did he just naturally sound that way.

As she reached for the latch, a stray thought came to her then sped off at warp speed. She froze, staring at her hand, trying to recapture whatever had bothered her. Something about Rooker? But it was gone. Probably she was just irritated the man was intruding upon her privacy.

She opened the door.

Rooker stepped through, shut and relocked the door. Strangely, that didn't make her feel all that safe. Not that *he* frightened her. No. Of course not. It was just that the man had a habit of rubbing her the wrong way. His ability to think through a problem seemed less cerebral, more of a physical reflex. Some part of him was always in motion—his eyes, his hands, a foot tapping—never totally at rest.

Today, he was wearing jeans and a black T-shirt under a leather jacket that seemed totally inappropriate for July. She suspected its purpose was to cover whatever hardware he carried beneath it. A plastic ID badge from the security gate was alligator-clipped to the jacket collar.

No Mercy

She moved away from the door, toward her desk. He followed.

"You all right?" he asked.

She dipped her chin in answer, then narrowed her eyes at him, feeling the dampness lingering in them. She hoped they weren't also red from crying and, if they were, hoped he wouldn't notice. "How did you know I was here?"

"The all-seeing eye." He motioned toward the security camera high in the corner of the room. "We got it working again. A wire had frayed and tugged loose, or was cut. When you walked in here a few minutes ago, I was at the guard house talking to the electrician who's fixing the alarm."

Did that mean he'd witnessed her breaking down and crying her heart out? *Damn.* "What did he say was wrong with it?"

"Not a thing." Rooker's roaming eye settled on the amethyst crystal paperweight on her desk. He picked it up, gave its butterfly shape a quick once over, then tossed it from one big hand to the other like a baseball. "Same guy checked out the system half a dozen times last week when Security reported it sounding off."

"I remember them showing up one day while I was working."

Kate recaptured the pretty crystal insect midflight and placed it back on her desk, out of his reach. It had been a gift from a dear friend. Ellen had lost her long struggle with cancer. Kate took it with her whenever she traveled, as a good luck charm and a reminder of the fragility of life. *Live for today, because time is fleeting.*

"Security was going from office to office, asking if everyone was all right. At the time I assumed they were just being extra vigilant, making the rounds."

He grinned as if she were a little kid who'd just said something cute.

"What?" she asked.

"Nothing." He shrugged, making his shoulders look even more massive in the black leather.

Kate took a step toward him, irritated that he seemed to find anything at all funny about the situation. "No, really. What were you thinking just then?"

Rooker shook his head but kept the grin. "I'll never understand you scientific types. You live in another dimension. Nothing outside of your work gets through to you." He laughed. "Hell, the building could burn down around you and you wouldn't even know it."

She crossed her arms over her chest and narrowed her eyes at him. "The absentminded professor is a dated stereotype. I never lose touch with my surroundings." But, she recalled, it had taken her precious seconds to react to a man with a gun breaking into her lab. "Besides, I knew the alarms sometimes went off on their own. I saw no reason to be concerned."

His normal blank expression turned serious. "Who else knew?"

"What?"

"Who else was aware that the alarms appeared to be malfunctioning?"

Kate frowned as she leaned over and turned on Cambridge's computer. "Everyone in the building, I suppose. I mean, when armed guards come charging down the hallway, you take notice. It's not as if sirens and bells go off in the comm center or offices. They're only heard in the security monitoring station. Unless you're the one who hit the panic alarm you wouldn't know why they'd shown up."

"Hence the reason it's called a *silent* alarm?"

"You've got it, sport." She winked at him and felt her annoyance fade. "After a while, we all assumed the guards were bored and looking for something to do. Or maybe they were running a drill. Checking badges at the gate and searching cars for explosives, which they never find, has to get old fast."

He nodded, as if satisfied for the moment, then looked around the lab again. "Your team is where?"

Kate leaned back against the burlap-and-metal sound partition behind her. Every muscle in her body ached, less from physical fatigue than from the emotional tension of the past twenty-four hours. She would have liked to sit down but suspected she'd feel even less comfortable with this big man standing over her. She watched the computer finish booting up, its screen brightening.

No Mercy

"Personnel contacted each member of my team to tell them to stay home at least until tomorrow morning. Then, if they feel okay with coming back—"

"I thought you needed them here to scan for signals to the satellite."

"DHS has both the FBI and NSA cyber-techs covering that for now, and I can work through the night on my own. It's better that way. Team members who were here during the intrusion need recovery time with their families. And I didn't want the others showing up at the lab because I didn't know when Security would release the area." She paused, swallowed with difficulty. Her throat felt tight. Her eyes burned, presaging more tears. She sniffed them back. "You have no idea how traumatic it was. Those monsters bursting in. Waving around weapons. Gunning down two of my people."

"But *you* are here," Rooker pointed out.

Kate let her gaze drift back to Cambridge's monitor. Figures scrolled down a black screen. With a glance at the encrypted language, she could see that HW-l's systems were still in Safe-Hold, no changes since the readings of the night before. Good news for now. That meant Zed hadn't yet accessed the satellite.

"Why am I here? Because..." This would be hard to explain to a layman, but she'd put her thoughts in their simplest, least scientific form for him. "You see, I've been thinking a lot about what might be happening. From the terrorists' viewpoint. It's unlikely Zed will try to contact the satellite this soon. He's on the run, right? First he has to get somewhere he feels safe—maybe even out of the country—or pass along the information on the flash drive to the people who intend to use it. Only then will he, or whoever got him to steal it for them, try to contact Heat Wave."

Rooker studied her. "But you still feel it's important for you to be here."

"Yes."

His eyes narrowed, then darkened to an intense blue-black. "Why?"

Because I feel responsible! Because I need to know what diabolical scheme these lunatics intend to hatch.

But she didn't say any of that. A man like Rooker wouldn't understand something as crippling as *guilt*. She doubted if he ever questioned his own motives, ever second-guessed himself or suffered as she was suffering. He was the kind of man who acted, and then moved on. Been there; done that. Next job.

"Have any demands been made yet?" she said.

"You're changing the subject, Doc. *Why* are you here *now*? Tell me what's going on in that pretty head of yours."

She glared up at him, refusing to let him goad her. Or was he flirting? It was hard to tell with him. Either way, she didn't like it.

"I need to know," she began carefully, "if Zed's people have communicated with Washington. Have you heard yet what they want in exchange for return of the satellite's control? Or what they intend to do with it if they keep it?"

Rooker continued to scan the room, as if he might have missed something. She was sure he'd canvassed the entire room, inch by inch, the previous night. "There's been no communication." He turned away, looking as though he had been distracted by the rows of blinking monitors above his head. "What are these for? They look as if they're flashing random streams of numbers."

She almost smiled. The macho ex-soldier was out of his element. And she was in hers. "Not random at all. This is how we view stars, planets, satellites, moons...the universe around us and beyond."

He chuckled, hands on hips, swinging back on the heels of his boots. "Can't fool me. That looks like nothing I've ever seen through a telescope."

"In a way, though, those numbers represent our lens focused on space. I can *see* HW-1 by reading the data its computers send me. I know precisely where it is in its orbit and what onboard mechanisms are functioning or have shut down."

"Just from numbers and codes? Dang!" He managed a brooding scowl for her benefit but couldn't mask his interest. "And I have trouble programming my VCR."

"Oh, please." She didn't believe that for a minute.

Kate suspected Rooker had perfected this self-effacing, I'm-just-a-simple-country-boy routine for a reason. She didn't much care what that reason was. Higher on her list of priorities was getting back to work and finding a way to retrieve her satellite. Only then would she feel at peace with herself.

"Tell me," she said. "If I pick up a signal connecting with the HW-1, and can get a fix on the origin of that signal, what's your next move?"

"You mean if you can tell me where Zed is? Hell, we scramble an assault team, move out and nab them."

She pursed her lips and gave him a skeptical look. "Easy as that."

"Pretty much." His expression waxed from smug to concerned to pissed off at her silence. "Look, if you're going to warn me that these people are ruthless and slippery and God knows what else— save it. I've dealt with worse."

"How can you say that? You don't know anything about those three?" She tilted her head up and studied his face. "Or do you?"

"It's my business to know, Doc." His blue eyes, only marginally lighter than moments before, were in motion again, taking in the room as if still unconvinced only the two of them were there. "For instance, if they really were as dangerous and out of control as everyone's making out, no one in this fucking lab would have walked out alive."

Had his intention been to shock her? He'd succeeded.

Kate swallowed, closing her eyes for a moment against the disturbing image of corpses sprawled across the floor. How close had she herself come to death? It was a question she hadn't chosen to face until now, forced to it by this strange man.

It took her a moment to catch her breath and mentally regroup.

"I wasn't going to warn you to be careful," she said at last. "Don't flatter yourself."

"Oh?" The arrogance gone, now something like a twinkle in his eyes made her think he was amused.

"I was going to tell you, when we do discover where the stolen USB's date has gone, you'll need me to go after it with you." The words came out of nowhere. And once she'd said them, she wished she could take them back. The last thing she wanted was to be involved in a manhunt. But she remembered

Kathryn Johnson

what the ASEC rep had said, and it made sense. Without a scientist on board, one who knew Heat Wave and its technology, any chance of regaining control of the sat would be lost.

Kate jumped when Rooker burst into laughter. "In your dreams, lady!" She opened her mouth to protest, but he plowed on. "*You* are staying right here. End of story."

"I don't think so." She met his gaze and held it. No way would she back down. She was right; he was wrong.

Kate explained Jerry Reingold's concerns, which by now had become her own. "The man can be a pain in the ass," she admitted, "but he knows what he's talking about where that satellite is concerned."

Rooker stared at her, for a rare moment at a loss for words. "I can take one of the FBI or NSA cyber-techs with me."

"No doubt they're good when it comes to anything earth-bound. But they won't know how to re-deploy or shut down a satellite. There may be literally only minutes to act once you recover the data."

This time Rooker's laugh sounded forced. For a moment, she thought she'd gotten through to him.

"Don't you think," he said, "you're getting just a little possessive about a chunk of metal?"

"Possessive?" she snapped.

He took a step back, as if surprised by the force of her reaction. "Calm down. All I'm saying is...you being physically in on the capture isn't necessary. Just tell us where the signal is coming from. That is, if you can find it at all. We'll take care of the rest."

She sighed and rolled her eyes. *Unbelievable.* Could anyone be this pig headed? She glared at him.

"What now?" he groaned.

"It will be a lot harder than you think to find what you're looking for. First—" she intentionally slowed her words, to make sure the big guy understood the importance of what she was about to say "—Zed can run a signal through a series of remote computers to mask his real position."

"I knew that." He blinked, shrugged. "Hackers do it all the time. So it takes a little extra time to follow the trail. After all,

No Mercy

how many computers can there possibly be with the sophistication and power to talk with a goddamn satellite?"

"That's just it. Theoretically, anyone who has the flash drive, the knowledge to use it, and access to the right kind of antenna—" she kept her voice quiet but forceful "—can link with the satellite through any home PC or laptop computer with a modem. Anyone. Anywhere."

Satisfied she'd repaid him in shock value, she let the words sink in. Then watched the tightness return to the sun-weathered skin around his mouth as the color leached out of his face.

"You're telling me," he began slowly, as if only now working out all of the ghastly implications, "that Zed and his crew have unlimited mobility. They can jump from computer to computer anywhere in the world...and still control your satellite?"

"Hey, I think he's got it."

If possible, his face turned a shade grayer. "Shit."

Kathryn Johnson

Rooker worked fast without stopping to think whether fast made any difference to the outcome of this scenario from hell. He checked in with Homeland Security; they'd brief President Garcia. He texted his own people at Worldwide Security: *Alert! Brief @HQ 1500hrs.* His elite team of six would be waiting for him. After meeting in DC they'd be ready to move out from Andrews Air Force Base as soon as he got coordinates for the Zed's. A Black Hawk helicopter was already fueled up and waiting.

He prayed, although he wasn't a praying sort of guy, that whatever voodoo Kate Foster performed on Heat Wave's programming would buy them enough time to retrieve the flash drive before its information was copied and spread around. He was counting on the strong possibility that, if this Zed didn't intend to use it himself, he would auction it off to the highest bidder. And getting the word out on what he had to offer would take time.

As he headed for his truck, Rooker mentally checked off other arrangements, already made. In case Zed was outside of the chopper's four-hundred-mile range, General Kinsey had put on standby one of the corporate- style government jets, painted in the same Presidential livery as Air Force One. The decoy planes were often sent up when the President was in the air.

But if Zed made it out of the country everything changed. Everything became more difficult. Without the necessary extradition agreements, he couldn't lay a hand on Zed, or remove him and his gang from a foreign country.

Not legally anyway. Then again, it wouldn't be the first time he'd skirted international law.

"Hey, Rooker!"

At the sound of his name he spun around, one hand reaching for the door handle of the black four-by-four, the other beneath his jacket to the holster. You never knew when a friendly sounding voice was an ID check before bullets started flying.

Mercy O'Brien strode across the asphalt toward him. He let his gun hand drop to his side.

"I thought you'd headed back to DC hours ago," he said.

"Back again. Spare me five?"

A woman after his own heart. Not a wasted a word. And she wasn't bad on the eyes either. Stunning, really. Blonde, green eyes...or were they hazel? But they didn't have the warmth of her cousin Kate's pretty dark eyes. Between the two of them, he'd pick the doctor. Even though she drove him crazy. Even though he was pretty sure she didn't like him in the least.

"Sure," he said. "What's up?" But if he had any thought of this being a friendly chat, he soon found out otherwise.

Mercy an Ipad from her shoulder bag and brought it to life. "Of the members of Dr. Foster's team present during the intrusion, who do you know, personally?"

"Not a one," he said.

"Foster herself?" She looked up with an air of nonchalance, but her gaze penetrated.

"Nope. Never met the woman before last night. Why?"

"The NASA techs and our forensics team agree that something funky was going on with the alarm and security cams."

"I know. I was over there with them. Funky? That a technical term?"

She gave him a humorless smile and shook her head. "Not my forte, electronics. Let's just leave it that it's likely someone on the inside made sure Security wouldn't respond with any enthusiasm to the alarm." Which, of course, he already knew.

"Doesn't take an electrician to figure that one out. Someone with access to the building had to have been paid off by, or was cooperating with Zed."

"Right. So what have you done to follow up on that theory?"

"Me?" He put on an innocent face. "Not a damn thing, darlin'."

Mercy tilted her head a fraction of an inch, slanting him the same look she might give a pet cocker spaniel after it peed on her Kasmir rug.

Kathryn Johnson

"Not a damn thing...ma'am," he corrected his previous response. "Listen, I just fell into the middle of this mess. NASA contracted my company to handle security on a new solar probe project. When these intruders broke in, I was pulled from that job to oversee the recovery of Heat Wave. Priority one: recover the missing data. Priority two: capture Mr. Zed, whoever he may be. Base Security is handling the internal investigation. Your job is—"

"I know *my* job, Rooker," she said coolly. "One small part of it is finding out exactly what happened here last night. We need to know who is responsible and stop it from ever happening again. I just want to be sure you and I understand our roles and aren't working at cross-purposes."

"Right." He could see evidence of strain in the tight lines around her eyes, even as she tried to hide her concern. The job was weighing on her, and she wasn't about to take crap from anyone. He decided he'd best ease off. "So, do you have a theory as to who helped these people access the building?"

She thought for a moment, snapped shut her notebook. "A lot of people can get into the compound."

"True. But what about that specific lab? Regulations call for the door to always be locked. That indicates to me an inside job."

"I haven't dismissed that possibility," she admitted. "That's why I'll be in there tomorrow. I just got off the phone with Dr. Foster. She expects her entire team to show up for work tomorrow morning. I'll interview each of them. But—" she added, giving Rooker a look "—I want you to know I respect Kate Foster." She held up a hand when he opened his mouth. "No, let me correct that. I don't just respect her, I love her. She is my cousin, and I don't want to see anyone hurt her, *for any reason*. Got that?"

"And you're leaning on me, in particular, why?"

"You have a history of being—" her eyes flashed "—a smidge hard on persons of interest. I've heard that you and she have already engaged in at least one volatile argument." She watched him intently. "In the parking lot?"

He stuck his hands in his pockets and smiled. "You do get around, don't you?" He suspected there was a nice thick file on him, somewhere. He'd gone straight from high school into the

No Mercy

Marines, then accepted a few jobs from the CIA before his most recent missions as a corporate warrior. That file might make for interesting reading someday, if he could get his hands on it.

"It's a tough business," he said. "You were the one who said that someone in the lab might have been in collusion with Zed. Asking people politely if they've betrayed their country isn't likely to get a confession. I had to be sure that our traitor wasn't her."

Mercy shook her head, hard. "Kate has too much to lose. She wouldn't sabotage her own project. I'm warning you, Rooker, ease up on her. Let the woman do her job."

He shrugged noncommittally. He didn't see why anyone should get special treatment. Hell, Foster was already trying to weasel her way into tagging along with his team. *Ridiculous!*

"I'm serious, Rooker. You offend Kate Foster and she's going to be thinking about wringing your neck instead of locating her data. We need her cooperation."

"So you want me to play nice."

"Say it any way you like." She narrowed her eyes at him. "Just make it happen."

He felt as though he'd been pushed into a corner. He ached to push back.

"What are you thinking now?" she asked, looking even more suspicious.

"Nothing." He reached again for the truck's door. "You'll let me know the results of your interviews tomorrow, right?"

"If they pertain to this incident. Otherwise, don't hold your breath. You do your job. I'll do mine." And then she did a very proper about-face and marched away from him.

"Yeah, right," he muttered. If anyone thought he was going to babysit a Ph.D.-princess, they were out of their freakin' minds.

Chapter 10

Kate studied the monitor in front of her, too aware of the tension in the sat lab to be able to concentrate. She'd slept in her office the previous night, washed up in the ladies' room and grabbed a breakfast of vending-machine coffee and toaster pastries from the break room. By 8:00 a.m. her entire team of twenty-six had arrived. They hugged and told each other it would all be okay, but she heard the doubt shadowing their words of encouragement.

Everyone expressed shock and regret over the loss of David Proctor and the kidnapping of Frank Hess. No one said out loud what they all knew. Terrorists didn't give back hostages, not unless it served their purpose.

There was one bit of good news. Whoever held HW-1's codes, they hadn't yet broken through Kate's hastily configured firewall. The satellite's Safe-Hold status hadn't changed. And now it had been decided that Kate's own people, who knew the satellite best, would partner with NSA in cyber tracking them. Maybe there was still hope.

Kate's phone rang. She picked up immediately. It was Security, letting her know that Mercy was on her way to the lab.

"I thought the investigation here was done," Kate said to Mercy after she'd buzzed her in.

"This visit has nothing to do with physical evidence. I need to speak to each member of your team, whether or not they were working the night of the incursion."

Kate frowned. "I don't understand. Those who were here already gave statements. Those who weren't—"

"—might have seen or heard something in the days prior to that night," Mercy said. "An innocuous detail maybe to them, but something we could use."

Kate frowned. "Is that really why you're here? Don't lie to me, please." If she couldn't trust Mercy, whom could she trust? "If you think one of us had something to do with what happened here— Mercy, that's just...outrageous. Everyone on my staff is absolutely loyal to NASA, to this country." *To me*?

No Mercy

"I hope so. I really do." Mercy's smile did little to encourage her. "Listen, it's not just your crew that's in question. We're interviewing everyone with access to this building. If that doesn't turn up something, we'll broaden the investigation to anyone who has set foot on the Weston facility in the past six months." Mercy took Kate's arm and drew her toward the back of the room, out of hearing range of the others. "Someone familiar with this project is responsible for ISIS or an unrelated terrorist cell realizing the dangerous potential of Heat Wave. You must see that."

Kate looked away, not wanting to hear accusations about her own people. Just because Zed knew which lab to break into didn't mean he'd been tipped off by one of her people. Did it? As to the alarm and camera, couldn't an outsider with knowledge of such systems have messed with them?

It was then that it came to Kate—the thought that had bothered her that night. The one she hadn't been able to put her finger on. *Rooker's rescue team had to knock to be let in, but Zed just walked in.*

"The lab door automatically locks," she blurted out, feeling suddenly nauseous at the thought.

Mercy stared at her.

"The intruders, they just walked in. They must have had a key card."

Mercy rolled her eyes. "Great. Why didn't you tell me before?"

"I only just now thought of it." Or maybe it was something Rooker had implied but it hadn't sunk in at the time.

"Which means someone willingly gave them their card. Or they got hold of an employee's entry card without their knowledge." Her cousin drew a deep breath.

"I'm so sorry," Kate said. "Ever since that night, I haven't been able to think clearly."

"Never mind." Mercy rubbed Kate's arm. "We've got that covered. Human Resources is checking to see if anyone with access to the building has recently taken sick leave or been on vacation. They might not realize their card is missing."

Kate took three deep breaths. Time to calm down. Time to start thinking logically about the situation. To stop let her emotions rule. "I'm sorry for giving you a hard time. I know you're just doing your job." She massaged her throbbing temples. She hadn't slept any better last night on her office couch than she had the night before at home.

"Listen, I've already picked up personnel records for everyone in this building, including maintenance," Mercy continued, all business again. "If you don't object, I'll use your office for the interviews."

Kate nodded. She supposed this was necessary, even though it felt wrong to her. Was she supposed to trust *no one* now? "Starting with me?" she asked.

"Not unless you have something you want to add to your report."

"No, not really."

"Then let's start with your support tech." Mercy flipped open her notebook. "That would be Amanda Becker? Point her out to me."

As soon as the door closed behind a very nervous-looking Amanda, laughter broke out on the other side of the partition from where Kate stood. Startled by the sound of merriment, so foreign to the past 48 hours, she peered around the partition's edge.

Thomas Leonhardt, the youngest member of the HW team, stood holding his sides, wiping tears from his eyes. "Leave it to the Freakin' Bureau of Idiots to waste their time investigating the people least likely to have anything to do with terrorists!"

"Listening in on us, were you?" Kate shook her head in mild reproof. "Ms. O'Brien isn't with the FBI. And she's only doing her job, Tommy."

"Yeah, but—" he flipped his hands, palms up "—like, *us*? Aiding terrorists? Come on! We're extreme geeks not religious extremists." *Indeed*, she thought. Her young intern wore blue jeans and a T-shirt that looked like a relic from the 1960's. A peace sign on the front, something faded that might either have been a bouquet of flowers or an atomic mushroom cloud on the back. Customary workday garb for many in her lab on a weekend.

Cam looked over the top of her cubicle at them. "I gather we're all under suspicion?"

No Mercy

Kate shrugged. "The truth is, ISIS and al Quaeda have gotten sophisticated enough to be able to monitor all sorts of electronic transmissions. They may have just stumbled upon us and followed our signals here."

"Right," Tommy agreed. "Any decent hacker could have latched on to Heat Wave. Hell, drive around Capitol Hill with a mobile antenna in your car and you can pick up a dozen government wireless networks within four or five blocks!"

"And you know this from personal experience?" Cam asked. She wasn't smiling now.

Tommy's face colored. He looked away from her. "I quit black-hat hacking a long time ago. You all know that."

Cam exchanged looks with Kate.

"The FBI is just covering all bases," Kate said, hoping to soothe frayed nerves. "It's important that we cooperate."

The door from Kate's office opened. Amanda stepped into the lab, her eyes brimming with tears, hands clutched in front of her matronly body. She was visibly trembling. Amanda tapped one of the physicists on the shoulder and pointed toward the door. He left for his turn to be interviewed by Mercy.

Amanda made a beeline for Kate. "She wouldn't tell me anything about Frank!" she wailed. "Did she say anything to you? They must know something by now." Tears rolled down her cheeks. "All I want to know is if he's alive...if he's still got a chance."

"I'm sorry." Kate patted her plump shoulder. "We'll just keep hoping, right?"

"Yeah," Tommy scoffed, "like that's gonna do the dude any good."

"Dude?" Amanda exploded. "Have some respect for your elders. Frank's a good man. A *young* man, barely forty. He has his whole life ahead of him. And he's a brilliant scientist."

"I didn't mean anything by it," Tommy complained, looking stunned at her reaction. "It's just—he didn't have to get himself shot. If it were me, I'd have made my move way before that creep squeezed off a round. Zed wouldn't have known what hit him."

Kathryn Johnson

"Can it, Tommy," Cambridge snapped. "Any one of us could've got that bullet. He just picked on Frank because Frank irritated him."

"You think that was it?" Amanda asked Kate, her voice cracking with emotion. "Because Frank stood up to him?"

Kate sighed. "I don't know. How can any of us be sure what goes on in a mind that warped? I'm just glad all of you came through." Kate took in Amanda's distraught face, Tommy's wounded expression, Cam's anger. Her troops. She'd let them down. And now, somehow, she had to rally them and keep them on task.

She looked the length of the room toward Vernon's area. He alone, of those who had been here that night, hadn't come out of his cubicle all morning.

"Back to work, everyone," Kate gently prodded. "I want to know the second any attempt is made to contact HW-1."

She turned away and walked back through the lab toward Vernon. He was hunched over his keyboard, earphones clipped over his head. He and Tommy were supposed to be scanning ultra-high-frequency radio transmissions, hoping to pick up signals between an antenna selected by Zed and the satellite. Right now, though, Vernon's mellow brown face was turned toward the blank wall beside his cube. She couldn't tell if he was puzzling out a task or had drifted off to sleep.

She came up behind him quietly and tapped him on the shoulder. "You okay, Vern?"

His spine went rigid. He unclipped earphones and turned to look up at her, the muscles in his face relaxing. "Yeah. Cool." But his eyes were red-rimmed, the lids puffy.

"It's hard on all of us," she murmured.

"I didn't even know them," he murmured.

A warning alarm went off in her head. "Know who?" she asked.

Vernon Hernandez was the newest of the group, transferred from Silicon Valley. He kept to himself, except for occasionally talking to Tommy. She'd thought he was just shy, but something about the way he was acting this morning made her wary. Had he played a role in this disaster? Had he given out information he shouldn't have?

73

No Mercy

His voice shook when he spoke again. "Frank and Dave. I worked with them. And now they're dead and—"

The tension in her body released a little. "We don't know about Frank." She laid a hand on his shoulder. "He might make it yet."

"Right!" He scowled and looked away from her. "Those thugs dragged the man out of here, bleeding like a stuck pig. We all saw it! And all anyone can do is accuse *us* of—"

"Now wait a minute," Kate jumped in. "Interviewing us isn't the same as accusing us. The investigators are looking for answers to why this happened." She looked over her shoulder to see others were watching them with concern. "We all need to keep busy. Do our part. I'm sending Tommy back here to work with you. The two of you together scanning HF's are more likely to find a signal than anyone at NSA." In reality, she wasn't sure that was true. But she hoped that by partnering the two she'd restrain Vernon's depression and Tommy's impulsiveness. A two fer. "Is that okay with you, Vern?"

He nodded. "I guess."

By the end of the workday, Tommy and Vernon were still tag-teaming the UHF bands but had come up with nothing. The good news, if there was any—HW-1's status hadn't changed. Although NASA couldn't access the satellite, no one else had either. Yet.

The soft hum of voices in the lab as other scientists or support crew came on duty or left at the end of their shifts was periodically broken by a shout from Tommy: "C'mon, you creeps, show yourselves! I dare ya!" He might have been playing a video game in his parents' living room. If nothing else, his enthusiasm for the hunt broke the tension.

Two key members of her crew would oversee the mission through the night—one monitoring the satellite, the other scanning for transmissions. Cambridge and Tommy had 8:00 p.m. to midnight. Vernon and Kate would relieve them.

Four-hour shifts would continue around the clock, for as long as necessary. Kate's office became a dorm with wall-to-wall cots for those who lived too far from base to bother going home to sleep. In case something happened when she wasn't in the lab,

74

Kate wanted to be close at hand. Amanda, who didn't have the scientific training to do any of the most critical jobs, suggested she pick up Cam's five-year-old daughter after school and take her to her house so that her mother could remain at the facility.

Dave Proctor's funeral was planned for the following morning. Several of the team, who hadn't been working the night he'd been killed, volunteered to cover the lab so others could go. It was one of the saddest times of Kate's life. The flowers in the church were beautiful. So were the organ music and the sermon. But nothing could replace a lost life.

Afterward, back at the compound, they all pulled together, no one complaining about the extra hours. Kate saw silent prayers in their eyes—for their missing cohort, Frank. But she guessed that they were also thinking about the future. What would these desperate, violent satellite hijackers do with the power they'd stolen?

No Mercy

The next morning, everyone was hyped on coffee. Amanda delivered a generous batch of glazed donuts, adding sugar to gallons of caffeine without nourishment. Kate asked her to bring something a bit more healthy next time. Perhaps egg sandwiches. Fruit. Yogurt. Anything to keep up their strength.

It was during a change of shifts on the third day of their round-the-clock watch that Tommy shouted, "Bingo! I got you, sucker!" Everyone stood up in their cubicles and stared across the room at him.

Kate ran to her intern. "What?"

"It's them. Has to be." He was bobbing up and down on the toes of his Vans. "I've got a strong signal coming from a source west of DC. Are you picking up anything from Heat Wave's end?"

Kate ran back to Vernon's monitor, ignoring the worried stares of others in the room.

Vernon had returned to working on his own. He frowned at a stream of data dancing across his screen. "Most of this is garbage," he muttered. "No, wait. There! He's right. Looks like an entry code."

"It can't be coincidental," Kate said, her throat suddenly parched. She peered over Vern's shoulder. Felt her heart thumping like a jungle drum in her chest. Had they really found them? Or was this an aberration, a fluke of the atmosphere?

She narrowed her eyes at the screen. No, she was sure of it. The codes made sense. Someone was trying to contact the satellite. If they broke through her virtual barrier, all would be lost. There would be no way to stop them.

Kate reached for her cell phone. There were a dozen people she should contact. But she hit auto-dial.

Rooker picked up immediately. "Yeah, Doc?"

"We have a signal. Someone's making an attempt to bring Heat Wave online."

"Where? You have GPS coordinates?"

"We're working on it. Tommy? Anyone?" she shouted down the room. "Do we have an origination antenna?"

"West Virginia!" Cambridge called out. "I'm notifying NSA. They'll be able to isolate the exact location."

Kate relayed the information to Rooker. "But that's just the antenna. There's no telling where Zed is."

"Right. Okay." He sounded as if he was running while talking. "But Appalachia would be a smart place to hide out. Fugitives have gone missing there for decades, and never been found."

"Vernon, what do you think?" Kate shouted. "Can you track down the location of the computer they're using?"

He glared at his screen, a pained twist to his mouth. He typed information then shook his head. "Too soon."

"Wheeling!" Tommy called out.

"No way," Vernon grumbled. "You're just guessing."

Rooker was bellowing in her ear. "Give me a town, a county, anything!"

"You'll get it when we have it." Why was she snapping at him? They were on the same side. Every one of them in the room was close to breaking. She softened her tone. "Just hold on. Okay?"

But the man seemed incapable of understanding the concept of waiting for anything. "I'm at Andrews AFB now. We're scrambling as I speak. Be in the air in fifteen minutes, twenty tops. You sort out your directions then call me back."

"No, wait! I'm going with y—" But he'd already cut the connection.

Kate clicked off her phone, breathless, furious. Her head spun with frustration. The jerk was going to make it impossible for her to accompany him. "Do we have coordinates yet?" she shouted.

The lab was silent.

"Answer me, someone! Cam, do you have NSA on the line? Have they tracked the antenna or the computer on GPS?"

A shout went up from the end of the room. "Sweet Mary and Joseph, he's right!" Vernon jabbed a finger excitedly at his screen as Kate approached him at a run. "Look at this—the

No Mercy

antenna's in the West Virginia mountains not far from Wheeling."

"And I've got a signal between it and a computer. It's a freakin' dial-up service!" Tommy laughed, sounding manic. "You believe this shit? Dial-up? How low-tech can you get?"

Within an hour, cyber techs at NSA verified with Verizon the location of the computer that was sending signals to the satellite. Moments later, the DHS was all over it.

Tommy and Vernon high-fived over the tops of their partitions while Kate forwarded the information to Rooker, already in an Air Force chopper with his team.

For some reason she didn't feel as elated as everyone else. She sat at her console and stared at the new computer that had replaced the one the psycho-rocker woman had shot up. Something felt wrong. Very wrong. She just couldn't say what.

"You're a worrywart," her mother always used to tell her. "You worry even when there's nothing to worry about."

Did she? Maybe that was why she was a good scientist. She didn't take things at face value. She felt compelled to always dig deeper, ask more questions, double check answers, never be satisfied until every last argument to the contrary had been refuted.

Another thought occurred to her. Maybe that also was why she'd never succeeded at relationships. She had tons of friends– both men and women. But lovers? They were few and far between. Rarely were they around for long. And never in the romantic, take-me-I'm-yours-forever sort of way. Mercy once accused Kate of intentionally trashing her relationships, looking for her partners' faults and using them as excuses to break up. She shoved aside the troubling thoughts. Now wasn't the time to work the kinks out of her love life.

After the excitement calmed down, Vernon and Tommy went off to the break room, saying they'd be back soon. Kate contemplated the luxury of a nap. She'd slept hardly at all in the past three days. Mostly catnaps on her office couch. Her eyes burned, her butt ached from sitting too long. The muscles in her neck and low curve of her back felt as tight as piano strings. Even so, she strained to keep her eyes focused on her monitor.

She prayed Rooker would find Zed and stop him from passing along the codes or using them to hurt anyone.

Cambridge came and stood over her. "You should go home to bed. We've done our part. Now it's up to DHS and that hotshot mercenary."

"Can't." Kate shook her head. It swam with images of destruction.

"Why the hell not?"

"Because I don't trust Zed or...or any of this." How could DHS prevent misuse of her sat, without knowing the motivation behind Zed's crew or their affiliation? ISIS slaughtered without regard for nationality or religion other than their own. Al Quaeda was unpredictably violent, always finding new ways to terrorize. Then there were homegrown troublemakers whose goal was their own ten minutes of fame.

And Rooker? Cam was right; he was a mercenary of sorts. But, to her, the man was not much better than a cowboy, a loose gun. How had Homeland Security determined they could trust the man? So much could go wrong!

If only her head would clear. Her thoughts crawled like a lazy salamander through the river-bottom sludge of her fatigued brain.

"I'm scared," she whispered, forgetting Cam was there.

Cam leaned down and patted her hand. "I know, honey. We all are."

Think positively, if not for yourself, then for your team. "Maybe," Kate said, "after a few failed attempts to connect with the satellite, whoever is behind this will realize they can't bring HW-1 online because I've blocked them."

"Sure," Cam said. "Then they'll give up." They looked at each other. Did either of them believe that? "What are you thinking now?"

Kate shrugged. "They're still so close to DC. It was almost too easy to find them." Kate shoved herself up out of the chair and staggered more than walked over to Tommy's station. Lack of sleep was catching up with her fast.

Tommy and Vernon had returned by then with cans of soda and bags of potato chips. Vernon pulled up a chair beside the younger man at his console. The two of them were taking turns at the keyboard, looking more like two little boys sharing a video game than computer experts tracking a terrorist.

"Is there any chance that's a bogus signal?" she asked, pointing at their mnitor. "Or routed from somewhere else in the country?" *Or the world?*

"Finding out will take a while." Tommy looked up at her and wrinkled his nose. "And it's not exactly in my job description these days, ya know?"

She knew.

There was a time when Tommy had been on the other side—a black-hat Internet saboteur. He'd made the FBI's list of most-wanted hackers. The arresting agents had been shocked to discover a fifteen-year-old kid had hacked into the Pentagon's war-room database on a lark. And then they found he'd stolen over three hundred credit card numbers and passwords in one of the most aggressive identity theft schemes by any individual in the U.S. He'd used other people's credit to buy expensive computer hardware, pay for airfare, feed his college tuition fund, buy books, a car, a mountain of CDs, and gaming software.

Only the threat of jail time and an unusual proposition had persuaded him to change his ways. For four years Tommy out-hacked the best, working for the FBI's elite squad of cyber-techs to hunt down and trap scores of white collar criminals. His record cleared and loyalty proven, NASA officially hired him at the ripe old age of twenty-one. He'd been a godsend as far as Kate was concerned.

But hacking was like any addiction. Tough to beat. Some said impossible. Kate still was unconvinced that Tommy didn't dabble on weekends. It was a question she hadn't asked him, and wouldn't now. She didn't want to know.

He was looking up at her now, a glint of excitement in his clear gray eyes. "But," he said, "if my boss *ordered* me to hack a bad guy..." He shrugged.

"Do it!" Kate said, surprising herself at her lack of restraint. "If you find more computers than one, follow the trail until you hit the end." She'd warned Rooker that this might happen, but had he listened to her? If Zed wasn't in Wheeling after all, Rooker's team would have wasted precious time by flying there.

She punched his number again. The phone rang for a long time before he picked up.

"Got an address yet, Doc?"

"Soon, we hope. It'll be in Wheeling. NSA says they will be able to trace the location. They're working on it now. But—"

"Good."

"No, wait!" The roar of what she imagined were helicopter blades was deafening, even over the phone. She had to shout into her cell. "Listen. Whoever has contacted the sat may be nowhere near the antenna. Rooker, are you listening? Do you hear me?"

"Until we've picked up Zed's crew, I'm shutting down all communications except with NSA. After we get the coordinates we'll break off with them, too."

She still didn't know if he understood what she was trying to tell him. The man was maddening. No, he was insane. Past reasoning with. She opened her mouth to speak again, but he continued bellowing over what had become a high-pitched whine. She imagined the helicopter lifting off.

Rooker said, "Going silent now, Doc. Don't want to tip off the perps."

No Mercy

Kate slid down in her chair, dropped her phone on the desk and closed her eyes. Every nerve in her body burned with anticipation, with fear for what might come.

How long did it take to fly by helicopter from Washington, DC to Wheeling, West Virginia? She had no idea. She leaned forward with a groan and dropped her head into her hands.

"Yes!" a shout from Vernon sent her back onto her feet.

"What is it?"

Vernon stood beside Tommy, who was grinning up at him like a kid on Christmas morning and snare-drumming pencils on his desktop. She wondered if either of them was doing more than coffee. Perhaps riding an amphetamine wave? *Don't ask.*

"What have you got?" she asked breathlessly.

Vernon slapped the young intern on the back so hard he nearly knocked Tommy out of his seat. "He did it. He found the pot of gold at the end of the rainbow."

"Huh?" *Talk sense*, she pleaded silently.

Tommy unclipped his earphones and gave her a smug look, eyes bright. "They funneled their signal to the antenna in West Virginia through eight different computers. *Eight!* This is the first one in the string. This is where the fuckers really are, boss." He pointed at a satellite map on his monitor.

Kate stared at the terrain under his finger. "That's not mountains. That's ocean. Long Island Sound?"

"Close. The coast of Connecticut, nearly to the Rhode Island border." Tommy narrowed the focus, bringing more detail into the display. "See there? The signal's originating there—Groton, Connecticut. Got a street address and everything. Rooker will be thrilled."

"No, he won't." Cambridge stepped up beside Kate. "Mr. Rooker will be totally pissed. He's somewhere over West Virginia, on a wild goose chase."

Kathryn Johnson

"And we have no way to reach him," Kate said. The floor felt as if it was falling out from under her feet. She couldn't reach Daniel Rooker, but there was someone who would pick up her call immediately, and know what to do. She snatched her cell phone off the console and hit speed dial.

No Mercy

Kate barely had time to buckle herself into the wide leather seat before the little jet was airborne. "Don't worry about a thing," Mercy had said. "We'll get you up to New England so fast you'll hardly have time for a cup of tea between take off and landing."

Their conversation had been brief. Mercy said she'd take care of informing all involved parties—the FBI, DHS, Connecticut State Police. They'd agreed on a plan. Kate was to take one of her people as backup. As soon as the hijackers were neutralized (Mercy's word, which made Kate cringe at the violence it implied), she would disable the satellite. Kate had chosen Cam as her support. Dave Proctor or Frank Hess would have been her first choice; they had far more time on the project. But they were lost to her, and Cam knew enough to do the job. Kate just hoped they'd arrive before Zed did anything drastic. She'd failed her people once; she couldn't afford to make any mistakes now.

She looked out the plane's window. Andrews AFB dropped away beneath her, a jeweled pattern of lights as day turned to dusk. The plane banked and pointed its nose north.

Kate closed her eyes and tried to focus on the job ahead. There was no telling how much damage might have been done to the satellite's operating system, or how difficult it would be to reprogram it, to make it harmless again.

Before she knew it they were preparing to land. Kate looked across the cabin at Cambridge. Her colleague's warm-molasses skin had turned a milky tan. The woman stared at the back of the seat in front of her. Her fingers were locked around the arms of her seat.

"Why didn't you tell me you were afraid of flying?" Kate said.

"I'm okay. Maybe I'll take Amtrak home." Cam unstrapped her seatbelt. The plane rolled to a stop on the small commercial landing strip. She stood up and reached for her laptop in the overhead compartment.

Kate gathered her things. "I'm sorry I had to ask you. I needed to bring someone I trusted, totally."

Cam shot her a strange look. "You don't trust the others on our team?"

Kate hesitated. "I...I guess I just don't know." She bent down to look out the window. "Our welcoming committee awaits us." She pointed toward a black SUV with Connecticut State Police shield on the door, headlights on.

An officer in black SWAT gear met them on the tarmac at the foot of the plane's steps. "Lieutenant Jefferson Smith!" he shouted over the still whining jet engines. "We're to take you to the UConn campus at Groton Point. We have no orders beyond holding anyone who tries to leave the campus, by whatever force necessary. The FBI is staked out with us, but I have to say they're being pretty short on the details. So is DHS. Do you mind telling me what this is all about, ma'am?" He sounded irritated to have been kept in the dark, and Kate didn't blame him.

Archer, press-shy to the point of obsession, was no doubt insisting that everything stay on a need-to-know basis.

"I'll fill you in while we drive, Lieutenant," Kate said, and climbed into the rear seat of the SUV with Cam.

She couldn't help thinking how many things could go wrong in the next few hours. The police and FBI would be armed to the hilt, of course. And certainly, armed force might be necessary. But she felt dizzy and sick at the possibility of more bloodshed, more lives lost.

A metallic taste filled her mouth, burned her throat. Her pulse echoed in her ears as she thought about the confrontation to come.

She'd bet any amount of money that Zed and his people wouldn't allow themselves to be taken without a fight. The SWAT team knew the risks and, of course, would take precautions. But she'd have to find a way to protect Cam if it came to a firefight. She couldn't let her get caught in the middle. She began to regret having brought her. Cam was a single mom. What would her daughter do without her?

No Mercy

The lieutenant's driver hit the gas. They raced down a narrow road bordered on both sides by tall grass and salty marshlands. Even as the last of the sun's light faded, Kate could feel the August heat still radiating off the asphalt. The briny smell of sun-warmed ocean rose up around them.

"How much do you know or have you guessed?" Kate asked.

The lieutenant turned in his seat to look back at her. "All we've been told is that this is a possible terrorist situation. Keep it low profile, no press. Come to the party armed." He frowned. "What have we got here, ma'am? Sounds like war to me."

"Cyber-war, at least." Kate quickly described the assault on the NASA compound and the theft of the satellite. The man's expression, in profile, shifted from serious to incredulous as filled in more details. "And they sent two female scientists to deal with this maniac Zed?"

"That wasn't the original plan." There was no sense getting into Rooker's situation now.

"We've only just now learned the true location of the sending signal," Cam said.

"Time is of the essence," Kate added. "We had to move."

He nodded his understanding. "Hence, our involvement."

"Exactly," Kate said. "We have to stop these people before they power-up the satellite and choose a target. We can't be sure yet how they intend to use it. But it's my guess they've already worked that out."

"Otherwise, why steal it?" the lieutenant said.

She couldn't help wondering if any of this really made sense to him. How could he or anyone not involved in the HW-1 project understand the real power the satellite was capable of unleashing? "So you're here to retrieve your stolen information." He paused. "We've been given descriptions of your three intruders and orders to capture if possible."

"And if that's not possible?"

He hesitated. "Our snipers will be in place as soon as we know which building the target's in."

Kate swallowed. Shoot to kill. Isn't that what they said on TV cop shows? "I see."

Kathryn Johnson

She glanced across the rear seat at Cambridge. Their eyes met. Kate reached out and squeezed Cam's shoulder.

Because of the heavily forested mountains, the chopper had to set down in an open field about a quarter mile from their target. It wasn't yet dark but soon would be. Didn't matter to Rooker and his men; they'd come prepared with night-vision goggles.

"Sit tight," Rooker told the helicopter pilot. "We'll be back soon with a few guests."

He took his cell phone out of its holster, thinking he should check in one last time with Kate, then decided against it. Why give Zed any chance of knowing he was in the area?

There would be no moon tonight as they hiked in through the woods. That was good. The air was remarkably clear and cool for summer. Almost like fall up here in the mountains. A nice change from D.C.'s sweltering heat and humidity. If he hadn't been on a job, he would have enjoyed this little excursion. He thought of Kate again. Wondered if she liked camping out. Supposed she'd laugh at him if he invited her to go off for a weekend in the mountains with him.

Are you out of your mind, Rooker?

Why was he leaping into such fantasies? He'd been doing that a lot lately. Far too often. "Bossy woman," he muttered, trudging on through the trees. The brush was dense but they'd found an old path not yet overgrown. He'd told the men that Kate had wanted to tag along, and they'd agreed it wasn't a smart idea.

Patrick Donnelly, the young former marine walking beside him, must have heard him talking to himself. Patrick turned and grinned at him. "My sister's like that. A tomboy from the time she could walk. With five brothers, guess she and her Barbies didn't stand a chance."

Rooker hitched a shoulder. "Doctor Foster is in no way a tomboy. She's just a control freak." It sounded funny, saying it like that. Wasn't that what she'd accused him of being?

"Know what I think?"

"No, what do you think, kid?" Hal Peterson said.

"I think the woman wants the chief real bad." Patrick nodded sagely and stepped over a fallen tree trunk. "That's the first sign. They want to hang around you all hours of the day and night."

"Do they?" Rooker mumbled.

"Sure. Hey, Peterson, didn't you know, the chief's a babe magnet?"

They both laughed. Rooker didn't object. His men needed to release some of the tension they'd carried with them from D.C. He could handle a little ribbing.

But the possibility that the little blond scientist might find him appealing nudged at his libido. If nothing else, she'd be an interesting challenge. Why not try to get her into bed? No reason she shouldn't be attracted to him. He wasn't a bad looking guy.

But then he remembered how angry she always looked whenever he was around. To be honest, he hadn't exactly done anything to make her day since they'd met. Practically accused her of incompetence the night of the raid on her laboratory.

He winced at that thought. Maybe he'd been a little too hard on her. It wasn't as if she was used to standing up to armed intruders.

"The doc's got the hots for Rooker," Peterson chanted.

Enough, Rooker thought. "Won't do her any good. That's one woman this man is not going to tangle with."

Peterson frowned. "Why not? She's a good-looking female. Got all the necessary parts."

"Nice ones, too," Donnelly added. The path ahead seemed wider, more recently traveled. Now they could move more rapidly.

Rooker shook his head. "You ever try getting friendly with a dog that's got too much wolf in her? Beautiful fur, eyes that just pull you in and shine with intelligence. Gorgeous animals. But you move the wrong way, or even smell funny to her, and she'll take off your hand."

He thought about Kate's eyes. They scared the hell out of him. She knew things he'd never begin to understand. He hated that—feeling inferior because he didn't share her level of education. He'd always felt intimidated by super-intelligent people. Always felt they were testing him. Just waiting for him to make a slip and say something dumb.

Maybe it had something to do with having been kicked out of school three times. That was for fighting. Half the time, he'd been trying to defend some puny kid from bullies. School principals didn't understand that. Fighting was fighting, as far as they were concerned.

Peterson said, "A she-wolf, huh? I still wouldn't mind—"

"You come between her and her cub," Rooker warned, "you're dead."

"She's got a kid?" Donnelly took the path to the right, following the coordinates they'd already mapped out.

"No, you idiot," Peterson groaned. "He's talking metaphorically."

"Meta-who?"

"The chief means her satellite. She's, like, protective of it."

"That hunk of metal?" Donnelly laughed. "Strange thing to get attached to, if you ask me."

For some reason Rooker felt the need to defend Kate. "I guess it's sort of like us. You know, the team. What we'd do for each other. That Heat Wave thing is her life. You should have seen her up against the bigwigs at the briefing the day after the break in. She hung tough against all of them."

"Cool," Peterson mumbled.

"I still think she's a looker," said Donnelly of the one-track mind.

"Not worth the trouble," Rooker growled. He checked their position again. They were nearly there. "Cut the chatter. Focus, everyone. Let's get this job done."

Kate wondered if anyone had yet been able to reach Rooker. She supposed he'd realize their mistake soon enough. She also was pretty sure that Cam had been right when she said he'd be pissed to find himself hundreds of miles away from Zed. She put him out of her mind the second the lieutenant said, "We're almost there."

"Tell me about this place," Kate said.

"An old private estate, turned over to the U.S. Coast Guard in the early twentieth century. Used for training purposes for several decades before becoming an extension campus for the University of Connecticut. Here's the gate and main entrance."

No Mercy

He pointed to several unmarked vehicles and a manned road block. The SUV was waved through. "Classrooms, dorms, power plant, an old stone mansion made into administrative offices. This time of year, the place is pretty much deserted. Campus security doesn't expect students back for another month."

Good. If there was one thing she didn't want, it was a bunch of kids involved in a hostage situation.

"We've blocked all land exits, have officers watching the woods. Two boats are positioned off the point, in case anyone tries to slip away by water."

Kate pulled her laptop out of its case and onto her knees. She booted up. Cambridge was already on her cell, talking with someone back at NASA.

The lieutenant turned in his seat to watch her fingers fly across the keys. "What are you doing?"

"Downloading information from our database back at NASA-Weston. I need to check my satellite's status." She bit down on her lower lip, remembering Rooker's teasing. She mentally changed "my" to "the."

"Vern's online," Cambridge said, sounding breathless. "Says someone is still trying to contact Heat Wave but hasn't succeeded. NSA has pinned down the signal to one building on the campus. Tommy's sending us a satellite map right now."

Kate dared to hope that they might be in time. "Tell them to keep trying to reach Rooker's team. We have to let him know what's going on."

The police officer studied her with a frown. "You said earlier that the signal to your satellite has to go through an antenna. Can't your people just destroy the antenna?"

Kate shook her head without looking up from her keyboard. "That won't solve the problem. Destroy one antenna, and they'll find another. Any antenna from 5.4-to-10 meters will work, as long as it can be pointed at Heat Wave."

"Shit."

Exactly, she thought.

The SUV was beginning to slow down as they followed the narrow, twisting roads through the campus. The driver shut off the headlights.

The lieutenant was quiet for a minute more. "But satellites orbit the Earth," he said, and she could almost hear the gears of his mind working to understand the science. "Won't these creeps need to find more than one antenna, a whole series around the world, to keep following your satellite?"

"Not necessary," Cambridge said. "HW-1 is in a geosynchronous orbit. It keeps pace with Earth's rotation, basically tracks the East Coast of the US."

Kate explained. "That keeps it in a stable position in relation to NASA-Weston, which enables us to study it and run our experiments."

"Bloody hell," Smith muttered. "And they can use that thing like a weapon? Like some kind of big cannon in the sky?"

"Not exactly, but it's possible that they could do some real damage, hurt a lot of people if they somehow figure out how to control it."

Cam nudged her. "Here, I've got Tommy's satellite map. Looks like that's the building." She pointed out a two-story, red-brick dormitory several hundred feet ahead of them. Orange light glowed dimly from a single window on the second floor. The SUV rolled silently to a stop. Two additional State Police vehicles soon joined them.

"Good," the lieutenant said. "You two sit tight." And he climbed out to meet with his men.

Kate ignored the order and started to open the passenger door to get out.

"Better wait here, ma'am," the young driver said. "The lieutenant means it."

Kate forced herself to sit back in the seat, feeling as though the sides of the vehicle were closing in on her. More than anything, she just wanted to get this over with. Go back to her lab, where people she trusted worked with her. Sane people who weren't out to wreak havoc on the world.

Kate watched out the SUV's window. It was almost totally dark now, making it harder for her to see much of anything. Two armed men disappeared into the night at the lieutenant's orders. Four others split off in another direction. The lieutenant was speaking into his collar, she assumed a microphone. Positioning his snipers? She felt sick to her stomach. What if Zed's crew spotted them first? Would one or more of these young men not survive the night?

"Can you see any sign of life in that building?" Kate asked Cam.

"No. Doesn't mean they aren't in there."

Not a sound came from outside of the vehicle now. Only Smith and a final pair of men in black jumpsuits, Kevlar vests, and knit skullcaps remained in sight. Kate held her breath. Slowly her ears adjusted to the silence. She heard the soft splash of waves on rocks, so the ocean must be very close. A seagull gave a mournful call. Or was it an owl? A foghorn bleated in the distance.

Suddenly, Smith's face filled the window beside her, making her jump. He spoke through the glass in a whisper. "You two will wait in the vehicle until we've secured the building and taken control of whoever is inside."

"No!" Kate shook her head emphatically, pushing open the door, making him take a step back. "I have to go in with you. We can't risk anything happening to the data. If they've managed to connect with the satellite I'll need to intercept the signal and countermand the—"

"I can't let you do that, Doctor. Sounds to me as if you're pretty important to this mission. My head will roll if anything happens to you."

"Then give me the same protective gear that your men are wearing."

He shook his head, dismissing her request with a wave, then stalked away from her. Out of the corner of her eye she glimpsed Cam climbing out of the car, holding a hand out to fend off the driver who was trying to stop her.

Kate rushed after the lieutenant. "Wait. Ms. Cambridge is your witness. I'm refusing to follow orders. You're no longer responsible for my safety."

"Kate!" Cam appeared behind her. "What are you doing?"

"My job." She turned back to Smith, the words tumbling out of her in desperation. "We have no idea of the status of the satellite. This is exactly why we needed a clandestine response, not a battalion storming the building. If your men rush in there while Heat Wave is being deployed...the consequences could be disastrous. *I* have to be there when they go through the door. This isn't negotiable, Lieutenant!"

He swung around and stared at her incredulously. "Don't make me physically restrain you, lady." She was trying not to look at his hands. Big, strong warrior hands. Clenching and unclenching at his sides.

Kate stood firm. "You can't spare men to babysit me. Are you going to loan me protection, Lieutenant, or do I walk in like this? A polyester business suit won't do much to stop a bullet."

Giving her a disgusted look, he peeled off his flak jacket and flung it at her. She'd seen others in the SUV. He could have told her to take one of those. But it would have been less dramatic. She bit her lip, holding back that thought. "Thank you."

"Kate, no," Cam pleaded. "This is insane. You can't—you aren't trained to—"

Kate ignored her. She tugged the bulky, too-large vest over her suit jacket. She cinched up the waist strap and accepted a helmet the driver held out to her. Blood roared in her ears. Every movement she made felt supercharged. Adrenaline. She was swimming in it. Drowning in it.

"Kate?" Cam said again. "Listen, I at least know how to handle a gun. That's something. If they give me a weapon and I go in there instead of—"

"Absolutely not. You have a little girl at home waiting for you." She was having trouble getting the helmet to sit right on her head. It felt massive. Awkward. "I'm not going back to DC without her mother."

Cambridge looked to the lieutenant for support. "She can't go in there unarmed."

"I'm not carrying a gun," Kate insisted.

"I'll assign two men to cover her." Smith whispered something into his collar. Almost immediately two men in black appeared out of the dark. He gave them hasty orders. "Get her in fast...in one piece. Soon as the shooting's over, if there is any."

Kate glanced at the pair. They looked just as young as Tommy. Younger even. They were putting their lives on the line for her. Was she making as bad a decision as everyone else thought?

No Mercy

Rooker's team arrived at a clearing with a stream running through it. Three cabins, widely spaced, formed a small campground on a low rise above the little river's banks. Rooker thought they looked like strictly summer places, probably not winterized. But brick chimneys indicated fireplaces, maybe woodstoves. Lights were visible in only one cabin.

The dial-up connection had originated from one of them. Were the perps still attempting to connect with the NASA satellite? Again, he thought about contacting Kate to find out. But if this gang was sophisticated enough to hijack a satellite, they'd be able to listen in on nearby phone conversations. If he were Zed, that's what he'd be doing.

A Ford Explorer was parked beside the lit-up cabin. No other vehicles around. A plastic playhouse and children's riding toys littered the pine needle covered ground. If this was where terrorists lived, they'd put down serious roots.

If it wasn't?

A warning bell had begun chiming in Rooker's brain, softly at first, but persistent. Could they be walking into a trap? Or a home invasion? Had the gang forced their way into a house with kids in it? He'd need to move his men in cautiously. Go in hard and fast from all sides of the building at once, quickly assess possible danger to innocent civilians. No firing until fired upon.

He gave his orders. Men dissolved into woods and shadows.

"Light just went out, back room," Peterson whispered into his body mike from somewhere in the trees.

"Yeah." Rooker felt queasy. Something sure was wrong. He couldn't put his finger on it. But he'd given the orders: No damage to any equipment. First priority, recover data and any equipment. Second priority, capture Zed and his crew. Third priority, if it was still possible (which he seriously doubted), rescue Hess, the kidnapped scientist."

Rooker waited. Breathed. Waited.

"Ready on the north," Donnelly reported over the radio.

"Ready east," from Sanchez.

"Ready on..." At last they'd all checked in.

He pushed aside doubts and concentrated on the satisfaction of striding up to Kate Foster and dropping her precious USB thingy into her hand. How could she not thank him then? It would be a nice change to see a look of admiration in those cool green eyes instead of that critical glare she always leveled at him.

"Go," he said.

They stormed the cabin.

Fifteen minutes later things had calmed down enough for Rooker to figure out what the hell had gone wrong.

"I can't tell you how sorry we are, ma'am." He must have said that six times already. Probably would apologize another six times before they left.

Thank God they hadn't gone in firing. Thank God neither the man nor his wife had time to grab the shotgun off the wall and try to defend themselves.

A young couple with three little kids. *Shit.*

And all his guys had found as far as high-tech gear was an ordinary laptop, a TV, and an Xbox setup.

He'd immediately switched on his phone, contacted the lab at NASA-Weston. One of Kate's people—Tommy, he thought was the young guy's name—told him she'd been trying to reach him. Worse than an irate Kate: "The computer you found is just one of a string of innocent decoys. They're using them to mask the real location of the sending signal."

Hadn't she warned him that something like this could happen? Had he listened? *No.*

Did he dare imagine the look on her face when he slunk back to Andrews, tail between his legs, empty-handed? *Hell no.*

"Where is she? Let me talk to her."

"She flew up to Connecticut," the kid said. "We think that's where Zed's gone."

He listened, incredulous. What were Kinsey and Jessup thinking? They'd get the woman killed!

He hastily got the coordinates from Tommy. Checked to make sure he had Kate's cell phone number. Called it. It rang

No Mercy

once then went straight to voice mail. *Fuck*! She'd turned it off. Which meant she was somewhere she didn't want it to ring. Maybe already in the middle of a raid. Or it was over and she was injured. Or dead.

"We're moving out," he barked at his team, standing in embarrassed silence near the cabin's front door. "Now!"

He shot the father a final look of apology. "Send me a bill for the door," he repeated, pointing to the card he'd laid on the kitchen table, around which the family sat. The mom was still trying to calm the youngest of the kids, who hadn't stopped crying since his men burst in on their summer retreat. "Sorry. We're really sorry about this. Terrible mistake."

"Where we going, sir?" Donnelly asked.

"New England," Rooker said. "To college." He tried Kate's number again as they ran back along the dark, wooded path toward the waiting chopper. Rang her four more times in the next hour, on the way back in the Black Hawk to Andrews AFB and after they'd switched to a real plane.

Nothing. Nothing. Nothing. Nothing...

He felt sick. He shouldn't have gone dark. He should have listened to her.

Kathryn Johnson

The single dim light shone like a beacon through the second-floor window of the dormitory. Kate stared at it. Why no other lights? She felt a twisting in her gut, a visceral sense that something was very wrong with this picture.

Zed wasn't stupid. He couldn't be, and pull off the assault on the compound as smoothly as he'd done. Yet, as she stared at that light, she thought it was almost as if he was holding up a sign for their benefit: *Look here!*

Was she leading these men into an ambush?

She wanted to warn the lieutenant. But he had disappeared into the night. And her two escorts were already moving her forward in short runs—from behind a hedge, to the shelter of a brick wall, to the corner of another student dormatory only a hundred feet or so from the target building.

From nearby, Kate could made out shadowy forms in the moonlight. One figure crouched at the cement foundation of the suspect building. Another edged nearly invisibly toward a door. She imagined other men on the far side of the building.

Her heart beat harder, faster. Her mouth went parchment dry.

Kate felt, surreally, as if she'd been dropped into the middle of a true-crime TV drama. She was accustomed to long, quiet hours spent plotting trajectories, calculating positions of distant objects—satellites, moons, planets, stars, black holes—studying the lightless outer regions of known space. She'd interned on the Hubble Space Telescope team. She'd played a vital role in saving SOHO, the Solar Heliospheric Observatory. When that satellite, orbiting the sun, had inexplicably turned, throwing its cameras out of alignment and making them useless, she'd been on the recovery team. The Comm Center had exploded with cheers when, from thousands of miles away on Earth, her programming adjustments successfully repositioned the valuable lenses.

No Mercy

That was her kind of excitement. Adventures of the mind! Physical danger was utterly foreign to her.

She glanced at one of the young police officers at her side. He looked so calm, absolutely sure of his every move. Kate swallowed, felt heat rising in her face, the nerves at the back of her neck zinging. She must have started to straighten up from her crouch without thinking. A palm pressed down on her helmet, reminding her to stay low. Then one of her protectors closed a hand around her upper arm and scrambled her across the last few feet of open lawn. He signaled her to stay where she was.

Kate watched, transfixed by the pantomime in the dark. Figures converged soundlessly in the faint glow of a silver crescent moon revealed by parting clouds.

Dan-ger! Dan-ger! Dan-ger! Her heart pounded.

An extended hand. A raised finger. A quick jerk of one man's head—the lieutenant's?—and everyone shifted positions again. They all seemed to know what to do. She could only follow along. Pray that, in these few minutes since she'd last contacted Tommy in Maryland, Zed hadn't accessed Heat Wave.

There was a moment after they'd all reached positions outside of the building, as the first men slipped in, quickly, silent as death, when she was sure that her heart had simply stopped. The world held its breath. The wind ceased, as if in sympathy. Nothing moved or made a sound.

Suddenly, shouted warnings erupted from somewhere inside the building: "Freeze! This is a raid. Show yourself! Put down all weapons!"

She could hear the slap, slap, slap of running feet. The nerve-shredding noise of splintering wood. More shouts but no gunfire.

Kate's escorts reacted to something coming through their wireless earphones. One young man looked at her. "They've found the computer. You're on, Doc."

"What about Zed?" she gasped. "Did they get him?"

The young cop shook his head. *No.*

And Frank? Guiltily, she realized she'd stopped thinking about her colleague. She prayed none of the lieutenant's people had been hurt, then it struck her that she'd heard no shots. Not a one.

Kathryn Johnson

Why? Had they found the wrong building after all?

Her guardian angels in black rushed her through the front door and into the building.

Inside, a wide, tile-floored vestibule led to a stairway. Stopping her at the bottom, one of her guys spoke into his mic and listened for a moment, hand cupped over his ear bud. "All clear above," he said, beckoning to her to follow him up.

Along the second-floor hallway, a row of doors stood open. Most appeared to have been unlocked or already open. But one, halfway down and facing the front of the building, showed signs of having been broken through. A light shone from inside, throwing a brilliant orange stripe across the dark wood of the hall floor. The same light she'd seen from outside?

The lieutenant stood in the doorway, staring with a puzzled expression at something inside the room.

Kate moved cautiously forward, terrified of what she'd find. Bodies? An empty room with no computer? She stopped beside Lieutenant Smith.

"This what we're after?" he asked.

She stared at a Toshiba laptop sitting on a lone student desk that had been dragged into the middle of the nearly empty room, as if to put it on center stage. A message in bold white letters flashed against a black background: *Hi there, friends of HW-1!*

"What on earth?" she whispered.

She hadn't believed that human beings actually snarled, like you read in some books. But the lieutenant did. "Is this some college kid's prank?" His words came out in a low, dangerous growl.

Kate shook her head. "I don't think so." Although—she could almost hear Zed laughing.

As she stared at the creepy greeting it morphed into another image. Blue-and-white graphics mimicking the NASA logo. Words slowly faded in beneath the symbol: *Password, please.*

Kate took a step into the room.

The lieutenant's arm shot out in front of her. "Wait. We should call in the bomb boys first."

"There may not be time," she said.

He made another guttural sound deep in his throat but let her pass. Kate rushed across the room. Flung herself down in the

No Mercy

wooden chair in front of the screen. She entered her initiation code, praying it would work, aware of men entering the room behind her.

That'll do, the screen read. *Hiya, Dr. Kate. Watch this!* That sounded more like the Rocker woman than Zed. But she didn't have time to process what the words might mean.

Blinding yellow-orange flames erupted across the screen. An ear-shattering explosion echoed off the walls with Dolby-like volume, vibrating the floor. Everyone in the room, including Kate, ducked or hit the floor.

For a moment, she too believed a real bomb had gone off.

"What the hell!" the lieutenant shouted.

Boots thundered down the hallway toward them. Shouts of confusion. Orders to evacuate the building. Half the SWAT team stampeded toward the stairwell.

Kate didn't move except to straighten up in her seat. She couldn't stop staring at the screen. One word in big red letters: BOOM!

"A joke," she whispered. Swallowing once, twice, she caught her breath at last. "He's playing with us."

"What?" The lieutenant shoved himself up off of the floor.

"It was a trick to get our attention. Sound effects from the computer. Speakers." She looked up at the corners of the room. She hadn't noticed them before, but there they were—three little black boxes, no attempt to hide them.

"Christ. Why?" The lieutenant sounded more weary than angry now. He dusted off the knees of his pants.

"They want to make a point. To show us it could have been a real bomb. They're sending us a message."

"What?"

She sighed. "We're dangerous, unpredictable, desperate. Lethal? Who knows. They don't want to be ignored."

"He's going to make a demand," a voice came from the doorway.

Kate closed her eyes. She didn't have to turn around to know who it was. She would never mistake that raspy, far-too-cocky voice. "Welcome to the party, Mr. Rooker."

Chapter 16

Cam had led the Worldwide Security man up from the vehicles. She stood behind Kate now. Touched her on the shoulder: *Glad you're okay.* They both peered at the computer's screen. The image was morphing into something new. A message of some sort.

Kate angled the screen down, making it harder for others in the room to see what was slowly materializing before her eyes. She had a feeling it might include information that Washington would want to kept from the public, at least for the time being.

"Lieutenant, obviously Zed isn't in this room. Would you please ask your men to leave?" Kate kept her tone controlled. If she let her voice rise in pitch, even a little bit, she might sound hysterical to these men. "Their time probably would be better spent in other parts of the building." She couldn't let them think she was no longer in control of her emotions or, worse yet, had lost the ability to think rationally.

Moments later she could hear the SWAT team crashing around in more distant rooms and hallways, in search of the elusive Zed.

Rooker motioned the lieutenant aside. Kate turned her attention to the keyboard, started following directions that flashed up onto the screen. Cam pulled up a chair beside her. In the background she heard Rooker introduce himself to the police officer, but then his voice dropped. She strained to hear their conversation. Didn't trust their male secretiveness. But after a few more words between them, the lieutenant left the room, too.

Rooker placed two of his own men in the room. One at a tall window overlooking the ocean, the other at the hallway door. Neither within view of her screen.

"Do you need me to leave too?" he asked, keeping back a respectful distance. She couldn't imagine what had come over him. He was a different man than the one who'd left for West

Virginia. He'd actually taken her side. Without demanding explanations. And he was asking permission to stay.

"No. You'd better hang out here," she decided. "We might need someone outside of NASA to back up whatever—" She waved off the rest of her words, too busy hitting keys to talk.

The foghorn moaned again. From outside she heard engines, vehicles going or coming—she couldn't tell.

She wondered, was Zed's schoolboy trick only that? Or might it be the precursor of the real thing? Her next keystroke could be the one that set off a real explosion. Why not? Clearly these people had no respect for human life. They didn't care if people suffered. Maybe this night was the last she'd see. Ever.

"What are you thinking?" Cam asked, watching the screen over her shoulder.

Kate shook her head, as if the motion would disburse the cobwebs of her confusion. "I don't understand how Zed knew we'd track him down and then I'd fly here and discover his demonstration?"

"You don't think someone back at the lab—"

"A leak, you mean? I don't know." A traitor in their midst? God, she hoped not. But if not that—what then? It was as if he could read her mind. As if the man knew her far more intimately than a stranger who'd stood in a room with her for less than ten minutes.

That thought sent icy prickles through her. Terrified her. How did he know her so well that he could predict her reactions?

She should get up and walk out of this place this very minute. Leave the whole mess to Rooker and the FBI, NSA, DHS—anyone else who wanted it. They dealt with crazies, radicals, violence all the time, each in their own way. They knew how to deal with death and destruction. Wasn't she being presumptuous to think that she might be of any use at all?

Worse yet, she'd dragged Cam up here with her. Clearly a mistake. The woman needed to be back home with her little girl. For all they knew, Zed's crew was still on this campus. Watching the drama unfold through binoculars, night goggles, or cameras. Laughing at them.

She stopped typing and studied the new screen in front of her. It read: *Hit ENTER, Kate.* If she did, what chain reaction might it set off? Would she blow the entire campus sky high?

Her hand hovered over the keyboard.

She hit ENTER. And held her breath. Looked at Cam...who blinked then gave her a quick nod.

The screen went blank for two seconds. A video feed began to play. Zed's face appeared.

"We were never properly introduced, Doctor Foster. Al Ahmra Zed, at your service." He bowed his dark head in mock deference.

She froze at the memory of facing the man in her lab. How defenseless she'd felt, standing there while he robbed her of her life's work and terrified people she cared for. Helpless to stop him from killing one man and gunning down another.

Beside her she heard Cam draw a sharp breath, felt Rooker step closer, his body language telegraphing its tension.

"My cause," Zed continued solemnly, "is a worthy one, though I do not expect you to understand. What I do expect is that you will appreciate the tenuous position of your colleague, Mr. Hess. To my delight, he is still alive. And," he added with a smile, "able, with a little encouragement, to help us correct your tampering with the satellite's program. Mr. Hess believes that by helping us he will save himself. Such naiveté from a man of science, yes?"

"You bastard," Kate murmured.

The voice continued without reaction to her comment. "I come to my point. You see, now that you know you cannot stop us, or catch us, it is only a matter of time before we gain full control of your satellite. When we do, we will be in a position of unparalleled power, wouldn't you agree?" He glanced down for a moment, and she wondered if he was reading his statement. Had someone else written it for him? The word choices sounded unwieldy, coming from him. He'd stumbled over the word *unparalleled*.

"My demands are simple. You will instruct your government to deposit, within five days, ten million dollars into an account named at the end of these instructions. If they fail to do so, I will select a nice little American town to use as a

No Mercy

demonstration of my sincerity." His lips pinched at the corners, eyes focusing hard on the camera. "Let me assure you, I am a very sincere man."

A blank screen replaced Zed's face. Kate held her breath, her fingertips still on the mouse pad, trembling.

A page scrolled down without any prompt from her. A line of numbers appeared, followed by the words: *Banque de Belize.*

Rooker wasn't terribly surprised to see the type of demand the terrorists were making. Like any business, the bottom line was all about money. Without capital, they couldn't function.

What had surprised him was that Kate Foster had been right about West Virginia being a false lead. Until the moment he'd busted in on that family, he'd assumed she was simply obsessed with controlling the mission. Wanted this to be all about science, about outsmarting the enemy on some theoretical level beyond his comprehension. All about *her*. Whereas he was the one who knew only too well how the minds of men like Zed worked.

Fanatics didn't give a rat's turd about science. They were obsessed with power. And power meant doing anything they damn well pleased. Arrogant, mean-spirited bullies, that's what they were. They *liked* killing people who thought differently about the world than they did. They *liked* taking things that didn't belong to them then blowing up whatever they left behind. Violence was their currency. With it they enforced whatever laws and customs struck their fancy, and justified their fantasies of superiority.

But he knew what the Kate Fosters of the world—the tree huggers, the pacifists and isolationists —didn't know: *Only violence stops the bullies*. This wasn't about reasoning with other human beings or being smarter than them. And that's why she'd get herself and a lot of other people killed, if he didn't move her out of the picture somehow and regain control of this mission. And he would. But just now he had to be patient and let her do her thing.

He only had to look at her to see how the stress was wearing her down. When she was concentrating on the computer in front of her, her posture changed. The straight back slumped. She tucked in her chin and dropped it to her chest. Her green eyes faded to a washed-out gray and lost their shine.

Soon she'd be looking for a way out of the responsibility she'd taken on. And he'd give it to her. Then he could do his job the way it was meant to be done. He could stop worrying about her.

Though why he should worry about her at all made no sense. It wasn't as if she meant anything to him. It wasn't as though he even knew her. She was pretty. She was intelligent. But an impressive IQ wasn't what he usually required in a companion. He imagined she'd probably be pretty uptight in the sack. Analyzing his moves, her moves. The way scientists did. Probably no fun at all.

Probably.

His cell phone rang. Rooker checked the screen and nearly groaned out loud. He stepped away from the two women staring at the computer screen. The one called Cam was taking down the offshore bank account number in a small notebook.

"Rooker here."

"Max Archer." Homeland Security, just what he needed. He winced.

"Yes, sir."

"What happened, Mr. Rooker?" Bad news spread fast. "And where are you? Not West Virginia, I presume."

"We believed a computer-generated signal near Wheeling supported the probability that we'd find Zed's crew but—"

"But all you had was the Little House on the Prairie?" Archer's sense of humor left him cold.

"Something like that, sir. More like a cabin in the mountains, actually," Rooker said.

"So you got nothing for your trouble?"

"We learned something from the experience."

"We'd expected more from you."

Rooker gritted his teeth. "Yes, sir."

"Where are you now, and what's happening?"

Rooker filled him in. When he was done, Archer was silent. For one long, anxious moment Daniel Rooker wondered if he was about to be fired. ASEC and NASA were his employers, so only they could take him off the job. Technically. But the Patriot

No Mercy

Act gave the police, FBI and even individual government officials like Archer with the Department of Homeland Security, previously unheard-of power to act on behalf of the nation's safety.

Being taken off a mission this high-profile would kill his career. Everyone in government, and all of private industry that might be prospective clients, would hear about his fall from favor.

He couldn't let that happen.

He started to say something to lessen the blame, but Archer cut him off.

"Dr. Foster just messaged me from Connecticut."

"She did?" When had she done that?

"Yes, just now. About the demands," Archer said.

"Right. Yes of course, sir. I was standing right here when that message came in." Imagine, she'd acted that quickly. Even while her second-in-command was taking down bank routing numbers, she'd been on her cell phone with Washington.

He swallowed over a lump in his throat the size of his pride. He was hating this conversation more and more.

"We're taking this threat seriously, Mr. Rooker. I hope you are as well."

"Very seriously, sir."

"From now on, you will follow Dr. Foster's instructions, to the T."

Rooker felt the blood rush to his face as a flash of heat. "Now, wait a minute, sir. With all due respect, the woman is a scientist, not a terrorism expert. My team and I need to be free to move fast and without permission or rejection from a—"

"Mr. Rooker."

"Yes, sir?"

"Either you start cooperating with these experts, or you're off the job. Got that?"

He glared at the back of the woman still sitting in front of Zed's laptop. What was she doing now? "But she—"

"NASA hired you. The President can fire you. On matters of this sort, he takes recommendations from me. It's that simple. Got it?"

"Yes, sir." Rooker stabbed a finger at the End Call button on his phone. *Damn politics*.

There were far too many cooks stirring this pot. Nothing good could come of it. ASEC. NASA. FBI. NSA. DHS. And now the God damn Oval Office. All on the same side, technically, but fighting to be top dog, to be the one in charge. To be his country's savior.

Before the sun had risen fully over the horizon, Kate Foster announced that she had a plan. She said she doubted Zed would return to the DC area. Therefore it seemed pointless that they rush back to Washington. Instead, she wanted to set up temporary headquarters in the old mansion that doubled as Administration Offices on the deserted campus. Rooker agreed with her, at least on these two points. They might as well stay put until new data indicated the hijackers' new location.

He found dorms to settle his men into so they could get some much needed sleep, but only allowed himself two hours to rest before returning to find Kate Foster with Cambridge Mackenzie hunkered down in a small office overlooking a rocky cliffs rimming Long Island Sound. He stared suspiciously at the ordinary looking laptops on which they worked. Knowing Kate, her computer was probably crammed with enough high-tech gear to launch the Space Shuttle.

She looked up from her keyboard when he walked in. "Have a nice nap, Mr. Rooker? Some of us are working here."

"Don't even start," he muttered.

An uncomfortable looking wooden, ladder-back chair was the only seating close to her. It reminded him of the ones in his high school principal's office. He'd spent many an afternoon cooling his heels there, waiting for his customary reprimand. How had he gone from class troublemaker and clown, to hunting down bad guys? *Go figure*.

He stayed standing.

Cambridge observed him dubiously then slid back from her keyboard. "I got a question for you, Mr. Rooker."

"What's that?"

"Why didn't you let Dr. Foster go with you to West Virginia?"

No Mercy

"Why didn't you two ladies wait for *me* before flying to Connecticut?" he countered, feeling smug because it seemed to him they were just as much at fault.

"As I recall," Kate said without turning her pretty blond head to look at him, "you were the one who went all macho incommunicado. I tried to reach you and couldn't. You left me no choice."

He curled his lip at her, though he knew she wasn't looking at him. "You took unnecessary risks coming here alone."

She pushed her chair away from the table, spun the office chair and faced him. "I did what I had to do." Her voice was irritatingly cool. She crossed her arms over her chest. Her very nice chest.

He caught himself before he smiled. "Doesn't make it the right move."

"We had a chance to catch Zed. You weren't available, Rooker. What would you have done in my place?"

A good shouting match might have made him feel better. He needed to burn off pent-up frustration after Archer's reprimand. Apparently she wasn't going to oblige. Her voice remained calm. She seemed as cool as spring in Ketchikan.

Maybe he could rattle her. "Doesn't change the fact that Zed's crew disappeared before you arrived. People keep telling me you're the key to this mission, Doc. We lose you, we have no chance of recovering that satellite."

"That's not entirely true," she said. "Several of my team are perfectly capable of stepping in for me."

"And they are?"

"Cam here is one."

"And?"

She shifted her green eyes away from him. "Hess and Proctor would have been able to—

"But Proctor's dead and your other man will be soon enough." Unless Zed was lying and he'd already killed the other guy. He'd offered no proof that Hess was still alive.

"I'm trying to think positively," she said so softly he almost didn't catch the words. She gave a delicate sniff then sat up straighter and met his gaze. "As long as Frank can convince them that they need him, they may keep him alive until we can rescue

108

him." There was more plea in her tone than confidence. He felt sorry for her. She was so ill prepared for anything of this magnitude.

"All right then," he said. "How do we stand with the satellite? Anything happen while I was unconscious?"

"The situation with the sat is the same. They're still trying to connect with HW-1. But the rules of the game changed, Rooker."

Had Archer told her that he'd demoted him? Cripes! Rooker slanted her a look. "What rules?"

"Zed's game."

"What the hell are you talking about, woman?" He looked around, spotted a metal folding chair leaning against the wall, flipped it around and straddled the seat to face her.

She rolled her eyes, looking amused. *Men!* Her gaze shifted toward Cambridge, as if they'd already been discussing this. "I've been thinking. Ten million isn't a great deal of money for all the trouble Zed's going to."

"Sounds like a bundle to me," the other woman murmured.

Rooker nodded, but not in agreement with the dark-skinned assistant. This had been his first thought on hearing the figure. "No. Not a lot, in the scheme of political ransoms. I expect this is a dry run."

"Like a test?" Cambridge asked.

"Yeah." Rooker turned back to Kate and, in that flicker of an unguarded moment, he saw her not as a scientist but as a woman.

A petite, blond-haired, jade-eyed, undeniably attractive woman. Perched on the very edge of her chair, long legs crossed at slim ankles. Gorgeous, really. Just as the boys on his team had pointed out. A woman already getting under his skin in more ways than he wanted to admit. He took a deep breath, tightened his fists, and made a concerted effort to remind himself how much she annoyed him.

He said, "At first I thought Zed would aim for one really dramatic, newsworthy event to make a political statement of some kind. Threaten to zap the Statue of Liberty. Take out Congress. Roast the White House. If people were in his line of fire—too bad. They'd be part of his political message. A single, massive shot of microwaves from your satellite."

No Mercy

Kate looked deep in thought. She worried her bottom lip between white teeth. "But it's not about politics, religion, land, ideologies, or to force the release of political prisoners. It's just about money,"

He nodded. "Right. Zed may pretend he's sending a message to the world, but that seems not to be high on his agenda. Which makes me think we have more of a chance to catch him. Because he'll get greedy."

Kate's eyes fixed on his. "What you mean is, he won't be happy with a measly ten million. He'll come back for more?"

"Exactly. If it works once, why stop there? Pick another target, a different population of victims. Demand a billion, or more, next time." He shrugged. "Why quit when you have a good thing going?"

"That's sadistic," Cambridge spat, scowling at him, as if he were to blame for everything.

"That's having a golden goose," he corrected her.

Kate acted as if she hadn't heard their bickering. "So now we've learned something new about him. We know he's not crazy or, despite what he says, driven by a higher cause. He's just evil." She clamped down on her lower lip until he thought it might bleed. "I'm not sure knowing this really helps."

"Of course it does. We also know more about how he works," Rooker said. "He finds an antenna the right size and orientation then filters his instructions to it through a string of remote computers. The owners of these linking terminals aren't even aware they're being used. A classic hacker's technique, used to cover their trail."

Kate nodded. "Right. And once he has gained control of the satellite, he can give it instructions to use stored energy from the sun to generate microwave energy." She reached for a pencil and tapped out a nervous rhythm on the table's edge. "Until now, all of our tests have produced small amounts of microwave energy that we feed into the power grid. It's harmless, almost inconsequential. Just testing the process."

"But," Rooker thought out loud, "if they ramp up that energy—say, a hundred or even a thousands of times over what you've tested—what happens then?"

"A power surge like that could blow out the grid," Cambridge said. "That's one of Homeland Security's fears." She looked to Kate. "Right? Kill the grid and that leaves the country open to military invasion."

Kate nodded her head but added, "Or...they might concentrate and direct the energy at a highly populated section of a city. Used against people and property, it would become a weapon of terrible destruction."

Rooker was only now beginning to understand what the panic had been about. "So, it'd be like one big microwave oven? Buildings would burn? People too?" He didn't wait for an answer. The expressions on the two women's faces told him he might not have the details right, but he'd gotten the gist of it.

"Then," Kate said, "if we can't stop them, we need to know their target. So we can prepare— maybe evacuate, maybe shield the area. Though I don't know how yet." She frowned and rubbed her fingertips up the bridge of her nose.

Cambridge folded her arms over chest and leaned back in her chair, her attitude looking doubtful. "That might reduce loss of life, if we can get people moved fast enough. But once Zed's crew learns how to choose and actually hit a target, everything could happen pretty quickly. He might not give us enough, or any, warning."

Rooker swore under his breath. "So, what's your status on getting a new fix on Zed's location?"

Kate tossed her pencil down on the table. "It's a slow process. My team at NASA are doing the best they can. Honestly. The FBI is helping, and so is NSA. I think we could use more help from the private sector, if only to keep a lookout for Zed's bunch. But DHS wants to limit exposure to the press. If the public were to find out how bad things could get..." She sighed.

"It's inevitable." Rooker knocked a cigarette out of a soft pack and lit up. "Reporters eat up this shit—they'll pay for any information they can get to build a good headline. *Terrorists capture satellite! Reign of terror!* It's only a matter of time before they track you down, Doc."

She made a face. "They were already flocking around Weston's gates before I left. Waiting to pick Jessup's bones when they couldn't get to me. But back then, all they knew was that there had been an attack on personnel inside the compound. They might have uncovered the hijacking, but still would have no idea of the consequences."

"So." Rooker looked at her over the glowing end of his cigarette. "I understand you're making all the calls now. I'm good with that." *Not really.* But for now it's what it was. "Next moves?"

Kate looked a little startled at his admission that now he was willingly taking orders from her. She shifted around in her seat and appeared to refocus. "My people back in DC are good. They found Zed once, and I believe we only just missed him here, this time. They'll find him again." He wished he felt as sure as she sounded. "There's one thing I haven't totally figured out."

He laughed. "Just one?"

Kate gave him a teacherly look—*Shut up, wise guy!*— but otherwise didn't rise to his bait. "I keep wondering how they're going to point the microwave energy."

"What do you mean, point it?" He blew a puff of smoke in her direction, suspecting that'd annoy her.

She waved it off. "We have a massive array of solar panels up there, as part of the configuration of the HW-1. They catch the sun's energy, it's converted to microwaves then beamed to the ground where it's converted again to electricity for everyday use. But redirecting those microwaves would be a hit-or-miss thing. The energy likely would be too spread out to do any real damage. Zed needs a way to focus the energy, to direct it to a specific target."

He felt a jolt of hope. "You're saying you think they're scamming us? They can't do anything with what they have?"

Green eyes flickered around the room, as if searching for answers. "Maybe they think they can just scare Washington into putting up the money. We talked about that before, remember?"

Cambridge looked worried. "But what if the President decides to call their bluff? Not pay up."

"If it's a scam, nothing happens," Kate said.

"But if it's for real—" Rooker ground out his cigarette with a vengeance in a tin ashtray on the table "—they'll roast Cincinnati, or whoever their intended target is."

Kate suddenly got busy on her laptop but kept on talking. "They need a way to direct the energy to a specific target. Think of a laser beam as a highway, Rooker, with signs posted along the way: *This way to Vegas!*" She flashed him a grin. "You can relate to that, I bet."

He snarled, "Give me a break." But she was sort of cute, teasing him that way. He kind of wished she'd do it more often. He gave her a don't-mess-with-me glare in return, but she ignored him.

"If they use the onboard lasers along with GPS coordinates, theoretically they could run the waves down the laser beam. It could work."

Rooker stared at her. "You're serious. This is what you think they're going to do?"

"Maybe." She paused, her hands leaving the keyboard and resting in her lap as she studied information she'd called up on the screen.

So, things are looking worse instead of better, he thought. Some brainstorming session this was.

There was, though, something else he'd been tempted to bring up. The idea (more finely put, the suspicion) had eaten at him ever since the night of the invasion. But he had no hard evidence to suggest he might be right. And bringing it up now would only put Kate Foster on the defensive again.

For the time being, he'd keep further speculation to himself. If he found what he needed to prove he was right, he'd lay his cards on the table.

But not on Kate Foster's table. He'd have to go over her head. Because, in this particular situation, he couldn't trust her to do the right thing.

No Mercy

Chapter 17

The teleconference dragged on for over an hour. By the time Kate finished her report and the DoD and military types took over the conversation, she was whipped. At last, she clicked off the speaker phone, looked over her shoulder at Cambridge and groaned, "I've aged ten years."

"You did what you could," Mercy said. She'd arrived an hour earlier. Just having her there made Kate feel better. "You told them the truth. Let them fight it out in Washington."

Just the four of them were in the temporary office Kate had made for herself on the college campus. Kate, Cam, Mercy, and Rooker. Four exhausted souls with no game plan.

What worried Kate most was that Kinsey was gaining more support for shooting down HW-1, even though he admitted that no one had ever successfully shot a satellite out of orbit with a missile. ASEC was still arguing against the demolition of their pricey investment. And Kate reiterated her warning about the danger to the population from fallout debris if a strike on the sat was ordered. But no one seemed to be listening.

At first, Kate had felt oddly reassured by the squabbling because it meant they'd do nothing as long as they couldn't reach an agreement. That bought her time. But there was also the question of whether or not to pay the extortion fee. Archer, the voice of DHS, had stated flatly: "The President will stand by his zero-negotiation policy for dealing with terrorists."

Rooker had sat beside her the whole time, chin propped on his fists, his face thunder-cloud dark, brooding silently through the entire briefing. She assumed he'd been ordered to keep his opinions to himself and follow her lead. *It must be killing him,* she thought, taking orders from a scientist, and a woman at that.

It was almost enough to brighten her day.

Almost.

"Now what?" Cambridge asked after the call had ended.

"We wait," Kate said. "Nothing we can do until Zed or whoever is ultimately running this show is located."

"Right," Mercy agreed. "Which reminds me of something I need to do." She took off without saying where she was going.

Kate watched her slip out the door. As fond as she was of her cousin, Kate rather resented Mercy's clandestine behavior. Did everything need to be a deep, dark secret?

Rooker leaned back in his chair. He crossed boot heels over the desktop. It was if he was posing for her benefit. Demonstrating his ability to be patient. She didn't believe him for a minute. This was not a patient man.

She reached down into her valise for the small crystal paperweight she'd brought with her. Her connection to home. To a saner world. The purple crystal of the butterfly's body caught the light from the window. She ran a finger up and over its cool glass wings.

Rooker shot to his feet so unexpectedly she jumped. "I'm out of here."

"Nerves getting to you, Mr. Rooker?" She couldn't help taunting him.

He made that snarly face again, lip curling. "Nothing's happening here. I need a decent meal and a cold beer. Either of you ladies want to come along?"

Kate couldn't remember the last time she'd had a hot meal. Or a full night's sleep. Or a shower. She was pretty sure she must smell. She looked at Cam.

"Beats sitting on our hands while Washington figures out what to do. We all could use a break," Cam said solemnly.

Kate nodded. "All right. Everyone has my cell phone number. They can contact us as easily in a restaurant as they can in this room."

Her only fear that, as soon as she put warm food in her stomach, she'd crash. Four days, with only catnaps and junk food to sustain her, had left her feeling physically depleted.

Rooker made sure his men were taken care of, then borrowed an SUV from the local police. He always seemed to know how to get what he wanted whenever he wanted it—aircraft, weapons, men, information. Did he carry that ability over into his private life?

A disturbing notion, if she really thought about it. She decided not to.

No Mercy

They followed directions from one of the university's grounds keepers to a nearby Applebee's.

Steak—yum! Kate thought, catching a whiff of grilling meat as soon as she opened the car door. A thick, juicy medium-rare sirloin with lots and lots of hot, salty French fries. Her mouth reacted with Pavlovian predictability. She was nearly drooling by the time they hit the restaurant's front door.

They sat in a booth and ordered beers, a basketball-size fried onion bloom as an appetizer, and their meals. Fifteen minutes later, Kate was in heaven. She wolfed down her food and didn't even debate the wisdom of dessert. She ordered a warm brownie sundae with extra whipped cream. The combination of gooey chocolate, melting vanilla ice cream and fluffy sweetened cream was decadent and wonderful.

Thankfully, her phone waited to ring until she was spooning down the last bite of brownie, having successfully fought off Rooker's spoon attacks after he'd finished his own dessert. With a contented sigh, she punched her call button.

"Thought you could take a break, silly woman? Did you have their half-pound cheeseburger?"

Kate smiled. "The steak was even better. How did you know where I was, Mercy?"

"It's my job. Scary, isn't it?"

"I'll say. What's up?"

Rooker leaned over the table, trying to listen in.

"I'm on my way to you now," Mercy said. "I've been on the phone with Washington again, and I have information about Zed that you should know. And some things Rooker might need."

"Right." Kate closed her eyes and shook off the feeling that she was in way over her head. Oh, for the quiet solitude of her lab before all of this madness swept her away. "We're at a table in the back, to the right of the bar as you come in."

"Be there in five."

And she was.

Rooker stared suspiciously at the Red Sands agent when she arrived at their booth. For the first time it struck Kate that they probably thought of each other as competitors, each of them working for different but similar covert businesses.

"Have the powers that be sent you to haul me back to D.C. for flubbing the West Virginia gig?" he said.

"No." Mercy shrugged. "The general opinion is that you acted in the most logical way, as fast as you could. Trouble is, terrorists aren't always logical." She slid onto the bench beside Rooker, facing Kate and Cambridge across a mountain of empty plates. "Good to see you've all been well fed."

Kate felt her eyelids growing heavy. She shook her head, trying to wake herself up, and found Mercy staring at her with concern.

"You should catch some sleep while you have the chance. You'll be no good to us if you're sleep deprived."

"I'm fine. Seriously." But the carbs were kicking in with the force of a strong sedative. She hoped she could make it to a bed, any bed, before she keeled over.

"Well, soon maybe." Mercy folded her hands over the table. She gave the dining area a quick sweep with her eyes. Her voice dropped a few decibels. "Meanwhile, I have good news and bad news."

"Give me the bad first," Kate said, clinking the ice in her water glass with the straw, to give herself something to do. One minute pooped, the next antsy. Was she losing it?

"The *Post* reporters have dug up a few details about the HW-1, its capabilities, and someone has leaked the wording of Zed's threat. It'll be all over tomorrow's newspapers. It's already on the radio and online. On TV news tonight, you can bet. You can expect the media to be all over you, once they realize where you are."

"Crap," Rooker said.

"We really don't need this." Kate rubbed her eyes. Why weren't they focusing?

"What's the good news?" Cambridge asked hopefully.

Mercy leaned forward another inch. "We now know something about Zed's background."

Kate's heart sank. That was all? Her expression must have given away her disappointment.

"No, really," Mercy said, "this is important. We know he goes by the name Al Ahmra Zed but his real name is Gordon Jones. He was a small-time crook in Philadelphia—burglary, car theft, that sort of thing. Did some jail time, came out and went right back to his old routine. More jail time. Learned a trade in prison. Came out and worked in a car lube shop for a few months before being picked up for armed robbery. Skipped bail then disappeared. No one, least of all his parole officer, has heard from or seen him in months."

"Any intel about his being involved with militant groups or religious fanatics?" Rooker asked.

A waitress started to approach the table. Mercy gave her a sharp look and raised one hand a tick off the table. The woman about-faced and left them alone. Kate was impressed. It was like waving a magic wand.

"At some time, he came into contact with a domestic terror cell. They welcomed him with open arms. We don't know if he's still involved with them or acting on his own."

"And," Rooker added, keeping his voice equally low, "even though his message to Dr. Foster refers to his *cause,* he still hasn't said what that cause is."

"Exactly." Mercy turned to Kate. "Usually these types can't say enough about their supposedly good reasons for resorting to violence. They rationalize everything they do. Love having an audience."

Rooker looked around at the neighboring tables, as if to reassure himself that no one was taking an interest in their conversation. "A guy like Zed, he has wet dreams about making the six o'clock news."

Mercy nodded. "So although we don't know why he's doing what he's doing, we at least have some idea of who the man is. And we're beginning to think he might not have a political agenda at all."

Which, Kate thought, went along with her earlier conversation with Rooker.

"What good does this really do us though?" Cambridge asked with an irritable scowl.

"Every piece of information helps us target the guy. His personal and social contacts, places he feels safe and might retreat to. You'd be surprised how many Most Wanteds run back to their home turf, even though that's the most obvious place to look for them."

Rooker finished off his second beer and eyed the bar wistfully. "They think they have the advantage, knowing the territory."

Suddenly, Kate was having trouble focusing on the conversation. It wasn't that she lacked interest. She just kept feeling more and more distant from the group gathered in the booth. Almost as if she were floating above the table, looking down on the four of them, including herself.

"Kate?" It was Mercy's voice, but she sounded as if she were talking to her through a wall.

It took Kate a moment to realize her eyes were closed. With effort, she peeled them open.

"What?" The room swam blurrily. Traffic sounds, the clink of glasses, screech of a chair moving across tile floor, voices—everything blended together. *Annoying,* she thought. Her eyes wouldn't stay open.

"Come on, Rooker," a voice said, "help me get her into the car. Looks like it's shut-eye time."

Funny, Kate mused, *they think I need help to walk.* She smiled to herself, cracking open one eye as she felt hands grip her upper arms and lift her out of the booth. "We leaving now?"

"Nighty-night," Cam crooned.

No Mercy

Chapter 18

Everything felt wrong.

Her mattress, usually so cushy and comfortable, seemed hard and unforgiving against her hip bones and shoulders. She liked to sleep in the lovely blue silk pajamas Mercy had sent as a special luxury for her last birthday, but the slippery hand of the fabric against her skin was missing.

And the light. What was up with that?

No golden morning sunbeams slanted through her bedroom blinds. Yet Kate felt sure she had slept through the night.

She let her eyes drift open a little wider.

Only a thin, luminous strip seeped beneath the door that was placed too far to the right in the wall. The rest of the room? A pair of plain chests of drawers, two industrial-design computer desks, a second narrow cot like the one she was lying on. The lumpy shape on the other bed told her it was occupied.

For another breathless, semi-panicky moment, Kate had no memory of where she was. Then it all came back to her in a rush.

She bolted upright and then off of the bed, tossing aside the thin wool blanket someone had thrown over her fully clothed body. Even in the low light she now was able to identify the other sleeper: Cam.

If both of them were unconscious, who was monitoring communications from NASA and the rest of the world?

She stuck her feet into the plain navy-blue flats beside her bed.

Swinging open the door, Kate staggered into a wave of blinding fluorescent light in the hallway. She rushed, tripping over her own feet only twice, out the door of the dormitory, and across the grass yard to the stone house where they'd set up their temporary Command Center.

There she found Daniel Rooker, in what long ago must have been a formal dining room capable of seating two dozen guests, his boot heels hooked over the tabletop. Her laptop sat within arm's reach.

"Good afternoon, lazy bones," he tossed over his shoulder then turned and grinned at her.

"What the hell are you doing?" she gasped.

"Minding the store."

She raced to her laptop and hastily reviewed the screen. HW-1 was still on Safe-Hold. She breathed again. Immediately, she checked her messages—nothing critical. She fished in her suit jacket pocket then saw her cell phone sitting on the table beside her computer. When she picked it up, the screen lit: Battery low.

"The least you could have done was recharge it," she grumbled at him.

"I think it's called getting out of the wrong side of the bed," he said.

A dozen new calls had come in, and nearly as many gone out, while she'd been unconscious.

"Well, you've certainly been a busy little bee." He appeared to have been chatting with Tommy in her NASA lab most of the night.

"That's me!" He sounded way too chipper. But his eyes, red-rimmed and watery, gave him away. A line of foam cups stained with the dregs of cold coffee suggested hours of forced wakefulness.

"How long was I out?" she asked, pulling up a chair to sit down beside him.

"Oh, seven...eight hours. But who's counting."

Kate groaned and shook her head to dispel the final foggy traces of sleep. "I can't believe I crashed like that. I never sleep more than six hours a night. Never."

"You've been operating on fumes for days." He narrowed his eyes and looked her over. "Actually, you are a good deal more attractive with adequate sleep."

"Thanks, Rooker, like I really care." But she did, she realized. And she had to look away from his cocky smile to hide the small zing of pleasure his compliment brought. "Looks like you haven't gotten much sleep yourself."

"I'm used to it when I'm working."

No Mercy

"You didn't have one of your team cover communications so you could take even a short nap?"

He shrugged. "I'll catch up later. Figured you'd throw a fit if a stranger listened in on your precious NASA link. Top Secret, and all that rot. You already hate me, so I had nothing to lose."

She didn't argue the point about her protecting her information. But hate him? Had she ever said that? "You'd better take a turn on the cot while things are quiet."

He nodded. "Thanks." He stood up and stretched, reaching one hand behind his head to touch the opposing shoulder blade, then reversing the exercise. It looked like pure pain to her. "My guys are bunked down the hall. If you need them for any new emergency, wake me first. If you want something to eat, ask one of them to run to the Seven-Eleven for you, just down the road. They have a cafeteria on campus, but it's closed this time of year, like everything else."

She thanked him, then watched him out the door.

It was troubling, the way Rooker sometimes looked at her. She had disliked him from the start, of course, but he did have a way of unexpectedly entering her thoughts. She wasn't afraid of the man, or even wary of him, not most of the time. When he was in a combative mood, she could argue right back at him. But when he got quiet and drew into himself, she was unsure what might be brewing in that mysterious male brain of his.

At least when he was screaming at her she knew what he was thinking.

She decided it was a waste of time, trying to fathom the unfathomable. She checked in with Tommy at NASA by phone.

"Vern is sleeping now. I took over an hour ago. They're going nuts down here, boss. Reporters jumping people outside the gates, hanging out in the neighborhood bars during happy hour to try and corner NASA employees."

"At least they can't get into the compound," she said.

"No, but someone leaked the lab's phone number, and we've gotten a bunch of calls. NASA's Community Resources is preparing a statement, hoping to satisfy the vultures." He paused. "Rooker told us about your laser theory. You could be right, about using the onboard laser to aim the microwave stream."

"But the public doesn't know about the lasers yet, right?"

Kathryn Johnson

"Right." He hesitated. "You know, if it's really lasers they're going to use to guide the beam, we're cooked."

"Pun intended?" She was *not* amused. "You heard about the demands?"

"Right. I don't see how we'll stop them. Not so long as we've lost our ability to talk to HW-1."

Unfortunately, this was true. But there was one tool left to Kate. She could still track the satellite's telemetry. That is, she could physically observe what the spacecraft was doing. That might give them a general clue to Zed's target.

Meanwhile, she hoped someone—the FBI, most likely now—would locate Zed's crew.

Cam woke up an hour later and stumbled into the room. "What does someone have to do around here to get coffee?" She made a face at the collection of disposable cups with muddy liquid in their bottoms. "*Hot, fresh* coffee."

"Room service is down the hall." Kate explained Rooker's solution to such urgent missions. "The boys are resting up for action, I imagine. But you'll probably get at least one volunteer if food is mentioned. I could go for three eggs over easy, hash browns, bacon and a carafe of high test."

Cam's lovely molasses face lit up. "Until last night, I didn't think you ever ate. Now you're stowing it away as if there were no tomorrow." She blinked. "Sorry. Bad choice of words."

Kate smiled at her. "After you rustle up breakfast, why don't you give Amanda a call. Maybe she can put Kristi on the phone. I'm sure your little girl would like to hear your voice."

Cam nodded. "No more than her mother wants to hear hers."

The full, hot breakfast came from a nearby diner. A leap over the quality of convenience store rubber-egg sandwiches. It tasted like heaven to her.

One of Rooker's young team members, Adam Grabowski, came back to pick up trash and return the room to livable conditions. "You ladies let us know when you need anything else. We're just playing cards and watching the tube." He gave Kate a sweet smile. "You want to join us, Doc? Everglades Swamp Dudes is on."

"We have to take care of business," she said with a smile. "But thanks for the offer."

No Mercy

He turned and, giving her a longish parting look, left the room with his loaded trash bag.

Cambridge hummed to herself.

"What?" Kate asked.

"Boy's got the hots for someone in this room. Ain't me."

"Oh, stop it. I must be at least ten years older than he is. Probably fifteen. Adam's just a kid."

"He's a man. And you're an attractive woman. Or would be if you bothered brushing your hair."

"You're the second person today who's used that word on me," Kate said.

"Attractive?" Cambridge twinkled at her and leaned across the table. "Who was the first?"

"None of your business. You watch that screen. I'm calling Tommy again."

Cambridge sighed. "If I had a sex life as dismal as yours, I'd just put a gun to my head and pull the trigger."

Kate turned away, hiding the pain she knew must show in her face.

Guns, weapons, bombs. The act of killing another human being—whether by intention or accident—the mere idea sickened her. It didn't matter that Cam had been joking.

Kate had dreamt of giving humanity a means to virtually free and unlimited energy. But, as much as she loved that vision and the science that made it possible, she would never have taken part in the Heat Wave Project if she'd known it might be used to cause pain or destroy life.

That afternoon, things started to happen again. Vernon reported that the NASA team had detected a different antenna broadcasting to the satellite. The only good news: the intruders still hadn't broken through Kate's impromptu firewall. The bad news: no one still hadn't traced the signal back to its sender.

Again, a string of remote computers was being used to confuse the white-hat hackers. Refusing to pay the ransom that Zed demanded seemed a mistake to Kate. The government was gambling with people's lives. She didn't give a damn about policy. She'd seen the look in Zed's eyes. Witnessed the reckless insanity in the woman who accompanied him. Then there was the cavalier manner of the third intruder who hadn't so much as blinked when they'd shot Dave Proctor and wounded her second in command.

Clearly, these people would stop at nothing to get what they wanted. It was just a matter of time before they managed to gain control of the satellite. Another day or two. An hour. Maybe just minutes. Her body hummed with anticipation of that awful moment.

Then Zed would do exactly as he'd threatened: demonstrate the power of the sun's destructive energy, unleashed on innocents. She shuddered as her stomach curdled and mouth soured. It was all she could do to not run for the toilet and lose her breakfast.

Kate threw herself into her work. Refusing to give in to her body's reaction to fear. She reviewed every bit of data they'd accumulated so far. The terrorists (or extortionists, whatever one wished to call them) could be anywhere—that was true. But several indications pointed toward the Boston area. She relayed that information to Rooker but advised they not react prematurely to that possibility. He paced the room. Left it to talk on the phone with Washington. Returned to pace more, annoyingly, directly behind her chair.

He was driving himself crazy. He was driving them all crazy.

Late that same afternoon, the man finally lost it. "I'm taking my team to Boston," he told her. "It's not that far, a few hundred miles. We'll take a chance that it's Zed."

"No," Kate argued. "We can't risk a repeat of the West Virginia fiasco. Give Tommy and Vernon a little more time. They'll find him." But would they?

Still, she felt she had to voice confidence in her own people.

"We sit tight until we're sure—then you can scramble, Mr. Rooker. And," she reminded him, "this time I'm going with you, whether you like it or not."

He cast her a sullen look and stalked out of the room.

"That man is some po'ed," Cam said, picking at a carton of takeout Chinese with chopsticks. "I can't remember. Is this chicken or pork lo mein?"

"Does it matter?" Kate asked.

No Mercy

"I hate chicken."

"Then it's pork."

"I *am* hungry." Cam took a bite, chewed and swallowed. She stared at the noodle-filled carton. Kept on staring. And staring. Tears came to her eyes.

Kate reached out and touched her arm. "You miss your little girl."

"Yeah. Kristi, my baby."

"I offered before. You really should go back to DC. You could send one of the boys in your place."

"No, they need to be where they are. Doing what they're doing. I want to be here. It's just hard, you know?"

"Yes." Kate couldn't honestly imagine.

She'd never been married or had children. She wondered if she ever would now. At one time it had seemed an important part of her life-to-be. She'd been more than a little envious when Mercy married. She'd been her cousin's maid of honor. She'd been in the wedding parties of many of her girlfriends. Kate had, of course, dated some, but not seriously. Through her post-college years, her career had filled up the days, the weeks, the months...until her job, her beloved science was everything to her.

To her surprise, she had liked it that way.

At least, she had liked it until the day a crazy man stole her satellite and threatened to turn her life's work into a weapon.

"Besides," Cam said with a smile, "I can't leave you alone with Rooker. He'd eat you alive."

Kate laughed. "Let him try it. He's just sulking. Sooner or later, he'll get his chance to play commando."

"If we're lucky."

If we are very, very lucky. Kate sighed and rubbed her forehead.

The door opened, and Adam stepped through.

"Not another bite of food." Kate warned him off with a raised hand.

Adam shrugged and smiled sheepishly. Only then did she notice the long brown canvas bag slung on a strap over his shoulder. It looked suspiciously like a rifle case.

A jolt of terror shot through her. Rooker's men were breaking out their arms? "What's happened?"

"Don't worry, Doc. I just thought you might like to try a little target practice. There's a range on the navy base just the other side of town."

She stared at him, then at the gun case. "I—well, no. I've never...that is, I don't know how to fire anything as sophisticated as those things I saw you and the others with." She shook her head. "Or any gun really."

"C'mon, Doc. It'll do you good to get out of this room. We've got another three hours of daylight. It's beautiful outside."

"He's right," Cambridge agreed. "At least go outdoors for a little while. Your brain will atrophy, not to mention the rest of you, if you don't get some exercise and fresh air." She paused, waiting for Kate to respond. "When I went out for a walk earlier it really helped clear my head."

Kate bit her bottom lip. "I don't know."

"You don't have to shoot, if you don't want to," Adam said. "Rooker says you're supposed to go in with us when we find Zed's crew. You ought to at least get used to hearing rounds go off."

Kate knew what *that* sounded like. Only too well. She felt vaguely sick to her stomach but unwilling to explain her revulsion for firearms. It seemed easier just to go along with him. Get it over with. Besides, Cam was right, she did need to get out and move around a bit. The small of her back ached, and her shoulders had locked into a forward slump from hours of typing and screen staring.

"All right," she murmured. "But my name is Kate not Doc, okay?"

He winked. "Gotcha, beautiful."

Kate rolled her eyes at Cambridge as she followed the young mercenary out of the room. Cam gave her a thumbs up. The woman was hopeless.

It was still late August but some trees in Connecticut were already starting to turn after an early cold snap. The maples were the best, showing off deep purple-crimson leaves.

The drive to the navy base took only ten minutes. They passed through a checkpoint. Parking in the visitors' lot, they walked past barracks, the commissary, motor pool and several other buildings labeled only with numbers.

No Mercy

Adam talked a blue streak the entire time, about his high school days in Ft. Worth, playing football with his brothers who went on to college at the University of Texas, and the girl he'd gone with until he shipped overseas with the Marines. He'd seen heavy action in his fourteen months in Afghanistan.

"Four months after my discharge Rooker looked me up," Adam said. "The pay is great, better than making bread in my dad's bakery, that's for sure. In-country assignments—a thousand or more a week. Overseas, working security—sometimes that much in a day."

"But you're putting your life on the line," she pointed out. "How does your family feel about that?"

"It's my life," Adam stated, a little defensively, she thought.

They arrived at the range. Concrete walls divided shooters' positions. Paper targets had been set at various distances, backed by mounded earth to catch stray bullets. She could hear a soft pop, pop, pop from down the line. It didn't sound very threatening, not like the sharp crackle of gunfire she recalled from the day Zed broke into her lab.

Or the sound she'd heard that *other* day. The day she would never forget. For which she'd never forgive herself.

She swallowed, felt her eyes go hot and begin to tear. She told herself to relax. She'd just watch. This would be okay. Adam would finish practicing, and then take her back to the campus.

A nearby movement caught her eye. She turned, and Rooker stepped out from behind a barrier. Adam gave him a nod and backed away, as if to leave.

She'd been set up.

"I'm leaving," she said.

"No, you're not. This is mandatory training." Rooker held out his hand, and Adam gave him the rifle he'd just pulled from the canvas case. The weapon was fully assembled—a long steel barrel, composite stock, serious-looking scope, the requisite trigger—and it looked just as intimidating and dangerous as she'd imagined it might.

Kate stepped away, fighting the urge to turn tail and run. Her heart galloped, stumbled, raced. Adam said, "I'll head on back; see you later, Doc...Kate."

Kathryn Johnson

Rooker didn't miss a beat. "First thing to learn about any firearm is the parts." He stepped forward and held the rifle out toward her.

Kate's hands shot out in front of her defensively. She backed away another step. "I just tagged along with Adam for the fresh air and walk. And to get used to hearing rounds go off." Her pulse leaped to a marathoner's pace.

I can't do this. No way. Absolutely could not.

"Kate," he said.

"No, I'm serious. I *don't* want to do this. I'm going back now."

The past was suddenly there, in her face, every ugly detail. A family torn apart. Accusations. Threats. Fear of punishment. But even more than that, it was forever and always the guilt that had haunted her since childhood. It seemed a miracle it hadn't destroyed her.

Each time tragedy struck in the form of a shooting somewhere in the country, she was forced to revisit that horrid day. Bloodshed on a school campus, at a shopping mall, or in an office building. She and her neighbors had lived through the infamous sniper attacks that had paralyzed the Maryland and Virginia suburbs. Like everyone else in the targeted areas, she'd taken alternate routes to work, used the next-to-last drop of gas in her car's tank before forcing herself to stop for fuel, avoided going to grocery stores and mall parking lots. No one knew when or where the sniper would kill again. She'd held her breath whenever she turned on the radio, praying a new attack hadn't brought hell to another family. Altogether, ten people were murdered before the police caught the two men responsible. And always in the back of her mind was her own, earlier experience.

She jerked to a stop when Rooker's big hand closed around her wrist.

"It's a tool, Kate. A gun is a tool. Like any tool, you have to know how to use it safely."

"No." She shook her head. "This isn't fair. You made Adam lie to me, to get me to come here. You don't understand. I can't. I just can't."

Blinking, she wished away the images. A rifle in a child's hands. A game that ended in tragedy.

No Mercy

"Kate, listen to me. It's not safe for you to be in the middle of a raid when you don't know anything about the weapons we're carrying."

She shook her head. "Rooker, believe me, it's not something I can control. I can't—"

He pulled her gently toward a bench behind the shooting line. He sat down beside her and laid the rifle diagonally across his knees, muzzle pointed down and away from her. She was trembling, head to foot. Surely he must be able to see that. Why was he being such a bully, forcing her to do this?

"Just listen to me for five minutes," he whispered, "then you can decide."

She closed her eyes and tried to breathe without trembling, talk without a catch in her throat. "All right. Go ahead."

"What if Adam or I get hit and go down? What if we can't use our weapons to defend ourselves?"

She stared at him, her heart crying out at the thought. "I'll pray that doesn't happen."

"But what if it does, Kate? What if the bad guys take me out and this—" he patted the rifle "—*this* is lying on the ground and one of Zed's guys dives for it. If you don't pick it up before he does, you're giving it to him. You're giving him the power to kill you, finish me off, and hurt others on our team."

Kate squeezed her eyes shut against the movie in her head. Images of Rooker or sweet-faced Adam lying wounded, helpless. And she was standing there, frozen. Useless as a block of wood.

"Don't!" she gasped. "Okay, yes. Yes, I'd have to take the gun to keep it from them. I'd threaten to shoot them if they came near me. Near you. I could do that."

"Sure you could." His voice sounded even softer. So kind and patient and sympathetic that she was shocked. This was a side of him she would never have thought existed.

He pried her right hand off the edge of the bench seat and rested her fingers across the rifle's stock. "See, it can't hurt you."

It's not me I'm worried about! she thought frantically.

"Now," he continued with patience, his blue eyes locked on hers, "you've picked the weapon up off the ground. You warned the bad guy not to come any closer. But he's still coming at you."

"No!" she cried out reflexively. Two sailors standing down the line turned and stared at them. Rooker gave her a look of mild reprimand. "I'm sorry. I didn't mean to scream out like that. It's all right. Go on."

"Right. So you have my piece here because I've been wounded. The enemy has his own weapon. If you don't do something, Kate, he is going to put a bullet in my head while I'm lying there."

Oh, God! She didn't want this. Had never asked to be put in this position. It was too much!

He stared deep, so very deeply into her eyes she had to look away. "You have a choice, Kate."

"I'm a scientist, not a killer," she rasped, choking back a sob. "I do things to *help* humanity, not snuff it out."

He put an arm around her shoulders and squeezed. It felt good, comforting. Maybe he'd stop badgering her and let her go back to Cam. She'd bury herself in the work she understood and loved. The way she always did. Work crowded out the terrors. Work tired her out so that she could sleep at night.

"I know," he said. "And I bet you're brilliant at what you do. You do help humanity, I'm sure. But these guys aren't exactly humane, are they?"

"No," she agreed with a moist sniffle.

"So, do you want to know how to safely handle this baby?" He gave her an encouraging half smile. "You'll probably never have to fire it other than right here and now. But if it comes to protecting yourself, or one of us—"

"Show me," she said quickly before she could change her mind.

No Mercy

Kate told herself that looking through the scope of a rifle was just like looking through her first telescope. The one her dad bought her for her eleventh Christmas. She'd taken it out into the backyard that night and stayed outside for hours and hours in the freezing Chicago cold, enraptured, staring up at the heavens over the city.

Just concentrate on the mechanics of the thing, she told herself as she held the rifle. *Don't personalize it. It's a tool. Don't think about that other time.*

She focused on Rooker's sure hands and firm voice while he demonstrated the way to hold the weapon, placing the heel of the stock firmly against the fleshy part of her right shoulder, her left hand supporting the long barrel, her right fitting around the narrow section behind the trigger guard. Index finger straight out along the rifle's side, pointing directly away from her. Never on the trigger until the final moment. That's what he said. Never even moving her finger into the trigger guard until she had aimed and decided to fire.

He showed her where the five-cartridge magazine slid with a click into the belly of the weapon. He demonstrated how to slip the shiny, gold-colored cartridges into the black plastic clip. "You can hand-load one at a time through the breech underneath, here, if you have to. But it's better to have a couple of magazines prepped."

He made her snap an empty magazine into and then out of the breech, several times, until she could do it by touch, eyes closed. Then they practiced finding the target through the crosshairs, and chills crawled up her back. Her hands began to shake.

"Rook—"

"It's okay, just relax. Breathe," he encouraged her. "We're not killing anything today. Paper targets don't feel a thing.

132

Imagine yourself at the county fair. You want to win that great big purple doggy to take home and put on your bed, don't you?"

Okay, she thought, *I can do this. Win the stupid stuffed animal.*

"Now, hug the gun with the soft part of your cheek close to the stock. See the bull's-eye through the scope? Line it up on the crosshairs."

"Got it," she said.

He brought his arm around her from behind and rested his right hand over hers. He nudged her forefinger a fraction of an inch. "There's the safety. Feel it?"

"That little raised spot?"

"Yes. Press it."

She did.

"Now lever the bolt forward. It will snap itself back. That puts a round in the chamber. Move your finger into the guard and find the trigger."

"But we left the magazine out. It's not loaded," she reminded him.

"I know. You're going to dry fire until you stop shaking. It's a tool, remember? Like a hammer. If you hit me over the head with a hammer you could kill me."

"Don't tempt me," she muttered.

Rooker laughed—a deep, throaty sound that she found she liked. "You really do hate this," he said. "Okay, now breathe and think hammer."

She did. The shaking stopped. It helped that his body was wrapped around her. His chest felt warm and solid against her back.

"When you like where the crosshairs are, draw a picture in your mind of what you want to hit. Take a breath in, let it halfway out, then slowly squeeze the trigger."

Kate sighted through the scope, saw Zed in the crosshairs pointing his ugly assault weapon at Frank Hess. Saw him aim at Daniel Rooker.

Breathe in...out a little. Finger to trigger. Pull. Click.

It took her a moment to realize she'd done it.

"That's it?"

No Mercy

"Perfect. Now do it twenty more times. Make it pure muscle memory. You don't even have to think about what you're doing once you've decided to shoot." Rooker stepped back from her.

She positioned herself and the rifle without his support. She sighted. *Bolt. Breathing. Trigger. Click.*

Each time she felt a little steadier but, she reminded herself, the weapon was still empty.

"Would you like to try loading and shooting a few rounds?" he asked.

"Would you like to step into rush-hour traffic on the Washington Beltway?" she returned maliciously.

"You're still that keen on this, huh?"

"You'll never make me like it, Rooker." She sighed.

"You don't have to enjoy it. This is to keep you and the rest of us safe."

"Right." She swallowed, felt dizzy with indecision.

She couldn't think of anything she'd hate doing more than this. But the man wasn't going to let her leave until she did what he wanted. She turned her head to look up into his eyes. Steel blue. Determined. They chilled her. And she liked it. *Damn!*

"I'll do it," she whispered.

He gave her a quick that-a-girl grin and dug a set of earplugs for each of them out of his pocket. He pulled from his case a pair of clear acrylic protective eyeglasses. "Load up," he said.

While she wrestled cartridges into a magazine the size of a baby's fist, Rooker rambled on about the rifle's specifications.

"This is a Steyr SSG, twenty-six-inch barrel. Cold-hammer forged. Made in Austria. Used mostly as a counter-sniper rifle. It's extremely reliable and accurate. Won't knock you on your ass like a shotgun when you fire it."

"A nice plus." She snapped the magazine into the rifle's underside as he'd instructed her.

"Same routine," Rooker whispered in her ear. "Expect a little kick to your shoulder." He placed himself close behind her, as if to catch her should she lose her balance.

Kate braced herself and let the practiced actions take her through each step. When she eased back on the trigger, her hands were surprisingly steady.

The recoil was less than she'd expected, more like someone shoving her in the shoulder on a crowded Metro car. It took her a moment to realize she'd actually fired the Steyr.

"Did I hit the target?" She didn't dare look for fear of embarrassing herself.

"Bloody hell," Rooker muttered.

Her heart sank. "I missed the whole thing?" Her eyes darted up the dirt bank, expecting that's where she'd put her shot.

"No, you didn't miss. You're just off dead center by two or three inches." He grinned down at her. "Okay, Annie Oakley, now let's see you get the next four rounds inside your first shot."

Kate emptied three magazines before Rooker let her stop. She never hit a perfect bull's-eye, and a few shots barely made it inside the outermost circle. But not one totally missed the paper target.

By then her arms were aching from supporting the weight of the rifle. She still knew nothing about any other weapon, but this one she felt confident she could handle in an emergency.

It's a tool, she thought. *A really noisy, big hammer.*

She handed him the rifle, walked back to the bench and collapsed onto it, exhausted.

Rooker sat down on the bench beside her to clean and put away his rifle. "It was bad, wasn't it? The thing that scared you off guns. Whatever happened."

"Yes," she said.

"You don't have to tell me."

"I know."

She looked past the row of targets toward the horizon, washed in brilliant hues by the setting sun. This time when the past flashed back at her like a clip from a film, it didn't leave her feeling as helpless. She'd never told anyone about it—not all of it, and not after the day it happened, when the police questioned her. The child's parents had raged at her. And her mother had taken her back home, flinging at her the same accusations over, and over, and over again.

She hated anyone talking about that time, herself included.

To her surprise she felt like talking about it now. To *him*. To this man who had probably killed in battle. Because he might understand and not judge her.

No Mercy

She said, "I was right there, in the house, when he shot her. I should have been watching him. I should have stopped him."

"Stopped who?" Rooker asked, as calmly as if they'd been talking about neglecting to interfere in an ordinary schoolyard scrap.

She turned toward him on the bench and opened her mouth but nothing came out.

He set the rifle, in its case, aside and folded his arms around her. She rested her cheek against his muscular shoulder. He smelled of outdoors, of musk and sweat. Of strength. After a moment it was easier to speak.

"I was a junior in high school, babysitting my neighbors' kids. The girl was ten years old. Her brother was eight. I had no idea their father kept a shotgun for hunting in the house."

"Damn," he breathed close to her ear. He sounded as if he knew how it must have felt. As if the scene that repeated over and over in her nightmares had somehow become visible to him.

The dreams came less often these days. But in times of stress, they still revisited her with paralyzing intensity.

"Which one of the kids got hold of the gun?" he asked.

"Danny. I was making a snack for them after school." The words spilled out. "They were playing a game—tag, I think. Meghan was it. She came into the kitchen when I called them, but Danny was taking forever. I sent Meghan to get him."

Rooker tightened his grip around her, as if to squeeze the words out of her when he sensed she was faltering.

"I-I heard Meghan shouting at her brother. Warning him that he was going to get in trouble if he didn't stop whatever he was doing. She tended to be bossy."

"Aren't all girls?" She could tell he was grinning.

Her lips wobbled into an almost smile, but she was too deeply into the past to react to his teasing. "Danny had a habit of intentionally annoying his sister. Their squabbling was nothing new."

"Just being kids."

"Yes. I didn't have a clue anything was really wrong. I yelled at them to knock it off and come for their snack. That's when Meghan screamed. She sounded so frightened I tore out of the kitchen and down the hallway. When I came around the corner into their parents' bedroom, Danny was grinning, pointing the rifle at his sister."

"Christ."

"'Bang, you're dead!' he shouted. And then he pulled the trigger."

Her shoulders jerked within Rooker's embrace—the memory of the shotgun's blast obscenely loud in her memory. But there were no more tears. They'd been spent a long time ago. Rooker said nothing, just held her.

Kate finally gathered up enough composure to push herself away from his chest.

"Sorry," he murmured, trying to catch her gaze with his, "for upsetting you."

She shrugged.

"What happened to the little girl?" he asked. "She die?"

"No, but at the time no one expected her to make it." Kate started walking. Rooker hefted the rifle case and fell in beside her. "There I was, me with my ridiculously inadequate Red Cross childcare certification. The only thing I knew to do was call 911, put pressure on the wound, and keep Danny from running out of the house for fear of what his parents would do to him."

"So you took the gun away from him?"

"I guess I must have." She thought about that. "You know, I can't remember. But by the time the medics and police rushed in, it was sitting up on a high shelf over the stove. And I was back in the bedroom holding on to Danny with one hand while I pressed a kitchen towel over Meghan's chest."

"You saved her life."

"Did I?" She shook her head. "Her parents blamed me. Said I hadn't adequately supervised the children."

"That's a load of crap," he snapped, walking faster so that she had to speed up, too. "That gun shouldn't have been anywhere a kid could get at it. Was it loaded?"

"I think so. Danny told the police he had no idea how the shell had got into it. Anyway, I don't think he understood the difference between pretend shooting and the real thing."

"In the movies the guy who gets blown away in Doomsday 2 shows up in Doomsday 3."

No Mercy

They were in the van that Adam had left for them, and nearly back to the campus before she spoke again.

"In the end I think Danny had a harder time coming back from that day than Meghan. We've stayed in touch, the three of us. As an adult, he's still struggling with the guilt."

"And you're not?"

She gave him a look. "Point made."

It was strange, but as she slanted a glance over her shoulder and toward the rifle case in the rear seat, she didn't feel the same burning horror she'd felt on first seeing the weapon. She still hated all things created with the intention of killing. But the world was indeed a violent place these days. Like it or not, she lived in it and had to survive here.

Kate said, "That scenario you described—you wounded and down on the ground, Zed ready to finish you off. That's your personal nightmare, Rooker. Isn't it?"

He laughed, tight and short. "We each have our own bumps in the night. Monsters that haunt us. Or memories." He looked at her, and she felt a sudden sharp snap of connection. "Mine is some guy who comes at me when I can't fight back. But they say it never happens the way you expect it. Death, that is."

"I wouldn't want to be the one responsible for getting you or one of your men killed." She climbed out of the van. All of a sudden, sitting alone with Rooker inside it, the vehicle felt too intimate. She didn't want Rooker to take it into his head to hug her again. Or maybe she did. But then she wouldn't know how to react.

Something was happening between them. Something she didn't understand. She'd have to think more about what all that bodily contact back at the range meant. Just a nice guy comforting a near-hysterical woman? Maybe. No. She didn't think so.

She started walking toward the building where Cam was keeping watch over their communications. Rooker easily caught up with her.

"Have you given your men orders to protect me?" she asked.

He looked away as if he hadn't heard her.

"Rooker? Is that what you weren't saying back there at the range? That your boys, your men have been ordered to put their lives on the line for me?"

He rolled one shoulder, flexing the muscles. "You're the one who has to work magic with the satellite. If one of us buys it, the whole mission doesn't crash."

That was it then. If necessary, any one of the team would put himself between her and a bullet. And what was she supposed to do about that? Stand helplessly by without fighting back, because of a tragedy that happened nearly two decades ago?

She stopped and turned to Rooker, put a hand on his arm. "You have to promise me something."

"What?"

"The things I told you this afternoon, about the kids and the accident. You don't talk to anyone about that. You don't tell your guys."

"Why?" he asked.

"I don't want to give them another reason for feeling protective of me. They'll take more risks."

He nodded his head. The intensity of his gaze sent a warm shiver through her. He was staring at her lips. She sensed his body tensing, as if to take a step toward her. And what then? Was he actually going to kiss her?

She quick-stepped back and away from him. "Thank you for today," she said. *Coward!* She knew that's exactly what she was. Because it would have been nice to feel his lips on hers. But she still walked away.

No Mercy

The intolerable waiting came to an abrupt end early the next morning. Rooker's gruff voice, shouting orders outside the dorm room she shared with Cam, shattered Kate's pre-coffee, almost-out-of-bed stupor. Whoops of male excitement erupted in the hallway. Kate launched herself off of the cot.

Cam had taken the early-morning watch, leaving Kate in the room to sleep another few hours. Kate got as far as pulling on underwear and bra when boots again clattered down the hallway. This time they stopped outside of her room. But just for a moment.

Before Kate could pull on her blouse or snatch the jeans off the bed, the door flew back on its hinges, banging against the wall.

"We're moving out!" Rooker snapped at her. "With or without you."

"With. And your manners are atrocious. Didn't your mother ever tell you to knock?"

Rooker winced, his eyes traveling over her body. "Sorry." His voice dipped lower. "Umm. Never knew my mother." He blinked, a big man suddenly looking self-conscious. As if he hadn't meant to let that last bit slip out.

But he didn't seem in the least embarrassed by her near nakedness. And he didn't turn away. Now it was her cleavage that seemed to most interest him. Then her bare legs. Then boobs again. "Not a good enough excuse, I know," he mumbled.

Kate blinked at him, stunned motionless for a moment before remembering to continue dressing. "I'm sorry, I didn't know about—"

"Manners are hit or miss in foster homes." He gestured toward the jeans she was stepping into. "Don't hurry on my account. The view is, uh, not bad." He flashed her a wicked smile.

She quickly yanked her jeans up over her hips and zipped them. Young Adam would have been a puddle at such an opportunity. Rooker? She couldn't tell if he was really interested or just enjoying the chance to needle her.

Or maybe this was his way of changing the subject. Not wanting to reveal anything more personal about himself? It also struck her that a difficult childhood, might be one reason he was...well, Rooker. All gruff and needing to be in charge. Being bounced from one foster home to another did that to a kid. Didn't it? What does a child do in a situation like that? Be the controller, not the controlled.

"Where are we headed?" Her heart was already pounding. The chase was on! Kate shoved everything that wasn't already on her body into the overnight bag that was all she'd brought from home.

He gave her a mysterious look. "I'll let Cambridge fill you in. I'm making travel arrangements now."

She frowned at his departing back. Why was he being so obtuse? It was too damn early in the morning for mysteries.

She grabbed her things and dashed across the campus to their command center.

Cam was on the phone. It took Kate seconds to figure out that she was talking to Tommy back at NASA. Cam swiveled round to face her, still listening to whatever he was saying, her dark eyes worried.

"You're not going to believe this," she whispered, holding a hand over the phone.

"Try me." Kate steeled herself for bad news.

"They're out of the country."

"Zed and crew? Where?" Of course, it didn't have to be them at all. Not anymore. By now they easily could have transmitted the codes for the sat's guidance system to someone else anywhere in the world. Someone more capable of unlocking her firewall.

"Italy. They're in Rome, we think, or somewhere close to it." Cam refocused on the phone. "No, I'm listening, Tommy. Kate just walked in. I'll fill her in."

Kate gritted her teeth. Maybe that was it—Zed was no longer involved. After all, why risk trying to get through airport

No Mercy

security when he could do everything he wanted to do while still here, in the States? Unless he felt safer in Europe. No, she decided, it made more sense that someone else, an individual or organization or unfriendly government paid him to steal the data. Whoever that was, they somehow knew the capabilities of the satellite and planned this sophisticated scheme. Zed was just a hired hand, a thug. That's the only scenario that made sense to her.

"Give me the boys." Kate held out her hand for the phone.

"It's Kate," she said. "Has anyone verified a target guidance system?"

"We're still thinking laser. But nothing's gone active yet." There was commotion behind Tommy's voice.

"Vernon here." He was breathing hard, as if he'd run from the far end of the room. "Okay, this is the way it is. The FBI has been tracking the illegal use of green lasers to disrupt air traffic. They've recorded several laser trails that came *not from the ground* but from somewhere above Earth."

Pocketsize laser pens above 5 milliwatts had been made illegal for non-commercial use in recent years, due to their malicious use by pranksters. But that hadn't stopped them from getting into the hands of people who wanted them. Apparently more than a few idiots thought it fun to point laser beams at the cockpits of planes taking off or landing at airports, to annoy pilots.

Kate had recently read that over 4,000 laser/aircraft incidents in just the previous year had resulted in pilot issues ranging from glare-distraction to flash-blindness. Near and actual crashes had been attributed to such interference. A laser beam no stronger than 5 mW could conceivably guide a burst of microwave energy from HW-1 to a target.

Kate's mouth went dry. She rubbed and back of neck. *Oh, God!* It sounded as if someone was testing the satellite's onboard laser. That likely would be one of the final steps before launching the stored microwave energy. And yet, if they were still trying to figure out how to jump her digital roadblock, and they hadn't yet been able to coordinate the laser with the microwave transmission...there might be time to stop this madness.

"What's taking so long?" Rooker was suddenly at her back, nudging her with his hard knuckles. "We got a plane waiting for us."

She stuck her hand up in his face. *Back off!* She spoke into the phone. "So what are DHS and the others saying we should do now?" Hell, she didn't even know who was in charge in such a situation.

"I don't think anyone really knows what to do, except try to predict the intended target," Vernon said.

"But they could always change that at the last minute," she said.

"Right. And since a laser isn't able to be traced until it fires up, it's guaranteed we'll lose the game."

The game. Hacker talk. Tommy was rubbing off on Vernon. *Not good.*

Kate rocked back on her heels, thinking so hard she wouldn't have been surprised had her brain burst. She'd always hated mind games. And that's what this was all about to these horrid people. Money and games. "So our only hope still is to find whoever has the data and is attempting to use it."

"Right. We recapture the data before they can use it. With any luck, before they can sell it to more sickos like them, too. Then we use their programming to help us regain control of HW-1."

Kate turned to Rooker. "Looks like we're going to Rome."

No Mercy

At Roma-Fiumicino airport, three Carabiniere officers met and escorted Kate and the Worldwide Security team through Customs. Despite the presence of Italian officials, considerable confusion, dramatic arguments, and hand gesturing ensued when the crates containing the team's arsenal were opened. Bringing such weapons into the country, they were told, simply was not done.

What if criminal elements got hold of them? the Italian agents demanded. What if the very terrorists, which the U.S. government claimed the team was tracking, seized and turned these sophisticated weapons on Italian police and citizens? Kate didn't speak Italian, and the senior customs officer's English left room for wide misinterpretation.

After an hour of frustration, a government-provided translator arrived to assist in communications.

Kate stressed the urgency of their mission while keeping details on a need-to-know basis. Her information seemed to quell some concerns but resulted in another round of questions and more red tape. Kate sensed Rooker's growing impatience.

He'd barely spoken a full sentence to her during the overnight flight from New York and seemed intent on distancing himself from her. She supposed his grim mood might still be due to his resentment at being forced to bring her along, then having to play second violin in her orchestra.

As to the Italians' reluctance to allow foreigners bearing lethal weapons free run of their city, she understood completely. Certainly such a thing would never be allowed in the States, if the roles were reversed.

In the end, a compromise was reached. Ten assault rifles, five 36-barrel stacked projectile machine guns, two grenade launchers, and numerous side arms and crates of ammunition were all allowed through—with the stipulation that the operation was to be a joint effort between the Italian police and the Americans.

Rooker wasn't happy, having to coordinate with the Carabiniere. Kate was just grateful they'd come to an agreement.

Finally, they were cleared with a great show of reluctance by the customs officials, who seemed to view even the Carabiniere with suspicion. By the time the Americans were transported to accommodations in Rome proper, the sun had risen. Nevertheless, there were still more formalities to be satisfied at *The Abruzzi*, their hotel located on Piazza della Rotonda. The manager had been awakened early and insisted on greeting them in person in the lobby. Kate began to share Rooker's irritation. This was no longer a clandestine operation.

Her head throbbed as they stepped into the elevator. Every muscle in her body ached. All she wanted to do was crawl between cool sheets and sleep. But she knew she'd first need to check in again with Washington and also with Cam, whom she'd sent back to NASA in DC.

The translator accompanied them to their rooms. He kept glancing worriedly at Rooker. The security man's face had grown redder and redder, his silence more threatening at each delay during the early morning hours.

Now, standing in the hallway, as a sleepy-eyed bellboy opened the door to a suite of rooms that would be their new headquarters, the translator explained, "It is not customary, Signore, to rush about without properly greeting your host and satisfying local custom."

"Is it customary to drag your fucking feet while the enemy takes a bead on one of your cities?" Rooker lashed out, brushing past the man and disappearing inside the suite.

His men tramped after him, without comment.

Adam gave Kate a small smile of apology as he passed by.

"We're just very tired," Kate apologized, furious at Rooker for his rudeness. "And worried. You understand, these are very dangerous people we're after." He, of course, knew very little about their mission. Only that terrorism was involved.

The man bowed his head briefly. "I understand the urgency of your trip. I will try to speed things along.

No Mercy

Gradualmente, si?" A little at a time, Kate supposed. Faster, but slowly. *Only in Italy.*

The translator had taken a separate room, which suited Rooker. He had said he didn't want the man underfoot. Just nearby, should they need him again.

Kate stepped through the doorway and into the suite. She closed and locked the door behind her then turned to observe their new space. The ornate decor of the central salon—crown molding, oil paintings of the city displayed on each of the walls, chic modern furniture, ivory and gold color scheme. Too bizarre—populated as it was by young warriors popping open cases of firearms.

My worst nightmare. A superfluity of guns.

Perhaps it was just as well that her blood was boiling, her anger still overpowering even the hated weapons. She stepped over gun cases, zeroing in on Rooker.

"You didn't have to go ballistic!" she said. "That was childish and unbelievably rude behavior. The Italian government is being amazingly cooperative, considering we've tossed a live bomb into their laps."

He continued to fuss over his Steyr, his back to her.

Kate wasn't about to let him ignore her. "Unless you plan on learning Italian overnight, it might be wise to show a little courtesy to our translator."

Rooker spun on her, eyes ablaze. The male bantering in the room immediately ceased, as if his men knew the limits of his tolerance for criticism.

"Listen, Doctor, I don't trust anyone except my own people. Got it? We don't need to add anyone else to the mix. Not a translator. Not local police." He clenched his teeth so hard she could hear them grind. "It was a mistake to agree to outsiders taking part in the operation."

She stared at him. "Don't you think you're being just a little paranoid? We *know* who the enemy is. We can use all the help we can get."

"Do we know?" His features tightened, but he quickly looked away from her, as if he'd said more than he'd intended.

She studied him. What was he hinting at? Of course they knew the enemy. Zed and his two flunkies. Was he talking about the possibility of there being someone higher up in the chain on conspirators? The same thoughts she'd had about there being someone to whom Zed was reporting?

"I'd thought we knew," she said more quietly. "Or am I wrong? *You* tell *me*, Rooker. What do you think you know that you haven't told me?"

"Forget it."

"I won't." She circled around him to get a good look at his expression, but he refused to meet her eyes. "If you want me to be an effective partner in this mission, you have to be straight with me. I've been trying to educate you on the science. How about you return the favor. What have you found out that you haven't told me?"

Men started disappearing into the surrounding bedrooms.

Rooker laid down his rifle and straightened up to face her. His eyes had gone from their usual clear blue to a stormy, unquestionably violent gray. "It's not paranoid to think there might be a mole in the pipeline. I've suspected as much from the beginning. But I didn't have any evidence, until just before we left Connecticut."

She had to tip her chin up at an uncomfortable angle to meet his gaze. "What the hell are you talking about? A mole? You mean a spy?"

He looked uncomfortable, as if this was a conversation he didn't want to have with her. As if he'd been keeping secrets and he wasn't yet ready to let her in on them. He sighed, shifted his gaze toward the trio of tall windows overlooking the street, then to the ceiling, and finally the carpet. Anywhere but at her.

"I can vouch for every man on my team." He dropped his voice to just above a whisper. "They're loyal to the bone. Can you say the same for your people?"

"My people are totally dedicated to the mission. More than that, they're patriotic citizens. I've worked with them for years."

"Not all of them," he said.

How would he know?

His meaning hit her with the impact a gut punch. She felt her breath sucked away. "You've *investigated* my team?" She'd known that Mercy and the FBI were interviewing everyone connected with the project. Apparently Rooker had been given access to those reports. Or to other classified information, of which she wasn't aware.

"I think you'd better explain." She felt like strangling him. Sincerely and thoroughly.

"Vernon Martinez. He transferred from the Applied Physics Lab in San Diego less than a year ago."

"Correct. Vernon is a bright man, a serious and dedicated scientist."

"Did you know he entered the U.S. illegally?"

She crossed her arms and planted her feet more firmly, as if a small earthquake had just shifted the floor a foot to the left. "No, I guess I didn't know that."

"Neither did the people who gave him a top-secret security clearance at Weston. Then there's Miss Cambridge Mackenzie."

Kate felt as if pins were pricking her skin all over her body. "Cam is beyond reproach."

"You're friends with her, not just colleagues."

"Yes." And she was proud of their friendship. Proud, too, of Cam, whose mixed-race parentage had produced an exotically attractive woman with her father's Asian eyes and her mother's Jamaican complexion.

"She has a child," Rooker said.

"She's a single mother, yes, and a damn good one. You'd better not tell me that anyone's holding that against her. It's why I sent her back to DC instead of bringing her along with us. She needs to be home with her daughter."

"The daughter she gave birth to in prison? Or nearly so." He turned and walked briskly away from her, into the kitchenette at the far end of the room.

Kate stared after him, rocking on the pads of her feet. It took a moment for her to get moving and follow him.

"You can't walk away on a line like that. You'd better tell me where you're going with this, Rooker." *Prison? Cam? Impossible!*

"The woman seems to have straightened out her life, but she wasn't always the model citizen." He opened cupboard doors until he found coffee, a little stovetop espresso maker, sugar packets. "When she was sixteen, she got involved with a gang in southeast D.C. Police picked her up on possession the first time.

Then for theft. She and her friends were breaking into houses, stealing anything they could sell to buy drugs."

Kate's head was reeling. She said nothing. Could say nothing. She clasped her hands in front of her. *No, no, no! Security clearance investigations don't miss this kind of thing.* Rooker must be mistaken. Or making it all up. But why would he do that?

"Daddy arranged for bail until the trial. Meanwhile, Miss Mackenzie got herself high again, as well as knocked up."

Kate eyed the back of Rooker's head. She felt chilled. Vaguely nauseous. She bridled at his tone. Hated the judgmental clip he gave each word. She still didn't believe any of it. On the other hand, Cam had never seemed inclined to talk about her past. Which in a way did seem odd. They'd gone out drinking together—true, it wasn't exactly a binge or even a pub crawl. More like a glass of wine after work. And she'd babysat for Kristi, a time or two.

"So maybe she was a messed-up teenager," she allowed. "I understand there are a few others out there with troubled youths."

"Very messed up. The DC penal system detoxed her. The court found her guilty on multiple theft charges and transferred her to the women's unit at Jessup Correctional Institution in Maryland. Two months later, prison officials notified her parents that their daughter was pregnant. Mom and Dad appealed to the courts to shorten her term so she could have the baby in the hospital where her father, a doctor, was on staff, then come home to their supervision. A sympathetic judge agreed and sprung her."

Kate shook her head, confused. "But the woman has a degree in aerospace engineering!"

"She started taking undergrad courses while still in prison, then transferred to American University after the baby was born. From then on, she appears to have been a different person. Ideal student, perfect parent, respectable citizen—the whole shebang."

Kate looked down at her fists, wondering why they were hurting. As if of their own volition they clenched and unclenched, over and over. *Past sins,* she thought. *So what?*

Cam was a good and intelligent woman. Kate would stake her life on that much. But Cam had lied to her. Cam had hidden

No Mercy

her past from the government, from her employer, from Kate. Friends weren't supposed to do that.

And yet...she, Kate, had never confided in Cam as she had to Rooker on the gun range.

"So she has a history. If she was incarcerated as a teenager, her record probably would have been purged clean before she came to work for NASA."

"You're saying that omitting the fact she's an ex-con isn't the same as a lie?"

Oh! How she ached to punch this man in his oh-so-smug face. "Less than a year in detention for a juvenile crime doesn't make her a hardened criminal!"

"Doesn't make her Mother Theresa either. And the fact is: What happened that night in your lab was unlike any terrorist attack on record that I know of. Something stinks, Kate. Something about this plot of Zed's doesn't make sense. You've been trying to reconnect with your satellite but have failed, while the brainless bad guys seem to be making great progress. We've been chasing after the bastards behind this plot, but we're always three steps behind."

"That's all true, but—"

He stepped toward her, clamped his big, heavy hands down on her shoulders. Her knees nearly buckled but not from the weight. His touch alone would have done it. Somehow she stayed upright and faced him without flinching.

He said, "I think there's a reason we're making no headway. I think it's because someone close to you is working behind your back, behind our backs, for the other side."

"You *are* paranoid! You really are," she shouted and ducked out from beneath his hot palms.

Where were his men? Why didn't they reappear from their rooms and calm him down? They should step up and put their boss in line, remind him he didn't have the right to bully her this way.

Before she could move more than a few steps away from him, Rooker reached out a long arm. He seized her by one wrist and whipped her around to face him.

"Think about it, dammit! Use that scientific reasoning you're so proud of, Kate. There were *six* people working with you that night. One got blown away, one got shot up and dragged off against his will. The rest, including you, saw Zed's and his companions' faces. You five can identify them, but they left you unharmed. Doesn't that seem strange to you?"

Kate glared at him, remembering now that he'd made a similar point back at NASA. "So we count ourselves lucky?" She wished she sounded more sure of herself.

"No!" He released her with a halfhearted shake, but the tension in his face didn't lessen. "You were being protected. Kate. The team's survival was part of the bargain. Face it. Someone on the inside sold out."

She let out a whimper of denial.

He plunged on. "Whoever cooperated with Zed's plan must have been the one who tampered with the alarm system in the days before the intrusion. That person also cut the wire on the surveillance camera that night. But they also made one demand in exchange for getting Zed in: 'Don't hurt me or the people I care about."

"Oh, God," she breathed. Her vision blurred. The room swam in tears no matter how fast she blinked them away. "But wait! That can't be right. Someone *did* get hurt. David Proctor and Frank Hess." Just the mention of Frank's name and she recoiled, remembering the terror in his eyes, his hysterical pleading, the bleeding wound. Was he even alive now?

Rooker was shaking his head. "We can't know for sure that the mole was one of your team. Could have been someone else with access to the building. But at the moment it's the only explanation that makes any sense. Maybe Zed, or whoever he's working for, decided he didn't like deals. So he wasted two of your people as a warning to his inside contact. 'Screw with me, and this is what you get!'"

Moments ago, her entire body had been vibrating with fury. Now, overwhelming icy fear crowded out anger. Her stomach roiled and cramped at the thought: *What if he's right?* What if, all along, she'd been blind to the existence of a traitor within their ranks? When she left for Rome, had she left someone behind in Washington she never should have trusted? Someone who'd been manipulating her, plotting behind her back, all along.

No Mercy

Kate stared at the ceiling above the bed. *Rome, I'm in Rome,* she reminded herself.

As tired as she'd been—from jet lag, too few hours of sleep, the constant worry of not knowing whether they'd be able to recover HW-1 before it was too late—she hadn't been able to sleep after arriving in Italy. After tossing about endlessly in the sheets, she finally threw back the bedclothes, sat up, and stared at the wall—her mind whirring.

No matter how she tried to dismiss Rooker's allegations, she admitted they held an unfortunate and ugly ring of truth. And yet...

As a scientist she didn't believe in unproven hypotheses, conjectures, and certainly not wild speculation. She had to hold onto one reassuring truth: *Rooker has no proof.* He was all hot air and hunches. Yes, that was him exactly. He was doing what he always did. Talking big and bold, spouting steam, trying to take charge again. He'd never liked the idea of her outranking him, being the boss. It was so like him to try something sneaky.

But was there at least the smallest possibility that someone on her team might have betrayed her?

Worse than betraying her personally, though, this traitor among them—if indeed he or she existed—had compromised the entire Heat Wave project. Had already cost lives. Would likely be responsible for the loss of many more. She couldn't wrap her mind around the possibility that someone she'd worked closely with and thought she knew could willingly turn to violence.

She sat up on the edge of the bed, rubbed the heels of hands into her burning eyes, hard. No matter how she tried to argue away Rooker's accusations, the existence of a traitor among them held a warped kind of logic. And logic was the cousin of good science.

How else would Zed have even known of the existence of the satellite? How had he learned of its capabilities? The project

152

Kathryn Johnson

was a closely guarded secret. NASA had been diligent in keeping any news of the program out of the press. All tests had to be complete before this innovative source of power was announced to the world. So how had homebrewed terrorists outscooped the world press? How had they discovered anything at all about her satellite?

She stood up and paced the cold marble floor of the hotel bedroom. Her mind sparked, spun, reached for answers.

Once Zed's gang broke into the compound, how would they have determined which of three dozen buildings was home to the Heat Wave Command Center? Zed had known she was Chief Project Engineer. He knew *her name!* Someone had supplied that information.

Had Rooker, maybe even Mercy and others, assumed this much from the beginning, while she had remained blind to the possibility? A traitor among them. Someone she trusted. But who?

Kate ripped off the clothing she'd traveled in (and slept in) and stepped into the shower. She didn't wait for the water to come in hot. Cold spray shocked her body awake. As much as she hated the idea, she had to find out who among her people was capable of such unforgiveable deception.

Cam? Surely she had no motive for selling out to the Dark Side, Tommy's term for all black-hat cyber hackers. Unless... *No.* Kate pushed that thought from her mind, but it came back at her again, too insistent to ignore.

Cam had already deceived her, lied to her through omission. She'd never admitted the past that Rooker had revealed—her convictions and prison time. Wasn't a person who lied even once about important things like that likely to cover up the truth in other situations? A liar was a liar. It became a habit. A way of living one's life—one lie after another, just to make life easier.

Cam often complained about the challenge of making ends meet as a single parent. The high cost of living in Washington made it worse. Next year, Cam had admitted to Kate, she'd have to stretch her already tight budget to afford private school for Kristi. The public elementary school was rife with problems. Low test scores, racial bullying among students, inadequate teaching materials and teachers weary of a system that just plain

153

didn't work. Had Cam been tempted to take money in exchange for classified information?

But then, didn't everyone struggle with household and family expenses these days? Amanda and her husband worked hard to support their three kids. Last summer they'd had to cancel their annual family vacation.

She felt contaminated by her own suspicions. A virus of the mind. *Please, no, not Cam! Not any of them!* Kate soaped and scrubbed her body until her skin tingled under the steamy spray.

She reluctantly turned her questions in another direction. Vernon Hernandez. Solemn, nose-to-the-grindstone Vern. At thirty-eight years of age, he was a quiet, private man. He seemed mature beyond his years. Fatherly.

But he'd falsified information on his job application, which could result in his being fired. Maybe Vernon had more to hide than entering the country illegally. He never seemed to get too close to any one person in her lab, she'd noticed. His friendship with Tommy had been recent, only evolving after the break-in when she'd paired them up to more effectively hunt for Heat Wave's captors. But he was always considerate, soft spoken, seemed kind to everyone. And he'd been an asset to the team from the first day he came on board.

She drew a shaky breath and turned her face into the stinging prickle of water. Did Vernon's reserve mean more than natural shyness? Did it have more to do with a fear of his past being discovered? Or worse. A loner—that's how people often described neighbors or classmates who had slipped over the edge into violent fantasies? People who sent letter bombs or suddenly decided to buy a gun and start firing in the middle of a shopping mall.

He seemed just like anyone else. Kept to himself, never any trouble.

Then one day this person flips and takes out all of his frustrations and disappointments on innocents.

She turned off the shower with a jerk of her wrist. The hotel's old plumbing shrieked in protest.

If Rooker was right, Zed had bought one of her people. Or maybe it was even worse than that. What if he'd collected a cult of devoted followers over the years, planting them in top-security installations around the country? Could they have been watching for years for the perfect opportunity to create mayhem?

No, that was too far-fetched. She'd stretched reality too far, surely.

Then again, these days, was any atrocity formulated by one human being to harm others beyond the pale? When she was a kid, the idea of terrorists crashing passenger jets into skyscrapers would have sounded outrageous, like something out of a B movie. And yet, 911 had changed all of their lives.

Kate hugged the bath towel around herself. Who could she trust now? Anyone? If the people she had felt closest to in recent years weren't above suspicion, then maybe it was best to trust no one.

Not even Rooker, a voice whispered.

No, not even him.

Kate dressed, considered unpacking then shrugged the chore off. Why bother? She'd brought so little with her, and who was to say whether she'd be in Rome for a few hours, a couple of days, or weeks?

She checked in with her people back in DC. "I want a report every hour on the hour, day and night, from here on," she told Tommy. "Make sure the others know."

"What if there's been no change?" he asked.

"I don't care. We keep communications open. We talk about anything and everything. You see a blip on your screen, or hear anything suspicious, I want to know about it. Got that?"

"You're beginning to sound like Mr. Macho-man Rooker." He laughed.

Not funny, she thought. "Just keep talking to me. If at least one of you doesn't check in, I'm going to assume all hell is breaking loose over there."

"Gotcha."

She hesitated. "When is Amanda due in?" It was the middle of the night in Washington, DC, but they were taking shifts.

"She's here now. She decided to come in for a few hours before the kids have to get ready for school. Her husband is with them while she's gone."

No Mercy

"Put her on," Kate said. She wasn't sure how comfortable she was with the decision she'd come to. But she couldn't figure out another way to address Rooker's mole theory. Faintly, she heard Tommy calling Amanda to the phone.

"How are you holding up, Katie? Are you eating? Getting some rest?" The typical Amanda, playing earth mother.

"I'm hanging in there. How are the troops?" She tried to sound light-hearted, but the words came out flat and less unconvincing than she'd hoped.

"Tense. Exhausted. Biting each other's heads off." Amanda lowered her voice. "The FBI has been spending a great deal of time in here."

"Mercy, too?"

"Yes. Why do they keep coming back, asking more questions? Shouldn't they be out chasing down those terrible people?"

Kate wasn't sure how much she should reveal of their probable motive for watching her team so closely. On the other hand, if one of them had turned, it might not be a bad thing for that person to know that the Feds were looking over his, or her, shoulder.

"Amanda, I have a favor to ask of you."

"Sure, honey, anything you want. You know that."

Kate swallowed. "You know how to reach me on my cell phone, right?"

"Tommy and Cam have the number posted in their cubicles. I'll just ask them."

"No," she said firmly, "I want you to go to my desk and look in the middle drawer. Pull out my emergency numbers. I added Rooker's phone number at the bottom of the list. You may need to call me through him, without anyone else knowing that you're doing it."

There was a long pause from the other end.

Then, "I don't understand, Kate."

If she had to choose one person out of the entire HW-1 team she felt she could trust absolutely, it would be Amanda. The woman would never do anything to endanger her children or result in her being taken away from them.

"I'd like you to keep your eyes and ears open for me. If you notice anyone behaving strangely or doing anything in the least bit questionable, you call that number. Immediately."

"If you say so." Amanda sounded doubtful.

"I can't explain." Kate tried to keep the anxiety out of her voice. "Please. Just do this for me. I need to know if anything sets off alarm bells for you. You're a mother. You have eyes in the back of your head when it comes to your kids. Pretend the people you're working with are your children. Okay?"

"Okay. I guess."

"Seriously," Kate said. "I need this from you."

Next Kate checked in with Homeland Security. They had nothing new to tell her. Last of all, she called Mercy's number, but only reached her cousin's voice mail.

Mercy hadn't told Kate that they were now actively staking out the Heat Wave lab, and Kate resented that. She'd tell Mercy so, but she'd do it live, not in a recorded statement.

The message she did leave Mercy included the hotel's name, phone, and her room number, in case her cell phone failed. Unlikely since she carried an Iridium satellite phone, the same model DoD and the military used. It should find a signal virtually anywhere in the world. But you never knew. Something as uncontrollable as sunspots had been known to interrupt signals between towers.

When she finally walked out of her room and into the suite's sitting room, she found it empty, except for Rooker. He appeared to have passed out on one of the matching brocade sofas, still in his work fatigues. Apparently his boys were still asleep in the two other bedrooms.

Military types, she'd noticed, seemed to have no trouble crashing whenever and wherever they had dead time. Until the Carabiniere, with the assistance of the Italian telephone company, hunted down the address of a signal attempting to reach the satellite, there was nothing the Americans could do.

Anyway, it wasn't yet 7:00 a.m., Rome time. If what she'd heard about the lackadaisical attitude of Italian businesses was true, it might be hours before either the police or the phone company got cracking.

No Mercy

Kate was wound up so tight she couldn't sleep any more. It would be another hour before her people reported in again. She'd go crazy just sitting here, waiting. If something happened, they could reach her just as easily in a café down the street as shut up here in the hotel.

She scribbled a quick note on hotel stationary then stood over Rooker for a moment, observing the rise and fall of his broad chest beneath the olive-drab shirt. He'd undone the top two buttons for comfort, and he didn't wear an undershirt. His chest looked hard and muscled beneath the pattern of black hair.

Standing over him, she took her time admiring the rather pleasing example of male physique. So what if he was a jerk sometimes? She could appreciate the anatomy.

Smiling, she placed her note on the cushion beside Rooker's head: *Gone out for something to eat. Back soon, K.*

As Kate stepped out of the hotel lobby and into early-morning Rome, she breathed in the pungent scents of the ancient city. It was her first time ever in Rome, and the sights and smells were different than those she recalled from any other city she'd visited.

Air-dried linens flapped in the breeze from clotheslines strung between balconies. The sun had already begun to heat up the marble steps in long, twisting alleys, bringing out their chalky scent. Sidewalks gave off the odors of centuries of *passeggiatas,* the customary evening strolls. Then there was the heady, pungent aroma of warm wine, so thick in the air she could taste it when she opened her mouth and breathed in. Fish, even this early in the morning, cooking in an outdoor kitchen. Or maybe that distinctive odor just lingered in the air from the night before. Ripe cheeses, exotic herbs, and fermenting yeast from the day's fresh-baked bread—everything here was sharp and real, nothing subtle. Rome came at her like a fist, refusing to be ignored even when she closed her eyes for a moment.

Kate gave the streets and shop fronts her full attention. She tried not to think about what she'd say when it came time to speak with Cam and Vernon about what she knew. About what they hadn't told her. Their secrets. Their past. In the meantime, was she supposed to simply pretend she didn't know they'd lied to her? Apparently so.

What about the others? Who else among the nearly thirty scientists and techs who worked on the project had a private agenda?

It would do no good to flog herself with blame for not knowing everything about her people. Rooker could sleep away the tension; she would deal with it in her own way. By being on her own for a short time, away from the constant anxiety of the search. Away from Rooker's moodiness.

She'd found no time to call her own since the night of the attack on the compound. Healing solitude and a stroll through this beautiful city would be her small gift to herself.

As she walked, she observed the people around her. Some were obvious couples. Married? Lovers? Strolling with their arms around each other or, hand-in-hand, stealing a final few minutes together before rushing off to their workdays. Others were alone, preoccupied with getting somewhere.

She thought about her own life, so ordered and quiet. Well, it *had* been quiet before all of this.

She couldn't remember the last time she'd had a real date. Not one of those let's-do-lunch things with a colleague, crammed with shop-talk. An honest-to-goodness date, dressed up for the occasion. Candlelight, white linen tablecloth. Maybe a movie or concert after. How long had it been?

One year, she'd bought herself season tickets to the National Symphony at the Kennedy Center and loved every delicious performance, even though she'd gone alone. Another year, she dated a man who was involved in local theater. He'd taken her to productions at Wolftrap and Arena Stage.

Then along came Heat Wave. Suddenly there'd been no time in her life for anything else.

If the satellite was destroyed, she'd have all the free time she could possibly want, for dating and concerts and anything else she fancied.

Kate didn't care. Nothing had ever excited her as much as the pure, exquisitely beautiful science that had opened up to her while she worked for NASA. When the time was right, she'd make room in her life for romance. For the right man. But at this moment, all she cared about was getting her satellite back and

No Mercy

keeping people safe from its misuse. She wanted that so badly she hurt inside.

Kate passed two cafés, already filling with people on their way to work, stopping for their morning coffee. They chatted exuberantly with co-workers, friends, vendors. The streets were colorful, cheerful, lively in a comforting way. *This is normal,* she thought. *Normal is good.*

Another advantage to getting out of the hotel was removing herself, if only for an hour, from Rooker's mercenaries. It wasn't that she didn't like the boys. They were polite, intense but controlled. With several she'd shared no more than a few passing words. Adam continued to flirt; she'd caught him watching her more than once. Soon, all of them would risk their lives for their country. She felt the need to separate herself from them—physically for now, emotionally when the time came. If she let herself get too close and had to watch them die, something inside of her would be lost with them.

Then again, wasn't she also at risk? Why would she think she was any safer than Rooker and his team? She'd be right there with them, when they cornered these vicious, desperate people.

But she couldn't bear those dark thoughts. Not now. Kate shut them out, firmly as she turned down another street. She pulled her phone out of her purse and checked to make sure no messages had come through while she was walking, the ringing of her phone lost in traffic noise. Nothing. She wouldn't go much farther, in case she was needed back at the hotel. She still felt restless, but the darkest of her demons were retreating in the bright morning sunshine.

After looping the next block and coming out in a pretty piazza, with the requisite Roman statuary and fountain, Kate settled on a tiny café with a dozen small marble-top tables arranged along the sidewalk.

A waiter approached her immediately. *"Buon giorno, signorina."*

"Buon giorno. Un tavolo, per favore?" Kate requested, feeling awkward with her stumbling guidebook Italian. She'd studied a few phrases on the flight over, but was unable to form the luxurious mouth sounds she heard all around her from natives.

"Subito," the waiter responded.

Good, she hadn't flubbed things too badly yet. He brought her to a table with a good view of the piazza's fountain. The sun felt lovely. She ordered a *caffe* and *un cornetto,* a delicately flaky croissant.

She ate slowly, savoring the rich buttery flavor of the pastry. The coffee was heavenly, rich and dark.

The fountain splashed. Children chased a soccer ball around it. Was school in session here this time of year? She had no idea. She smiled to herself, liking the freedom of being anonymous, an uninvolved observer.

"Signorina," said a voice above her.

Kate looked up, startled when she saw it wasn't the waiter. *"Si?"*

The man was tall and elegant. He reminded her of Marcello Mastroianni in a score of old movies. Silver at the temples, a timeless smile, eyes that seduced.

"It is not right for a beautiful woman to eat alone."

Kate laughed because it was such a worn pickup line and she knew she wasn't beautiful. But it was lovely to hear the words. And his English was better than her Italian. She waved him to a seat. *Why not?*

They chatted for a while over more coffee and then, as she got up to leave, he asked to walk her back to her hotel.

She smiled and shook her head. "Thank you, no. Friends are waiting for me. I should hurry."

"Hurry on such a beautiful day?"

"I must," she insisted firmly.

A little innocent flirting had seemed safe enough in a public setting. But she wasn't sure she wanted a stranger to know where she was staying or why she'd come to Italy.

"Ciao," she said, cupping her fingers and giving her Roman admirer the backward wave she'd seen Italians do.

He started to protest, but she held up a hand and told a small fib. "Discreet. I must be discreet."

He smiled, no doubt thinking that she was married or traveling with a lover.

No Mercy

Rooker stood in the shadowed doorway of the *salumeria,* across from the *Café Bianca.* He tried to ignore his complaining stomach as the delicious aromas of spiced meats beckoned to him from within the shop at his back.

Back at the Abruzzi he'd felt Kate's nearness when she'd stood over him. What had she been thinking? He wouldn't have put it past her to give him a swift kick in retaliation for the grief he'd been giving her. But she hadn't touched him in any way. That had been a disappointment.

As soon as he'd heard the suite's door click closed, he'd read her note and swore. No more sleep for him. He had to follow her. To make sure she was safe, he told himself. Or to find out what she really was up to.

The first thing he noticed after she'd settled herself in front of the café was how relaxed she looked, sitting alone at the little pedestal table. She didn't wistfully ogle couples nearby, as if she missed having a companion with whom to enjoy her meal.

He remembered one of his foster sisters once saying she was never so lonely as when she had to eat alone. Carol had struggled through three disastrous marriages searching for a dining partner. Maybe Kate had the right idea. Be comfortable with yourself.

Just when Rooker had decided her excursion really was innocent, and he was debating whether to join her or return to the hotel, a man approached her and sat down at her table. Had she arranged to meet him? Who the hell was he?

Rooker glared at them. Maybe he should make an excuse and interrupt their little party. He'd tell her that something important had come up and she was needed.

No. He'd see how this scenario played out. Then make sure she wouldn't lead the guy back toward the hotel. If she did, he would have to intercept them. The team couldn't afford to advertise their presence. A whisper of covert operations to the local paparazzi, and the press would be all over them. For all he knew, the guy at her table could be a reporter.

At last Rooker saw, with relief, that she was moving off alone. He hung back to make sure the man didn't follow her. Although the stranger cast a regretful eye at Kate's long legs as she walked away, he didn't try to go after her. Rooker tailed her back to the hotel and into the lobby.

He waited until she'd stepped into the elevator then quickly followed her in and pressed the button to shut the doors before anyone else could join them.

"How was your date, princess?"

She flashed annoyed eyes at him. "It wasn't a date." She drew her lips tight against her teeth and narrowed her gaze. "You were spying on me."

"The team was instructed to remain in quarters until told otherwise. I ordered breakfast for everyone to be brought up at seven o'clock."

"I needed to get some air."

Yes, I saw your note. You didn't mention the Italian to go with your danish." He smirked, knowing he was provoking her. He didn't know why, but it felt damn good.

"I needed to escape for a while." Her eyes darted to the floor numbers overhead, as if she were anxious to get off. To get away from him? "All that testosterone in the suite was getting to me."

"That testosterone may save your butt," he commented as the elevator wheezed to a stop on the fifth floor.

She laughed. "Oh, please. Enough." And strode off down the hallway.

"What?" He ran to catch up to her. "You think analyzing the situation to death is what will get back your satellite? You think tracking Zed to his lair means the end of it? Someone has to take this guy down! Whether it's the Carbs or my team or the fucking U.N., you'd better hope they're hyped up on adrenaline, hormones, and whatever else it takes to stop these assholes!"

"Stop shouting," she said.

"I'm not shouting." Yeah, he was. So what? "I'm trying to make you realize that just because you have a sky-high IQ, it doesn't give you special privileges as far as this mission is concerned."

She spun to face him. "Let me remind you, Mr. Rooker. I'm the one in charge. I make the rules. Got that? I didn't lock your gang in the suite. If you think it's necessary to control your men, so be it. But—" she said with emphasis "—I'm not one of them. *You don't control me!*"

"Maybe not, but I have a right to protect the mission."

She stopped in the middle of the hallway and glared at him. "You're accusing me of jeopardizing the mission by going out for coffee?"

"I'm saying you were getting pretty cozy back there with Romeo. What did you tell him, anyway?"

She pushed past him and continued toward the suite's door. "Too bad you didn't have a wire on me. You could have heard the entire conversation." Her face flushed with anger. She whipped her key card out of her purse and reached toward the slot in the door lock.

Rooker grabbed her wrist.

She didn't try to pull away, the first mistake women usually make when an attacker makes a move on a victim. He felt the muscles in her forearm contract then almost immediately relax. She let her arm drop limply to her side, still resting in his grip.

Kate glared up at him, green eyes flashing, but her voice sounded more annoyed than frightened. "Let. Go. Of. Me."

He loosened his grip, not wanting to hurt her. But the stubborn little boy in him didn't want to release her. He liked the feel of her skin against his. "Listen, Doc, I'm not just being nosy. I have to know what you told him."

"Why?"

"Because he could be in league with Zed, or whoever put Zed up to this plot."

She closed her eyes and leaned against the metal doorjamb. "Why don't we go inside and discuss this without the strong-arm tactics." Her eyes dropped to her wrist, still encircled by his strong fingers.

He grimaced. Over reaction maybe? When he released his fingers he was relieved to see he hadn't left a mark in the smooth white flesh. He'd been trained to act fast, on instinct. Sometimes, he realized, his responses weren't appropriate. This was clearly one of them.

Kate marched into the suite, with attitude.

Adam, Kent, Travis, and Pete were sitting, albeit half awake, with their coffee at the table. Kip Boyt, senior member of Rooker's team, sat phone duty at the desk by the window. He looked up at Rooker, his report in the blank expression on his face: no calls. Wade, their newest man, was the only one not in sight, probably back in the room where the team had bunked.

Kate walked a straight course past the group and toward her bedroom. She turned in the doorway to crook a finger at Rooker. *Come here.* He followed her inside, aware of the sudden interest of his men as she closed the door after him. Aware, too, of the feeling of intimacy. His hopes, however outrageous, were short lived.

She tossed her purse on the bed and faced him. "Now, let's try having a real conversation instead of an interrogation," she said, keeping her voice low and under control even though she looked as though she wanted to scream at him.

He shrugged. "Kate, I'm not being unreasonable. I need to know. What was the substance of your conversation with that man?"

"It's none of your business."

"It *is* my damn business!" he shouted.

And suddenly, the conversation that had been going on in the other room stopped. Kate made a show of looking around the room in a bored way.

"Answer me!" he said, his face feeling as if it were on fire.

Kate dropped all pretense of calm. "Rooker, you're a royal pain in the ass, you know that? I'm telling you—nothing was said to that man that can hurt our mission. I didn't tell him where I was staying or why I was here. Unless he followed me back to the hotel, and I'm pretty sure you made certain he didn't, I'll never see him again. Now what is your problem?"

He stepped closer and leaned into her. "My problem is *you* putting *yourself* at risk!"

Kate blinked at him, momentarily stumped. Maybe this wasn't about the mission after all. "Exactly what risk are we talking about, Rooker?"

"You heard me." He turned toward the window that overlooked the street. Through it came the muffled sounds of taxis, buses, cars and people.

"No," she said, "I don't think I did. At least I didn't hear correctly. You were worried about *me?*"

"I'm protecting the mission, that's all. Drop it."

No Mercy

"No, I won't drop it. You were afraid Emilio or someone else might attack me, kidnap me...or what?"

He raked a hand up the back of his head and stared out the window with a pained expression. "All I care about is what's in your head, woman. If they get you, they have your brain. In your brain is all the information they need. After this is over, you can stroll through the slums of Calcutta at midnight, for all I care."

She stared at him, feeling her pulse thrum in her chest, the steady bump-bump-bump resonating inside her ears. The tips of her fingers prickled with a sensation she couldn't interpret. Why should it matter to her if he cared at all what happened to her?

"You must take me for an idiot," she murmured. "I wouldn't intentionally put myself in harm's way or jeopardize our recapturing Heat Wave."

"You might not have a choice." He turned and looked at her, hard. "Have you forgotten what happened in your lab? Could've been you they gunned down that night."

She bit down on her lip and had to concentrate on steadying her voice before daring to speak. The words came out as barely a whisper. "Of course I haven't forgotten. But walking a few blocks in a civilized city in broad daylight is not the same as facing a gun-toting lunatic in a locked room. You don't give me enough credit, Rooker." She drew a breath. "I'm not helpless."

He let out a huff of air, not quite a laugh. "Right. Well, I just don't want you going MIA on my watch."

"Understood," she said.

"Good."

Kate turned her back on him. She didn't look around to see him leave the room but heard his steps cross the room then the door open and shut. She let out a deep sigh, but the nervous strain of their argument remained in the form of heat. It radiated throughout her body, making her feel itchy, anxious.

Earlier, out in the hallway, she'd aborted her instinctive reaction to his grabbing her arm. If she had allowed herself to follow through, they wouldn't have needed to have this conversation.

His aggressiveness had triggered a chain of automatic responses Kate had thought she'd forgotten.

Apparently, she hadn't.

Kathryn Johnson

Back in college, she and her roommate had signed up for a women's self-defense course. The techniques were inspired by the so-called gentle martial art, Aikido. Based on the laws of physics and anatomy, it seemed a logical match for a scientist.

She'd never needed to use her training, but it gave her the confidence to drive alone through Washington at night, or walk the streets of Georgetown where Mercy lived. When Mercy wasn't off traveling, they sometimes ran together through Rock Creek Park. Some of the deeply wooded paths were less traveled and the scene of an occasional mugging or rape. They had agreed not to let the threat of violence control their world. They ran in defiance of fear. But only because they knew how to defend themselves.

Confronted by Rooker, she'd automatically recalled one of the Aikido drills: *Soften knees, relax arm, withdraw foot, turn body, palm circles up...* When performed correctly, without hesitation, the maneuver would force an attacker who had grabbed her wrist to fall off balance and release her.

But she hadn't followed through and broken his grip or sent him tumbling to the floor. Because it was Rooker.

Now she reminded herself that, in another situation, censoring her body's automatic reactions might result in her injury. Or worse. Next time she wouldn't check herself, wouldn't ignore her training and instincts.

No Mercy

Chapter 23

Time was running out. Zed's deadline rapidly approached. Everyone on Rooker's team knew it. No one talked about it.

Throughout the day, Italian military, police, and government officials moved in and out of the hotel. News spread of the Americans' presence. Rumors of terrorist plots raced through Rome faster than the Huns. Why else would an American security business be meeting with Italian anti-terrorist forces?

By noon Rooker had whipped himself into a rage. "Whatever happened to 'low profile'?"

"Maybe anyone watching the hotel will just think a law enforcement convention is in town," Adam suggested, sneaking Kate a smile.

"Shit," Rooker said.

At 8:00 p.m. the tension broke when word came, at last, that NASA had located another signal attempting to contact the satellite. This time the connection was long enough for the Carbiniere to match it to an address. The team moved out, Kate with them.

Kate kept a line open to people back at NASA-Westin, as they rode in a van across the city, with two other vehicles following, carrying the rest of the team and weapons. "I need to know everything, no matter how insignificant it seems," she told Cam. "I'm worried Zed might have booby-trapped the place where we're headed." Was that the intended warning of the fake explosion back in Connecticut?

"I've thought about that too," Cam said, concern thickening her voice.

"How's the code breaking coming?" Between her own team, NSA, and the FBI—it would seem they'd by now have untangled the encrypted message that captured her sat.

"Nothing yet. Everyone's pushing as hard as they can. It looks like a war zone here. No one's slept in days. We're operating on fumes."

Kate sighed, feeling guilty for the few hours of rest she'd been able to grab. But there was no way to give her people any relief. Not yet.

"Keep at it. Something's got to give soon."

She was aware of the others in their van, all of them Rooker's team except for the Italian driver and interpreter. They'd be able to hear her end of the conversation. Did they even care? No one else was talking. She sensed the men's minds were elsewhere.

The closed space smelled of sour sweat. And what else? Fear? No. Maybe. Yes, it would be natural. Was Rooker afraid? Or these young men who followed him blindly? Maybe the silence was their way of storing up courage to do the job they'd been sent to do?

"Tommy wants to talk to you," Cambridge said, startling Kate back to their conversation.

"Put him on." Kate listened to the former hacker rattle off the steps he'd taken in the past twenty-four hours to break through to Heat Wave.

Never before had she heard him sound discouraged, by anything. Every task she'd ever given him had been accepted as a challenge. *A game.* It must have suddenly hit him. *This is real life.* This time, figuring out the puzzle counted, big time.

The penalty for losing would be human lives.

Her people back in DC kept passing the phone around, filling her in, updating her one at a time. Another idea came to her. A different angle, a set of commands that had the slimmest chance of working. Whoever engineered Zed's takeover had known what they were doing. Had, in fact, been nothing short of brilliant. Somehow, her team had to be smarter. She asked to speak to Vernon again and sent him back to try something new. A work around.

Five minutes later, Vernon reported back to her in a dull and disappointed monotone. No, her idea hadn't worked.

She peeked out of the corners of her eyes at Rooker. He sat on the bench seat on her right, Adam on her left. Their hard hips pressed into hers. Neither seemed aware of the contact. Remarkable, at least for moony-eyed Adam. Marco, their translator, rode in front with the driver. The rest of the men had crammed into the remaining seats. All remained silent as the van sped on.

She told Vernon to keep at it and then rang off. She had to remind herself to breathe. *It will be all right. We'll beat them. Somehow, we 'll beat them,* she told herself over and over. Less than one hour of daylight remained.

Rome rushed past her: antiquity on fast-forward. The Coliseum, the crumbling ruins of the Forum—marble columns snapped off and left in mammoth chunks or cemented back in place, leaving visible scar lines in the stone. Rome had gloried, then died. One day, would the same be said of the United States of America?

Kate closed her eyes and prayed.

The van turned down broad, voluptuous Via del Corso with its many monuments and glittering modern shops. As they flashed past the corner of Via della Muratte, Kate caught a breathtaking glimpse of the immense bas-relief sculptures of the Trevi Fountain. Then they turned right, into a maze of tiny back streets.

A few blocks farther on, the van stopped in a residential area cordoned off and guarded by Carabiniere officers. They looked crisp and official in their tan uniforms, red stripes up the side seam of their pant legs, snap-brimmed caps pulled down over foreheads, serious expressions on their faces.

"Wait here." Rooker threw himself into the street before the van had completely stopped.

Kate watched out a side window.

An Italian military officer approached him.

She could hear most of the conversation. "We have cleared the perimeter. Evacuated lower floors." The something about limiting danger to civilians. The man spoke excellent English, with very little accent.

As he listened, Rooker slipped off his leather jacket, revealing the Glock beneath it. When he opened the vehicle's door to toss the jacket inside, Kate started to push her way out and past him.

Adam reached out a hand to stop her. "Better wait, Doc. He won't take you in on the assault anyway."

"The hell he won't!" She signaled their interpreter to join her outside, in case she needed help in getting her point across to the Italians.

Rooker flashed her an irritated look but stepped aside to let her out. He was suiting up in flak jacket, strapping on a helmet. He started to say something but she turned her back to him and addressed the Carabiniere officer.

"Before any of your people go in," she said, "they must understand that they absolutely cannot touch or harm any electronic equipment that might be in there."

The interpreter started to repeat her words in Italian.

The officer waved him off. "I can assure nothing of the kind, *signorina*. If the shooting starts, there will be no way to protect furnishings of any sort." He looked offended at the very thought of not being allowed to blow away anything he liked.

"But—" she began.

The Italian took a step closer and glowered down at her. "Our orders are to apprehend or eliminate these fanatics. This is at your own government's request. We will cooperate and do the job."

She shook her head violently. "The data! Rooker, tell him how important it is." But she knew she couldn't count on the mercenary. She kept her eyes locked on the Italian and jabbed a finger into the air. "A satellite. Up there. Your bosses must have told you about it. It's been hijacked. I need the data that's on a thumb drive, a USB stick, or possibly has been transferred to the hard drive of a computer. Without it thousands of innocent people may die!"

"She's right, Commander." Was there reluctance in Rooker's voice? She didn't care, at least he'd come to her defense. "These are ruthless characters. They have access to a very powerful device that—"

"I was told nothing of a bomb!" The Italian's eyes widened. Although a satellite didn't seem to concern him, a bomb was a concept he clearly understood.

"Worse," she said. "Potentially far worse than any traditional bomb or IED you can imagine."

The officer studied Rooker for a long moment. "Your men know what they're looking for?"

No Mercy

"Yes, sir. I'd appreciate your letting us take the point. If we go in first, there's a better chance of recovering the property."

Kate groaned, nearly jumping out of her skin with impatience as the two men jockeyed for position. *Get on with it!* she begged silently.

Finally, an arrangement was reached. The Italian officer took a contingent of his own men and disappeared up the street as dusk enrobed the buildings around them. Rooker's men already had piled out of the other vehicles in their convoy and stood waiting for orders in their night camos.

Rooker passed out orders and they were off. He turned to Kate. "I can't leave anyone with you. I need all of my people. Will you promise to stay here until we've cleared the way?"

Kate opened her mouth to protest. Hadn't she learned to shoot his stupid rifle so that she *could* go with him?

"I promise I'll get you in as soon as possible," he said, as if he knew she was about to argue with him. "Someone will come for you when it's safe."

"Seriously?" She really wanted to pull rank on him, for what it was worth. But she didn't want to jeopardize the mission by leaving him a man short. Frustrated, she busied herself by checking the radio receiver clipped to her blouse. It's blue-tooth ear bud would allow her to hear Rooker, in case he needed to consult with her before she could be brought into the building.

He reached out and touched the pin-size gadget clipped to her neckline, as if to adjust its angle. His fingers brushed her left breast through the fabric as they drew away.

Her breath caught in her throat. She tensed. "It's fine," she said and took a step back.

He smiled. Blue eyes sparked at her, as if he knew what his touching her did to her insides. "Keep your radio on. Things may sound pretty frenzied in there, but don't worry." He adjusted the chin strap to his helmet. "We'll all be having fun."

"Sure you will." She guessed that the bravado was an intentional cover for nerves. Battlefield humor.

Still, it infuriated her that he refused to listen to her. He'd edged her out of the way again. Kate only hoped that, one way or another, by the end of the evening she'd have what she'd come for. Then this nightmare would be over.

"Yo, *signore, avanti.*" Rooker waved the translator over. "We may need you."

The man frowned, looking unhappy with the prospect. But he followed docilely along behind Rooker, clumsily pulling on the heavy, padded vest he'd been holding on his lap during the drive across the city.

Kate wondered why they didn't have a dedicated police translator, a man accustomed to situations like this. As if there ever had been another. She paced the pavement beside the van, one ear tuned to NASA on her cell, the other listening to Rooker's clipped orders to his people, and each of his men reporting in as they closed in on the target building and took positions.

Her stomach clenched. She felt vaguely dizzy with anticipation. The street appeared totally empty of human beings now. How had that happened? Were the police cordoning off still more streets leading into the area? Had they discreetly evacuated this part of the city?

A cat yowled from somewhere in the dark. From a distance came the motorized murmur of city traffic. Rooker's voice in her ear, talking to his men, suddenly went silent. She wondered if her receiver was still working. Should she test it by trying to talk to him through the mic? No. Best to keep quiet.

Oh, God! If anything was worse than violence, it was anticipating it. The next few minutes might turn ugly-bad.

What was wrong with people? Couldn't they just get along? Couldn't they be kind to each other? Human nature confounded her. This was why she'd stopped reading newspapers years ago. The suffering and pain was unending. It made her physically sick.

And now here she was, overseeing a raid that would likely end in a loss of lives. How many, and whose, she couldn't say.

Blood pounded in her veins. Its pulses filled her head, her ears, until they were ringing. She paced along the line of empty vans, wishing she was anywhere but here.

It's like this, she told herself. *There are times when circumstances force a person to act. Even if responding to violence with violence is against your nature, you have to protect yourself and those you care about. Right? You can't always run the other way.*

173

No Mercy

Maybe that's the way Rooker thought, at times like this.

Suddenly the ear-splitting chatter of firearms burst from the bud in her left ear. Even without her radio connection, she could hear the report of guns echoing off nearby buildings, louder and louder. Through the blue tooth: warning shouts, orders to freeze and throw down weapons in English and then Italian. Wood splintering, glass shattering. Thundering feet. All of it a hundred times more terrifying than the mayhem at the Groton campus.

Kate stood stock-still on the sidewalk. Someone was calling her name, as if from miles away. *The phone, stupid!* She was still hooked up to NASA. She brought the cell phone to her other ear.

"Kate? You still there?" Cambridge. "What's going on?"

"The raid's on and they're in the building. Rooker wouldn't let me go in with them. No surprise there. I don't have a clue what's going on in there. It's horrible, waiting. What about you?"

"Same stuff. We're jammed out, and someone is still trying to bring up the sat's power systems. So far, no— Oh, jeezuz! Hold on."

"What?" Kate shouted into the phone. The noise from the earpiece connecting her to Rooker was so loud she had to pull off the earpiece to be able to hear Cam. "Say something! What's happening?"

"They've done it." All hope left her colleague's voice, as if swept away by a gust of wind.

Kate's heart sank. *No. No. No!* She couldn't breathe. Literally. Could. Not. Breathe. At last, she gulped down air and gasped, "Zed's established control of Heat Wave? You're sure?"

"Him or whoever he's given the codes to. The sat's powering up now." Cam's voice cracked with emotion. "And...now it looks like there's a live signal from the satellite. I repeat *from the satellite*. The readings are changing fast now." A locked-down, unresponsive satellite had been, at the very least, a thorny problem. Now they had a hot satellite on their hands. A satellite with enough power to cause unimaginable damage. And no control over it.

"If you can't access HW-1," Kate said, "can you at least decipher the commands?"

"It will take time."

"We don't have time!" Kate shouted. She could hear raised voices in the background at the Comm Center, calling out readings. Her team, no doubt, trying to make sense of the data streaming in from the satellite.

Cam broke into sobs. "I'm sorry, Kate. I'm so, so sorry. I'm doing...we're all doing everything we can!"

Kate pressed a hand to her throbbing forehead. "Of course you are. I'm sorry. I shouldn't have screamed at you. Please don't think this is on you. It's just that I..." *I have no more answers. I'm as terrified as you are, girl.* "Just do everything you can. That's all anyone can ask."

"I will. I will." Sniffles. A Cough. "Best get off this line, boss. I'll be back once we know more."

Kate drew a long, shaky breath, and watched her phone return to its home screen. She tried to breathe normally. Ironic. How long had it been since anything felt *normal*?

She slipped her phone back into her purse.

All she could hope for was that Rooker and the Italians would catch Zed's gang and bring her in to recover the sat's control before any real harm was done. It might not be too late to abort whatever release of emissions was being programmed into the onboard computer.

She stretched her fingertips down her left-side pocket and fished around for the blue tooth. She found it and looped it back over her ear.

An agonized scream nearly deafened her.

She clapped a hand over her ear as if that might shut out the horrible wailing. But that only made the noise louder. She pulled the blue tooth thing off her ear but, a beat later, she shoved it back on. She had to hear what was going on. No matter how awful it might be.

Had someone inside the building been shot? Absolutely. What else would cause a human being to screech like that?

Please, God, don't let it be Rooker. Or Adam. Or...any of our boys.

Tears burned in her eyes. Her guys were in hell. And here she was, useless, pacing the empty street. Her chest felt so tight every breath came with aching ribs.

No Mercy

Would any of those young men walk out whole? Would Daniel Rooker?

She'd traveled with them, joked with them, shared cold pizza and long talks to pass the time.

Who among them was dying at this very moment? The thought drove her near mad.

She had to find out what was happening.

She felt for the receiver clipped on her dress. If she flicked it on. If she called out to Rooker, he would reassure her. Or yell at her to leave him alone. At least then she'd know he was still alive.

And she'd be glad. Exuberant! Because there were things she wanted to tell him. Questions she needed to ask him. And she really, really would like for him to, accidentally, just like before, brush his strong fingers across her breast.

Kate clicked on the mic. She wet her lips. Opened her mouth to speak, then clicked the mic off again. *No.* It was foolish of her to distract him at this critical moment, just to reassure herself. She bit down on her lower lip, thinking.

Then she remembered the surveillance van.

Inside would be at least one man, an Italian police officer using sophisticated electronic equipment to track the assault team's progress throughout the building. She could ask him to tell her what was happening, if Rooker and team were all right. But she, a stranger, couldn't just walk in on him, on them. God only knew how they'd react!

The gunfire had become intermittent. Coming in short bursts followed by an unsettling silence. Kate looked around the deserted street. The dark spaces between streetlights seemed less dense and intimidating; the moon had slipped out from behind clouds to cast a pale gray light over buildings and street and potted geraniums in front of a florist shop. Shadowed storefronts were easier for her eyes to penetrate. Nothing moved. But from somewhere came a soft scuffling sound.

She let her eyes sweep from building to building, and then saw a narrow alley between what looked like an apartment house and a factory of some sort. She took a few more steps so that she could look down its dim length. *It's a cat,* she thought. *Rome is full of cats.* At the far end she could just make out a narrow backstreet that appeared to run parallel to the street on which she stood. Why she even noticed it, she couldn't have said until...

She glimpsed something in motion. A shadow, a shape, a figure—but definitely too large to be a cat. It had been absolutely still one minute—one with the shadows, invisible. But now it darted toward her. She stepped back into the dim entrance of the shop front across the street, and waited. The figure stayed low, crouched and compact. Edging along cautiously.

Maybe this was an unfortunate civilian left behind in the evacuation. Terrified, running for their life. The person—she could tell now it was definitely human—wore what looked like an Italian military jacket and cap, but they didn't quite match the pants. In the dark, she could make out no facial features.

The figure stopped at the mouth of the alley, turned left then right, as if to make sure no one was watching.

It couldn't be one of the assault team, she reasoned. He, if it was a he, was moving in the wrong direction, away from the fighting. The stance and broad shoulders made her think it must be a man. Should she call out, wave the person to safety? Instinct told her not to. She shrank farther back into the awning-covered shop entrance and held her breath.

The man cautiously stepped out into the street, straightened up, and immediately started walking away from the gunfire.

He passed beneath a street lamp and, for just a second, the yellow glow illuminated the lower half of his face beneath the hat brim. A thick mustache, dark skin, slightly down-turned lips. A face she would never forget.

Zed.

No Mercy

Kate stifled a gasp. What should she do? Without a weapon and alone, she had no chance of stopping him.

She waited until he'd moved out of hearing range, then she triggered the send button on her belt radio and urgently whispered into the tiny microphone clipped to her blouse. "Rooker, Zed's getting away. What do I do?"

The cacophony of battle went on uninterrupted.

"Rooker!" she rasped as loudly as she dared, keeping an eye on the departing figure.

Zed was still taking his time, a man out for a leisurely evening stroll.

A few blocks farther on there would be the official police line, a few officers left behind to make sure no one escaped the raid or wandered back into the neighborhood before it was safe. But if Zed managed to slip past them, he would disappear into the city. And with him, she had every reason to believe, would go the vital data she needed to recapture Heat Wave.

She tried her radio again. "Zed is walking north of Via del Tritone. I'm not sure of the cross street names." Some weren't labeled, others too far away to see. "Rooker, do you copy Anyone?"

How Zed had escaped from the raided building, she didn't have a clue. But did it matter?

Still no response. Was she operating the damn radio correctly? Maybe the noise from the battle was drowning her out. Or, worse, maybe Rooker had been hit!

Desperate, she looked toward the surveillance van, in the opposite direction from where Zed was headed. If the communications man had overheard her message he wasn't responding. The thing to do was pound on the rear doors and shout that their man was escaping. Let him raise the alarm.

But if she took the time to do that, she'd lose sight of the fugitive. Precious minutes would be wasted while Rooker extricated himself from whatever action was going on inside the building.

She couldn't risk losing Zed, losing whatever data he might still have.

There was nothing to do but follow him.

Kate turned toward the departing figure and started walking, just as casually as he. His strides were much longer than hers. The space between them gradually widened. She shifted into her exercise pace. Perhaps it would appear she was out for her evening exercise. She tried to look intent, athletic, although she wore a skirt-suit and panty hose.

The wind picked up as Kate's faster gait ate up the stretch of smooth paving stones. A cool drizzle descended on the city. She looked up and down the streets, into narrow alleys for any sign of the police.

Where the hell were they?

She walked faster and faster, all the while hoarsely whispering into her collar. "Rooker, Rooker, Rooker...anybody, do you hear me? It's Kate, I'm following Zed."

Nothing.

She started naming landmarks and reading street names into the microphone, when she could see any, marking her route for anyone who might be listening. "Still heading north, now passing over a narrow footbridge. Crossing a tiny piazza with a circle of statues in the middle. Looks like an abandoned fruit stand up ahead. Anybody there yet?"

She wondered if she'd already moved beyond the range of the little radio's signal. She kept walking, hanging as far back from Zed as she dared. If she let him get too far ahead, he might slip away. If she clung any tighter to him, he'd hear her footsteps and suspect he was being followed.

She was almost certain they should have run into the police line by now. Then she realized he'd been taking a circular route, as if he was intentionally staying within the protected area. The streets and houses seemed less affluent here. The alleys stank of urine and fetid garbage. Three small, black humps darted between torn plastic bundles set out on stone stoops.

No Mercy

Zed was still barely within sight. Then he rounded another corner and disappeared up an alley. Her heart leaped into her chest.

She ran toward the corner, hoping he wouldn't turn again before she caught sight of him. A second later she realized how vulnerable she'd be if she stepped around that same corner and he was waiting there for her.

She stopped and stood very still, trying to think of a way to handle the situation. What would a cop tailing a suspect do? Keep on walking, she thought. Pass the corner without hesitating or looking down the side street. Move fast, as if she had no intention of turning there. Then find another route to intersect with his.

Just to be safe, she crossed the street so that she'd be on the opposite side. At least then, if Zed were lying in wait, he couldn't reach out and grab her. On the other hand, if he had a gun, she'd be out in the open, an easy target as she passed the mouth of the alley.

Kate became aware that the sounds of gunfire had stopped. Through her ear bud she could hear harsh, stressed breathing. Rooker's? Men started calling out to each other, checking in:

"Adam here."

"You whole, boy?" Rooker's voice. *Thank God!*

"Not a scratch. Sanchez and Donnelly are with me."

Then it was like a rapid-fire roll call, including the Italians and ending with Rooker's report, "I have two perps in the basement. One dead, one wounded. Locals. We need an ambulance. Anyone find Zed?"

"I have him!" Kate whispered into her mike. She'd already passed the alley and kept on moving.

"What? Who's that?" Rooker again. Confused. Everyone else silent.

Kate smiled at his shocked tone. "It's me, Kate. I'm following Zed. Where the hell is my backup?"

She could imagine Rooker trying to place her in the building. "I thought I told you—"

"I'm north of your location," she said. "Zed slipped past you. He's wearing what looks like an Italian officer's uniform jacket. Our local friends may have lost a man."

"What the hell do you think you're doing?" Rooker bellowed so loudly she had to pull the bud out of her ear for a moment or go deaf in that ear.

"Pass by the vans and keep going another block then take the first left then another left." Was there one more turn? She couldn't remember. "I'm just past the fruit stand. He's disappeared down an alley that curves out of sight. I'm going up the next street to see if I can intercept him."

"The hell you are!" Rooker yelled. She could tell by his breathing that he was running. Toward her, she hoped.

Other voices broke in, asking what he wanted them to do.

He barked out orders to the surveillance van, to their translator for the benefit of the Italians, to his own men. "No sirens. Silent approach. Do nothing to alert him. And Dr. Foster, you stay right where you are. Don't move!"

Did he think she'd worked this hard to keep their quarry in sight only to let him disappear into the night? She kept on walking.

She began to see other people on the street. But still no sign of the police. She couldn't understand how Zed had managed to lead her out of the secured area. Perhaps back at the little footbridge, which had taken her, just for a moment, below the main street level?

A few cars sped past her. She looked both ways then crossed a street. Three young men lounged on the next corner despite the thin rain, smoking cigarettes and laughing. One made crude kissing sounds. The others laughed, elbowed each other.

She rushed on, wiping raindrops out of her eyes, still not seeing Zed. Had she lost him?

Through open windows she heard voices arguing, the sound of car tires squealing from a TV drama, a baby crying, a woman letting out a high-pitched wail—of agony or ecstasy?

Frantic now, Kate searched for an opening between buildings that might lead her to the other end of the alley into which Zed had disappeared. Her own footsteps echoed, duplicating themselves. Or was the second set just a little faster, a little weightier? She looked around. Saw no one. The street began to climb.

No Mercy

At last she saw it in the dim light from a low window. A very narrow passageway between gray stucco buildings. It was only wide enough for two people to walk through, shoulder to shoulder. The path was formed of stone steps so ancient the foot traffic of centuries had worn a hollow in the center of each one. Rain water puddled in each stone cup.

Kate stood for a moment, suddenly less sure of herself. She might have lost Zed already, but if there was any chance of tipping Rooker off to the fugitive's location... She took two steps up the narrow stairs and dipped her head toward the mic.

"Rooker, are you anywhere near?" she whispered.

"Closing on your last stated location. Stay put."

"He'll get away."

"Stay—"

An indistinct shuffling sound turned her attention to the stairs above. Footsteps were coming down the hill out of the dark at a rapid pace. She pressed back against the damp, moldy wall just in time as a young boy darted past her. Trembling with relief, she released a held breath.

"Kate, where the hell are you? I can't see you, damn it!"

She hadn't told him about her last turn.

Leaning one shoulder against the wall to face the street, she brought her lips down to her collar to murmur instructions. It was then that she heard a single footfall and felt the presence behind her.

Before she could turn around, a hand snaked around and clamped over her mouth, driving her teeth into the tender flesh inside her upper lip. She tasted a metallic saltiness, her own blood. Strong arms dragged her up steps, deeper into the narrow space between crumbling building walls.

"Dr. Kate," a voice hissed in her ear, "you are out much too late for your health."

She swallowed blood.

Wrestling with the man would gain her nothing; he was twice her bulk, double her strength. She let her body go slack, waiting for a next chance at freedom. A change in his grip. A moment when he reached for a weapon.

At least he didn't have a knife at her throat. It could have been worse. Though not much.

"You should leave the spying to the professionals," he snarled. This was a different Zed, without the thick Eastern accent. The Philly street punk was back. "Maybe I should have, too." He laughed. "But the money was too damn good."

What would he do to her?

"So are you alone?" he said.

Her mind flew in a dozen directions. He didn't release his hand from her mouth to get an answer. She shook her head.

"No? How many? And if you scream, you die. *Capisce?*" She could hear his pleasure in using a word he'd probably picked up from a TV mob movie. "Whisper," he said. His thick fingers unrolled one at a time from her lips.

She breathed in through her mouth and tasted his sweat on her lips. Was he at all worried? The possibility that he might be capable of fear but refused to show it, made her braver. "Ten men...maybe more."

"Is that s-s-so-o-o." The final word lingered, a reptile's hiss in her ear. "You are a crappy liar, Dr. Kate. Two blocks. That's all it took before I knew you were following me. Another and I was sure you were alone."

So he'd intentionally led her away. Trapped her by circling around and beating her to this deserted place when she thought she was being so clever and outfoxing him.

She blinked, tried to breathe without whimpering. His left arm bit painfully into her ribs. The fingers of his right hand had shifted from her lips to her throat. If she shouted for help he could easily silence her, forever.

Then her radio burped and crackled. Kate went rigid.

"Ah, yes. I thought so." He reached down and ripped the tiny mike clip off her blouse, the wire and earpiece going with it.

Even as the bud was moving away from her in his big hand, she could hear Rooker's voice bleating faintly at her.

Zed tore the radio unit from her skirt waistband and threw it down on the pavement. He stomped on it, grinding the little black box beneath his boot. "Not exactly the cavalry, are they?" he chuckled. But something caught his attention, and he shot a wary glance toward the end of the street.

No Mercy

A shadow passed in front of the alley's opening, momentarily blocking the dim light from the street before moving on, distracting her captor. *My chance. Now!*

Kate let the muscles in her legs go limp. She fell like a rock, straight down to the pavement. "Rooker!" she screamed.

Zed must have been prepared for her to try and break away from him and run. But her unexpected descent to his feet took him by surprise.

The slick fabric of his coat helped her slip out from between his body and arm, down to the rain-damp stones. When he bent forward to reach for her she braced her legs like coiled springs, locked them, shot up at an angle, aiming the hard top of her head for his crotch. And connected.

Zed let out an agonized roar, the sound of a wounded lion. It echoed down the alley's walls. Clutching himself, he staggered sideways, dropped to one knee, bent double.

Kate scrambled away on hands and knees, over sharp-edged rubble and clumps of garbage. She kept on screaming a random mixture of Italian and English, hoping someone, anyone would respond, *"Assassino!* Rooker, help! *Polizia!* Rooker!"

The end of the alley suddenly was no longer visible, as if something had blocked it. Was it Rooker? The Carabiniere? Or strangers incapable of helping her?

Frantically, she struggled to her feet and tried to run toward the alley's end, away from Zed. A hand clasped around her ankle before she could take a second step. She went down with an audible crack. Pain shot through her knees and jaw where they struck stone. Stunned, she lay helpless for a moment. Then it was all she could do to twist around and kick with her free foot. She hit air.

Zed on his hands and knees, gripping her ankle harder, leering at her. She kicked again. The heel of her shoe connected with his jaw.

She heard teeth clack and grind. The fingers loosened just long enough.

Kate was up on her feet again. Tripping down steps, two at a time. Nerves all the way up her spine tingled with the premonition of Zed's big hands seizing her from behind. Any moment now. Dragging her down again. Holding her helplessly on the ground. Pummeling her with his big fists until she couldn't move, couldn't breathe. Until she lay bloody and dead.

She kept on running, heart ripping through her chest. She tore into the street, even as shapes flashed past her like ghosts in the dark. Men running hell-to-pay in the other direction, disappearing into the alley from whence she'd come. Men she paid no attention to. Needing to escape a madman. She plowed into the side panel of a Carabiniere van.

Kate collapsed against the vehicle, gasping, seeing stars.

Hands grabbed her by the shoulders.

She fought them off, her fists flying, fingernails clawing. In the vaguest of dreamlike ways she was aware of voices shouting at her. Then coalescing into a single, voice, barking at her, demanding she listen. Until the words slowly started to make sense.

"Kate! You're all right. It's Rooker. We've got you now." He pinned her arms and torso to his chest, as if for his own defense from her flailing as well as to calm her. "You're safe. It's over."

No Mercy

Chapter 25

As it turned out, it wasn't. Not by a long shot.

By dawn's first light, Kate sat with a mug of hot tea warming palms, Rooker's leather jacket draped over her rain-drenched blouse and chilled shoulders. Adam stood beside her as she stared through a one-way mirror into an interrogation room where the Carabiniere had brought Zed.

Three Italians, one she suspected might be the equivalent of a District Attorney back in the States and other two Carabiniere officials, crowded into the closet-size space with them. On the other side of the window Rooker was questioning Zed with little success.

Neither the thumb drive nor any other incriminating evidence was found on him or anywhere within the raided building. To Kate's dismay, NASA verified that the satellite's onboard computer had been moved out of Safe-Hold and was responding to signals sent by an antenna somewhere on the Adriatic coast.

Kate slanted a quick look at Adam. He looked years older than he had a few days ago. He'd come through the raid with bruises on his face and arms, and a cut perilously close to one eye that would require stitches. Even worse, one of Rooker's team, Travis Peterson had taken two rounds, one in the throat, one in the thigh. He lay in a nearby hospital, in critical condition. Rooker wasn't happy.

Before capturing Zed in the alley, his team and the Italian police had rounded up three more men in the building. They seemed to know nothing about the satellite. Claimed they'd been hired by an American businessman for protection. They identified Zed as that man.

"I still don't understand what those men thought they were protecting him from," Kate said.

Adam squatted down beside her chair. "He told them he was a wealthy entrepreneur afraid of being kidnapped."

"Really."

"Yeah. It probably made sense to them. Snatching and ransoming foreigners is considered a legitimate business in some parts of the world. It's definitely profitable."

Kate took another sip of tea and turned her attention back to on what was going on in the interrogation room. Rooker stood facing Zed, who was shackled to a chair leg and in handcuffs. The Italians looked on grimly but their occasional questions seemed to get them nothing useful. Zed was playing a believable role as a man swept up by mistake in an ill-planned raid.

"This could take a long time," Adam said. "You sure you don't want me to take you back to the hotel?"

"No." She studied Zed's expression. He had been on the verge of killing her. Only his delight in tormenting her briefly before he did it had given her the opportunity to escape. What was going through his mind now? "He doesn't look at all worried that we've caught him."

"He thinks he's tough shit," Adam said, then blanched. "Sorry, Doc."

She smiled weakly and looked at her watch. Back in DC, it was already morning. Zed had given them until noon, East Coast time, to make payment. Would his threat be carried out regardless of his capture? Was that why he looked so smug, despite shackles?

"If we'd only found your USB stick on him," Adam said.

"By now, I'm not sure it makes any difference."

He frowned at her. "Why not?"

Kate sighed. "They're in now. The don't need that data any longer. It's my guess he's full of himself at the moment because he's already instructed someone to proceed with their plan, whatever that might be."

Adam dropped his eyes to hands folded between his knees. "Then we're beat."

She wished she could tell him he was wrong. But she felt as if their opportunities for stopping a terrible tragedy had finally slipped away.

Rooker stepped out of the interrogation room, leaving the Italians in the room with Zed. He must have heard the tail end of her conversation with Adam. His frown deepened. "You think that having caught him we haven't stopped his plan?"

"I'm afraid so." She brought him up to speed on her thoughts about their status. "According to my team back in DC, whoever is in control of the sat is bouncing the signal from an antenna here in Italy over to another one in the U.S. That's necessary since they can't reach Heat Wave directly from here. They may even be using another satellite to make the Atlantic connection."

Rooker glowered at her. "You got any more cheerful news for me?"

"Not news...just thoughts." She stared through the one-way glass at Zed. "Look at him, Rooker."

"Yeah. What?"

"How would you rate that man's intelligence after talking to him for over an hour?"

Rooker smirked. "He ain't no rocket scientist."

She made a face at him. "Exactly. Which means he probably had very little to do with the planning that went into hijacking the satellite. When he grabbed me, he said something about the money being too good."

"So, he was just a hired gun. We guessed that much from his background."

"That leaves open the question of exactly who is behind this. Remember how after the nine-eleven attack we heard that the preparation for that day must have been complex? This is no less so. It must have taken years to work out the details. It's brilliant even if it is warped."

Rooker studed her expression. "You've figured something out, haven't you? Something about the brains behind this?" His blue eyes sparked with hope. "Tell me. We'll get the jump on them before it's too late." For the first time in days he looked excited.

"I can't give you a name yet. I'm not seeing each move they make fast enough." Kate felt only irritation with herself. "Someone, an unfriendly country with one hell of a grudge against the U.S.—or al-Qaeda, or maybe ISIS—has supplied the brains behind this. Yes, it's about money, like Zed himself said. But it's more than that. I just wish we knew what that man in there knows." She hitched her chin toward the glass partition between her and the interrogation room.

Rooker tucked his hands into his rear pants pockets and rocked back on his heels. "Want me to beat it out of him?" he offered helpfully.

"Rooker." She studied him, not at all sure he wasn't serious.

"The Italians would do it in a minute, if I let them." He glanced behind him through the glass. One of the Carabiniere officers was leaning over the table, shouting in Zed's face. "They're pretty pissed off, him using their city as a staging ground for an attack."

"No doubt." She sighed and stared down into her empty mug. "Rooker, it's time we faced it.

"Faced what?"

"They've been two jumps ahead of us all the way. There's no reason to think, now that they've established control of HW-1, that they won't use it. Whatever they intend to do, it's going to happen, with or without Zed."

"We don't know that. He may be bluffing."

She looked away from him, fighting back a wave of emotion. "I just have a feeling he isn't," she whispered.

He turned away from her for a moment, as if letting the deadly consequences of her words sink in. When he looked back at her, he still appeared worried, but something had altered in his rough features.

"Sorry," he said brusquely.

She frowned. "For what?"

"I've given you a bad time from the start, and not nearly enough credit. We wouldn't have Zed now if you hadn't followed him last night." He hesitated. "Sometimes, I can be a jerk."

Adam was pretending to be busy checking his gear, his back to them. She couldn't imagine what he thought of their conversation.

"Yes, you can," she said, but couldn't help softening her words with a weak smile. "But then, we've all been under a lot of pressure."

"Right." He winced. His blue eyes, the only feature that ever seemed to give away his emotions, dimmed to a stormy gray. "We've missed our window of opportunity, haven't we? Four

No Mercy

more hours to their deadline, and the U.S. government isn't paying. It's official. I just got word from ASEC. No concessions to terrorists."

She pulled his jacket tighter around her shoulders, scared out of her mind for the innocents at the other end of Heat Wave's powerful energy, whoever they might turn out to be. "All we can do now is wait," she murmured.

"No." He stared through the glass pane at Zed. "I think I need to nurture a more forthcoming conversation with our prisoner."

Kate didn't ask how he intended to encourage this forthcomingness. She didn't want to know.

Chapter 26

An hour later, after Rooker had finished his conversation with Zed, to no avail, Kate and the remaining Worldwide Security team, returned to the hotel, licking their wounds and demoralized.

"We haven't failed," Rooker tried to reassure them in the van. "We did what we came to do, capture Zed. The rest of the job is on hold. We'll get the bastards, just not today."

But Kate could hear the disappointment in his voice and feel his anxiety, a mirror of her own. If Zed's threat was carried out, hundreds, possibly thousands of people would be injured or killed. And she could do nothing to stop it.

She showered and changed into jeans and a sweater to wait in the solitude of her hotel bedroom for news from the States. Her knees and chin were scraped and bruised. Her neck felt wrenched from Zed's strong grasp. She popped a couple Tylenol and tried to ignore the shadow of pain that didn't go away. But the discomfort seemed inconsequential when she looked at the battering Rooker's men had taken. And the suffering of others to come when broiling microwaves struck an unnamed city.

More than anything Kate wanted to call her mom and dad. But contact with anyone outside of the mission was strictly forbidden. She'd tried calling Mercy, but her cousin wasn't answering. God knew what clandestine assignment had pulled her away. What could be more critical than a rogue satellite? Kate's frustration matched her fear. She couldn't eat, couldn't sleep. Never had she felt so utterly helpless.

At last, she walked out of her room and into the suite's salon to find Rooker seated at a table, his phone lying in front of him. He was staring it down, as if he expected it to leap up and attack him. She set her cell phone on the table beside his and sat in the chair to his right.

"Wanna race?" he muttered.

191

No Mercy

She played along with his sarcasm. "My people will call before your people. Bet you a dollar."

Why did human beings in times of great stress fall back on humor? *And sex,* she added silently. After funerals, disasters, and a multitude of other emotionally devastating situations, sex often happens. Or so she'd heard. Friends or even complete strangers took comfort in the intimate touch of another human being. Was it just a distraction from pain? A shared connection no more intimate than a hug? Or something more.

Something raw and needy tugged from within her. She glanced at Rooker, then quickly away. A sensation of warmth spread up from her bottom. She squirmed a bit on the chair to make it go away.

Rooker stared at her. "Something wrong?"

"Umm...no." She grimaced, embarrassed. Such thoughts! What had gotten into her?

When she met his eyes again, they were a deep, disturbingly perceptive blue. She looked away quickly.

"Well, well," he said.

She slowly drew a breath. "Well, well, what, Rooker?"

"Your pheromones are showing, Doc."

"Where'd you learn a big word like that?" she snapped back but couldn't look him in the eye.

He didn't respond. What was the man thinking? Did he find her appealing? More than just casually interesting? She couldn't let the thought go. "And yours aren't?"

"What do you think?" Was that an invitation to check him out?

Kate started to bite down on her bottom lip, still raw from her confrontation with Zed, then quickly released it. She turned to face the man.

He lounged in the wooden chair. Long, blue-jeaned legs straight out in front of him beneath the table. Boots crossed at the ankles. The image of a man at ease.

But she could feel heat radiating off of him. An underlying tension in the muscles of his body telegraphed lust.

Her gaze drifted awkwardly, curiously to his lap for an instant then away. "Oh." She didn't think she was imagining an abnormal bulge.

"All your fault," he said, his voice low and deep.

Okay, she thought. *The right thing to do now is get to your feet, pick up your phone, and walk out of the room. Just don't let him know he's getting to you.*

But then she'd have been avoiding the issue. Which was what? Their shared arousal? She forced herself to meet his gaze.

"Do you get *that way* after every battle?" she asked, conversationally.

"Not every time." A whisper of a smile. "There isn't always an appealing partner to help out with the release mechanism."

She opened her mouth. Closed it. Tried again to come up with something witty. Nothing.

"What about you, Doc? After discovering a new star or launching a probe to Saturn, do you feel horny?" His eyes locked on her face. One corner of his lips ticked up in amusement. "Do you jump the nearest physicist's bones?"

"Rooker!"

"Took it too far, huh?" He shrugged but didn't look at all remorseful. "Well, any time you feel the urge, you know where to find me."

"Sure." She laughed, hoping he'd think she was taking it all as a joke.

But when she glanced back at him, he wasn't smiling. He reached out and touched one finger to her lips, once, lightly. "You won't forget?"

"No," she whispered, heart fluttering. She looked away hastily. "No, I won't forget."

The call they'd all dreaded came at twenty minutes after noon, Rome time—6:20 a.m. on the U.S. East Coast.

Kate's cell phone, sitting on the table in the hotel suite, rang and vibrated. Rooker turned immediately to her before looking down at her phone's glowing screen.

"It's NASA," she said when her lab's number came up on the screen. She picked it up, pressed the speaker button so that others in the room could hear. Most of the WSS team had gathered in the sitting room. "Foster here."

"It's happened." Cam sounded out of breath.

Rooker swore.

No Mercy

Kate closed her eyes. "God help us." Her ribs felt as if they were wrapped round by metal straps and cinched up so tight she could hardly breathe. "Rooker's here with me. What's going on? What happened? How bad is it?"

"The target wasn't a specific town or city as we'd expected."

"Where?" Rooker barked.

Kate pressed a hand to his shoulder, urging patience she knew neither of them had.

"Microwave surges disrupted then shut down the major power grid serving portions of the eastern U.S.," Cam continued. "So far it looks as though at least eight states are affected, from Maine to Virginia, and all major cities, including New York City, Boston, Philly, and D.C. are without power. It happened about half an hour ago."

Rooker looked puzzled. "So it's not that bad, right?" Behind him, his team was gathering to listen in. "I mean, people can live without their lights for a while. Happens all the time after a bad storm. No human casualties so far."

Kate shook her head solemnly. He didn't get it. "We're not just talking about doing without the AC or TV for a few days. If the energy from Heat Wave was sufficient to knock out the grid, it's also interfering with every vital electrical system."

Cambridge continued. "Homeland Security has started to hear from hospitals and metro transit systems. Air traffic control at Kennedy and Dulles are down. Probably other airports in the region too."

"Operating rooms and life support in critical care units—" Kate was thinking out loud now, focusing on the phone "—they can switch to their generators for a limited time."

She'd failed to think about so many possible complications. *Damn!* Why hadn't she seen this coming?

Kate stared at Rooker, who looked confused. Her voice cracked but she forced out an explanation. "Anything electrical is affected by high-level microwave emissions. Pacemakers, medicine released through implanted dosing mechanisms. People are dying over there. We just haven't heard about it yet!"

Kathryn Johnson

Rooker's expression turned lethal. His eyes hard as steel, lips pressed together in fury. This, Kate thought, is a man the wise wouldn't push too far. Zed had crossed that line long ago.

"Is Mercy O'Brien with you there?" she asked.

"Yeah, how'd you know?"

"I just hoped she'd stay close. Put her on."

Mercy's voice sounded grim and half an octave lower than the last time Kate had spoken to her. "I'm sorry I've been out of touch. Things have been pretty busy here. How are you holding up, Katie?"

"A little battered, but okay, I guess."

"I heard you opted in for a little hand-to-hand combat last night?"

Kate laughed wearily. "Not my choice." It wasn't a topic she wanted to dwell on. Besides, there were more important issues. "Are there reported fatalities yet?"

"Too soon to say. I've just checked with Johns Hopkins and Washington Adventist hospitals. They're beginning to get some E.R. admissions but haven't had enough time to evaluate the causes. We expect serious radiation burns to anyone in the immediate area struck by the microwave emissions. Not here in DC but near the Hudson Power Station, upstate New York. The Red Cross has been alerted."

Kate nodded and pressed a hand over her eyes. The elderly, infants and, possibly, fetuses in the womb would be most vulnerable. But direct and prolonged exposure to high-intensity microwave energy could kill anyone.

Mercy continued speaking, but all Kate could focus on was the misery she might have prevented.

"Katie, you still there?"

Rooker cleared his throat. "The doctor got a taste of hell last night. I think she needs to be relieved of her position as—"

"No!" Kate objected, throwing him a furious glare although she was even now fighting back tears. "This is *my* responsibility."

Mercy's voice came across low, solemn and controlled.

"Kate, *you* didn't do this. These bastards with no respect for human life did it."

"You don't understand. If I'd ever once thought that I might be creating a weapon, I'd never have supported this project. I

No Mercy

believed I was only doing good." She gasped, holding onto the table's edge, so close to losing it. Losing everything.

Kate sensed Rooker waving the men away from them. They silently retreated to the other end of the room. His hand rested on her back, reassuring. But unable to make the evil, the wickedness go away.

"It's not your fault," Mercy repeated. "Rooker, you there still?"

He leaned toward the phone. "Yeah, here."

"Get Kate into bed. See that she gets some rest. There's nothing she can do at the moment. And we may need her fully functioning later."

"The first part I can do. Whether or not she'll get any sleep is—"

"Not funny, Rooker!" Kate said pulling away from his hand.

"Yes, ma'am." He turned his attention back to the phone. "Ms. O'Brien, are we to stay in Rome or ready up to move out again?"

"As soon as I know anything more, I'll let you know. The situation could change at any moment. Meanwhile, sit tight."

Kate rested her elbows on the table, head in her hands, eyes closed. "Mercy, please tell whoever's in charge that I should come home now. I need to be with the team in Heat Wave lab. It might make a difference."

Mercy's sigh was unmistakable through the phone. Was it from frustration with her? Or the exhaustion they all shared. "Hold on. Let me ask."

The line went silent for no more than a minute then Mercy was back. "Sorry, cuz. The powers that be want you where you are for the time being. If it's any comfort, your gang here is amazing. They're doing everything they can, I'm sure."

Kate's heart dropped. "But—"

"We can't let them win, Katie. We *won't*!" Mercy, always so strong. How did she do it? "Hang in there. We'll beat them. Somehow."

"Okay," she managed to whisper. But it was hard. So very hard to believe they could do anything at all to stop this fiasco before things got even worse. Because, when all was said and done, sometimes the dark side won.

Three hours later Mercy called back with an estimated casualty count. So far, directly related to radiation sickness, over four hundred people had been admitted into various hospitals, twenty-six more were DOA. Police, fire and rescue workers were evacuating the area bombarded by microwave rays as quickly as possible. Assorted other injuries related to the strike on the power grid numbered in the thousands, all up and down the East Coast of the U.S.

Meanwhile, the entire country was in a state of panic. Congress demanded to know the facts behind the attack. The press, politicians, religious leaders were criticizing the President for not having acted quickly enough. For keeping knowledge of the threat from the public.

Kate stayed with Rooker and his men in the suite. Unable to sleep, she waited out the hours, hoping against hope for some good news. She couldn't have kept food down, she was certain. Her stomach felt as if she were riding an endless amusement park ride. Hot tea was the most she could manage.

As she stared out the window at the busy streets of Rome, at people unaware of a handful of foreigners using their city to stage a crime against humanity, Mercy's words sank in. And with them, Kate felt renewed determination to prevent further suffering.

She would find a way to take back what was hers, her satellite. And if she couldn't, she'd destroy it. Or die trying.

No Mercy

Chapter 27

Rooker didn't wait for Washington to provide new intelligence and tell him where next to deploy his team. As far as he was concerned, his government had blown it with its ridiculous noncompliance stance. Not that he thought extortionists should be rewarded for their efforts. Far from it.

To his way of thinking, you didn't play fair with the Hitlers and al-Qaedas of the world, you played them. Tell them, "Yeah, sure, you'll get your money. Yup, we're so scared, we'll hand over a country or two."

Promise them the world. Match lies for lies, deceit for deceit. That was the only way to outfox the devil.

Rooker had lured, trapped, captured or killed a dozen Zeds. When it came down to the moment of truth, some chose not to be taken alive, others possessed egos so immense they believed they could outfight anyone. He hunted them down. He pulled the trigger. He lost no sleep over it.

The truth was: You didn't go after maniacs and killing machines in a half-assed way. You went at them as hard as you could. Because if you didn't, they sure as hell would keep on bringing misery to the world, loving every minute of it.

He'd known from the beginning that calling Zed's bluff by refusing to pay the ransom was a mistake. As it turned out, the cost in human lives and loss to the American economy was far greater than the ten million that had been demanded.

But Rooker was certain this was only the beginning. There would be higher demands made by whoever had taken over for Zed in the organization, and other strikes. Maybe far more destructive.

Meanwhile, the U.S. Department of Energy and regional power companies would need weeks to fully restore the damaged electrical grid. Any unfriendly country observing this weakness might see this as an opportunity. Take advantage of the temporary paralysis of the American government and economy.

Kathryn Johnson

A country without communications or reliable transportation was vulnerable.

That was why he'd contacted a man as dangerous as Antonio Ricci.

Rooker had first met Ricci in Naples, nearly ten years earlier. After Rooker left Iraq and cut his ties with the CIA, he'd done freelance work for Ricci. On the surface, the Italian ran a legitimate Rome-based private investigation and security service, providing protection for Italian industrialists, bankers, politicians and visiting celebrities. In every country around the world today, fortunes were being made in security. Italy was no exception.

But Ricci played the game with a twist. People who chose to hire bodyguards from competing services sometimes ended up being kidnapped anyway, their families running in desperation to Ricci for help in recovering their loved one. Ricci had a suspiciously high success rate of working out deals with kidnappers and rescuing victims. Usually in one piece or, at least, with nothing more vital missing than a finger or two.

Rooker suspected that a good chunk of the ransom money often ended up in Ricci's pocket, along with his substantial finder's fee.

However corrupt the Italian might be, Ricci could be useful. Because he knew how to find virtually anyone in Italy. Rooker contacted him and was invited to drive out to his villa.

He rented a little red Fiat and drove into the Sabine hills, toward Tivoli. He passed beyond the industrial areas immediately outside of Rome, through rough terrain riddled with travertine quarries, and thirty kilometers on into agricultural land of gray-green olive groves outlined in centuries'-old stone walls. He knew only enough of the local history to remember that these ancient hillsides were where the wealthiest Romans, two thousand years ago and more, had built their homes to get away from the pressures of city life.

At last he reached Antonio's estate—the mansion a vision in pale marble and Corinthian columns, gleaming in the sunlight. Ricci himself greeted him at the door. They walked through the house and sat beside one of three outdoor pools surrounding the villa, sipping Camparis in the warm sunshine while Rooker explained what had been happening in Rome and the States.

199

No Mercy

Ricci had, of course, heard the news of the attack on America and the raid in Rome, but was eager for more information. Rooker suspected that any crime, or reaction from law enforcement, might be critical to the Italian's own business, legitimate or not.

"Diabolico!" Ricci exclaimed, looking properly disgusted. He made a dismissive gesture with one hand. "But these *criminali* you seek, they certainly will have left Italy by now. No? "

"That would be the logical thing to do, keep moving," Rooker agreed.

Ricci peeled a blood orange. The patio around him was already littered with the red-flecked skins and orange pits.

"A pity. I'd like to be in on this." No doubt the entrepreneur in him saw a possibility of profit. "I resent outsiders. Does not matter whether they are ISIS or al Queada or garden variety hoodlums. I don't want them in my country. Besides, Americans are good customers. I wouldn't like to lose potential clients." His gaze fell placidly over the pool. He observed one of several young women who had been sunbathing when Rooker arrived. She struck a pose at the pool's edge then dove into the clear blue water. Their host delicately tucked another slice of juicy fruit into his mouth and chewed.

"I was hoping you might circulate word of our problem among your associates," Rooker said. "They may hear something useful on the streets. Bragging is half the fun of pulling off something this big. Someone involved will want others to know."

"An indiscreet word in a bar?"

"Or in bed." Rooker knocked back the rest of his Campari. He was a vodka martini man, but this stuff had a bitter kick that wasn't half bad. "This isn't the kind of effort that could have been mounted without involving more people than just Zed and the two thugs he brought with him into the NASA installation."

"Si, " Ricci murmured, turning his attention back to his guest. "Those four men you took in the raid in Rome. Word reached me before you came today. They were members of a local *banda.* No brain, just muscle. This Zed, I do not know at all."

"He's definitely an American. And not the brains behind this either. Whoever is ultimately responsible for the satellite-jacking won't be the one to brag about his exploits. But henchmen might."

Ricci nodded. "I will let you know."

"It has to be soon," Rooker reminded him.

"Of course." The Italian smiled and tossed a crimson skin over his shoulder. "I will do this for you, my friend, as a personal favor."

Rooker winced. Being indebted to Antonio Ricci wasn't a comfortable position to be in. Unfortunately, he had little choice.

No Mercy

Kate looked up from where she lay on the couch in the hotel suite. She must have fallen asleep. Someone had thrown a blanket over her. She needed a shower badly. She needed food, but only in the way an engine requires fuel to operate. She still had no appetite.

Adam was cleaning his rifle, sitting in the armchair nearest to her. No one else was around. The suite was dead quiet.

"Where is everyone?" she asked, pushing herself up and stretching. Her gaze automatically slid to her cell phone. No messages. But no news, in this case, wasn't necessarily good news.

"Rooker gave them shore leave."

She smiled. "Watch out, women of Rome!"

Adam grinned. "Yeah. The boys are a little wound up."

"Why aren't you out with them?"

He shrugged. "I had stuff to do." He nodded at his Glock and the Steyr.

She didn't point out that he had plenty of time to tend to firearms. He'd stayed behind why? To look after her? To spy on her for his boss?

"Is Rooker on shore leave too?" The thought of him with a woman—the shore leave kind of woman—made her heart ping, although she didn't know why. Ridiculous the way her emotions were toying with her lately.

"He said he had a meeting."

"Oh." She stood up and combed her fingers through her hair. Like everything else she did, it seemed a useless effort. "I think I'll take a walk to wake myself up. Or has your boss ordered you to keep me here?"

Adam looked unsure whether he should answer or not. "I guess so long as you take your phone it's okay. Don't go too far."

"Right." She went off to find her athletic shoes.

Kathryn Johnson

Five minutes later, she stepped off the elevator in the hotel lobby...and found herself nose to nose with Rook. "We need to talk," he said, taking her arm and spinning her around to walk her back into the elevator before the door could close.

"I was going to get some exercise." She pulled her arm out of his grasp and hit the Door Open button. "Can't we talk while walking?"

He shrugged. "I guess. Yeah, why not?" He gave her a brief smile but it failed to light up his face. He didn't look like a soldier returning from R&R and the attentions of a cooperative female. Dark circles shadowed his eyes. The lines at the corners of his eyes and mouth appeared cut into stone. He followed her off the elevator and out the hotel door.

By the end of the first block Kate had revved up to a long, loping stride, her arms pumping at her sides. By the middle of the second she'd hit her normal workout pace. Rooker had to break into a jog to keep up with her.

"So, what do we need to talk about?" she asked.

"I have to know exactly what will happen if we can't run to ground these bastards. What if General Kinsley gets his way and orders your satellite blown up?"

She assumed since Rooker wasn't off chasing down new leads with the Carabiniere, the Italians had gotten nothing useful out of Zed—such as who had enlisted him or names of others in his organization.

"I don't believe the White House will let him destroy it." She had already given this deep thought. "But, theoretically, if Homeland Security gave nod and the President went along with Kinsley's plan, their best bet would be to put a missile in a trajectory that matches Heat Wave's." She hated to even think of this option, but it was something they all had to consider.

"Not just hit the thing head on?"

She shook her head. "Characters in movies blow up stuff like meteors and invading spaceships as if they were sitting here on Earth. You can't really do it that way when there's no atmosphere. Explosives don't work the same way in space."

"So how does one take out a satellite?"

"Ram it with something bigger. Destroy it by impact." Her insides knotted at the thought. Her life's work, shattered.

No Mercy

Daniel Rooker looked thoughtful. They kept on at a half-run, weaving between slower moving pedestrians, Kate murmuring an occasional *"Mi scusi!"*

"I gather from what you said before, the rubble doesn't just flutter to Earth like harmless snowflakes."

She laughed. "As long as the pieces of metal are in orbit, the wreckage will likely keep circling in the same path in which the satellite had been traveling, or in a parallel orbit into which it gets knocked. But there are all sorts of international implications we haven't even begun to take into account."

"Like who owns what orbital paths?"

Kate glanced at him, surprised. "Impressive, Rooker."

"I do use something other than a gun to think with, sometimes."

"I'm sure you do," she said, dropping her eyes down his body, unable not to tease.

He grinned. "That, too."

She grinned and shook her head at him, keeping her stride fast and long. "I'm sure."

"So what are some other international problems?" he asked.

"The missile or shrapnel from the sat might accidentally strike another country's satellite. That could be interpreted as an act of war."

"Really?"

"Really. And that might make the other satellite fall out of orbit, plummet to earth and cause property damage or loss of life. Will the country where it lands just shrug off the incident as bad luck? Not if the government is looking to instigate an international incident."

"A government like North Korea?"

"Exactly."

"But," Rooker said, "if it's done right, if we demolish Heat Wave in the proper way, we could abandon the remains up there. They'll just keep going round and round. We wouldn't have to worry about wreckage falling on populated areas."

She shook her head. "Orbital space is too valuable. More than eight hundred satellites circle Earth already. They've been launched by dozens of governments and private companies. Each

Kathryn Johnson

one is chock full of sophisticated, priceless equipment. It's too dangerous to leave junk floating around."

They crossed another busy street. He was breathing easily, keeping up with her now with no noticeable effort. "So how do you clean house up there?"

"Do you remember the satellite the U.S. intentionally brought down that made the news a few years back?"

"The one that crashed into the Utah desert?"

"Right. It had collected immensely valuable information and samples. We'd hoped to learn a great deal from it when we retrieved it. We still had full control of the computers, so we altered the trajectory and brought it back within our atmosphere. Parachutes were supposed to slow its descent."

His dry laugh took her by surprise. "I remember now! They even had a crew of Hollywood stunt guys who were supposed to snag the thing from a plane as it came down. To keep it from getting busted up."

"Right. But the 'chutes never deployed. What didn't burn up on re-entry into the atmosphere hit the ground at full force. The capsule disintegrated on impact and left one heck of a crater."

"Not the best outcome for you geeks, but—" He shrugged. "You could do that with the HW-1, couldn't you? That would at least take the satellite out of enemy hands."

"Yes, but we first need to regain computer control. And bringing it down safely would be a very tricky job. This satellite, with all its gear attached, is about a fourth of the size of a football field. Can you imagine what would happen if it survived reentry? What if the calculations were off by just a few degrees? Instead of coming down in a desert or the ocean, it might plow into Brooklyn or LA."

"Or in China," he said, "or somewhere in the Middle East." When she glanced sideways at him, his face had taken on an ashen color. "Talk about international incidents."

"Exactly." Kate was starting to breathe harder now, and it felt good. Deep inhales. Long, full breaths out. She imagined oxygen reaching corners of her lungs that her anxious, shallow breaths had been unable to supply for days. Moving, doing *something* instead of sitting in a room and waiting for the next

205

horrible thing to happen, energized her mind as well as her body. The tightness in her chest loosened. Her head felt clearer.

"I think," she said, "our best hope is still to find whoever is controlling Heat Wave."

They sped on, crossing streets, circling back now toward the hotel. The sights and smells of Rome all around her, begging her to explore. *Not now,* she told them. *We've got another civilization to save.*

Neither of them spoke for several minutes. Rooker broke the silence. "One more question. What if, in the process of catching up with them, we end up inadvertently killing the only person who knows how to access your sat? The guy in control."

She grimaced. "*That* would complicate things."

"Right. Like they aren't already."

Kathryn Johnson

Kate tucked the cell phone between her shoulder and ear while she pried off her athletic shoes. Reaching Jessup, the Chief of Operations at NASA-Weston, hadn't been easy. But she wanted to clarify her role in the ongoing hunt. "Just because the FBI wants me to stay in Italy doesn't mean I have to, does it?" Kate asked. "I mean, you are my boss, not them."

"It wasn't their decision." Jessup's voice sounded unusually stressed. She didn't doubt that he was taking a lot of flak for what had happened. He'd have to answer to everyone, from the Oval Office to the Pentagon and Congress, for the security breach. "Homeland Security is making all the calls now."

"Good grief." She tossed her shoes in the general direction of her luggage and gently rubbed her knees, still sore and bruised from her scuffle in the alley.

"What's happening with that man Dan Rooker's team nabbed?"

"Zed? Last I heard, the U.S. State Department and Italian government were haggling over legal jurisdiction."

Zed had been on Italian soil while committing an act of terrorism. It didn't seem to matter to the Italians that the power grid he'd struck was located on American soil. She could see a whole new can of worms in international law opening up and, honestly, she wanted nothing to do with it.

Kate finished talking with Jessup, checked in with her people at NASA again, then decided it was time for a shower and food.

She still felt the places where Zed had grabbed her, leaving deep, purply-green bruises at her throat and across her ribs. But the hot spray of the shower felt soothing, and hours of sweat and city grime washed away, leaving her skin feeling rejuvenated.

Some of her best ideas came to her beneath a steaming rush of water. The first step toward inspiration was always wiping the slate clean. She firmly put the problem of Heat Wave out of her mind and turned her face up into the hot prickly droplets. Then she gave her subconscious permission to take over while overworked ganglia recuperated.

She toweled off and returned to her bedroom, found a clean bra and underwear and put them on. She was debating between her navy-blue pants suit or something more casual when a voice called out from the other side of her door.

"You in there?"

"Yes, Rooker, I'm in here." She sighed. All she wanted was a few more minutes of peace. Alone. Was that too much to ask?

"There's something I need to say to you," he said. The door flew open.

Kate stared at the man as he stepped into the room and closed the door behind him. "You're doing this on purpose, aren't you?"

"What?"

"You wait until you think I'm naked and then walk right in without knocking."

"Do I?" He grinned, eyes brighter than they'd been in days.

"You are so obvious. This is the second time you've pulled this stunt." She shook her head in exasperation. At least she was as decently clothed as most women when wearing a bikini.

Daniel Rooker's gaze took in her scantily covered parts, then skipped back to observe her face. He grinned. "Best view in the city!"

"Give me a break. You don't even like me." She crossed the room to her closet to retrieve her blouse and suit.

"I never said that."

"It's obvious. We're like oil and water. And to tell the truth, I'm sick of bickering with you. Sick of this whole business. I just want someone to catch these monsters so I can go home."

Although home would never seem quite the same. Certainly not as safe as it had once felt. It must be mayhem in DC now. She wondered if the electricity had been restored everywhere, if critical support systems were functioning again. Even if they were, nothing could replace the lives already lost.

"We all want to catch them." He stuffed his hands into his pockets and tipped his head to one side, slanting blue eyes up to study her body openly. And then his gaze settled on her bruised ribs. He stepped closer. His expression hardened. "I didn't know he'd hurt you that bad."

"It's nothing. I'm fine. Now get out of here so I can finish dressing."

He didn't move.

"Rooker."

"Is that what you want?" His smile came back, but his voice sounded different. Tighter. Lower, with a little rasp to it. "What do you really want, Kate? Because it's hard to tell with you. You keep so much inside. Hard to read a woman like that."

She blinked, remembering their banter earlier in the day, and then again as they'd walked through the city. How turned on she'd felt. How annoyed she'd been at feeling that way.

"Out," she said.

"Funny—" he strolled toward her, hands out of pockets now "—you're trying to look pissed. But I have an entirely different impression of your mood."

She snatched clothes out of her closet, without paying attention to what they were, and brought them back to the bed. She refused to look at him but could imagine his eyes—dark, dangerous in a playful way. Seductive. "I didn't ask for your opinion on my moods or anything else."

If he'd heard her at all, he didn't let on. "I think you're horny as hell, Kate."

"Oh, give me a break, Rooker!"

Had there been anything handy she could have thrown at him—preferably something hard, with sharp edges—she would have heaved it at his head.

"Just because I admitted, in a very weak moment," she tossed over her shoulder, "that I might have had a brief trauma-induced sexual fantasy, doesn't mean I'm lusting after you."

He moved quickly, wrapping his arms around her gently from behind, avoiding her bruises.

Kate spun within the circle of his strong arms and braced her palms against his chest. She pushed away but gained barely an inch of space between them. "What the hell do you think you're doing?"

"I'm taking the edge off. For both of us."

No Mercy

"The hell you are!" She jerked her knee up with purpose between his thighs, but he shifted his hips. She came up in empty air.

"Now, now," he scolded. "That wasn't very nice."

"Let me go or I'll scream. You don't want to set a bad example for your men by behaving dishonorably."

"They're still out carousing."

"Adam then."

"I chased him out. We're alone."

"Damn you, Rooker." But she didn't put a lot of conviction into her cussing.

His expression softened. She could almost believe she saw tenderness in those blue eyes. "Kate, I'm not going to hurt you. I just wanted to get your attention. So I could make sure you were listening when I told you something important."

"What?" She closed her eyes and dropped her forehead onto his chest. Leaning into him was just easier than fighting his strength. Or so she told herself. The truth was, he felt good. Really good. All of him up against her this way—solid and hard in all the right places.

Of course, she wasn't about to share that with him. He'd never let her forget it.

"I just wanted to tell you," he began again, "that you scared the hell out of me when I couldn't find you. When you took off after Zed."

She laughed. "Thought I was going to lose him, huh?"

"I thought I was going to lose *you.*"

Her eyes flashed open but she didn't pull her cheek away from his chest. Warmth seeped into her flesh from his, through her pores, spreading through her body. This man's words, so unexpected, sent a flush of heat and longing to every part of her.

Who would have thought? Rooker was being kind, sweet.

"Kate. Things can only get worse," he whispered. "This situation, I mean. I don't want you in the middle of it."

Her hand crept up between their bodies. She played with the top button of his shirt. Thought about popping it open and pressing her fingertips to his breast bone. "I've been ordered to stay in Italy. Remember?"

"You can refuse. It's not as if you're in the military. You're a private citizen. You said you want to go home. Do it. Go to the airport. Take the next flight out. Let us take care of things here."

How very tempting that was. "You know that's impossible, Rooker."

"Daniel," he said.

"Daniel." His name felt so strange on her tongue. And his attitude? Could this be the same man? "What if someone has to disarm Heat Wave? We've gone over this a dozen times."

"I know but..." She could feel his body tense. "Kate."

"Yes?"

"I want to make..."

Make what? she thought. Make me leave? Make up for the arguments and bossiness? Make...*love*? She felt dizzy. She squeezed her eyes closed, trying to steady herself.

"Aw, hell," he said, "we've probably both got warrior's itch. That's all."

Kate turned her face into his shirtfront and breathed in his musky male scent. Nice. Very, very nice. Yes, this could be just about sex between two people thrown together into traumatic circumstances. Sex and nothing more.

Or not.

Because there was one truth she couldn't let go of. *He cared.* The arrogant, overbearing man cared about her. That much she understood from the way he was holding her, talking to her.

"I have a suggestion," she whispered.

"What?" He sounded prepared for the worst.

"Kiss me."

Daniel Rooker went absolutely still for a moment. She was sure he'd stopped breathing. Then his chest filled and he levered her a few inches away from him. He slowly lowered his mouth over hers.

Her insides liquified.

Damn. He was right. She wanted him...or sex in some form...or maybe just to be held. It was so confusing and unexpected, these emotions.

They kissed—long and hard, and then sweetly. Their lips started to part, but he came back for more and she was glad. Her body was a rocket, launched on a new trajectory. Out of Safe-

No Mercy

Hold, shooting off in hyper-drive. She felt sexually sentient, awakened for the first time in...how long? Years?

The last relationship she'd had was during the second year of the Heat Wave Project. Kate couldn't remember why it ended. She only knew she hadn't been particularly sad at the time. In the months that followed, she'd told herself that she didn't miss male companionship. Her science had consumed the days and nights. Her staff had become both family and friends. She'd been satisfied with the life she had.

But now...now as she stood in this man's embrace, feeling his unmistakable physical reaction to her, her own body responded with a fierceness that shocked her. Compelling her to get even closer to him. Although that was physically impossible without...well, actually, yes, without stripping off the remainder of her clothing and letting him inside her.

And. of course, that was such a preposterous thought. Allow him to make love to her? She'd never *just have sex* with a man. Without any sense of commitment. Without believing they shared interests, philosophies of life. Choosing a lover, like everything else in Kate's world, was the result of a series of logical events. In college, she'd even written a sexual attraction formula: $[(M + F) R] L = S$

As silly as it sounded now, she'd applied this formula to every man she'd ever dated. Most didn't pass the test. Only two had ever gotten farther than a kiss at her doorstep. Now though, as Rooker's hands started to wander her body, she found it difficult to recall what the stupid equation meant.

Rooker's hand slipped up inside her blouse. He flicked two fingers behind her back, and she felt her bra pop open. She gasped at the intimacy of his hand on her flesh between her shoulder blades.

Concentrate. The equation. Yes, that was it. *M for male. F for female. Factor into the relationship R for respect, then Love. The result was S—Sexual gratification.*

Respect Rooker? Love him? Did she?

"Oh, my!" She was having considerable trouble breathing. "That feels so...won-der-ful." She opened her eyes. He'd gone down on his knees. She looked down at the top of his head. Her blouse was open, bra pushed up. His mouth was over her breast. His tongue moved across her nipple. She quivered. Gasped.

To hell with equations!

Kate let her head drop back. She released a gasp of pleasure.

"Doc? You okay in there?" Adam. Back in the suite. Outside her door.

Oh, my God!

And now she could hear other voices, and a loud clack. The door into the suite from the main corridor had closed.

Rooker swore under his breath and pressed his head between her breasts.

"I'm fine, Adam," she managed to answer through the thankfully-still-closed bedroom door. But her voice sounded far too breathy to her own ears.

There was a moment's hesitation from beyond the door. Whispering. She could imagine the men exchanging looks. A wink? An elbow jab? And Adam's pout: the infatuated boy-man...jealous.

"God, what are we doing?" she rasped, embarrassed beyond words.

"Don't know, but it sure is fun." Rooker, still down on his knees, looked up at her and raised a dark eyebrow in supplication. "Do we need to stop?"

She reached down and wrestled him to his feet. "Yes, of course we need to *stop*!" She stifled her own whimper of remorse. "They must know what we're doing."

"But—"

She raised her voice to project beyond the bedroom door. "Rooker, I told you! Whether you like it or not, I'm staying right here in Italy until this crisis is settled."

"Oh, that'll fool 'em," he whispered in her ear.

"Shut up," she hissed. She reached both hands around to reconnect her bra, slipped on the blouse she'd pulled from the closet.

Rooker made an agonized face, punched the air with both fists—one, two—like a frustrated prize fighter. He scuffed at the carpet and finally paced away from her while making low, growly sounds of frustration.

No Mercy

"Oh, come now." Bad choice of words. But she didn't dare laugh at his temper tantrum because she was paying too, in her own way.

Hormones alerted and flowing, she'd been just as ready as he. And now her body was trying to deal with a barrage of potent chemicals that had no place to go. She knew the biology, just wasn't sure what to do about it.

Kate snatched the rest of her clothes off the bed and ducked into the bathroom. She came out fully clothed, five minutes later, to find Daniel Rooker still standing in the middle of the room.

She rolled her eyes. "I can't do this. Could never even think of doing this, with anyone. Not with a cheering section in the next room."

Rooker's expression brightened. "Right. No onlookers. Plenty of other hotels in Rome."

But by now she'd regained her sanity. "Rooker, we have work to do." She ignored his copycat eye roll. "And I have to figure out what just happened here."

The hard edges of his face softened, but only a little. "You mean about us? You think too much, Doc... Kate."

"Probably," she admitted. But she couldn't help who she was. Even if curling up in his arms seemed like a great way to escape the insanity that had swept her away this past week.

Kathryn Johnson

Kate plugged into the NASA database. Although a massive effort was being made at home to drive a wedge through the hijackers' control of HW-1 and reclaim the satellite, the white-hat hackers kept hitting cyberwalls. She couldn't simply sit and wait for the next strike.

Kate propped herself up in bed with her laptop, blocking out the chatter and male energy beyond the bedroom door. She had eaten finally—crusty Italian bread, slices of cheese and spicy, hard sausage. A carafe of hot, black coffee sat on the bedside table. She focused on her screen and drank cup after cup until her head buzzed and the figures streaming before her eyes vibrated on her laptop screen.

No matter what combinations she tried, nothing worked. Maybe, after all, they had lost the game. She felt sick at the thought.

There was a knock on her door. She looked at the clock: 2:38 a.m. If it was Rooker, she didn't have the strength to fend him off. Maybe she didn't even want to. But she pulled her robe closed across her breasts out of habit.

"Yes?"

"Saw the light under your door. You decent, Doc?" Adam cautiously poked his head around the door's edge. "I made some herb tea. Noticed you sometimes liked it. Maybe time for a change from the high-test?"

"You're a wise man." She smiled and couldn't help thinking how much he reminded her of her younger brother. Light colored eyes of an indeterminate hue. Slim build. Strong, but in a wiry, way—no bulky muscles. It didn't matter how good-looking he was. She'd never be able to react to him the way she had to Rooker. The way Adam undoubtedly fantasized. "Thanks, Adam."

No Mercy

He set the steaming mug on the nightstand but didn't leave. After an awkward moment he said, "The guys and I...we all wanted to say we're glad Zed didn't hurt you bad."

She'd overheard them talking in the sitting room beyond her door earlier. Peterson was still in the hospital, but it looked as if he'd be able to fly home within a few days. He'd asked Rooker to let him rejoin the team to finish the mission, but Rooker refused. He could have called up another man to replace him, but decided the team would work just as well with a tightly coordinated six.

She thought people must be insane to voluntarily go into this line of work. How did you live any kind of normal life while on a constant state of alert? Never knowing when circumstances would force you to use violence to protect others or save your own life.

"Thank you. That's very kind of you," she murmured. "All of you."

Adam nodded. "Better get some rest, Doc. Soon as they lock down on another signal we'll be on the move again."

She smiled at him. "I know."

Kate drank her tea then leaned back against the pillows propped up behind her. She wasn't aware of closing her eyes.

Kate woke up with a start at the sound of her computer screeching at her. She sat up on the bed, pulled the laptop over to her, shut off the e-mail alarm and checked the screen.

Cambridge had been trying to reach her. Messages with little red exclamation marks crowded the screen. *Urgent! Urgent! Urgent!* She grabbed her cell phone from the night table. "Damn!" How could she have forgotten to charge it? The thing flashed an angry "low-battery" symbol at her. That's why it hadn't rung.

But why hadn't NASA contacted Rooker if something critical had happened?

Quickly Kate scanned Cam's messages, plugged in her phone and connected with the lab.

Cam picked up before the first ring died. "Where the hell have you been?"

"Right here. Passed out cold."

"I hope the party was worth it."

"No party. What's up?"

"A lot. Bad news all around, I'm afraid."

Kate's heart sank. "Hit me with it."

"They've found Frank."

It took her a moment to equate finding her chief physicist with bad news. The lining of her mouth suddenly tasted vinegary. Locating Frank Hess should have been good news. Unless...

"He's dead?" she whispered.

"I'm sorry, Kate. His body was found in a stolen car out on some country road near Olney, Maryland. Maybe fifteen miles from here. He was..." She choked up. "They said it was made to look like he'd crashed into a tree and the car had caught on fire. But the fire investigator is pretty sure the fire was intentionally set, after the collision. There wasn't much left of him."

"They're sure it was him?" She didn't want to believe it. Until now, she'd held out a slim measure of hope.

"A NASA ID and key card were melted into him."

"Oh." She felt as if the last of her strength had seeped from her body. Tears welled in her eyes.

"Are you all right?"

Kate pressed her fingertips into her eye sockets and rubbed away the burning. There was more. Cam had said there was more. She had to hold on. Couldn't fall apart over Frank. Not when she'd already known, deep in her heart, that they must have killed him by now. Gotten rid of him before leaving the country. Of course they would have.

"I'll be okay. What else?"

"While I was trying to reach you, a new demand was made."

"Yes?"

"The *Chicago Tribune* received an anonymous call about an hour ago. Chicago is their next target."

Kate winced. The Windy City. The city where she'd grown up.

"At first the newspaper didn't know if the call was legit or a hoax," Cam continued. "They contacted Homeland Security anyway. The FBI ran the recording and believe it's for real. Archer got word to us."

"Where in Chicago?" Kate asked.

No Mercy

"No specifics. It could be another major power grid or something else entirely."

Kate imagined the awful possibilities: Wrigley Field, filled with thousands of people; the downtown Loop jammed with office buildings, hotels, condos. But mostly she thought about her parents in the big old house off of Lake Shore Drive that had been her grandparents' home. The house of her childhood.

Her insides felt raw. She swallowed once, twice, before she could speak again.

"How much time do we have?"

"Forty-eight hours. They want ten billion this time."

So Rooker was right after all. They'd shown their strength. Now they were going for the big money. And maybe a worse catastrophe with more lives lost? Why not? They were having fun.

Kate's thoughts whirled. She tried to reach out and pluck anything coherent out of the maelstrom. "Forty-eight hours," she breathed. That gave them a little more time. But how to best use it?

"Don't your mom and dad live out there somewhere?" Cam's voice had lost its usual crisp self-assurance.

"Yes, and my brother and his family."

Kate couldn't wrap her mind around the idea that she might lose all of them in one immense burst of energy. Of her own making. *Oh, God!*

"Kate. "

She forced thoughts of burned flesh and agonizing pain from her mind. Thoughts of jets attempting to land at O'Hare without benefit of guidance systems and air traffic control. "Do we know yet where the command signal is coming from?"

"NSA says it's still originating from somewhere in your part of the world. Not Rome. In the Veneto region. The Italian government is trying to get a fix on the actual location."

Kate shoved herself off of the bed and flew across the room. She pulled a map of Italy from her traveling case and shook it open. "The Veneto. That's Venice but includes a wide area around it and to the north. Right?"

"Yes."

Kathryn Johnson

"How long do they estimate it will take to find the signal's source?"

"No telling. Days, maybe."

Kate closed her eyes and focused on nothing. Nothing but forty-eight hours. She willed thoughts, possibilities, a clue to come to her. Nothing.

Cam whispered through the phone. "Kate, are you all right? Tell me what you're thinking."

All she knew was that everything they'd done so far had been wrong or too late. They'd only succeeded in feeding the enemy's ego and greed by allowing them a taste of success.

Whoever that enemy was. Zed appeared to be just a pawn, not the ringleader at all. Rooker seemed to think there was a major power behind the plot. A sophisticated terror cell or possibly even an entire country bent on destroying the U.S.

"Did Archer say whether or not the government will pay the ransom this time?"

"He expects they will, but the White House hasn't officially given the go-ahead."

Kate nodded. "Good. Call Archer and suggest that if the President is seriously considering paying the ransom, he can help us by stalling as long as possible. Assure the terrorists they'll get their money, but it will take the full forty-eight hours to produce it. Government red tape. Congress needs to pass an emergency bill. He can make up anything he likes."

"Stall them?" Cam's voice came out as a squeak, verging on hysterical. "Why bother? Kate, it's not like there's anything we can do."

"I can't explain now. Just do it. Please."

Kate broke the connection. Cam's question rang in her ears: *Why bother?*

Because it's personal now.

Maybe Rooker was right when he'd accused her of taking Heat Wave's theft to heart. *My satellite. Mine!* That's how she'd always thought of it. So, if that were true, if she had made the project her own, made it personal—might someone else identify her with Heat Wave? Or was that too farfetched to even consider?

No Mercy

Thinking back, she recalled the taunting message left on the computer screen in Connecticut. It had been meant for her, no one else. And now Chicago was a target. A coincidence that she'd grown up there and still had family in the city? Was she just imagining connections where none existed?

What if Rooker was right? What if the entity behind this plot wasn't making a political statement? Say, they were doing this purely for money. The hijackers had hit on an ingenious, high-tech, ruthless form of extortion. That might be all there was to it. Criminals cashing in on technology. But might there be another underlying motive? Was there a reason why she felt the prick of a blade with every move these people made?

She sat on the floor, letting these new and doubly disturbing thoughts run through her mind. "It isn't all about you, doc." That's what Rooker had said to put her in her place. But what if it *was* all about her—in some warped and wicked way she hadn't yet figured out?

She squeezed her eyes shut and clasped her hands together, hard, willing their trembling to stop. If, in theory, this plot did have at least something to do with her on a personal level, then what was happening had to involve someone who *knew* her. Someone from her past, maybe? Or someone close to her in her present life. Someone who, even now, was working against her. Rooker had questioned the loyalty of her team at the very beginning of this mess. But she had refused to accept the possibility of a traitor.

"God, no," she breathed. Was that really possible? One of her own? Or had she become so desperate she was reaching for the most outrageous explanations possible? She was letting her imagination rule when logic and fact should be all that mattered. Her head spun.

Forty-eight hours. That's all they had. She had to make the best use of the time. What could she do in two days?

Only one possibility came to her: Fly back home to DC and confront the only people she knew who had the ability to plan and execute the theft of a satellite.

"You can't do this." Rooker stared down at the petite, brainy blonde—the same one he'd kissed and fondled and almost, but not quite, bedded—who now had clearly gone mad. "And we can't afford to sit here, doing nothing, while you hop on a jet." Never had a woman so thoroughly annoyed him. No, this was worse than annoyance. Kate Foster always chose the one path that crossed his.

She'd told him she was flying back to Washington and instructed him to delay a raid in the Veneto until she returned to Italy. Now she was throwing clothing into her overnight bag despite everything he'd said to dissuade her.

"I need to eliminate a black hole, Rooker. A gaping, super-destructive black hole in our system."

"Don't start spouting astronomy jargon to me!" he growled, pacing away from her to stare out the window.

Rome suddenly felt hellishly hot and oppressive. He wanted out of this hotel. Needed to move on the latest intelligence. Giving her the lead on this mission had been a mistake. What were they thinking in Washington? She was adorable, he had to admit. And smart. But the woman didn't have a clue how to deal with a situation of this enormity.

"Honestly, what's this all about, Kate? Why not stay here? You wanted to be here to recover your data. That's here, in Italy, not in DC."

She threw a pair of slacks into the case and closed it. She showed no signs of having heard him.

He tried a gentler approach. "If you're worried about your folks, tell them to get the hell out of Chicago."

"I can't explain my reasons for going. Not yet. If I did you wouldn't..." She shook her head.

He couldn't take any more of this. "You think I'm too dim to understand your fancy science?" he shouted, bearing down on her again. If he got in her face she couldn't ignore him. "Put it in English."

She rolled her eyes at him. "It's not that, Daniel." At the unexpected sound of his name on her lips, he took a breath, closed his mouth. He liked it. The way she said it, long and musical. No one ever called him that any more. She said, "I just have to be sure I'm right before I accuse anyone."

"Accuse someone?" He squinted at her. "You know who's behind this?"

No Mercy

"I can't be sure of anything, not yet. I have to talk to a few people."

He shook his head, reached for her and gripped her arms before she could pull away. Her eyes flashed with fright. "Kate, you owe me an explanation." If scaring her was the only thing that worked, fine. But she didn't look intimidated, just wary. "You're hanging us out to dry here. What am I supposed to do while you go off to—"

"It's time we get to the root of this insanity." She shook off his hands the moment his grip loosened. "I'm beginning to think I'm the only one who can do that. And, no, I'm not being egotistical or arrogant. You have to trust me." She brought her eyes up to his and kept them there until he had to look away.

"Damn it, Kate! There's so much at stake."

"That's why I have to go." She lifted the suitcase off of the bed. "You know how to reach me. If I'm right and everything works out in DC the way I hope, we'll have the answer to who is behind this. Then we'll have a chance to end this. If I'm wrong, I'll meet you in Venice within forty-eight hours. Archer has assured me he can keep negotiations open that long."

Rooker shook his head. This was bad. Real bad. But they'd tied his hands. Except for Ricci. He still had the Italian's network looking for the satellite's captors.

"Okay, the team will set up in Venice and wait for word from you," he agreed. "But what if we locate an address tonight? Or tomorrow?" He stepped between her and the door, his fists tight at his sides because if he lifted one of them it would end up through a wall.

"Move, Rooker," she said.

"You think I'm just going to sit on my goddamn ass and not go after them because you say so?"

Kate gave him a severe look. "You're waiting, because those are your orders. You're a soldier at heart. You take orders." She stepped around him. This time he didn't try to stop her.

"I don't know why I ever wanted to screw you!" he growled as she passed him by.

She reached for the doorknob. "I don't know why I'd ever let you."

Kathryn Johnson

Mercy O'Brien was waiting for her at Dulles when Kate stepped through the gate and into the glass-and-steel terminal. Whereas normal human beings weren't allowed through airport security without tickets, apparently special people with high-level security clearances and connections with the FBI had no trouble accessing the passenger gates.

Mercy looked at Kate's overnight bag and broke into a brisk jog-walk that Kate easily matched. "You check any luggage?"

"Nope."

"Good. I have a car waiting. We'll go straight to NASA-Weston."

"No. I've asked my team to meet us at La Hacienda."

Mercy frowned. "The Tex-Mex restaurant near the compound?"

"I don't want this conversation we're about to have feel like the Spanish Inquisition," Kate said firmly. "We're here to uncover the truth, not place blame." She didn't like her cousin's sudden silence. "You have to promise me, Mercy, not to do anything rash. Listen to them. Please. These are good people."

"*Good* people who may have already killed? That's what you're thinking, isn't it? You think one of your team is behind this mess."

Kate turned to study her expression as they rushed through the busy terminal. A blank wall, eyes straight ahead. All the softness gone from Mercy's face. Kate wondered what had happened in just a year that had so changed her cousin from the joyful artist and contented wife of an American diplomat. It couldn't have just been her marriage breaking up, could it? Although she still wasn't aware of the reasons behind that. Now there was a toughness, perhaps even a bitterness in the girl she'd grown up admiring and loving.

"I don't really know anything yet," Kate admitted. "I'm honestly just grasping at straws. But I'm beginning to think that someone close to me, someone who knows both me and the satellite has to be involved in this plot." She took a deep breath. "When you limit suspects to the people who fit that profile, doesn't it sound a lot like the people I work with?"

"All right. But as soon as you think you know who it is, you tell me," Mercy said, shooting her a look. "You can't protect them, even if you think of them as a friend or colleague."

"I know." Kate drew a shaky breath. And she would turn him or her in, even if it ripped her heart out. "Has anything been done to prepare Chicago if we're unable to stop Heat Wave in time?"

"O'Hare is on orange alert. They'll shut down the entire airport—no incoming or outgoing flights—starting twelve hours from now."

"In case the power grid is hit and they lose their guidance systems?"

"Exactly. After what happened at Kennedy and Dulles, we won't take any chances. Other precautions are being taken, but you don't need to know about those now."

They speed-walked out through the terminal's electric sliding doors and straight up to a black sedan, its motor idling. Mercy gave the driver instructions. He hit the gas. The car sped east on I-60, heading toward Washington, DC.

Kate looked out through the car's tinted side window. After vibrant Italy, the late-summer landscape of Maryland appeared parched and bland. But her surroundings faded from consciousness as she focused on the task ahead. A task she loathed. She was about to confront a killer...and a friend.

At last they passed over the Maryland state line, turned into the dense flow of traffic heading north on I-695, the infamously clogged Washington Beltway. Between rush hours, and without construction, the trip was blessedly short. Soon they took an exit into Beltsville, a mixed commercial-residential area less than a mile down the road from the NASA compound where it had all begun.

"What about evacuation of the city?" Kate asked, picking up the conversation where they'd left off.

"Mayor Reston claims it's impossible to evacuate a city the size of Chicago in two days." Mercy shook her head. "Anyway, where do you put three million people?"

Kate sighed, thinking of her parents. They'd stay, even if she called and begged them to leave. Just as people will ride out a hurricane, her father would stand by his family's home. She knew others would too, concerned about looting or vandalism, thinking they could somehow physically protect what was theirs against natural forces, as well as from other humans.

Kate looked across the seat at Mercy. "You ordered everyone on the Heat Wave team to be investigated. Didn't you?"

"I'm not in a position to order anyone to do anything." Mercy squared her shoulders as if she was prepared for Kate's anger. "I suggested to Red Sands, my employer, that it would be appropriate. They consulted with DoD, and they agreed. Under the circumstances, no one should be eliminated from suspicion until—"

"But no one, not even Cambridge or Vernon were arrested when you discovered they'd lied about their backgrounds."

"True," Mercy said.

"Why not?"

"I assume it was because no evidence was found of their collusion with Zed or anyone else involved in this operation. And their continuing to work at the compound was critical to resolving the crisis."

Kate looked at her. If Mercy had been wearing makeup earlier in the day, it had worn off, leaving physical signs of her exhaustion and the immense strain she must be feeling.

Mercy said, "We decided that watching them was enough unless we saw them doing anything suspicious."

"So you...what? Tapped their phones? Tailed them?"

"Both," Mercy admitted without hesitation. "Didn't do any good. Maybe you can shake something loose today."

"I hope so." They didn't have much time left. Little more than one day. She felt physically ill at the thought of the price to be paid for her failure.

The car pulled into La Hacienda's parking lot. The restaurant was a popular hangout for employees of nearby high-tech companies and government branches. She looked around for familiar cars, glad to see at least two of her people had already arrived.

Inside, Kate looked around but didn't see familiar faces. She asked the hostess for a table near the back of the dining room, where they would have privacy. Amanda and Cam soon appeared from the ladies' room. Tommy and Vernon showed up moments later. They each gave Mercy a quick, surprised look. None of them made eye contact with Kate.

Guilt? Or just nerves?

When they were all seated, Cam cleared her throat and said, "We've got a deadline, Kate. Why the hell are we sitting around chatting in a Mexican restaurant?" She looked as tired as Kate felt, but a cloud of anger hovered over the fatigue. And there was something else in Cambridge Mackenzie's eyes. A flash of defiance? Secrets?

"We're here because," Kate began, keeping her voice low and controlled, "we need to talk. This time without holding anything back."

Amanda stared at her with a confused scowl. Tommy and Cambridge shifted in their seats and looked at each other.

Vernon shot to his feet. "If you're going to accuse me of lying or having anything to do with—"

"No one's accusing anyone," Kate said firmly. "Sit down, Vern."

He didn't. "So what's the freakin' Bureau doing here?"

"I'm not FBI," Mercy said.

"Whatever," muttered Vern.

Kate groaned inside. This was not starting off well. "Mercy has agreed to come as a witness to this discussion, off the record if necessary." The second part was definitely stretching the truth. She had few doubts by now that Mercy O'Brien's first loyalties were to her employer and the U.S. government. Family and friendship was no longer top of the list.

"Off the record?" Cam laughed.

Mercy leaned across the table, looking the other woman in the eye. "Off or on doesn't matter, Ms. Mackenzie. If someone at this table has either intentionally, or inadvertently, done anything to aid the enemy, they need to spill now." She looked around the table. "I have the authority to offer immunity in exchange for whatever you know that might help us stop these people."

Vernon dropped back into his seat but didn't look any more cooperative.

"Listen." Tommy leaned forward, elbows on the tabletop between napkin-rolled utensils and sweating glass of ice water. His eyes filled, mouth sagged, all of his youthful arrogance gone. "You can save the rest of them the grilling. I'm the one you think is behind this, right?"

Kate touched his arm. "We haven't singled anyone out. We just need the truth. We're out of time. People are going to die. A lot of people."

A waitress approached, armed with her order pad, but Mercy gave her a look that sent her scurrying meekly back into the kitchen.

Tommy inhaled deeply. Wiped at his eyes with the back of one hand. "Everyone knows my background. Once a hacker always a hacker—that's what you're thinking."

"We recognize the addictive behavior of Internet hacking," Mercy said, her voice soft while her eyes never lifted from his. Kate could feel their intensity even from the end of the table where she sat. "The thrill you feel is powerful. Seductive. At least, that's what the hackers I know tell me."

Kate watched helplessly as Tommy nodded his bowed head. "You break into a system, and there's this power rush like you can't imagine. You're higher than you get on any drug. Secrets unfold before your eyes. It's like you're...you're Master of the Universe. Or something."

"And there's the money," Kate said, barely daring to breathe the words. "You stole from people by stealing their identities."

"That, too," he admitted. "It was just so damn easy. There isn't anything you can't buy 'cause you can put your hand in anyone's pocket. Bank accounts, credit cards, stock portfolios..." He looked the length of the table at her with pleading eyes. "But I stopped all of that a long time ago. I swear I did!"

"Except for one last adventure," Mercy said, her voice suddenly steel-edged, cold as a January day in DC. Everyone at the table stared at her as if she'd sprouted horns.

No Mercy

Tommy's face went white. "I...yeah. Just once. 'bout a month ago."

A chill crept up Kate's spine. She'd trusted this young man!

Mercy said, "You busted the Pentagon. Again."

Kate closed her eyes and heard Cam moan. Amanda let out a whimper of distress.

"Shit!" said Vernon.

Tommy was sobbing now. "But that's all I did, I swear. I broke in and ducked out fast. Didn't mess with anything. Honest!" He gasped for air, hiccupped and stumbled on. "Didn't think they'd even detected me. It was just to prove I could still do it, you know?"

"Yes, I know." Mercy sounded almost sympathetic. Her pretty eyes flicked toward Kate with much less empathy. Did her cousin blame her for not foreseeing the weak link in her team? Why hadn't Mercy mentioned this to her before? Did she not even trust her own flesh and blood?

Kate stared at Tommy before turning back to Mercy. "Then he didn't have anything to do with hijacking Heat Wave?"

Mercy shook her head. "Right, Tommy?"

"No, I didn't. Oh my God! I swear I didn't." He was still sobbing but looked suddenly relieved. "Jezzus, I've been so scared. Afraid you'd come after me thinking my Pentagon hack had something to do with Heat Wave."

Kate didn't know whether to believe him or not. "You claim, except for that one relapse, you did break the habit? Then tell me how," Kate said. "Make me believe you."

"I've found a new drug." Kate frowned. *What?* Tommy's face took on a little more color. He swiped again at his leaking eyes with his shirtsleeve. He said, "Space. That's my drug. Using the computer to reach out and talk to satellites and discover stuff. It's like owning the universe. A new, better kind of high."

A high. An addiction. Yes, Kate thought. She'd felt like that sometimes, too.

Mercy didn't let the relieved silence last long. "Fine. Let's say, for the moment, that we believe you. One down, three to go." She glared at the rest of Kate's team.

"You can't be serious!" Amanda shrieked. Amanda, who never raised her voice, never questioned authority. "You actually think one of us helped Zed steal the satellite?"

Kate rested her hand over the older woman's trembling, ice-cold fingers. "Please, Amanda, we have to consider every possibility, no matter how far-fetched it might seem . The aim is to trace unconscious remarks or events you may have forgotten. I don't need to tell you how desperately we need your help."

Even as she said those words, Kate new she was lying. What she was asking of them was far more. Somehow she had to convince these people to open up, if not to reveal their own involvement in what was happening, at least to share information that might implicate a workmate or friend.

"Well, I didn't friggin' leak information to anybody," Cambridge stated flatly. "I never discussed mission-critical data with anyone on the outside. Not even my little girl. And if I had, I wouldn't try to cover for myself by lying."

Kate turned to her friend. This was the moment she'd most dreaded. "Maybe your lies weren't directly linked to the mission. But they *were* critical to my ever trusting you again."

Cam's eyes flashed black fury. "What the hell you talking about? Are you accusing me of being part of this?"

The noise from the bar continued, but not a sound came from anyone at their table in this dim end of the room.

"We'll come back to you in a moment," Mercy said with a cautionary glance at Kate. She turned to Vernon. "I'd like to hear from you now, sir. You came into this country illegally."

He startled but immediately segued from surprise to defiance. "Yes. And so have thousands of other immigrants. What of it?"

"You were how old?"

"Six."

"Tell us about it."

Vernon released a long breath and shook his head. "My father brought us over the Mexican border one night. We moved into a crappy apartment in Los Angeles with three other families, all of us terrified of being sent back."

"And you grew up running with gangs," Mercy said.

No Mercy

Kate leaned back and opened her mouth at this new information. But she said nothing. She watched Vernon's face work itself through a range of emotions.

"Yes," he admitted at last. "Until I was sixteen. When the cops picked me up for the fourth or fifth time. Instead of sending me to jail, the court put me in a program for kids like me. I was still locked up, at least for a couple of years, but I met a new friend."

"Who was that?" Kate asked softly. The way he said it, with gentle reverence, she expected it had something to do with religion.

"A computer." Vernon shrugged at her surprised expression. "Listen, I didn't know shit. I thought the world was the streets. Black and white and misery. Then I hooked into the Internet, took classes my counselor suggested. I saw what was out there and I couldn't believe it. Man! So much color and intelligence and...possibilities. I didn't want to run scared all my life, live in a rat-trap with a bunch of losers and illegals."

Kate smiled. "So you somehow educated yourself."

Vernon dipped his head to one side and met her eyes. "I picked up some inner-city scholarship money and worked for the rest of it. Got an internship after college with the Applied Physics Lab, worked my way up, then this job came along." He looked pleadingly at Kate. "I wouldn't risk losing everything I have. I've come too far."

She nodded and looked at Mercy who seemed satisfied. But then, you never knew with her.

Cambridge shifted forward on her chair. "All right. If he can do it." She shot Vernon a brief smile. "I falsified my job application with NASA. I wanted to work here more than anything in the world, but I didn't think they'd take me if they knew about my past."

"You had a rough childhood too," Kate said, wanting to move things along. She was all too aware of precious minutes leaking away.

"Yeah, but not like Vern. My parents were both educated professionals. I had every advantage in the world, and I blew it from the day I hit fourteen. I started running with a rough crowd and got myself tossed into juvie for doing drugs, then a real jail

230

for a robbery that went sour. Someone was hurt. Bad. So they threw the book at us. Trouble was, by that time I was pregnant."

"With your daughter."

She nodded. "My parents pleaded with the court and got me out early so I could have the baby at home. It nearly killed them, what I did to them." Her head dropped to her hands but she kept on talking into the tabletop. "God. I couldn't explain all of that on a job application! How could I?"

Kate sighed. "You could have come to me."

Cam looked up at her. "And put you in a tight spot because you knew I'd lied? Ex-cons don't get Top-Secret security clearances these days."

Kate sighed. That was certainly true. She turned to the woman beside Cam. "Amanda? Do you have anything to tell us?"

Her plump, grandmotherly Project Tech drew herself up with dignity, her violet eyes telegraphing their indignity. "Money gets short sometimes with a houseful of kids. But I've never stolen a thing in my life."

Mercy cleared her throat. "So, everyone's 'fessed up. And no one can think of a word they might have let slip to anyone, ever. Nothing that can be connected to what happened in the Heat Wave lab that night or in the days that followed." She took in the entire table with one sweeping glance.

For a moment nobody said a word. Then—

"Frank and David." Cambridge tucked in her lips thoughtfully, then slowly let her gaze drift toward Kate. "They're the only members of the team who were there that night and haven't cleared themselves."

"Christ! What are you saying?" Tommy yelped. "One of them helped Zed steal the HW-1? They're freakin' dead!"

"That's plain crazy talk." Vernon snorted. "Even if they weren't dead. They were professionals, through and through."

"You can't ask us to pick on those poor men when they aren't here to defend themselves!" Tears rolled down Amanda's cheeks.

"David Proctor and Frank Hess are all we have left," Mercy insisted, her voice tight. She folded her hands on top of the table. "Just because they were killed by Zed's people doesn't mean they weren't somehow involved at the beginning."

No Mercy

"She's right," Kate said, regretting she had to say the words. Hadn't Rooker said it seemed to him the intruders had help from inside? And now, something else was coming to her, a scrap of memory she couldn't yet form into a coherent idea. She worked it around in her mind. Nothing.

Mercy said, "Think back to any conversations you might have had with Hess or Proctor. Forget about how bizarre their being involved might seem. Did either of them ever express political or personal dissatisfaction with NASA or with the U.S. government? Any motives at all for taking advantage of their specialized knowledge?"

After several minutes' silence, Kate spoke hesitantly. "Maybe I've known something all along, but I didn't think it mattered."

Mercy hitch an eyebrow at her. "Yes?"

"This goes back years." Kate swallowed, still unsure. "Before most of the others on the team were working with me. I wanted this job, Chief Project Engineer, more than anything. It was everything I hungered for professionally—the extraordinary level of science being done at NASA, the chance to challenge myself and grow in a field that offered unlimited potential. I went after the position aggressively."

"So?" Tommy said. "No one can blame you for that."

"Others wanted it, too." Kate looked down at her hands and consciously untangled her knotted fingers. "Frank wanted it."

Tommy's soft blue eyes skipped from her to Mercy, then to Amanda and Vernon. "Well, yeah, so? Lots of us compete for jobs. But that doesn't mean the guy who loses goes on a vendetta and—"

"Wait." Kate drew her tongue across dry lips, cleared her throat. "There's more. He, Frank, was really angry at first. You remember his temper." Heads nodded around the table. "Then he went from obviously angry to just sort of sullen."

"I was there. He used to argue with you over decisions you'd made," Cambridge recalled.

"That doesn't prove a thing. Hell, I give you grief, too!" Tommy bounced in agitation on his seat.

"No, this was different," Kate said. "It was almost as if he was trying to rattle me. Make me less sure of myself so I'd make a mistake. But I hung in there. Faced him down a few times. After a couple of months he calmed down. Things went smoothly between us for the most part."

"Do you think someone might have approached him during that time?" Mercy asked. "Someone made him an offer: 'Help us capture this satellite and you can get back at that woman who took your job.'"

Kate sucked in a deep breath. "I really don't know. It just never occurred to me that Frank Hess would ever be anything but loyal to the project. Even if he wasn't loyal to me."

"But Frank wasn't a computer expert," Amanda argued. "He was a physicist. Besides, they *shot him* right in front of us!" She broke into sobs, weeping into her napkin. "And then they *burned* the poor man. Killed him! How can you say such horrible things about—"

"The shooting could have been faked," Vernon said, and everyone looked at him. "Right? Like in a movie."

"Yeah," Tommy chimed in. "They tuck a squib, a little plastic bag filled with red liquid, inside an actor's clothing. Shoot a blank at him. He punctures it with something sharp and it looks like he's bleeding."

"But David really *was* murdered," Amanda objected. "He...he died right in front of me."

Kate thought about that night. How every detail had played out. "Yes, but he was shot by the woman. Zed shot Frank. So only his gun might have had blanks."

Mercy nodded. "We ran a test on the stains on the carpet where Hess fell. It's real human blood and matches his type. He could have drawn some before the invasion and prepared a squib. Or he might really have been shot. It sounds from the testimony as if it might have been a less than fatal wound."

Vernon turned to Kate. "Frank knew I lived in L.A. We used to talk about Hollywood, how stuff didn't seem real out there sometimes. I think I told him about being on a set once, seeing how they faked gunshot wounds."

Cambridge swore.

"I might have said stuff to him, too." Tommy looked worried again. "You know, without realizing he was going to..."

"What?" Kate asked. "What did you talk about with him?"

No Mercy

"Frank was *the man* as far as astrophysics, you know?" Tommy drum-rolled his fingertips on the wooden tabletop. "I mean, like a genius, right? Everyone knew that. But he was a little lame when it came to computer stuff. I helped him out. Gave him some tips and suggested a few books that might bring him up to speed."

"And?"

Tommy's face flushed. "The man had a sponge for a brain. Amazing."

Amanda's eyes looked wild with horror. "I can't believe... I can't think that Frank..." She gulped air. "He wouldn't have let them kill David! He wouldn't!"

"Maybe," Kate said gently, "things got out of hand." Hadn't Rooker remarked that he thought it odd the terrorists left the rest of them alive? "It's possible Frank made a deal with them not to harm us, but once it all started to go down he lost control of the situation." She recalled the look of shock that crossed Frank's face when they gunned down his fellow scientist.

Mercy turned to Tommy. "Do you believe Frank Hess had the necessary knowledge to mastermind this hijacking?"

Tommy shrugged, but still looked visibly shaken. "Maybe?"

"Absolutely," Vernon said. He suddenly looked like a believer. "But if he did this thing, if he was a traitor and turned on us...I guess he's paid for it now."

Ten minutes later, Kate and Mercy were back in the sedan outside of the restaurant.

"So," Mercy said, "we agree that it's possible Frank Hess dug his own grave by conspiring with Zed and friends. Maybe it was even his idea. What do you think?"

Kate reluctantly nodded, her heart lying shattered in her chest. Everything that could possibly go wrong, had gone miserably, nightmarishly wrong. "Yes, maybe it was his plan. How else would someone like Zed even become aware of the satellite?" She stared at the traffic jamming the ramp onto the Washington Beltway, visible from the restaurant's parking lot.

Kate's phone vibrated against her hip. She'd set it on silent page. She unclipped it from her belt and checked the screen. Homeland Security—Archer's office. Perfect!

A text: *Laser deployed from sat. Targetted Chicago. Shut down before we could track exact location.*

"God," she murmured, "they're testing the laser." *My family!*

"We're getting you on the next plane back to Italy." Mercy tapped her driver on the shoulder. "Dulles, fast." She started punching numbers into her phone.

"Why? They've probably moved on from Venice by now."

Kate had never felt so weary, so inadequate and useless and frustrated. She wished she could hop a plane for Chicago. Gather up her loved ones and rush them as far away from the city, from any major city, as she could. But what about the rest of the innocents there?

No Mercy

Rooker wasted no time moving his men. Within two hours after Kate's departure from Rome, the U.S. Air Force brought a chopper down from the NATO base at Vicenza. The team and their gear landed in Chioggia just south of Venice.

Had he wanted to, they could have set down in the middle of St. Mark's Square to a welcoming flurry of pigeons and, no doubt, paparazzi, but he was determined to keep their arrival as quiet as possible. That hadn't worked in Rome, but maybe here.

From the lower tip of the Laguna Veneta the WSS team took a *vaporetti* into the city proper. The high-speed power launches the Venetian version of taxis.

Once again Rooker requested the help of the police in locating civilian accommodations and staying low-profile. Happily, the only attention they attracted was from the desk clerk, who raised a questioning brow when he saw the ominous weapons shipping cases.

Although the Dolce Aqua was a very old hotel, probably unnoticed by tourists because of its nondescript exterior and backstreet location, it wasn't as grim or run-down inside as Rooker had expected. The lobby might once have been the great hall of a sixteenth-century palazzo. The guest rooms were enormous and, although there were no closets, a huge wooden armoire with ornate carvings graced each one, matched by equally massive furnishings.

The place smelled of aged oak, candle wax, wine and citrus oils. Marble floors throughout of rose-and-verdigris marble with glittering black flecks, polished to an icy sheen. Rooker felt as if he were walking on a thin layer of water, flowing over flower petals and ferns. Such elegance he rarely found in his accommodations.

He thought of Kate and what she might say if she saw the place. Would she call it romantic? Was this the sort of hotel she'd expect a lover to take her? He remembered their kiss, imagined

236

her eyes sparkling as they took in the luxurious interior. He wished they hadn't argued. Wished they had met at another time. At any other time that didn't involve the anxiety and danger of thwarting madmen.

She was back in the States now. Good. For her sake, he hoped she stayed there. He'd continued to think about Kate far too often in the hours since she left. As he stood in the middle of his men, noisily unpacking their gear, he made himself acknowledge the pointlessness of what had become his obsession with her. How likely was it a smart, sophisticated woman like her would care about a brute like him? Not very.

Now, with effort, he put her out of his mind. He focused on the work ahead of them.

In his bones, he felt the enemy close by. Felt the nearness of his prey, the way other men sensed a good fishing spot or instinctively listened for a warning knock in their car's engine. The hunt was on, and he was back in his element.

As soon as Rooker had sorted out his team, he left them to see Ricci again. They had arranged to meet at a nearby café and exchange information. He was striding across a sunny piazza when his phone rang. He checked the screen. *Kate.* His stomach lurched at the thought of her giving him hell for disobeying orders, then he smiled. Even angry, she did something magical to his insides. He sat down on a low stone wall surrounding a Bernini-style fountain. Hit the answer button.

"Hey there," he said.

"I'm on my way back." Her voice sounded dull, washed out, barely there. "Alitalia. Flight 8011. The plane takes off in twenty minutes."

His first thought was *NO!* But he contained himself. She never reacted well to his orders. "A wasted trip, huh?" He couldn't help feeling a little smug that he'd been right.

"Not exactly," she said slowly.

Something in her tone worried him. "What's that supposed to mean?"

"I think you were right from the beginning...about the mole. We believe Frank Hess was in on the plot."

No Mercy

He squeezed his eyes closed, to better concentrate against the sun's glare. "Damn. Tell me more."

"There's no time to talk now. I'll be in Rome in less than eight hours. A charter will bring me to the civilian airfield outside Venice." So word had reached her, where he was now. "Have you located Zed's buddies?"

"Yes and no. The Italians are working with NSA to narrow the area. It's a slow process. But I have another source."

"What's that?"

"You don't want to know."

"Rooker." In the background he could hear an amplified voice announcing a final boarding. "I have to go."

The signal cut off. He stared at the phone. *Frank Hess? Damn.* Like everyone else, he'd assumed Hess was a legitimate hostage. But hadn't he sensed something not quite right about the scenario the night of the invasion? Maybe the suspicion that had been nudging at him was all about the scientist.

Someone was messing with the camera in the lab and the alarm system. Why risk trying to sneak an outsider into the compound if an authorized employee was already there and willing to cooperate? Whatever the man's motive, it no longer mattered. They'd promised him something, or maybe threatened him. They'd used the man then disposed of him. Predictable.

Ricci was waiting for him at the Caffè Lavena in the Piazza San Marco. The Italian said by way of greeting, "If the Lavena was good enough Wagner and his father-in-law, Franz Liszt, it's good enough for me. Besides there is more sun on this side of the piazza." Ricci was practically purring; a big cat, loving the sun.

Rooker pushed suspicions and theories from his mind and focused all of his attention on the man seated across the table from him. "So, my friend, what have you found? A rat or two in the canals of Venice?"

Ricci blew smoke from his cigarette and kicked back an espresso, as black and thick as molasses. The little cup looked like a child's toy between his thick fingers as he set it down.

"Three foreigners. Americans. They've rented space in a warehouse connected to a local glass factory. One of them, a man, has been hiring locals as guards. He tells them he is worried about industrial espionage."

"Could be our guys." Three, he thought, so...Zed's two sidekicks and a wild card?

"They claim to be chemists, working for an American glass-making firm."

Rooker ordered a coffee and then, at Ricci's suggestion, a plate of little veal meatballs with sliced potatoes and radicchio. When the waiter left he asked, "Is there any chance they might be legitimate?"

Ricci shrugged. "It would be wise to make sure you don't attack innocent industrialists."

"Where are these innocents?"

"In Murano. You are familiar with this place?"

"One of the islands across the lagoon."

"Si. In the sixteenth century the glass artisans moved their factories and studios to Murano, to prevent the furnaces from burning down the city. It is a short trip by *vaporetti.*"

"What makes you think these are the people we're after?" Rooker asked, sipping his *caffe corretto* while he waited for his food. The added shot of Sambuca woke up his taste buds and carved a nice edge on his mind.

"One of the bodyguards they solicited is a cousin to one of my men. He says he wishes he'd asked for more money before agreeing to take the job."

"Why?"

Ricci lifted a shoulder and looked away. "One develops a sixth sense in this line of work. There are easy jobs. Then there are the kinds of jobs where one might get killed if careless."

"That doesn't tell us much."

"Also—" Ricci held up a finger "—there is a woman in charge. And that is never a good omen."

Rooker stared at the Italian. "A *woman*?"

"Si." Ricci slipped a hand inside his jacket pocket and pulled out an envelope. "I thought a few photographs might be helpful. The cousin, apparently, is not averse to playing both sides."

"If I were a religious man you'd be in my prayers tonight." Rooker tore open the envelope and took out a half dozen digital

No Mercy

prints. There was no woman in the first few shots, and he didn't know if any of the men might be the third in the hijacking assault.

"If you are going after these people, you had better say your prayers, religious or not." Ricci pointed to several shots of thick-necked thugs standing on a corner and smoking in front of what looked like a medieval storehouse. "I assume you have the support of the Carabiniere when you go after them?"

Rooker nodded. "Where exactly were these taken?"

"Outside of the glass studio."

Rooker flipped to another photo. "Holy shit."

Ricci looked over his shoulder. "She's a tough one, isn't she?"

The tall, pale-skinned woman with white-blond hair shaved close to her head was looking nearly straight into the camera. *Snake eyes,* he thought. She was a dead ringer for the woman Kate and her team had described after the invasion of the lab.

Kathryn Johnson

Chapter 33

Approaching Venice by plane felt surreal to Kate. An iridescent cloud of pigeons rose up out of Piazza San Marco as the commuter aircraft dove down out of the clouds and circled the city. The S-shaped Grand Canal wound between ancient stucco and stone buildings. Even from a thousand feet in the air Kate could recognize and name some of the bridges she'd studied years before in her college art-appreciation class—the Rialto, the Bridge of Sighs, the Scalzi, the Accademia. Hundreds of years old, their designs eternal and exquisite.

Before she'd settled on a major, she fantasized about becoming an architect. Just as Mercy had dreamed of becoming an artist. Mercy's dream had come true. Her paintings were magnificent. She'd even landed a position with the Smithsonian in DC, as a curator. But, at that time, few scholarships were available for women interested in design and architecture. Many more had begun to be offered for the sciences. She'd decided to go with the flow and take a few courses in physics and astronomy, see how she liked them. By the end of the second semester, she was hooked.

Architects were earth-bound. As an aerospace engineer she could build bridges to the stars. Space had virtually no creative limits.

But now was not the time for dreaming of worlds and universes yet undiscovered. By tonight Rooker and his team would need to make their move on this planet. And she needed to be with them.

He had left a message on her cell phone, which she'd retrieved on landing in Rome. A man, who sounded like a northern Italian version of a Sicilian godfather, claimed to have located the terrorists on one of the islands close to Venice proper. She prayed their intelligence was on target.

241

No Mercy

By nine-fifteen darkness had descended on the city. Rooker moved his team to the Fondemente Nuove, the wharf area on the northernmost edge of the city. From there they would take police power launches across the lagoon to Murano. Once there they'd need a less obvious mode of transport.

As in Venice proper, the collection of islands that formed Murano were connected by a series of narrow canals. Merchants and tourists used gondolas as a matter of course to reach many locations, including the famous glass studios. At this time of night the factories would be closed, only a few watchmen drowsily keeping an eye on the precious art and the ever-burning furnaces.

Kate gazed across the Laguna Veneta. The water that night seemed to her as smooth as a telescope's optical mirror. The moon hung low over the city, huge and orange and angry looking behind the church spires of the city. Patches of stars appeared between clouds, then were swept away again.

Kate stepped out of the police launch and onto a wharf on the island. Here the night air seemed steamier. The sun's heat lingered in the stone of the buildings and the wood of the piers. Rooker's party exchanged the noisy power launch for traditional black lacquered gondolas—the next best thing to being invisible because the long, elegant boats floated everywhere in the night.

Kate sat on one side of the garish red-velvet passenger seat, Rooker on the other. His right hand rested on his Steyr SSG—the same anti-sniper rifle he had shown her at the range. She remembered how heavy it had felt to her, how terrified she'd been at first, looking through the crosshairs of the scope.

Now she was glad Rooker had it, and that she knew how to use it.

She didn't exactly feel safe because of the gun or the armed men with her. But being surrounded by enough weapons to fight a small war did have a strangely calming effect on her knotted stomach. She looked around her.

Carabiniere, dressed in gondoliers' costumes, poled the boats along a Murano canal. A lantern burned in each bow, lighting their way, casting eerie amber shadows over passing walls and wharfs. Ancient buildings on either side of the prong-bowed hull of her boat reminded Kate of a set from a Shakespearean play.

Adam Grabowski and the wounded Travis Peterson, who'd talked his way into coming after all, hid beneath a tarp in the bottom of Kate's boat. Each carried a 9 mm Glock in a shoulder holster, a smaller pistol strapped beneath a pant leg. Adam also hugged his Steyr. Travis was one of two machine-gun men. She could see the weapon's bulky shape beneath the olive green canvas. Before boarding the boats she'd noticed other shapes clipped to belts. Some, she assumed, were hand grenades or, possibly, smoke bombs.

Several gondolas disappeared down side canals. She knew they were to cover the rear of the factory. Three others glided languidly down the central canal, each with a gaily attired pole man and two passengers.

"Rooker, let's go over the plan one more time," she whispered. "First thing we do is..."

"I tell you to wait in the boat." She made a face at him. "Forget that," he grumbled. "Never does any good."

She rested a hand on his knee. "Please, let's not fight now." She tried to ignore the raw nerves tugging at her insides. "If this doesn't work, if something goes wrong I don't want our last words to have been angry ones."

"Fine. I like your classy outfit. Happy?" He glowered into the dark.

He'd been in a mood since they left the hotel, when he'd begged her one final time to stay behind. And she, of course, had refused.

Kate looked down at the plain black uniform she was wearing, the smallest of the SWAT team style fatigues in Rooker's supplies. She still had to roll up the pant cuffs and sleeves, and cinch in the waist. Why was it, in movies, heroines always found sleek catsuits into which they poured themselves?

"Signore," their gondolier said.

"Yeah?" Rooker looked up at the man.

"You are supposed to be *innamorati, si?"*

"I guess." Rooker glowered at their driver.

"You do not look like lovers, sitting so far apart. You will bring suspicion, don't you think?"

No Mercy

"Oh, Christ," Rooker muttered.

"He's right," Kate said, "we don't look terribly affectionate. More like squabbling spouses."

"Sit closer to her," the Italian suggested. "*Si*, now put your arm around her."

"Anything else?" Rooker complied but didn't look happy about it.

"It would seem far more convincing," the man added with a straight face, "if you kissed the *signorina*. Passionately. That is, if she does not object to so disagreeable a man."

Kate smiled back at the Carabiniere officer who seemed to enjoy annoying Rooker.

"It's all right," she said. "I've kissed worse." But she felt a little ping of anticipation as she remembered the one time they had kissed.

"Good grief, let's get it over with." Rooker's hand came up behind her neck. He pulled her toward him. She'd expected a quick brush of the lips to satisfy their audience. His kiss was long and deep, sending her insides tingling. She leaned into him, letting herself savor warm lips against hers. He didn't break the kiss until she'd started to feel dizzy from lack of air and pressed her hand lightly against his chest.

A very convincing piece of acting, she thought as their lips parted. Had she been acting too? Puddles of warmth spread through her body. *Oh, my!*

When his big hands at last released her, it took Kate rather too long to catch her breath and settle herself back down into the velvet cushion.

Rooker looked around restlessly. He said nothing but positioned one arm across his lap. To hide a telltale bulge?

He's turned on! she thought, stifling a giggle.

"For the cause, right?" he said, but wouldn't meet her eyes. "The kiss, I mean. It's all for show."

"Of course," she agreed, still smiling into the darkness.

"Just don't go taking it seriously," he warned. "Because it felt like you were putting a lot of, you know, heart into that kiss."

The good feelings washed away. Her irritation with him rushed back in their place. "Do you honestly think I could ever fall for a man like you, Rooker?"

Kathryn Johnson

"Plenty of women have."

"Give me a break," she groaned, sliding back and away from him as far as the seat allowed. "When I fall in love, it will be with a man I can spend the rest of my life with. A companion. A soul mate. An intellectual match."

He got very still and looked away across the water. "Sure. He'd have to be Einstein to please you."

"Obviously, you don't have a clue about such things." She sighed. "It's just as well. You'd make horrible husband material."

"You got that right." His voice sounded tight, but not really angry. Hurt? Was she being mean to him? Maybe. She couldn't help herself; he just rubbed her the wrong way, warning her off from taking their kiss seriously.

No, she couldn't imagine Rooker's feeling ever truly got hurt. And yet...

She sighed. "Rooker, I just want..." Where were the words that kept chafing at the back of her throat? Why couldn't she just blurt them out? "I need to say one thing before we go into that building." She drew a breath and stared down at her hands, folded tightly in her lap. *He'll laugh at me,* she thought. *But it doesn't matter. Some things just have to be said.* "Rooker, we haven't always agreed. But I respect what you've been trying to do. And the risks you and your men are taking. Also, I want you to know that— "she swallowed, then forced out the rest, all in one breath "—you don't totally turn me off."

His entire body went rigid beside her. She couldn't tell if he was still breathing.

Adam poked his head up from beneath the tarp and scowled at the two of them.

"Get down!" Rooker ordered.

For a long moment there was only the whoosh, whoosh, whoosh of water splashing against the boat's hull with each push from the gondolier's pole.

Kate told herself she hadn't been looking for a response in kind. Nevertheless she studied his chiseled face, glowing in the torch's light, wanting to read his reaction. It had seemed important to let him know she didn't hate him. That, in fact, she sort-of-maybe liked this gruff, unpredictable, often brutish,

245

No Mercy

frequently rude man. Yes, he irritated her at times, but he also moved her in ways she couldn't express. There had been a few times, she now admitted, at least to herself, when she'd actually felt a sensual ache for him.

At last Daniel Rooker turned back to her. His oh-so-blue eyes locked on hers. And the breath simply left her body.

She knew *that* look. It was the way a man who wanted a woman gazed at her. His eyes told everything. There was hunger in them.

She anticipated words of passion, of longing. But, knowing him, was equally prepared for sarcasm or even laughter.

Instead, he spoke as calmly, as emotionlessly as though he was issuing a command to one of his men. "You'll stay with me, this time, Kate. Inside the building. Understand?"

"Oh, okay." She couldn't think of what else to say. If she'd wanted to expose the tender side of him, she'd failed. Maybe, being Rooker, this was as close as he'd let any woman get. He was promising to protect her. That was good, right? She'd at least feel safe.

But feeling safe, she suddenly decided, wasn't enough. She wanted to revisit his embrace. Wanted the roughness of his beard against her face, the strength of his hands on her body. *Why the hell are you thinking such things? And at a time like this.*

"The B team will clear the way," he was saying, his voice low, all business now. "Your only job is to mess with the electronics once we've secured the area and taken prisoners."

"I know my job," she said dully. "Do you know yours?"

"Keeping your ass alive until your rogue satellite is powered down."

She nodded. "Sounds simple enough." He was tuning her out, emotionally. She would have to do the same.

"A cinch," he said. But the dark places deep within his eyes told her he didn't believe it either.

One by one, the gondolas drew up to a dock alongside the glass factory. Stealthily, figures in black moved up from the bobbing hulls, onto the pier and then the narrow walkways between the dark water and crumbling rock walls. The commercial district, at this hour, was bereft of tourists, workers, locals. Not even a single stumbling drunk or stray dog loomed out of the shadows.

Kate wished for the reassurance of any normal sound—a blaring TV, a slamming car door, a cat's yowl—anything to break the unbearable tension. Maybe Rooker's intelligence was inaccurate. Maybe they'd walk into an empty factory, surprise a sleeping guard and no one else.

Or maybe this was a trap.

We should have considered other options, she thought belatedly, frantically. But they were all here and there was nothing to do but proceed with their plan to search the factory. The price of failure was simply too high to delay action.

Briefly, she considered her life's work. So precious to her. There was every possibility they'd never recover the HW-1 prototype, setting back alternative energy research by many years. If they failed tonight, the military would have their way. They'd destroy her satellite. Losing it would just about kill her. But it was a sacrifice she would make without regret if it saved lives.

As she followed the men up the splintery pier, she looked up at the ancient walls of the glass factory, imagining what lay inside. These men would be like bulls in the proverbial china shop. Focused on their mission, they would take little care of the precious treasures inside. She'd read about the collections of centuries' old Murano glass in some of these studios. Of the priceless, irreplaceable molds and records of artisans' techniques stretching back centuries. If a firefight broke out or explosions shattered the interior, a history of beauty might be lost. A fire could set the entire island aflame.

"Come on," Rooker whispered in her ear, nudging her urgently from behind.

She turned to look at him. He wore night-vision goggles and an armored vest, as did all his men. The goggles were bulky, difficult to use and required training. Kate had opted against trying to use them, but she did wear the weighty chest protection that was crushing her breasts.

Her job would begin when theirs ended. First Rooker's men had to find the computer that might, even now, be sending an encrypted message to Heat Wave, telling it to launch a strike on

No Mercy

Chicago. Once the team secured the area, she would work on reversing the program. But until the assault was complete, and the infrared units no longer necessary, she'd have to keep the flashlight she was carrying turned off, so as not to blind men wearing night goggles or alert their enemy.

She ran blindly in a crouch, down the alley alongside the low wall, keeping up with Rooker's bursts of motion. They moved from shadow to shadow. She lost track of the rest of the team. They'd melted into the darkness. Only a soft scurrying sound, which might have been a man or an animal frightened by the sounds of their steps, broke the silence. Occasionally she saw the flash of a gloved hand in a beam of moonlight—maybe the lead Carabinieri officer, signaling: *Go right, go left...hold up!*

Rooker stopped abruptly, turned to her and pointed at two immense wooden doors. They looked as though they'd been designed in the Middle Ages to accommodate wagons and teams of horses. "Ready?"

"Yes." *No!* Blood surged through her body. The surface of her skin prickled, felt blazing hot, then turned to frost.

Kate pressed her back to the stone wall while Rooker waved two of his men inside. The black mouth of the open doorway swallowed them up.

She held her breath and strained to hear anything at all that would tell her they were making their way safely through the building. Had one of them been Adam? She was almost certain the second of the two had been him, although with their faces blackened they looked so much alike.

"Now!" Rooker huffed into his microphone. Then he rushed through the gaping black maw, and she followed.

They came out on the other side in a dirt-floored, unlit storage area. Only a little moonlight filtered through dusty skylights high above them. It was enough to reveal a vast, shadowy place piled with crates and pallets and shelves soaring thirty feet or more above her head. For all she knew, the rows stretched on for miles. Even in the moonlight it was too dark for her to see much more than vague shapes.

She ran forward a few more steps to keep up with Rooker. Her toe caught on an uneven place in the floor. She stumbled forward, hand extended to catch herself. Rooker spun around, gripped her arm and pulled her along with him until she'd regained her footing.

With his night vision, he seemed to have no trouble picking his way through the maze of crates. She took more care to step only where he stepped. After a few minutes, her eyes slowly started to adjust to the dark. She could see a little more.

Kate strained to identify a new sound. A constant, dull roar. They moved on. The sound grew louder. At last, from the far end of the room, she spied the red-orange glow of a furnace. Even at this distance she felt its heat on her face. Along unfinished plank shelves on either side of her she could make out the fragile shapes of glass pitchers, bowls, goblets and vases stacked to amazing heights. From behind the furnace grates, flames backlit the priceless collection, sending a rainbow of hues flashing around the empty workspace.

She marveled at the glittering beauty of the treasures around her. Would have loved to inspect them now that Rooker had stopped moving forward. She reached out toward a delicate crystal figurine.

The chatter of gunfire brought her back to the point of their mission. She snapped her hand back and turned to Rooker. Their eyes met. *Quiet*, his warned.

Boots clattered along floorboards some distance away. Were they moving away or toward her? She couldn't tell. Neither was it possible to know whether they belonged to Rooker's team or the enemy.

He shifted suddenly, knocking her backward and into an alcove she hadn't noticed before. Silicon sand, soot, and powdery chemicals used to color the glass filtered down from the rafters like gray snow, filling her nostrils. She coughed and started to choke. He pressed a hand over her mouth, silencing her.

Two men ran past them without seeming to realize they were there.

"You all right?" Rooker whispered.

"Yes," she croaked.

The gunfire, running steps, and more shouts came closer then faded. Rooker held a hand over his ear, shielding the Bluetooth earpiece. Listening. "They've made it up a freight elevator to the second floor," he said. "There's a locked room up there, someone barricaded inside. They think that's where the communications are set up. They're going to blow the door."

"Let's go," she said.

"No. Adam says someone came up behind them and is guarding the staircase. My guys will clear it first and—"

A deafening explosion drowned out even the gunfire. Rooker flinched; his face froze.

She gripped his arm. "What? Did we do that? Or..."

His grim expression mirrored her fears. "Report in! Repeat, all units report," Rooker hissed into his headset.

Kate waited. Prayed. Breathed. Prayed.

"Carry on," Rooker said at last. He glanced quickly at her. "The staircase was booby-trapped."

"The guys, they're okay, right?"

"We can still make it up to the second floor."

A chill swept through her. "Rooker! Are Adam and the others—"

He ignored her. "We take the freight elevator up the back side of the building. Come on."

As they ran past the rubble that had once been a long flight of open-back wooden stairs, Kate stared up at the splintered remains. Although the explosion had ripped away most of the outer treads, a six-to-eight-inch tongue of wood stuck out from the stone wall where each step had been. She estimated the remaining size and stability. Most looked wide enough for someone with a small enough foot to climb, although the handrail was completely gone.

She grabbed a handful of Rooker's shirt, hauling him to a stop. "They won't expect anyone to come up this way. Not now, in this condition." He was staring at her as if she'd lost her mind. "I can make it up this way. You go around the long way. Make lots of noise."

"What are you talking about?"

"Let whoever is up there know that you're coming. And radio your guys not to shoot me."

Rooker stared at her in exasperation.

"It's the most direct route," she insisted, "and I have to get into that room ASAP."

"Aw, shit." He seized her by the arm and started dragging her across the hard-packed dirt floor, away from the remains of the steps.

"Stop!" she protested. "I'm serious. It's the safest way, now that they think they've made the steps unusable. Your feet are too big and you're too heavy, but they'll hold me."

He released her, rolled his eyes toward the jutting planks, groaned. "I don't have time to argue with you. Take this." He shoved his Glock at her. "You've got a magazine with ten rounds in there."

She stepped back from the gun. "I can't."

"Take it or I throw you over my shoulder and carry you to the elevator."

She narrowed her eyes at him and blew out an annoyed breath...but took it.

"And don't put your finger on that trigger unless you mean it. Two-hand it, arms straight out in front, point and squeeze. Fastest lesson you'll ever get."

No Mercy

Kate watched him take off at a run toward the back of the building. She tried to find a way to stick the Glock in her belt, at the back, like they did in the movies. Then decided against it. She'd probably shoot off her foot, or worse.

Kate held the gun in her left hand, pointed down and away from her body. She used her right hand to steady herself against the stone wall as she started up the shattered steps. In her left hand, Rooker's weapon felt heavy enough to pull her off-balance. She kept it tucked close to her body. One cautious step at a time, she hugged rock and edged her way upward.

Step. Step. Step.

Kate forced herself to breathe evenly, slowly. In. Out. In. Out. In rhythm with her snail-like tread. She could still taste the metallic tang of glass dust on her tongue. The shots fired now sounded as if they were coming from a more distant part of the building.

This might be the best scenario she could hope for. Maybe the gang had abandoned their electronics, leaving their computer to her. She looked up and was relieved to see the second-floor landing just above her head. Then something else caught her eye.

Dangling over the edge of the landing was a hand and wrist, the fingers limp. Blood trickled from the uppermost stair treads from the floor above. She swallowed back a bubble of bile, unable to move for a moment. The uniform cuff was of tan fabric, not black. One of the brave Carabiniere down. Her heart sank but she was secretly glad it wasn't Adam.

Kate took another four steps up. Stepped over the man's body and onto the landing. She was standing on the second floor, breathing hard, feeling lightheaded. Now she could see a section of hallway stretching away from her, filled with smoke, pungent with burnt gunpowder. She stood still and listened.

From a distance at first, then moving closer came shouts from a familiar gravelly voice, the crash of breaking glass and tat-tat-tat of a machine gun and answering fire. Rooker, she imagined. Doing his job. Making noise, as requested. She nearly smiled.

Kate looked down to see men burst across the lower room, dodging between shelves of glassware, firing at each other across the vast work area between furnaces. Glass shattered as bullets flew. Jewel-colored shards flew into the hazy air, catching what little light there was and making them look like fireworks in the darkness.

Kate ducked, stooping over the unmoving Carabiniere officer she'd seen from below. She felt for a pulse at his throat, found none. A single bullet hole marked his temple just below the band of his cap. Blood had already stopped flowing.

Her heart racing, Kate ran down the hallway, past a row of open, dark rooms. A thin, yellow light showed beneath a door farther along the hall. Was this where the computer was? But Rooker had said his guys were going to blow open the door. Why did it appear to be undamaged?

When Kate reached it, she looked up and down the corridor. No one in sight. All sounds of combat came from below.

She tried the knob. Locked.

She threw herself against the heavy oak panel, crusty with age, paint long gone to reveal bare wood. The door didn't even budge. With a sigh, Kate looked down at the Glock in her hand. *Well, it's a tool, right? So use it.*

She took a step back, held the gun in an overlapping grip, lined up the two pin sights with the door lock and hoped to hell the bullet wouldn't ricochet and hit her. She fired, the crack of the gun deafening so close to her ears. Wood splinters flew. The door shivered. She kicked it with one foot, and the door swung open.

She had started to step through and into the room beyond when a white-hot sensation burned through her left shoulder, just at the edge of the heavy vest. Stumbling forward, she turned to look for the sharp object she must have run into, unnoticed in the dim light. Nothing. *What the—?*

Kate leaned her hip against the nearby edge of a heavy worktable. She reached up to touch her shoulder. The burning sensation morphed into fierce pain that set her gasping. She brought her hand away, fingers wet, bloody.

"It's too late, Doctor," a voice said.

Kate spun around, but with the motion of her body, the room swirled, too. A figure with spiked white hair stood in the doorway, smiling at her. The woman held a Kalashnikov, identical to the ones the intruders had carried when they'd broken into the compound. Belatedly, the reason Kate's shoulder hurt became clear to her.

"You shot me, you—" Suddenly short of breath, Kate tried to lift the Glock. It felt unwieldy, too heavy for her wrist. A sinking feeling in her stomach. She couldn't seem to heft it higher than hip level.

The woman smiled. "Put it down. You look silly, carrying that thing around like it was a snake about to bite you."

Kate hesitated, not because she meant to be defiant. It was just that, suddenly, it seemed extremely difficult to convert any thought to action. Her coordination felt off-kilter. Just staying on her feet was a challenge.

The scientist in her understood what was happening. Loss of blood. Her body had gone into shock. Try as she would, she was unable to override her muscles' natural reactions and force herself to move.

"All right. Hold onto the damn thing then, and I'll put a bullet in your other arm."

Ah yes, Kate thought blearily. The vest protected her vital organs but left her limbs open to injury. She released the handgun; it clattered onto the table.

"Listen," she said as she slowly straightened up, gripping the tabletop for support, "if you give yourself up, I'll make sure they don't hurt you."

The woman laughed. "Hurt *me?* It's you who's hurt, bitch. And I'm not going anywhere until I get my money."

Kate frowned, letting all of her body weight rest against the table. It was either that or fall down. "*Your* money?" Had Rooker said something about this to her? About the woman in the trio possibly being in charge? She couldn't remember.

"Did you think Zed or that wimp of a scientist Hess planned this? Don't be ridiculous."

Kathryn Johnson

She smiled, her silvery eyes slipping out of focus for a moment as she assessed another burst of clamor from below. They snapped back to Kate—lizard eyes narrowed. Dangerous. Unpredictable. Apparently, whatever was happening downstairs didn't concern her.

"Funny how men always underestimate women, isn't it?" she said. "Bet you had a tough time convincing the good old boys at NASA you were the right 'man' for the job. Frank Hess certainly didn't think you deserved it."

Kate stared at her but didn't respond. The woman was messing with her.

White Hair moved toward a wall of shelves. She smacked the butt of her weapon against one corner. A panel slid open revealing a stone passageway. "Medieval Venetians were ingenious. They've left us their wartime escape route. Now move!"

When Kate didn't respond, the woman came around behind her, shoved her roughly through the opening then followed. Behind them, the wall slid shut with a wood-on-stone grating noise. They moved through a cavern lined with stone. The air smelled musty, of clay and mold and rot.

Kate cradled her injured arm, trembling, tears streaming down her face the pain was so bad. "Frank agreed to help you steal Heat Wave because I got the job?" His potential jealousy and bitterness were motives she'd briefly considered then dismissed. Only too late taking them, and him, seriously.

"All because of the job? Well, not entirely." She snorted. "Frank and I were lovers. You do things for a lover you'd never think you would. But he was very upset about losing out to you."

Kate's vision blurred. She felt herself slipping away even as she staggered along the low-ceilinged passage. Rooker would never find her now. Not down here in a tunnel he didn't even know existed.

The tip of the rifle's barrel jabbed Kate from behind, forcing her to keep stumbling forward.

The woman rambled on, as if for her own amusement. "He needed direction, poor dear. I gave him a way to repay you, and to punish NASA for not appreciating his talent. At first he

No Mercy

thought it might be too much. A little over the top. Stealing a satellite, even for just a few days, to make his point."

"He wouldn't," Kate insisted. "You're making this up. You kidnapped him then killed him."

"Did we? Or did I convince him that you would be fired as a result of losing the satellite? What do you think? And who would be the big hero if he got NASA's baby back for them?"

Kate could barely follow what the woman was saying. The words buzzed in her head. They made no sense. Frank was dead. She'd seen them shoot him. She'd seen the look of fear and confusion in his eyes as the trio forced him from the lab. And what about the body in the burned car?

White Hair said, "Can't you see the headlines? 'Kidnap Victim Eludes Captors! Returns Stolen Satellite to a Grateful U.S. Government.'"

"But," Kate gasped, finally understanding, "you never intended to let him surrender control to NASA."

"Of course not. Are you mad? Not once I realized what he was capable of making the thing do! I could name my ransom. No amount would be too high to save a city."

Kate stared at her feet. A steady dribble of blood fell from her fingertips to the rough stones with each step. She glanced back over her shoulder. Two platinum-haired women followed her. Then three. Hallucinations? She blinked. Now just one woman, glaring at her, prodding her forward. Pain radiated like lightning bolts, from her shoulder, down her arm and across her chest. She coughed. And stumbled.

A hand gripped the back of her vest and steadied her. "Feeling a bit woozy, are we?"

Kate fought the effects of shock, desperate to keep her head clear. "You shot David Proctor that night," she said, "for no other reason than to show Frank who was boss."

"Did you see his reaction?" The woman laughed. "He probably wondered if I'd do him next. Until then I don't think he'd even considered that I'd eventually kill him, too."

Gulping down air, Kate wavered to a stop. "I can't...can't go on." She planted both feet, braced herself against the stone wall with her good arm, unsure how long her legs would hold her. The agony of the wound was unbearable.

"I'd put you out of your misery, dear. But someone wants to see you." White Hair shrugged. "Now move your ass!"

They emerged a minute later from the tunnel and into a small, brightly lit, plaster-walled room. A man was sitting at a laptop computer with his back to them. Before he turned around Kate knew who it was.

"You're not dead!"

Frank Hess turned and smiled weakly at Kate. He looked exhausted, disheveled, and not particularly happy for a man whose ingenious plan to blackmail his country for millions had succeeded. One shoulder of his shirt appeared bulked up, from bandages beneath.

His gaze stopped on her blood-soaked arm, and lingered. In commiseration?

"Good God! What have you done to her, Mona?"

"I warned you she wouldn't cooperate," Kate's captor said. "What do you need her for anyway? I thought you had everything under control."

"I do...I do," he said quickly. "Like I said, there's this one little hiccup in the system. Then we can power up the laser. She can help do it faster." He gave Kate a quick, unreadable glance. "Are you all right?" he asked softly.

"Do I look all right?" Her voice shook, and she felt sure she was about to vomit. Dropping into the chair next to her very-much-alive chief scientist, Kate stared in disbelief at him. "The body in the car wasn't you. Your ID and key card were planted?"

"Well?" Mona snapped, ignoring her, bearing down on Frank Hess. "They haven't paid up yet and they've sent their goons after us. It's payback time. Are you going to do it or not?"

"The deadline we agreed to is nearly an hour away," he said wearily. "You want your money, don't you?"

She glared at him. "Fine. We give them fifty minutes more, but that's it. We can still get away through the lagoon. They don't pay...Chicago suffers. Next time they'll know they can't play games with me."

"You'd better get the boat ready then," Hess said. "Just in case your brother and his men can't stop them."

Mona shot the bolt on the Kalashnikov, and Kate felt the metallic clack vibrate through every nerve in her body. She

No Mercy

closed her eyes and leaned back in the chair, conserving what little strength she had left.

Mona's steps moved away from her. The door squeaked open and then shut. Kate heard the lock engage then steps retreating down the secret passageway.

Kate swallowed and drew a shuddering breath. As long as she kept her hand pressed over the bullet wound the pain seemed a little less. The blood wasn't flowing as fast but it hadn't stopped. She whispered, "Was it worth it, Frank?"

"I never intended it to go this far! You have to believe me, Kate."

"Why does what I think matter? You opened Pandora's box when you gave these people the key to our satellite. You gave them a weapon so powerful—"

"I know...I know! I'm sorry. I just thought if I..." He raked a hand over the top of his bald head. A gesture from an earlier life with bountiful hair? "I don't know now what I was thinking. I believed her when she said I could make them notice me. I'd be a hero, you know? *She* made me feel brilliant. Important." He sighed. "I thought she loved me."

Kate pressed harder with her hand. She calculated she'd already lost at least a pint, probably closer to two. Before long, she'd lose consciousness. Then she'd bleed out.

"God, Frank! You must have realized after you left the compound with the three of them, after she shot Dave, that it was..." she gasped, caught her breath, "...it was about something more than making you famous."

He dropped his head into his hands. "I did. I knew. But then they talked about all of this money. Enormous sums. And I thought, well, make the best of things, Frank. Who needs a job when you have millions sitting in a vault?"

Kate drew a shaky breath. He just didn't get it. "She's already ditched Zed. What do you think she'll do to you when she no longer needs you?"

"Oh, God," he moaned.

He ground the heel of one hand against his forehead. His eyes looked sunken and watery when he looked up. The ring of hair, what little he had of it, seemed thinner than she

Kathryn Johnson

remembered, unwashed. His beard had grown in unevenly. He was a wreck, but she didn't feel in the least sorry for the man.

"I just...I just don't know how to fix things now. You've seen what she's capable of."

"You can stop it here and now," Kate said. "Do you hear me, Frank? You have the computer. You are at the controls. You can *stop* this!"

"Too late...it's too late," he groaned, rocking on his chair.

If she'd had any strength left at all, she would have gladly strangled the man. "Frank, she's going to kill both of us. Don't you realize that? She'll kill anyone who gets in her way. You have to refuse to make the final connection."

"No." He shook his head. When he lifted it from his hands, his face glowed a deep, angry red. "Don't. You. Tell *me* what I have to do! You're in the same boat, Kate. The only reason she hasn't already killed you is because I told her I needed you."

Was he insane? He was only making things worse. "And what happens when we do make contact? Or even if we pretend to try and can't? Eventually, she'll decide we're useless to her. She'll find a work-around. She's not stupid!"

Kate drew her head back and squinted at him; the room was out of focus, he looked like a blurry photograph of himself. Everything going gray, as if the room had suddenly filled with a dense fog. In another moment she'd pass out. An inner voice whispered: *Not much time. Have to do something. Anything!* The woman with the gun would be back any second.

Kate locked her eyes on the computer. "It's there, isn't it? The altered FARM. You've already set up the link." Which meant Kate could access the satellite's onboard computers, if she could get to the keyboard.

"Yes," he said miserably.

She nodded, listening for the thud, thud, thud of the woman's boots coming back to them. Mona, with her nasty Kalashnikov. Coming back to make sure Frank finished the job with Kate's help.

Oh, God!

Either the President would have already ordered the ransom deposited into the account in Belize, or he'd soon announce his refusal to do so. If Mona got her money, she'd kill both of them on the spot. End of story. If the President called her bluff, she'd order Frank to burn Chicago and keep him around for her next assault, knowing the government would eventually cave to her demands. But she'd kill Kate, for sure. Nothing she or Frank could say would convince her not to.

Kate leaned forward in the chair, as close to Frank as she could without tumbling out of the seat. "You can make it up to your country," she whispered, her voice hoarse with pain. "Go to the door. Listen for her. I'll shift the HW-1 back to NASA control."

"No!" His eyes flew wide with terror, his mouth flapping soundlessly for a moment before words emerged. "She'll be furious. You don't know how ruthless she is! She killed a man for no reason except he was the same size as me. To make it look like it was me that burned in my car."

"Let me do it, Frank." Kate let go of her throbbing shoulder to push herself up out of the chair. She winced as the nerves in her shoulder stabbed and zinged. "Go to the door. Tell me if you hear her coming."

He stood up with a robotic motion, turned toward the door as directed, but seemed to change his mind. He paced the room, staring hopelessly at the floor, muttering to himself.

"Frank! She's going to kill you. Now or later." How many times did she have to say it? "Archer has authorization for the money." Did he? She didn't know. "He'll hold payment until the last possible moment. But once Mona has it, she won't need you anymore."

He was whimpering, tears flowing down his unshaven face as he continued pacing. "Yes, yes, she will if she wants to keep on using the satellite. She can't kill me if she wants to keep the money flowing. She's greedy. She won't let the golden goose slip through her fingers." He thrust a thumb at his chest. "Without me, she can't control the satellite. We're a team!" He sniffled loudly. He was babbling now. Stuck in a sound track of his own despair.

Shut up, Frank. She'd given up trying to talk sense to him. Now she had to concentrate. Had to make her brain work even though her body was shutting down, rapidly losing its ability to function. Already her peripheral vision gone from gray to black, leaving her only tunnel vision.

Kate focused on the computer's screen. She scanned the visible codes. Just as he'd said, he had already made the connection with Heat Wave. But she had to reprogram the FARM, enabling NASA to again access the sat. The scripts necessary to do that were complex. She'd memorized them, of course. Any other time she wouldn't have trusted her memory. She'd have one or more of her people check her input. But not this time.

They didn't have the luxury of caution. No time for double or treble checking. No time for anything but acting.

Kate watched Frank Hess turn to pace once more across the room, away from her and the computer. She steeled herself against the inevitable jolt of pain that moving would generate. Then thrust herself up and out of her chair. She fell forward onto the keyboard, shielding it with her body from Frank.

She hit keys, blanking out everything but the precious codes, even as a voice—her own?—begged for relief from the agony of her wounded shoulder.

Her peripheral vision miraculously sharpened, caught Hess as he froze, open-mouthed, in a soundless wail of horror. Then, "N-no! No, you can't do—" He lunged for her, his face a mask of fury.

But by the time he'd seized her and pulled her away from the keyboard she'd hit *Enter*. All she could do was hope that her team in DC realized they were back in control. Frank seized her by the waist, wheeled her around and threw her across the room.

She hit the floor hard. It didn't hurt as much as she'd thought it might in the second before she landed. She didn't even try to get up. The last drop of strength had left her body. Kate closed her eyes, didn't even open them when something else crashed to the floor. The keyboard? The computer? Did it matter?

She hugged the hard marble floor, content to wait for the end. She was done.

But Frank, apparently, was not. He started screaming, "She's coming! Oh, God. I hear her coming. What do we do?"

Kate didn't move. Their fate out of her hands. Her blood-deprived body had used itself up. A gentle numbness stole

No Mercy

over her limbs. She became one with the floor, then drifted slowly upward as though an immense hand was lifting her above the room. She closed her eyes. *This would be almost pleasant, if I weren't dying.* Then another even more amusing thought occurred: *It's up to you now, Rooker. You always wanted to be the boss.* Her lips tweaked up in a weak smile.

Heavy boot treads were approaching the room. A door slammed. Open of shut?

Kate didn't have the strength to open her eyes. Didn't matter. She knew it was Mona, standing in the doorway, eyes afire, jaw clenched. "What did you do, bitch? Frank, what happened?"

His answer was so soft Kate couldn't make out the words. But she knew the essence of it. He must be explaining that she'd passed control back to NASA. Her team would reprogram Heat Wave, render it harmless. A single deafening crack brought an abrupt end to Frank Hess's explanation.

Sleep. Just let me sleep now...and forever. Good-bye, Mercy. Farewell, Rooker. Mom, Dad, everyone.

Kathryn Johnson

The room was dark because Rooker wanted it that way. Sunlight, the cheerful chatter of the nurses as they made their rounds to patients—he wanted none of it. He'd just come back from the morgue. Arrangements had been made by the U.S. Embassy. All he'd needed to do was sign off on the paperwork.

The body would be shipped home, military transport. Draped in an American flag, in preparation for a hero's burial. That's the way the government wanted to spin it.

He thought about Kate Foster. Who would have guessed that little Einstein could have put up such a fight. She'd hung on till the end. Somehow, in those final nightmarish moments before he'd reached the subterranean room, tracking her by the trail of her blood, Kate had worked her techno-magic and returned control of the satellite to her people at NASA.

How she'd done it, as severely wounded as she'd been, he'd never know. He'd seen heroism in his lifetime, but never anything like this. Never anything that hit him this hard.

He slumped in the chair beside the shuttered window and dropped his head back to stare, wet-eyed, at the ceiling. "God, Kate."

"Yes?" A faint voice came from the hospital bed.

Rooker squeezed his eyes closed, opened them again but couldn't look at her yet. He'd stood over her bed for hours, praying—mind you, he *never* prayed—for this moment, fearing it too. She'd hate him for what he'd put her through.

He'd sworn he'd protect the woman. But he hadn't been there for her when she most needed him. If it had taken him another ten seconds to find her, Mona Lescroat would have finished Kate off. Instead, when she heard Rooker and his men approaching, Mona chose to run.

"Rooker, don't pretend you're not there. The room may be dark, but I can see you."

No Mercy

He had to cough and clear his throat before he could trust his voice. "'Course I'm here. One of my guys gets messed up, I always come by to say 'hey.'"

Kate looked at the water glass on the bed tray and started to reach for it. He jumped to his feet. He held the glass to her lips while she sipped. She let her head fall back on the pillow and frowned up at him. "I'm one of the guys?"

"Officially. As of yesterday." He shrugged. "They voted you in. Said you proved yourself. Wasn't my decision."

"I see."

"So you don't consider me a *guy?*"

He smiled. How could he not, as beautiful as she looked? "Not by a long shot."

She nodded. "What, then, do you consider me?"

Daniel Rooker stuck his hands in his pockets and tried to find something safe in the room to focus on. "Listen, I just thought if you woke up I should be here. To brief you, you know."

"I missed something?" she murmured.

"Yeah." He laughed because it was something to do other than sobbing like a little kid, out of sheer relief. "You fell asleep on the job. Been out close to thirty-six hours. I had Cambridge call your folks, tell them you're okay."

"Thanks." Lifting her right hand from beneath the sheet covering her, she beckoned to him. "Come closer."

He took her hand and squeezed it. It felt warm, and that was amazingly reassuring. Back in Murano her skin had gone as cold as death. He thought he'd lost her. Now he was glad when she let him keep holding her hand.

"After I passed out, what happened? Did you get Mona?"

He shook his head. "She escaped, unfortunately. Those old buildings are like rabbit warrens. The Italian police are pretty sure she's left the country by now. A woman matching her description was seen at the Austrian border. Interpol has been alerted."

"And Frank?"

He shook his head. "They're shipping his body back home tonight. I just took care of the arrangements."

264

He decided the rest could wait. How Homeland Security and the President wanted Frank Hess to be seen by the public as a patriot. Kidnapped, forced to aid his captors, he valiantly tried to disarm the terrorist who held him and another scientist, Kate Foster, at gunpoint. Rooker couldn't quite figure out why they wanted to whitewash Hess, but supposed it had something to do with preserving the appearance of solidarity on the home front. Who could figure politicians.

"Poor Frank." She blinked, took a deep breath, winced.

"Shoulder hurt?"

"Like hell. Painkillers must be starting to wear off."

"I'll grab a nurse." He started to move away but she latched her fingers tighter around his.

"No, wait. I have to say something, and I don't want you to think it's the drugs talking."

He moved back to her side and looked down into her soft green eyes. Eyes he'd thought might never open again. "Yeah?"

"What I said in the gondola about not being able to imagine why I'd ever let you...you know."

"Let me sleep with you?" He intentionally used a more refined choice of words than he would have around the guys.

"Make love to me," she said, meeting his eyes. "I just want you to know that, given the right circumstances, if you had a mind to...I might not object."

"Dr. Foster, are you trying to seduce me?" He tried out a serious pinch of his lips, nearly a frown, but felt the loopy grin breaking through.

She laughed, then groaned as her face went white. "Damn, that hurts."

"Bullets will do that to you." He leaned down and kissed her on the forehead. "I think a little recuperative time is in order before we venture into hay rolling."

"Okay." She smiled up at him, breaking his heart and warming his soul all at once. "In that case, bring on the drugs."

Kate soaked up the view from the balcony of the house in Treviso. The ancient town northwest of Venice had its own, less famous web of canals, but the land around it rose to meet low

No Mercy

green hills. In the distance, the majestic, snow-tipped Alps sparkled in the sunshine.

Treviso attracted few tourists in comparison to Rome or Venice. It was a busy, friendly town, a mixture of modern and ageless, with delicious restaurants and singing in the *osteria* late into the night.

They'd been there for over a week, and Kate regained more strength with every day. She loved strolling through the village streets on Rooker's arm. Less for support, these days, than for the welcome feeling of companionship. Her Waterford butterfly rested on the antique dresser. A huge bouquet of flowers had arrived from her parents, along with a collection of cards from siblings, coworkers, and friends, wishing her a speedy recovery.

Today she'd wrapped a light cotton robe around her body and stepped out onto the balcony of their room. She gazed out over the Piazza dei Signori. Amused, she watched a woman shoo the family goats out through the kitchen door, to be led away by her children to graze. Kate marveled at planks of bread dough being taken to communal ovens by two other women. Not everyone had a stove in their own home. The air smelled of olive oil, grapes, yeast and wood smoke from the ovens. Scrumptious!

Since they'd been here she'd eaten as much and as often as she liked, and it was all a delight. They often visited the *Caffe ai Soffioni,* just across the square from the hotel where they were staying. She knew she'd never again be satisfied with frozen pizza when she went home. Which wouldn't be for another three weeks.

Jessup had called from NASA while she was still in the hospital in Venice. She suspected that Rooker had already spoken with him, perhaps exaggerating her condition. "I don't want to see you back in the compound in less than thirty days," he told her firmly. "You need a good, long rest after what you've been through."

"What will I do?" she asked him. "I'll go crazy hanging around my house for a month. I can't stay here in the hospital; they need the bed for other patients."

"I'm sure there are other accommodations in Europe. Tour the continent."

Kathryn Johnson

"I could," she said. Or she could just find a pretty place in which to nest...perhaps in Naples, or on the French Riviera, or in London. She loved London.

Rooker had made the choice easy. "My friend Ricci has a cousin whose mother runs a hotel in Treviso. She has a room for you." He actually blushed. "For us...if you like."

"Perfect," she agreed, feeling a warm tingle at the thought of sharing a room, a bed, with this man.

She ran her hands along the wrought-iron balcony rail, then over the crimson petals of geraniums growing in pots hooked over it.

"What are you doing?"

Kate turned back to face the bed where Rooker lay, the sheet tossed casually away from him, revealing plenty of man. "Touching things."

"Touching things." His entire face puckered. "I thought we'd taken your mind off of analyzing stuff."

"You have." She smiled, her body still tingling and alive from their last encounter in those sheets, less than an hour ago. "I just want to remember all of this. It's so beautiful. Like being in another world."

He laughed. "Like that's unusual for you?"

She went back inside to sit on the edge of the bed. She laid her palm over his naked stomach. He went still.

"Science is different," she said. "Space is endless, exquisite in so many ways, but we can't touch it. Not yet anyway."

"You like touching things, I see." He looked down the length of his body.

"I like touching things." She moved her hand again. Lower.

"Damn, you're good."

She stood up and slipped off her robe. "I know."

And then she took her time, proving it.

"I'm starving," Kate murmured, stretching lazily. Hours had passed since they'd again made love. It was still light, but the marble buildings beyond the window were beginning to go pink with the lowering sun. "Feed me."

"Do I have to get out of bed to do that?" he asked.

"I expect so. Signora Pasquino doesn't offer room service."

No Mercy

"Damn." He made a show of flinging himself off of the bed and stepped naked across the polished stone floor. "What do you feel like eating?"

"It feels like morning, but I know it isn't."

He looked at his watch as he buckled it around his wrist. "Breakfast food then. How about a *cornetto,* fruit, and coffee. We can go out for a big dinner later."

"Perfect." The buttery Italian versions of croissants had become her favorite way to start the day. She stretched out between the sheets. "I'll take another nap while you're gone."

When Rooker had finished dressing—a spectacle worth staying awake for—and left the room, she closed her eyes and let her mind drift pleasantly to thoughts of his body weighing down over hers, entering her, filling her, tenderly bringing her to climax. Too soon, these memories slipped away, replaced by the stark realization of how close she'd come to death.

It would take a very long time for her to forget. Perhaps she never would.

Get up and move around, her subconscious told her. Keeping busy she'd be less likely to dwell on the terror of the past weeks. That's how you made nightmares go away. You got up and got on with your real life.

Forget Venice. Forget Mona and Zed and the men who gave their lives to stop them. It was over. Thank God.

Instead of reaching for her robe, she pulled one of Rooker's T-shirts over her head. It fell nearly to her knees and felt cozy. Something of him in her, something of him on her. Good stuff.

She wandered to the window and stepped out onto the balcony to look down into the piazza, gently rolling her left shoulder to encourage circulation in the healing muscle. It felt better every day, although it still throbbed when the Tylenol wore off.

The fountain in the middle of the piazza spouted water from a trio of nymphs' mouths. A carved stone Diana, holding her bow, rose from the froth. Directly below the balcony, Kate could see Rooker—Daniel, she corrected herself—striding out across the piazza.

She smiled as she watched his strong back and shoulders in retreat. His dark hair was still appealingly mussed. Her fingers had clenched and tugged at it earlier. She wished she could see his face. She would wait here until he came back toward her with their breakfast. Maybe he would look up, sensing she was there without her calling out to him. That would be a good omen.

Did she love him?

It was too soon to say. She'd never before felt so intrigued by a man, so in tune with him in the most unconventional ways. And yet they were so very different. Whereas he was all about physical strength, she was all about her brain. Nevertheless, he was good at using his mind in tight situations, and she had discovered a strength in her body that she hadn't known she possessed.

She'd always been thrilled by her discoveries—out there in space. Now, miraculously, she was discovering herself.

Rooker continued away from her. In another few moments he'd disappear into the café.

Just then, a sudden movement caught her eye. At first it seemed part of the usual flurry of activity: zipping Fiats, running children, grandmothers knitting in doorways, men smoking on the curb and gesturing wildly with hands as they argued politics.

Kate looked straight down toward the cobbled street beneath her and saw the driver's door of a black VW slowly open. A figure stepped out, straightened up.

Her heart stopped.

The tall, slender woman with a scarf tied over her head stood very still in the V between the driver's door and the open side of the vehicle. She watched Rooker. Gradually, her arms rose. Gloved hands braced themselves on top of the car door. They sandwiched a silver-gray pistol between them.

Kate knew that stance, that wisp of white-white hair that escaped from beneath the back of the scarf, the stillness of the woman.

Mona. Not in Austria. Here!

You've seen what she's capable of doing! Frank's prophetic words.

Mona had hunted them down, vengeance on her mind.

Instinctively, Kate knew what wouldn't work. If she called out a warning to Rooker, it would be too late. He wasn't armed. The Italian police had insisted that all firearms be packed for

No Mercy

shipment back to the States as soon as the mission was over. Ammunition too, in separate parcels. The airline's rules.

All of it, except for Rooker's personal weapons, had already flown back to DC. His sniper rifle was broken down and stored under the bed in its crate.

Rooker was about to pass behind the fountain. Mona would have to wait until he reappeared on the other side of Diana to make her shot. Kate calculated she had maybe twenty seconds, no more.

Frantic, Kate rushed back inside the room, dragged the rifle's crate out from beneath the bed. She clawed away tape, tore open the box.

Rooker's Steyr, the one he had forced her to practice fire.

Ammunition?

Stacked beside the French doors were the remaining boxes to be shipped. With any luck, the magazines would already be loaded. Snap one into the gun's breech and she'd be ready. But there were no magazines in the first package, none in the second one. Seconds ticked past.

Beside herself with terror, Kate leaped up and peered down over the edge of the balcony. At any moment Daniel would step out from the other side of the fountain. She dropped to the floor, shredded another package. Only boxes of loose shells!

She remembered Rooker saying something about loading individual shells, but then she'd only have one round in the chamber. What if she missed? Once that shot was spent the delay of reloading would give Mona a chance to take down Rooker.

One shot's better than nothing. Kate rushed to the balcony.

Supporting the rifle against her bent knee to aid her weak left arm, she slipped the single brass- cartridge up and into the breech, slid the bolt home, stood up straight and aimed over the railing. The crosshairs lined up with the red kerchief over Mona's head.

Finger to trigger.

One shot. One shot! she warned herself.

Mona reached a hand up to tug off the scarf, presumably to show herself. So that the man she hunted would see her and know she'd won. "Rooker!" Mona shouted.

Kate didn't look to see if he turned.

Kathryn Johnson

Breathe in, let it halfway out. Target image. Pull.

The rifle kicked hard against her good shoulder. She staggered backward under the impact.

Please, God. Please, oh please! she thought, as she listened for other shots following hers. But none came.

Kate lunged for the balcony rail and stared down at the scene below. People were running toward Mona Lescroat, lying on the pavement. She wasn't moving.

Kate slowly lowered the rifle to her side. It had happened so fast. She had reached for her nemesis. A gun. A weapon she'd hated all of her life. She had killed a person. A human being. A living thing.

An evil thing.

Her hands stopped shaking. She expected to feel remorse. She didn't. Not an ounce. Not yet.

THE END

No Mercy

Dear Reader:

I hope you enjoyed this third adventure in the *Affairs of State* series. If you missed the first two books, starring Mercy O'Brien, Kate's lovely cousin, I hope you will find both *Mercy Killing* and *Hot Mercy* in your preferred reading formats--either print or digital.

The fourth novel in the series will be available soon. In *Mission of Mercy,* Mercy O'Brien responds to her love of art by taking on one of the most famous unsolved art thefts in the world. While attempting to crack this cold case and restore seven priceless masterpieces to humanity, she runs afoul of a ruthless Montreal gang. And discovers her lover, Sebastian Hidalgo, may finally have turned to the dark side.

Whether you're a reader, a writer, or both--here are a few ways to connect with me, if you like. By signing up for my newsletter, you'll receive advance notice of new books, special writing and travel tips, and make me terribly happy to be able to "meet" you!

Get the *For the Love of Fiction Newsletter*:
http://eepurl.com/D8so9

Or find me on the usual social networks:
Facebook: Kathryn Kimball Johnson
Twitter: @KathrynKJohnson, or
         @Mary_Hart_Perry
Or on LinkedIn or GoodReads

www.ingramcontent.com/pod-product-compliance
Lightning Source LLC
Chambersburg PA
CBHW031612240626
47153CB00002B/729